DRAGON'S TEMPTATION

NICOLETTE ANDREWS

THIS NOVEL IS MADE POSSIBLE BY

Andrew Trushinski ☾ Alexandra Corrsin
Alexandra Perreault ☾ Ambi C ☾ Anthony Lewis
Ashley Jean ☾ Bats1239 ☾ Billye Herndon
Blizoria ☾ Brenna Greenfield ☾ Brittnay King
Caitlin Millsaps ☾ Carolee S ☾ Caroline Roth
Caroline Seidel ☾ Cayla H. ☾ Chanel Holm
Cheyenne Thompson ☾ Chris Munroe
Courtney R. Delgado ☾ Daphné Melanson
Elisha Padilla ☾ Elizabeth W. ☾ Emilie Garneau
Emily A. ☾ Emma Radovich ☾ Finley Ymir
Franchesca Caram ☾ Hannah Barnes
Hilliary Lipsig ☾ Hope Terrell ☾ Hunter Malone
J. R. Frontera ☾ Jackie Kilby ☾ Jennifer B. Law
Jessica Hoyal ☾ Julia ☾ Kai'lee ☾ Kass
Katarina Forster ☾ Katherine Malloy
Kayla Stonecypher ☾ Keisha Marie
Kerrie Koopmab ☾ Kerstin Wanke
Kimberly Sudbrink ☾ Kristen White
Kristina Mazur ☾ Lindsay Ross ☾ Lorelai Isabelle
Lorena ☾ Lori Wolbrueck ☾ Mal
Marina Hatfield ☾ Megyn "Sapphi" MacDougall
Melinda Trimble ☾ Melissa Williams
Michael H. ☾ Michelle Huang ☾ Morgan G.
Natalie H. ☾ Nicole B. ☾ Nicole Haarstad
Nijeara "Ny" Buie ☾ Polinchka ☾ Qavee ☾ Rac
Raleigh D. Froeber ☾ Rebecca Hill
Rebekah Deats ☾ Renee Portnell ☾ Ron T
Samantha Keil ☾ Samantha Landström
Samantha Newberry ☾ Shannon J
Stacy Ward ☾ Starr Z. Davies ☾ Steffy
Summer Seeds ☾ Sunny Side Up ☾ Susan Rackley
T. L. Price ☾ Vera Soroja ☾ Virginia Phillips
Xiomara Reyes ☾ Zeb Berryman
Jordan Clifton ☾ Vannessa

TRIGGER WARNINGS

Multiple violent scenes, mild gore, animal sacrifice, religious deconstruction, references of past infertility struggle of a POV character, references/memories of a verbally abusive marriage, mentions of drug use and addiction recovery from side and background characters, detailed description of consensual sex acts, mild torture/pain inflicted through magic.

N
Feral
Lands
Sundland
Neolyra
Porreque
Soccicio
Artria
Basilia
Ageless
Sea
Xi'an

Erich, prince and heir to the kingdom of Sundland, has been living six years in self-imposed exile after he lost control of his inner dragon and killed a man. During the full moon, he transforms into a dragon and he's been searching the continent for a cure. Rumors lead him to Atria, the capital of Neolyra, and a Miracle Worker who can cure him. The Miracle Worker, an elf named Fritz, offers to heal him if he'll steal the Empress' magic golden blade. Elves are the empire's enemy, and Corrupted like Erich are executed if they're discovered. Working with the elf, he risks death, but getting the sword means breaking the curse.

Erich reclaims his title as Prince of Sundland and enters the palace intent on getting close to the royal family and the sword. Then he meets Princess Liane. The middle daughter of Empress Eveline, second in line to the throne and unmarried at twenty-six. Liane has suffered from a chronic illness since she was a child. It frequently incapacitates her with fever and debilitating pain. Because of that, her mother never arranged her marriage, but she's increasingly pressuring Liane to choose a husband. But Liane would rather focus on exacting her personal vengeance for her childhood friend's untimely death by catching the magic drug dealers who plague her city.

Liane is at first suspicious of Erich, but his charm, and their mutual frustration over their meddling parents, bonds them. And she agrees to pretend to be engaged to Erich as a cover for her revenge plot. While they each work toward their individual goals, things get serious. Tensions rise with the elves, and Liane's younger brother, Mathias, must risk his life to uncover the Elven plot, devastating Liane, who leans on Erich for comfort, deepening their bond.

Then Liane attempts to expose the drug smugglers and discovers her best friend, Ludwig, was working with her brother-in-law, Prince Consort Heinrich, to spread drugs and plan a coup against her mother. Amidst this chaos, Erich realizes that the sword he came to steal is a forgery and the actual sword is missing.

Liane tries to expose Heinrich and Ludwig's plot, but he betrays Ludwig, who takes the fall. Liane confronts Ludwig about his apparent betrayal and learns that he was under Heinrich's spell. Before she can exonerate Ludwig, Heinrich kidnaps her and plans to hand her off to the elves because the golden blade was inside her spine the whole time. And why she's had fevers and pain since she was young, she fused with the sword.

Erich left the city behind for his monthly transformation, when he learned Liane was in danger. Despite it being close to the full moon, he rushes back to save her. He rescues Liane from Heinrich, killing him as a dragon. Erich escapes the Midnight Guard thanks to Liane's intervention. But cannot forget her. Fritz informs him that Liane and the sword are part of a world-ending prophecy, that he needs Erich's help to prevent. While Liane works with the Church of Sol to master her latent powers, Erich swears to free her from their grip.

I

The *Dawn Skimmer* sliced through the harbor's blue-green water and sailed beneath the founding twin oracles' statues that acted as a gate to the harbor. Salt-crusted chains dangled limply in the statues' hands, hiding mechanisms that might be pulled taut to stop a fleeing pirate ship or merchants evading harbor duties. The bronze statues watched them sail past, their metal patinated with age and the hems of their robes crusted white by the sea. Their outstretched arms cast long shadows on deck. Liane had read about them while preparing for her trip. Depictions of them were scattered throughout the city, though the harbor statues were the most well-known. They were famous healers whose vision of the future had helped establish the first church in Basilia after the Corruption. They'd traveled the continent spreading the word of Cyra's holy light by performing healing miracles.

Liane turned her eyes from the statues to the sprawling holy city of Basilia. It was early, and heavy banks of fog hung low, bright-white stucco buildings emerged like crooked teeth, leading Liane's eyes toward the gilt resplendence of the temple, Liane's new home, and the church's first holy temple. Cyra's golden star atop the highest spire reflected the sun into Liane's eyes, forcing her to look away, and she turned back to the open ocean. The sun had just started to rise over Basilia, but the waning gibbous moon still hung defiantly in the sky, as if the Nameless Goddess refused to give up her place to her golden sister. Liane wouldn't admit it to anyone, but she'd become enraptured with the phases of the moon, hoping like a fool that Erich would risk coming to see her once more. Just to give a proper goodbye. That was, until she'd set sail for Basilia. He wouldn't risk his life for her in the holy city. The Midnight Guard had plastered his wanted posters across Artria, and if he were smart, he'd disappear from the continent for good, just as she should banish him from her thoughts.

Their weeks at sea were meant to have acted as a time of reflection. She'd never traveled more than a few days from Artria. And at the outset of her journey, she'd been confident in her decision to leave. Basilia was known as the city of healing. Many came in search of impossible cures offered by the continent's best healers. Mother had summoned some of their best and brightest, trying to cure her fevers, all while keeping the secret of the sword in her back and the source of her illness from them. Her frustration at the secrets and lies, had fueled her through the first leg of their journey—that, and righteous purpose. But as days and leagues had passed, and the familiar snowcapped mountains had softened to rolling hills dotted with sheep and cows, the pang of homesickness had crept over her.

Her life, until now, had been thoroughly entwined with her family's. They shared at least one meal a day together. They'd talked, laughed, and fought. They'd also lied to her face for thirteen years. The first time she'd seen a dolphin surfing the wake of their boat, Liane had turned to point it out to Aristea, only to remember she was alone. Then she'd remembered why. Aristea,

Mother, Father, and even Mathias all had known. Everyone had hidden the truth of the sword embedded in her back and let her believe she was afflicted by a mysterious illness—one that might have been cured by Basilia's miracle workers. But they'd rather keep up appearances than let her live a full life. The sword was Cyra's blessing, but it felt more like a curse. It sapped her of strength and plagued her with fevers and an aching back.

She loved her family, and a small part of her understood why they'd hidden the truth. But a greater part of her was still mad at them. She'd thought distance would lessen her anger and resentment, but it hadn't, and instead, she was filled with a strange concoction of longing for him and resentment. Perhaps her family being flung to the winds was inevitable. Mathias was on a quest to uncover the elven plots in the feral lands. Liane was in Basilia seeking answers; Aristea was in Artria doing her duty as future empress. Was this all the goddess' plan? Maybe Liane could answer that in Basilia.

She gripped the railing tighter as they rocked along the wake of a passing merchant ship. And she thought sympathetically of Luzie, who was below deck, clinging to a bucket. The choppy harbor would only make her seasickness worse. She turned around and nearly collided with Ludwig.

His expression was shuttered, and his gaze was fixed on the distant shore. It was a guard's expression—professional, cool, and detached. Before he'd resumed service, she'd thought they'd repaired their bridges, but betrayal was a slow wound to heal. They'd made amends, but the easy camaraderie they'd once shared felt far off. She couldn't look at him without thinking about the secrets he'd passed on to Heinrich, or fearing he was using again. Stardust always eventually killed its users, and yet somehow, Ludwig had recovered, unlike Elias, who'd wasted to nothing.

Their eyes met, and she felt a wash of guilt. She should be glad he'd survived despite the odds. And doubting him after everything felt cruel.

"We're nearly there," he said, nodding toward the dock slowly coming into view.

"Mm," she replied. Few words came to mind. Maybe she was exhausted after a long journey, or the unacknowledged hurt and suspicion froze her tongue.

"Nervous?" Ludwig asked. It was an olive branch, and not the first he'd offered.

"I'm not worried about you using again…" Liane said and regretted it instantly. It landed wrong, and she watched the goodwill wither in his gaze. Things were different now, and she didn't know how to fix their friendship. "I mean, what's there to be nervous about?"

"Does my vow inconvenience you?" he asked, evoking the promise he'd made to their deceased friend, Elias. Their mutual love for him had bonded them, but even that was tainted. Ludwig had loved Elias, but Elias had loved her and begged Ludwig to protect her on his deathbed. The very foundation of her and Ludwig's friendship had been built on a lie.

She held her hands behind her back and leaned into the railing as she wrestled with her churning emotions. Now wasn't the time. Later, when she'd had more time to reflect, they'd have a talk. But not today. As it was, she should be heading below deck to check on Luzie and change out of her sweaty, salt-stained traveling gown and into her procession gown.

Sailors scurried about the deck, shouting instructions to one another. As she passed them, they ducked their heads and made the sign of the star against their brows. Liane's cheeks flamed. They'd been doing that since she'd stepped onboard. Everyone treated her with this strange sort of awed reverence. It made her feel a bit like she was up on a stage and didn't know her next lines. Being a princess, she expected gawking, but that was when she was beside her family. Now Liane was alone in the spotlight, the wielder of an unknown magic and the goddess' chosen.

She felt like a freak. She was a bit of an anomaly within the church, too. The Avatheos had assured her he'd foreseen her coming, but he hadn't really explained what her role was within the goddess' grand plan. She'd pressed him early on in their journey—as much as she could press the Avatheos—but he'd been vague about the details and assured her all would be revealed once they reached Basilia. If she were being honest, the Avatheos still terrified her. She'd never seen his face despite having lived in close quarters with him for weeks, and he'd hardly left his cabin, presumably because he was in deep religious contemplation. Liane didn't get seasick, but she craved the sun. She needed to feel it seep into her skin, and the more time she spent in the light, the fewer fevers and less pain she had. That was all he'd told her. But it wasn't a cure. She wouldn't feel better until they'd drawn the sword from her body.

Their progress slowed as they approached the dock, and she spied a crowd gathering to greet them. She'd been paraded in front of crowds her whole life. It shouldn't bother her. But a swarm of butterflies erupted in her stomach. This was her first public appearance since the Sun Ceremony, where she'd glowed. Had rumors of her power preceded them, and had the crowd come to catch a glimpse of her strange ability? Or were they hoping to beg the Avatheos for a miracle?

"They know we're here," the captain shouted. "Look alive, boys."

The crew seemed to have had a fire lit under them because they moved faster, grabbing ropes and shouting to one another.

Liane scampered below deck so as to not be underfoot and met Luzie at the entrance to their cabin. Her complexion was sickly-green, and there were dark circles under her eyes. Luzie clutched a bundle beneath her arm, which she thrust toward Liane without ceremony as Liane approached.

"The Ava—" Luzie gulped, then inhaled, eyes closed, as the ship rocked. "The Avatheos has ordered you to be veiled for your procession through the city," she managed in a gasp, before rushing over to her bucket and retching.

The cabin smelled of sickness, and Luzie's clothes hung loose on her frame. Thank the stars they'd arrived. Liane wasn't sure how much more Luzie could take.

"I'll help you in—" Luzie said before retching again.

"Rest. I am capable enough to dress myself."

She left Luzie and went to their cabin, where she unfurled the veil and robe the Avatheos had provided. She crinkled her nose at it. The veil was a thick material and would fall down below her breasts, obscuring her face like the priests and priestesses of the Church of Sol. Liane wasn't a priestess, and wearing a veil seemed sacrilegious.

"He can't be serious," she murmured to herself.

With a shake of her head, she tossed the veil on her cot and compromised by putting on the robes. When she returned to the deck, the veiled priests and priestesses were waiting for her, along with a green Luzie and stern Ludwig. The Avatheos turned toward her and raised a hand that halted her in place.

"Where is your veil?" the Avatheos asked, and though she couldn't see his face, she felt his stare slide up and down her body, sending pinprick chills down her arms and neck. "A piece of the goddess lives within you. The common folk shouldn't look you in the eyes. It is unseemly."

"I've had the blade for thirteen years. Thousands of people have looked at me." Liane threw up her arms, searching the others' faces for support. But none would raise their eyes to meet hers, not even Ludwig or Luzie.

"But that was before they knew. Your image and how you present yourself are crucial. How do you think your mother inspires such love and devotion?"

"Her excellent statecraft?" Liane ventured.

"It is the mythos of wielding the blade. The way she is presented as Cyra incarnate. You are the successor to the blade. You must look the part."

"I'm not my mother, and I'd rather look the people in the eye if they're expected to worship me." Though she had serious qualms with the idea of people worshipping her. She crossed her arms and stared at the Avatheos, waiting for his counter-argument.

He inclined his head. "As you wish, your divinity."

Liane looked around the crowded deck, surprised her argument had worked. But the sailors shuffled off, avoiding her gaze, as they focused on tying the ship to the dock and lowering the gangplank. The crowd pressed closer, necks straining to see over the shoulders of the Midnight Guards struggling to hold them back. Beyond them, carriages awaited to take them to the temple. The party on the ship lined up, and on instinct, Liane took her place behind the Avatheos, but he glided aside.

"It is not the avatar's place to walk behind me. You outrank me, your divinity."

The comment felt pointed, but she decided to ignore it and stepped in front of him, bracing for the unmitigated stares of the crowd. Their hungry gazes seemed ready to devour her like a succulent piece of meat, and a cold sweat broke out on her brow. Taking one large breath, she stepped onto the plank and toward the buzzing worshippers.

When she reached the bottom, the crowd surged, pushing the guards until their backs were brushing against her shoulders. The guards made a narrow path out of their flesh, but grasping hands reached through the gaps, pulling at her clothes.

Liane could do this. The carriage was merely a few feet away. Someone held up a baby, thrusting it over the heads of the guards, as if they'd toss it toward her. For what? A blessing? What could she possibly give them? Bile caught in the back of her throat. This wasn't theater. These people believed her capable of miracles. Enough to risk their infant being squashed in this press of bodies. The horror of it struck her, and she searched their desperate faces—dirt-smeared, bandaged, and sunken. What could she do for them?

Among the press of people, she caught a glimpse of a familiar face moving through the crowd. She craned her neck, searching for Erich's gold-flecked brown eyes. He shouldn't be here. She moved closer to the wall of Midnight Guards, which was her first mistake. It emboldened the crowd, who pushed through the guards to reach her.

They grasped her arms, her ankles, her hips, her neck—anywhere they could grab a fistful of fabric, hair, or flesh—and pulled. She was lifted off the ground, yanked, and then dragged into the mob.

Their hands were everywhere; her screams were trapped in her throat. She couldn't untangle from the crowd—as soon as she broke free of one person, someone else had hold of her. They were screaming, pleading, crying, and pressing things into her hands that she couldn't grasp. Her scalp burned, and her joints ached as the crowd pulled. Tears streamed down her face as she struggled in vain to escape. The guards struggled, but they couldn't reach her.

Then, from the middle of the fray, he appeared. He grabbed hold of her, wrapping her trembling body up in his arms and shielding her until she was surrounded once more by a wall of

Midnight Guards. Liane stared in wide-eyed astonishment up at Erich as he cupped her cheek and offered her a crooked smile, saying not a word.

The Midnight Guard beat back the crowd with clubs, and people screamed as they fled. Ludwig pushed through, grabbing her by the arm and yanking her from Erich's grasp.

"We have to get away," Ludwig said, his hand at her elbow, guiding her forward.

She turned her neck to call out to Erich, but he'd disappeared into the crowd. Six guards flanked her and Ludwig as he escorted her into the carriage, where the Avatheos awaited her.

Her heart was thumping against her ribs, and her hands wouldn't stop shaking.

"They were going to rip me apart," Liane said, wrapping her arms around her body. If Erich hadn't been there...

"The veil could have shielded you from it. Perhaps you will remember this next time we venture into public," the Avatheos said serenely.

She didn't care if the Avatheos was the head of the church; she shot him a death glare. But he either didn't see it or didn't care. Liane pulled back the curtain, hoping for one more glimpse of Erich, but as mysteriously as he'd appeared, he'd vanished once more.

2

She'd been in Erich's arms. The impression of her against him lingered. Her phantom scent, rosewater and sea salt, intoxicated him still. And all Erich could do was watch her carriage disappear up the hill, sliding farther and farther out of reach. His decision to see her disembark had been ill-conceived from the start. The Midnight Guard might have noticed him, or worse. He'd come all this way to extract Liane from the church's grasp. He wanted to see what sort of challenges they might face in rescuing her. Fritz's visions hadn't given any insight into how they should proceed.

Erich might have started out as a casual observer, but when the crowd had swarmed, he'd lost his head trying to protect her. Foolish, reckless, dangerous. He was lucky the Midnight Guard was more preoccupied with protecting her than wondering who he was.

With Liane gone, the faithful turned on him.

"You touched her. Did she impart a gift upon you?" a man holding a thin child in the crook of his arm asked. "Will you lay your hands upon my daughter? Maybe some of the avatar's holy light will transfer onto her." His eyes were hungry and hollow, and the child's eyes were closed, and her face was ashen gray. He smelled death on them, and knowing he could do nothing felt like a knife twisting in his gut. And yet he felt compelled to offer them a small measure of blind hope and laid his hand on the child's forehead.

It was a mistake. After seeing that, they crowded closer.

"My arm hasn't been the same since my accident," a man with a skeletal arm hanging loosely at his side said. "What about me?" He shoved closer.

Erich had no power to heal them. If anything, he might transfer the corruption of his dragon curse to them. He shook his head to deny them, but the crowd's fervent desire for a miracle threatened to swallow him whole. The crush of bodies and dozens of voices talking over one another made his skin twitch, and the dragon, already too close to the surface, roared within him. Erich sought the hilt of his dagger for comfort, but there wasn't room to bend an elbow, and instead, he was left with his palms itching. He had to get away. Erich thrust his shoulder between people, forcing a path out. But their hands grasped for his clothes, tearing open his tunic and dragging his vest off him. Clothes that had touched their avatar seemed to appease them because once they had them, they descended upon each other like a pack of wolves, tearing them into strips. Erich drew his dagger and pointed it at the stragglers on the fringe of the crowd who eyed him. But they lost interest and left him to skulk away like a beaten dog.

They'd scratched his chest and neck, but the flesh was already mending, though it itched. He'd expected obstacles, but hordes of fanatical worshippers hadn't been one of them. The next logical step was to regroup and report what he'd learned to Fritz. They'd feared the elves would attempt an assassination on Liane to prevent her rise to power. They hadn't planned on the people assaulting her out of desperation.

Though his head told him to return to the inn, dragon wings beat in his skull like a second pulse. The waning gibbous moon should've soothed the dragon, but ever since Artria, it'd been closer to the surface, harder to control. Erich pulled taut the chains that held his dragon power in check. He didn't head back to the inn as would have been wise, but rather joined the crowd of worshippers trailing Liane to the temple.

All knowledge was worth having, and the risk of the Midnight Guard taking note of him in the crowd was low. They had enough on their plate keeping the masses under control. People stood on rooftops and hung out of windows to watch the closed carriage as it inched its way toward the temple. Erich caught glimpses of it from the alleys and back ways he traveled to avoid the bulk of the crowds. They kept the curtains drawn, robbing him of an opportunity to see her en route. When the carriage reached its destination, the crowd surged again. They were pushed back by the Midnight Guards. Erich had to elbow his way to the front of the temple steps. The guards stood, arms interlocked, in two rows, preventing anyone from getting close enough to touch her. Despite the well-armed wall of flesh in their way, the people grasped at her. Their desperation was reaching a fever pitch.

The stench of unwashed bodies and sickness turned Erich's stomach. He was jostled as hands pulled him back in an attempt to steal his place. Under normal circumstances, being this close to strangers would make him uneasy, but this time, his dragon twisted and thrashed against its chains, and he feared it'd break loose among the crowd. The effort to maintain control was making his head pound more. He couldn't so much as bend an elbow without accidentally jabbing someone in the ribs. He'd thought the crowds in Artria were bad, but Basilia was unbearable.

But he wanted to see her safely enter the temple. With this many guards around, they'd keep her party safe. As much as he hated to admit it, she was safest in the church's care, for now.

The carriage doors opened, and Liane stepped out, looking shaken and terrified. Six guards escorted her up the temple steps as the people cried out for her to turn their way. She didn't glance at the crowd, even as Erich's gaze burned into the back of her skull, willing her to find him. Which was for the best. Erich had a sinking suspicion she'd seen him at the dock, and when she'd stopped to find him, the crowd had swarmed. The thought made his chest constrict. Even when he was trying to protect her, he endangered her. Attempting to see her was a selfish indulgence, and yet he couldn't tear his eyes away until she passed through the temple doors and they slammed shut behind her.

With Liane's safety ensured, he retreated. As he did, the pilgrims chanted her name, a rising chorus demanding to see the goddess' avatar. When their demands were not met, they grew agitated, pushing harder and harder. The line of guards retaliated with clubs, dispersing the crowd, who let out a scream that rippled like the tide. Erich was nearly out of the square when the pilgrims fled. He knew they'd be back. The city was swarming with the devoted, seeking a miracle. More would arrive as the word spread. They would not be dissuaded, and Erich had to admit he shared their sentiments. Fritz couldn't heal his curse, but maybe Liane could.

It was what had driven him, against his better instincts, to come to Basilia. He'd made a deal with a rogue elf and risked capture by the Midnight Guard all because of his vain hope that he might be saved.

The crowds thinned away from the temple, and the tension in his chest eased a measure. Though he doubted he'd be able to unclench his jaw and relax his shoulders until he, Liane, and Fritz were out of this Trinity-damned city. He and Fritz had arrived in Basilia by a swift merchant ship shortly before Liane, and by then, rumors had already been swirling about the goddess' avatar. They spoke of her miracle-working and her ability to heal the ill and, perhaps, heal corruption. Fritz said her power had awakened, and Erich wondered how much she'd learned since they'd last spoken. Could she perform miracles, or had the gossip twisted the truth? Erich had to know.

First, they needed to get Liane away from the Church of Sol. The church would wield her like a sword to exterminate the elves and everything they deemed unholy. Fritz had seen it in a vision, and though Erich didn't trust much, he trusted Fritz.

Erich's footsteps dragged as he walked. Summer had passed its peak, and he felt the gray cloud of autumn looming on the horizon. They'd spent weeks planning and preparing, but he felt woefully underprepared. The Church of Sol had a mountain of magic, influence, and arms, and Erich felt as if he were standing at the foot of it, unsure how he'd reach that summit.

The wind blew down the street, and he caught a faint sour odor. The hairs on the back of his neck stood on end, but rather than look over his shoulder and alert his stalker, he kept walking. Residents passed him by, disinterested in him and muttering about the influx of pilgrims in the city. Without seeing his stalker, he couldn't say for certain, but with the lack of metal clinking or the sweet smell of magic, he assumed whoever was following him wasn't part of the Midnight Guard. He'd felt eyes watching him from the shadows before. This town was crawling with Midnight Guards, and at first, he'd chalked it up to paranoia. But now, he could hear leather-booted footsteps echoing behind him on the cobbles. When he stopped, pretending to examine a shop window, the footsteps halted as well. A tingle raced up his spine, and he made an abrupt turn down an alleyway.

The footsteps increased their pace as they followed. Two sets of them—large men from the sound of their footfalls. The dragon, already too close to the surface, roiled beneath Erich's skin, seeking to break free of the tight chains that kept it in control. The mental barriers that he held it in place with were meant to prevent a transformation before the full moon, when the dragon became too powerful and overcame him. He turned a corner, hurried down an empty street, and abruptly met a dead end. It would appear to them that he was cornered, but he'd led them there for a reason. These ruffians were doing this outside the law, and he wasn't about to alert the Midnight Guard to his presence with a street brawl.

Erich turned to face the empty alleyway. There was nothing there but shadows. But he could sense the stalkers close by.

"Come out. I know you're following me," he said.

Silence answered, and for a moment, he thought he'd imagined the footsteps. Until three people stepped into view—one more than he'd counted. Either he was losing his touch, or there was mischief afoot. The largest of them had a jagged scar bisecting his face and an empty, puckered socket where his eye used to be. The second man was missing a thumb and pointer finger, as if they'd been bitten clean off. The smallest man was well-dressed and unscarred, a strange juxtaposition to his comrades. Erich also realized, as he tried to study the smallest man, that his eyes kept drifting away from the man as if some spell were repelling him from looking too closely. Not good.

"You're rather brave, corrupted," the smallest man, and the presumed leader, said in a silken tone.

"I'm impatient, is what I am. Why are you following me?" Erich asked, his hand resting on the pommel of his dagger.

"I'm doing what all men must—earning geld. Your head will fetch a good price, I think."

Hunters. He should have known. He'd been so preoccupied with the Midnight Guard that he hadn't thought about the Hunters' Guild. Basilia had the largest group of organized hunters and smugglers on the continent. He hadn't been as inconspicuous as he'd thought.

"I think I'd rather keep it, thank you."

The man shrugged. "Suit yourself. Watching these two fight is half the fun."

The largest man was wielding an axe, twice the size of his head. It would have a slow swing but a deadly, bone-crushing strike. The best thing Erich could do was try to avoid it.

Erich drew his dagger from its halter, and the axe man laughed at the sight of it.

"Is that all you have?" he asked.

"It's all I need."

Erich lunged at the leader. As expected, the big man swung his axe toward Erich. He dodged and backed up a step, and the smaller lackey pinned him between him and the larger one. What he hadn't expected was for the leader to move, lightning quick, out of harm's way. Erich slashed the axe wielder at the elbow, and his massive weapon sagged. Erich turned to the smaller one, who blew a cloud of something foul-smelling into Erich's face, which rendered him partially blind.

Stumbling in the dark, Erich narrowly avoided another crushing swing of the large man's axe. Someone let loose a bloodcurdling scream, and Erich jabbed in the direction he last remembered the big man to have been in. He heard a loud thud as the axe fell to the ground, and using his heightened sense of hearing, Erich rushed the man, grasped him by the neck, and twisted. A sickening crack sounded as the man fell to the ground. Erich could hardly see through the haze of poison, and his sense of smell was impaired. The dragon inside him roared, eager for bloodshed, hungry to destroy them all, but the sensible part of him held on. It had been long enough since the last full moon that he had greater control. Erich used his dragon sight to find an opening, sliding in close enough to stab a dagger into the poisoner's ribs. He crumpled to the ground.

As soon as they were dispatched, Erich stumbled away, half blind, for several city blocks before he found a fountain that he could dunk his face in and wash the poison from his eyes. His dragon blood would take care of the rest. But even with his quick healing, his vision remained blurry. A disadvantage he couldn't afford should the men recover and come after him. Erich took the long way back to the inn. He was afraid that he was being followed and had to loop around several neighborhoods before he was confident that he wasn't leading the hunters to Fritz. If a corrupted like him fetched a high bounty, he could just imagine the geld they'd offer for an elf.

That was why Erich preferred being alone. If you didn't have companions, you didn't have to worry about risking their safety. Worrying about someone else only made his job more complicated. By the time he returned, the sun was high, and he was exhausted.

The inn they'd chosen was a shabby, run-down establishment in one of the more unsavory parts of town. When Erich entered, Fritz was sitting in the common room. His body was angled toward the flames, and there was a blank expression on his face. It was a painfully uncanny scene, and Fritz may as well have waved a flag over his head that declared him nonhuman. Thankfully, the innkeeper was the sort who accepted bribes, and Erich, anticipating this, had paid her extra when they'd rented the room, just in case. She was the common room's only other occupant, and her gaze was averted.

Erich fell heavily into the wooden chair across from Fritz,

startling him from his vision. Fritz blinked at Erich in a haze, before shaking himself like a wet dog. How Fritz had survived this long among humans was a mystery. At times, he seemed wise beyond his years, while at other times, he seemed terribly young and naive.

"We might need to change inns," Erich said by way of greeting. Living with the constant fear of attack was normal for Erich. Watching another person's back was unfamiliar. If it weren't for Fritz, he wouldn't have gone back at all.

"Getting into trouble already?" Fritz asked.

"It finds me. Or rather, it found me today, on my way back from the docks."

"That *is* trouble. I told you to stay away from her until we've formulated a plan."

Erich grunted in acknowledgment as guilt gnawed at him. He trusted Fritz's intuition, but he trusted his gut too, and he was glad he'd been there.

"You don't have to stay. I can get her out and bring her to you," Erich said, though he already knew what Fritz's answer would be.

"Trying to get rid of me again?" Fritz said with a single raised eyebrow.

"Better we break apart than get caught together."

"This only works if we do it together," Fritz said, pinching his brow. He looked skinnier and paler than when Erich had first met him.

Erich leaned forward to whisper. "Did you *see* something?"

"No. There are too many possible outcomes, a thousand tangled threads." He sighed and leaned back to slump in his chair.

"Well, you keep trying, and I'll do what I'm best at." Erich stood and grasped Fritz's shoulder.

Fritz looked up at Erich with a quizzical stare. "And what's that exactly?"

"Find information. I'll search for a way into the temple."

"You make it sound so simple. Do you really think you can simply carry her out of the temple?"

"I'll do whatever is necessary," Erich said, with a nonchalant shrug. But on the inside, his gut was churning.

3

There were no rules for how a widow-princess might dress if her husband died a traitor, but Aristea had chosen to wear a black veil. In Neolyra, widows wore a sheer black veil for a year and a day to mourn the passing of their husbands. It was an ancient tradition that was thought to have originated with the first Empress Consort, whose devotion to her husband had been unparalleled. After her husband had died, she'd slept inside his tomb in the catacombs for a full year. Thankfully, the tradition of lying next to the corpse of one's husband had ended half a century ago. The thought of lying beside her husband's mangled corpse for a year made Aristea's skin crawl. It'd been hard enough sleeping next to him when he was alive.

Heinrich's plot to overthrow the empire through cultivating an army of stardust-enhanced soldiers had failed, and he'd paid the price. But apart from a few minor officials, his co-conspirators remained at large, though officially, the case was considered closed.

Aristea felt as if she were poised on a dagger's edge. She hadn't put on the veil out of love for Heinrich, but rather wore it like armor. Her ill-fated marriage had been the ribbon that'd tied up the loose ends of a civil war that had begun before she was born, but whose threads were woven into the tapestry of the current court's political climate.

Heinrich had been fourth in line to the throne before he died, and the figurehead of a rebellion that had attempted to steal the throne from Aristea's mother. Because of that, Aristea had been destined to marry Heinrich before she'd taken her first breath. A faction of dukes didn't want an empress at all, and then her mother had made the audacious choice to name her eldest daughter heir even after a healthy son had grown to maturity.

If Aristea and Heinrich had produced a son, their two factions would've been united. But after years of marriage, Aristea hadn't borne a son, nor any children. Her womb had never quickened. Each month, her courses came, and hope withered in her chest. Now, at nearly thirty and a widow, her position as future empress seemed shakier than ever. By Aristea's age, Mother had had two children and had squashed a rebellion.

What did Aristea have? A veil to hide behind and a desperate scheme to keep her husband's followers loyal to her by pretending to be a grieving widow. On melancholy days like this, she wandered the cold rooms of her and Heinrich's apartment and was reminded of the times when he'd been sweet. When he'd kiss her gently on the brow or lay his head against her stomach and wish for a son. She'd tried loving him, she really had. But then he'd turn cruel and bitter. He'd stumble in, stinking of alcohol and another woman's perfume. Aristea would get angry and shout, and he'd find some way to twist her anger into being about her mistakes. If only she'd given him a son, if only she'd been better, sweeter, more pliable.

His study was dark, but she didn't bother lighting a candle

or opening the curtains. She hadn't gone in there since he'd died. She stood in the center of the room, her arms wrapped around her waist in a protective stance. Her gaze flicked over to the drawer with the false bottom. The same one where he'd kept the letters she'd written to him when they'd been engaged, when she'd been a teenager desperate to make their marriage work, and his responses had been sweet and flattering. She'd been hopeful, if not in love, and convinced their marriage could heal the empire. Could protect her mother's legacy and her right to the throne. It had been romantic to the girl she'd been that he'd been the prince in exile, waiting for their wedding day to return to court, ready to make amends for his father's sins. Then once they had been married, he'd used those same words against her. She walked over to the drawer, pried open the false bottom, and grasped hold of the letters.

"But now you're dead and I'll be empress," she said to the empty room.

She turned her back on the study and returned to the sitting room, where she'd asked her lady's maids to build up the fire. It burned bright and hot, warming her cheeks and flushing her face. She tossed those letters into the flames and watched them curl and burn.

She hated herself for having trusted him, having listened to the lies, the excuses. He'd been plotting to kill her and usurp her mother, and she'd suspected but said nothing. But she wasn't going to stand idly by anymore.

She'd win over Heinrich's allies, unify the dukes' council, and spearhead an attack on the elves before they could strike at the empire again, ending the threat and solidifying her rule. No one would question her ability again.

The letters turned to ash, but Aristea wasn't satisfied. Her lady's maid Yvette entered the room with a black gown draped over her arm. As was her usual routine, Aristea dressed and prepared for her morning walk around the gardens. After which, she would have to meet with Duke Mattison from Sundland, a notable, wealthy bachelor whom Mother was angling to pair with Aristea.

It was another reason Aristea had taken the veil. While she was in mourning, she wouldn't have to entertain suitors. But Mother had found a loophole. As he was an important royal dignitary, it was natural that they'd have lunch together.

Liane's fake engagement had given Mother the idea of bringing Sundland and their army into the empire's fold, and she wouldn't let it go, especially after learning, from Duke Mattison, that the real Crown Prince of Sundland was missing, and the king was dying. It was presumed that Duke Mattison, the king's brother, would take over the throne.

When their husbands died, most widows retired to the countryside, where they might enjoy newfound freedom and autonomy. That had never been an option for Aristea. It wasn't a matter of if she'd remarry but how long she could delay it. For now, Mother was indulging Aristea's mourning period. It wouldn't last forever. If she must marry, she'd rather it be to a man of her choosing, perhaps from Heinrich's former faction, preferably close in age to herself.

As crown princess, Aristea should have a choice. But the fraught political climate meant every move she made was scrutinized, leaving her paralyzed at times, terrified of making the wrong move. Unlike her sister, Liane, who had freedom. Liane chased vengeance and took lovers without repercussions. Mother always let her do as she pleased because she wasn't the heir. Now, as the goddess' avatar, she'd escaped their gilded cage and was flying free, unburdened by political intrigues.

It wasn't fair.

Aristea stuffed those thoughts down. She would claim her power, in her own way. She wasn't like Liane. Nor was she like her younger brother, Mathias, who was a jokester and peace-keeper. His charm had won him many fans at court, but he'd distanced himself from court politics by joining the army, and now he was risking his life to uncover the elven plot.

They each had their roles to play, and hers was to become empress. *But you're nothing without a man by your side. No one would bow to you alone.* Heinrich's vicious jabs haunted Aristea from beyond the grave, like old scars that wouldn't heal. He was dead and he'd been wrong, she reminded herself.

Outside, courtiers meandered through the rows of hedges and flowering bushes. They swiveled their heads to watch her as she passed, whispering behind their hands when they thought she was out of earshot. She took note but pretended not to notice. Some were bold enough to greet her, and she smiled but didn't linger, her gaze fixed on the old oak tree where she and her siblings used to play. Its large boughs drooped, wilting from the summer heat. Her lady's maids followed behind her, their shoes pattering on the cobbled paths.

Aristea was never alone. Guards, maids, courtiers—all their eyes watching, judging, circling like birds of prey. Normally the fresh air calmed her, but today even the sound of her lady's maids breathing was agitating. She needed to be alone, to clear her head before the lunch with the duke.

"Leave me," she said.

"Your majesty..." Yvette started to protest.

"I want to be alone," she reiterated. Yvette bowed, and they all backed away, giving her the space she'd requested.

Aristea breathed in the fresh air, perfumed by lavender bushes. If her siblings had been with her, they would have run off into the nearby hedge maze. But Aristea wasn't like Liane, who followed her own rules, or Mathias, who floated wherever the wind blew. Aristea was a rule follower.

But there were no rules against wandering closer to the fountain. Her ladies and guards were well within sight, and she was perfectly safe inside the garden. She inched closer to the fountain in question, resisting the urge to look over her shoulder to see if they'd noticed.

She was so preoccupied with seeming nonchalant that she didn't notice the branch dipping into the walk until it caught her veil and it pulled taut. Aristea tumbled forward and would have fallen onto her face, making a spectacle of herself, but someone grabbed her arm. But her forward momentum was too great, and they both toppled over.

Her would-be rescuer managed to switch their positions, and she fell on top of him. They were both tangled up inside her veil, and they thrashed about, pulling it free. This exposed her face and rumpled her blond hair, which fell from the pins that had held it back so that her hair now partially covered her face. This was her divine punishment for bending the rules, surely.

"Are you hurt, Aristea?" His familiar voice sent a wave of shock through her.

Aristea pushed aside the curtain of her hair and, for a moment, was transported back in time as she looked into the face of the first boy she'd loved. He wasn't a boy any longer, but a man. He'd grown out a neatly trimmed beard, and his hair was a bit thinner at the temples, but it was still him, Jonathan Sommerfeld.

Heinrich had banished him from court not long after they'd been wed. She'd foolishly confessed to having feelings for him. Nothing had ever happened, of course. Her purity couldn't be compromised. They'd danced a few times at court balls and shared a few impassioned glances. It was innocent, young, and naive love. By the time she'd wed Heinrich, it'd meant nothing to her. But it'd enraged Heinrich. She'd never seen Heinrich angry before then. Their first year of marriage had been sweet and tender. But that night, he'd grabbed a vase off the mantel and shattered it at her feet before she could calm him down by swearing Jonathan meant nothing to her. After that, Heinrich had arranged for Jonathan to marry the daughter of some allies, and Jonathan had been living in the countryside in informal exile.

Her breath caught and her tongue was tied. She recalled vividly the last moment she'd seen him. It had been the day before he'd left to marry. Oh, how she'd shed tears over her careless confession that'd ruined his reputation.

Guards, having witnessed her fall, rushed over and helped her up. Then her lady's maids were swarming, urging her to put her veil back on and straightening her hair. Aristea waved them off, and they backed up a few steps—not enough to give them the privacy she truly craved, however.

Aristea sat on one of the nearby benches and tried to catch her breath. Her heart was racing. And she'd rather die than make a further spectacle of herself by fainting.

Jonathan approached, leaning heavily on his cane. Jonathan had been born with a clubfoot and had relied on a cane to walk since he was a boy. "I didn't mean to startle you. Forgive me, Aristea." The familiar use of her given name sent a shiver through her. No one, apart from her family, called her that. It warmed her to see that their familiar childhood bonds remained. She wanted to apologize, and she also wondered what'd brought him back to court, but the question came out as, "I'm sorry, what are you doing here?" She'd blurted it out and felt the blush crawl over her entire body. If she could've torn off her mouth and thrown it away, she would've.

He rubbed the back of his neck and wouldn't look at her directly. "I've been hoping to speak to you," he said, his gaze burning as it searched her face. "But perhaps I shouldn't have —" He turned as if to walk away.

"No, don't go." She reached out for him on impulse before letting her hand fall to her side, feeling like an impulsive child. The lady's maids had stepped back, but they had a full view of them both. And their allegiances were dubious at best. They were daughters and sisters of powerful men whom Heinrich had placed in her household to keep their eyes on her. And she had no doubt that they reported every move she made back to their fathers and brothers. She needed to be careful.

He turned toward her, face inscrutable. "Your majesty?"

She lamented the return to formal address, but it was a necessary evil. "What is it you wanted to say?" she asked, against her better judgment.

He leaned heavily on his cane, his grip white-knuckled. "I told myself I would come and give my condolences for your loss. But now that I'm looking at you face-to-face, I don't think I can. I'm glad he's gone..."

Her lady's maids gasped. It wasn't treason, but it felt close to it. It was impetuous at the least. And she shouldn't allow it, but it secretly delighted her.

"I will remember this," Aristea said. It could be construed as a threat or as praise. And judging from the small twist of Jonathan's lips, he understood her meaning. He'd said what she'd been thinking all along. Though she dared not say it out loud, she was grateful he was brave enough to say it.

"Your majesty, it's time to meet with Duke Mattison," Yvette said.

His expression fell. "I should go—" He gestured over his shoulder.

They stood awkwardly for a few moments, neither saying a thing.

Yvette cleared her throat.

Aristea ignored it.

"Are you staying long—"

"Shall I escort you inside then?" he said at the same time.

They both laughed, and it seemed to ease some of the awkward tension between them.

Yvette cleared her throat again.

"You've been clearing your throat an awful lot, Yvette. Perhaps I should summon a priestess to examine you."

"That won't be necessary, your majesty. But your appointment... We cannot keep him waiting..."

Aristea had lingered too long. They said their goodbyes, and she didn't express her wish that they'd see each other again, though the sentiment was on the tip of her tongue. They parted ways, and she risked one last look at him over her shoulder. He stood in place, watching her, and when he caught her errant look, he waved a hand at her. Her blush burned hotter, and she was grateful for the veil covering her face.

By the time she returned to her room, her skin was buzzing, and she felt her heart racing. She hadn't even realized Jonathan was back at court. Was it really because of Heinrich's death? She wished there'd been time to talk alone, but they weren't teenagers anymore. No more time for secret meetings in the garden. As it was, she hardly had time for a morning stroll. But maybe they'd stumble upon one another in the garden. She'd like that.

Yvette fixed Aristea's hair and smoothed the wrinkles in her black gown. Then, when she was primmed and prepped, they positioned her on her couch in her receiving room. Once more, the porcelain doll, prepared for empty greetings and statecraft. The duke arrived right on time, which was a point in his favor. Whether she liked it or not, she knew her mother well enough to know this was the preamble to a future engagement, and she might as well get a read on her potential future husband.

Duke Mattison was a handsome man, middle-aged with blond hair gone mostly silver. His neatly trimmed beard, the intentional choice of silk and brocade, and the jewels on his fingers marked him as a man of wealth.

He bowed low upon entry and extended his hand with a flourish.

"Your majesty. It is an honor to make your acquaintance at last."

"A pleasure," Aristea said, with a courteous bow. She wished she had Liane's ability to slip out of fussy meetings. But she was forced to put on a polite smile and offer refreshments instead.

"Thank you for agreeing to see me. Your beauty is famed across the continent, and I couldn't resist the chance to gaze upon you," he said.

"I fear you'll miss out on seeing my visage as I am in mourning for my late husband."

He nodded. "I'm sorry for your loss. He was a great man."

Maybe it was because of Jonathan's earlier comments, but she winced.

Duke Mattison noticed and commented on it. "Am I wrong to think you're not grieving your husband's passing?"

"We shared many years together. That he died before we could start a family was tragic," she said by rote.

"You do not have to pretend with me. In fact, I'd prefer if we were honest with one another. I've known many women who celebrated their husbands' deaths. It gives a widow great freedom to choose her own path, don't you think?"

It'd been presumptuous of him to comment on her feelings during their first meeting. Ruder still to push the issue. She wanted this meeting to end, but feared pushing for such would cause offense. So instead, she smiled coyly and said, "That is not typical of Neolyrian women, I'm afraid. It is traditional that we grieve a year and a day. Sometimes longer."

The duke smiled as if she'd revealed something about

herself. "Then I suppose it would be too forward to invite you to a party I am hosting at my rented home? You would be the guest of honor, of course."

"I thank you for your offer, but it is against customs for a woman in mourning to attend gatherings."

"And for her to entertain would-be suitors," he said.

Aristea did not reply to that.

"You will be missed. Many influential dukes shall be there. I believe many of them were your late husband's friends?"

The smirk on his face sent a chill down her spine, but he'd dangled a tempting carrot before her. There were few natural chances to talk with Heinrich's allies, so the duke had just offered her an opportunity she couldn't refuse.

"Then I'd be delighted to attend," she said, plastering on a fake smile.

4

Liane woke up screaming. In her dream, hands dipped into her flesh as if she were made of soft clay, tearing pieces off her, bit by bit, until there was nothing left of her but a golden sword lying on the cobble. Her scar throbbed as she sat up straight in bed, eyes wild, taking in her unfamiliar surroundings—The stark white walls, a single wooden stool, and Luzie sitting up in her cot, hair mussed as she reached for a candlestick. Luzie leapt to her feet, brandishing the makeshift weapon at unseen assailants.

It would have been funny if the pain was not still shooting up Liane's spine and the specters of her dream weren't lingering at the edges of her memory.

"No one's here." Liane bit down on a gasp. "Just a nightmare and a back spasm. Can you get me willow bark or anything for the pain?"

Luzie dropped the candlestick with a clatter and ran out the door. Liane slumped over onto her side, trying and failing to find a position in which she might lie that'd cause her the least amount of agony.

Luzie returned with willow bark tea and a warm stone

wrapped in a cloth, which Liane applied to her back. Heat seeped into her aching muscles, and they relaxed a tiny bit. When she could sit up, half hunched, she sipped the tea, waiting for the worst of the pain to ease. Aside from the nightmares, her first two days at the temple had been uneventful. She'd spent most of her time in her chambers under the Avatheos' orders that she rest. But the problem was, she wasn't getting much. Nightmares of the dock attack had been impacting her sleep. For the past couple of nights, her dreams had been haunted by disembodied grasping hands tearing her apart. If she weren't trapped in her room, she could have distracted herself. The blank walls and hard bedding reminded her of her miserable bedbound childhood. But the Avatheos was being cautious to not let her overexert herself. Even so, things were progressing too slowly. She'd come to Basilia in hopes of a cure, but she feared she was regressing instead. She needed to get out of this room.

"Luzie, I need to leave this room, or I will go mad."

Luzie shook her head sadly. Liane was hardly able to move as it was. The warm stone was helping, as was the willow bark. In a few minutes, she might be able to muster enough energy to shamble about.

"You need rest."

Dark circles marred Luzie's eyes. Liane wasn't the only one suffering from the nightmares. Luzie had spent the entire boat ride here sick, and now she was being kept up by Liane's nightmares. If Liane left her alone for a bit, at least Luzie would be able to relax. And maybe Liane would pay the price for overexertion tomorrow, but it would be worth it.

"I'm rested enough," Liane said and attempted to sit up to prove it. A jolt of pain ran through her back, and she winced. But once she was up, the throbbing was tolerable, at least.

Luzie clicked her tongue. "Keep this up and you won't be able to sit up for days."

Liane frowned at her, ignoring her good sense. Luzie was the one who would tend to her when Liane inevitably overexerted herself. But the Avatheos had told Liane that pain was a symptom of her unused power. Convalescing wouldn't make it better, action would. If she started her lessons, then surely all her problems would be solved.

"Perhaps I could go to the temple to pray. Surely the Avatheos won't argue against that," Liane said.

"Knowing you, you'd be searching out hidden passages and getting into mischief," Luzie said, crossing her arms and studying Liane with narrowed eyes.

"Why would you assume such a thing of me?" Liane pressed a hand to her chest in a show of false shock and horror.

Luzie narrowed her eyes further, making Liane squirm.

"I promise to not crawl into any strange holes—not that I think I'm capable of much mischief in this condition. I'll lean on Ludwig... Wait, where is Ludwig?" Normally, he'd rush in, sword drawn, at the slightest commotion.

"Now that you mention it, he wasn't outside when I left." Luzie frowned.

It wasn't like him to abandon his post. Especially after what'd happened the other day. A sinking feeling came over her. He couldn't be... could he? Liane got up and flung the door open, certain he would be there with a surprised look on his face, but he was gone. Liane stared dumbly at the empty doorway.

Ludwig was gone...

"I have to go find him," Liane said.

Luzie was faster than Liane in her current condition and placed herself between Liane and the hall, arms crossed.

"I'll go find him. Rest." She gently shoved Liane toward the bed.

But knowing Ludwig was missing felt like an itch inside her skull. Even if pain slowed her down, she had to know what he was up to.

Liane changed tactics and grabbed Luzie by both her hands as she jutted out her lip and fluttered her eyelashes at her. "Please, Luzie. I will go mad if I spend another minute in here. Don't you want some sleep? You haven't rested since we left Artria."

Luzie looked around the room as if the walls would guide her. Then she sighed heavily. "As if I could stop you."

Liane hugged her tightly before turning to leave. She hadn't taken more than a few steps when Luzie grasped her by the wrist.

"What about your veil?"

Liane looked skeptically at the sheer bit of cloth draped over a nearby chair. She'd tossed it there after a priestess had delivered it and hadn't looked at it since. The Avatheos might think it protected her, but it was just a bit of fabric. She might be the goddess' chosen, but she felt anything but divine. Covering her face felt silly. She'd made no vows and was hardly a priestess.

Erich had saved her. If he hadn't been there, she would have been torn to shreds. After the incident, she'd hoped to see him again. Even if it was reckless. If the Midnight Guards discovered him, they'd kill him for being corrupted. As magnificent as his dragon form was, it was corruption. Normal humans didn't turn into winged beasts. As the goddess' avatar and chosen vessel, she represented the light, and he the darkness. But it was hard to separate the man she knew, who'd risked his own life to save her, and the force of evil she knew he was supposed to be.

She pushed thoughts of him away and focused on her

acquired mission. Not even the Avatheos could question her visiting the temple to pray. And should she happen to get lost along the way and discover secrets about her new home, while looking for her errant guard, who could blame her?

Her chamber was at the end of a long hall lined with doors. The corridor ended in a stairwell that led down to the main floor. Liane's first impression of the temple had been a bit of a blur. She'd been surrounded by Midnight Guards as they'd hustled her into her rooms, and then there'd been a flurry of priestesses and priests in and out of her room checking that she was unharmed. By the time the initial shock of the incident had worn off, the visitors had stopped, and the boredom set in. Now that she'd had time to soak it all in, she was surprised by how different the interior of the temple was compared to the one back in Artria. While her room was stark and plain, the halls here were covered in mosaics depicting different moments in Neolyra's history. From the tale of Cyra and the Nameless Goddess to more recent events like the founding of Neolyra.

The temple itself was made of many interlocking circles, and spires. Most of the halls curved, and she couldn't see anyone coming until they were nearly on top of her. The ceilings were vaulted, and each footstep she took had a faint ringing echo. But the priests and priestesses she came across didn't seem to make a sound, and she was startled more than once on her way to the shrine.

They bowed their heads at each other as they passed, but no one spoke. And despite the stillness and silence, there was a frenetic energy in the air that prickled over her skin. She passed by a room with an arched doorway, a ceiling painted with vibrant frescos, and rows upon rows of hooded acolytes sat over scrolls, working, the only sound the scratching of quills on parchment.

Around the next corner was a smaller room, where a

hooded priest instructed a group of children. Liane lingered for a few minutes, wondering what it would have been like had she gotten instruction from a young age. But the thought was too depressing, and she wandered off in search of Ludwig, or at least a hidden passageway.

There were none to be found, it seemed, and she was about to give up on uncovering secrets and finding Ludwig when she saw him speaking with a Midnight Guard. The guard's back was to Liane, but the conversation must have been serious because Ludwig's brow was pinched and he was dragging his hands through his hair, as he often did when he was upset.

He noticed her and said goodbye to the guard before marching over.

"What are you doing?"

"You weren't outside my room," Liane said.

Ludwig sighed. "I had something to do."

She raised her brows, urging him to continue, but he pressed his lips together.

Liane sighed. "You're keeping secrets again."

"No, I'm not." He wouldn't look at her when he spoke.

She wanted to press him, but a crowd of priests passed them by, heads bowed. This wasn't the place to argue. A part of her was afraid to know. Ludwig placed a comforting hand on her shoulder, but she shrugged it off. Let him keep his secrets.

Since she was out, she decided to head to the shrine after all. On her and Ludwig's way, they passed through a garden filled with verdant bushes, arches laden with flowering vines, and a few marble fountains. The pathways, benches, and shaded spots were a place where worshippers and temple residents could sit in quiet meditation if they wished. It reminded her of the garden back home, and a sudden wave of homesickness overtook her.

If she stopped to bask in a sunbeam, she might be transported back home. But when Liane tried to close her eyes and do just that, the stillness and quiet felt too dissonant. Priests and priestesses didn't linger in gossiping circles the way courtiers did. In fact, they seemed to move with single-minded purpose, as if they all had somewhere more important to be. And the only other people in the garden were Midnight Guards standing before the entrances. It left the entire palace, though full of people, feeling cold and lifeless.

She gave up and continued to the shrine. The main shrine room, where they held ceremonies and sunrise services, was twice as big as the one back home. It was a large circular room with a domed roof painted like the sky. A few priests and worshippers were scattered about the pews, heads bowed in prayer. None of them looked up as she entered. Liane slid into one of the pews near the back and sat down to gaze up at the statue of Cyra. It was a massive gilt statue that loomed over the curved rows of pews. In Cyra's right hand, she clutched the Golden Blade. The same sword that was embedded in Liane's back. Liane hadn't come here to pray, not really, but she felt so overcome by the sight of Cyra's golden glory that it felt wrong not to.

She knelt at Cyra's feet and bowed her head. Liane wasn't someone who faith came easily to. Oftentimes, she found excuses to skip sunrise rites and drifted off when the Vice Premier preached. She didn't have words to say in prayer, but she hoped Cyra understood her heart. She had many questions for the goddess. *Why choose me? What do you plan on doing with me?* But as she stared into the farseeing, impassive face of the goddess, no answers were forthcoming. It seemed being the goddess' chosen wasn't as simple as the Avatheos had made it out to be.

Someone cleared their throat from behind her, and she turned around. Ludwig placed himself between her and the interloper, but he relaxed when he realized it was a veiled priestess wearing acolyte yellow.

"Forgive me for interrupting your worship. I went to your room in search of you, but your maid informed me that you were out."

"And you are?"

"Sylvie, your grace. The Avatheos said I was to give you a tour of the temple."

"Oh." Liane looked at Ludwig, and he gave her a slight shrug. "I was eager to get out and stopped to pray."

"I can wait until you finish your prayers." Sylvie bowed to her and took a few steps back to allow her privacy.

Liane stared up at Cyra once more. She could be imagining it, but it felt like maybe this was a sign of the goddess. Liane took a few more minutes to wrap up her prayers and made a show of performing the nine-pointed star before rising up and smiling at her soon-to-be escort.

"Where shall we start?" Liane asked.

"Here, I suppose," Sylvie said. Liane couldn't see her face properly, but what she could see of it looked young.

"You'll see on the ceiling a depiction of the judgment. It shows that when we die and pass through the veil, the Nameless Goddess will judge our souls, and should there be a taint of corruption, we shall remain trapped and tortured for all eternity. But if we live good and pure lives, then we shall ascend to the golden beyond to live with Cyra among the stars." She said this all in one breath, as if she were trying to say it as fast as possible before she forgot what she was supposed to say.

"I'm familiar with church dogma," Liane said in a light, teasing tone. "I thought maybe you could show me the interesting parts of the temple. Maybe tell me a bit about yourself? How long have you been an acolyte?"

A blush was burning on Sylvie's cheeks, and she turned

away. "My life before was nothing; my life among her chosen is eternal," she muttered. It sounded as if it were something she said by rote.

Liane reached out to touch the girl's shoulder, but she flinched away from her. "Please, your divinity. I'm not worthy."

Liane let her hand fall limply to her side. "You don't have to call me your divinity. Liane is fine."

"Your holiness, it is unseemly. You're the goddess' chosen."

"And aren't you? As one of her servants who's dedicated her life to the church?"

"It wasn't much of a choice. Either I came to the church, or I died of corruption when I was older—" She clapped her hand over her mouth as if she'd said too much.

Liane's interests were piqued. "What's that?"

"Nothing. Promise you won't mention it to the Vice Premier? I wasn't even supposed to be here, but I begged Klara, who would have done a better job of this than me, I've always wanted to see a real avatar. And well..."

A group of priests had entered the temple, and Sylvie turned her back toward them, her shoulders slumping. Liane, noticing her fear, moved the conversation along.

"Where's the library? I heard there isn't a grander one than the Library of Basilia."

Sylvie latched onto the distraction and used it as a segue to get them out of the temple interior and into the hall. Liane didn't prod her further into her past, afraid of flustering the poor girl more. She knew from the priests and priestesses back at home that they went into service as children. Some had an aptitude for the mystic arts, reading auguries, healing, or other small hearth magics. She'd never heard of an ultimatum being given.

Sylvie filled the silence by reciting her memorized script,

mostly about the history of Neolyra and other religious dogma Liane had heard hundreds of times before.

"Of course that's before, when the country was called Lyra," Sylvie said, finishing a thought Liane had only been half paying attention to.

"Are you a historian? I never hear people refer to Lyra outside of my stuffy professors."

Sylvie flushed again. "I haven't taken my vows yet, and I may not pass my exams to become one. But being a scholar is my hope…"

"I'm fascinated by the time before the Corruption," Liane confided. "There's not much in the way of information, as so much was lost in the chaos after. But I heard there were rumors that the Library of Basilia had collected what fragments remain of the great library, which contained the world's history on magic before the fall."

She sighed wistfully. "Yes! There are some in the archives. I've never been in there myself, but my mentor has shown me fragments!" Her tone shifted from shy to excited and animated as she waved her hands as she spoke. "And there are books by scholars who've studied them. I can show you a few."

They continued their conversation as they toured the many shelves of the library and by the time Liane returned to her room, Ludwig's arms were overladen with books on corruption, the formation of the empire, and the church's history, which Liane planned to peruse. If she was going to be the goddess' chosen, she ought to know more about what that meant.

5

The sun cresting over the domed roof of the temple cast a glare, forcing Erich to shield his eyes. For two days, he'd been searching for a way into the temple. Each day, the line to get in grew. They arrived before sunrise, waiting their turn for a chance to enter the temple and hopefully meet Liane. Erich hadn't joined the queue on his first day but had stood back and observed the Midnight Guards as they inspected each supplicant. Nine out of ten were turned away, and they would leave offerings on the temple steps. Fruit, wheat, caged chickens, candles, and small piles of valuables. Members of the priesthood gathered them up at sunset, before it started over again the next day. Some had brought their sick or dying relatives and laid them among the offerings, perhaps hoping the priests would take them inside.

There had been no more riots. The Midnight Guard's presence was enough to keep the peace for now. Opportunistic merchants had opened shops in the square, selling hot food, fruit, incense, and other trinkets for offerings. One man even claimed to have strings of beads blessed by the goddess' avatar herself. The smell of food, incense, and the sick was a stomach-churning concoction, and Erich tried not to linger in the square longer than necessary.

Though Erich never got in line himself, he'd talked to those who did, and many were convinced the rich and powerful were being given preferential treatment. No surprises there.

The dragon was restless, weeks away from the full moon, and none of the usual tactics would soothe it. It got worse when he was close to the temple, as if an invisible thread tethered his inner dragon to Liane. It was concerning. The dragon's attention could be deadly. The sooner he could save Liane and heal his curse, the better.

Other than interviewing the common folk, Erich spent his time surveying the perimeter of the temple. Its large towers and main building had a few narrow windows, and even if he could get through one, the walls were tall, smooth, and impossible to climb. He hadn't uncovered any sewer grates or hidden entrances, which had surprised Fritz when Erich had told him. According to Fritz, all church temples were built atop dead veins of magic; there should have been something under it, but there wasn't.

Erich had observed that while worshippers came in and out through the front, no tradesmen, merchants, acolytes, or priests came out. Even the temple could not provide everything they needed to survive and bought from butchers and artisans from outside the temple. Which led him to a back entrance where deliveries were made; it was unassuming, faded orange, and installed in the side of the hill on which the temple was built. There was a young, disinterested Midnight Guard on duty, watching the door.

Erich talked with the merchants coming and going and learned the delivery schedule and about an upcoming celebration they were receiving deliveries for. With that many people coming in and out, Erich thought it was the perfect time to sneak inside the temple unseen.

There was a line of merchants at the back door when he arrived. And the young Midnight Guard lazily checked his ledger, scratching at the scraggly hairs on his chin as he waved merchants in.

"Hello, my friends," Erich said to a pair of merchants sitting in a cart at the back of the line. They were transporting what looked like barrels of wine. He had no goods of his own, nor was he on that ledger. But his plan was to slip in with another group.

They looked at him from the corner of their eyes.

"You're not selling anything," said the younger, and it sounded more like an accusation than a statement.

"But you're selling something worth having, I can see." Erich flashed his bag of geld at the man. "My master would be most interested to know who the Church of Sol has deemed worthy of its patronage."

Geld and compliments were powerful motivators. While he didn't have much of the former, he had plenty of the latter.

"Who do you serve?" One man looked Erich up and down. He wasn't wearing shabby clothes. Thanks to his short stay with Ivar, his clothes were finer than they'd been before he'd arrived in Artria, but they were a bit travel-stained.

Erich leaned in to whisper in the man's ear, and the drama of it caught the attention of several nearby merchants, which was more than he'd expected. The more hooks on the line, the better. One of them was bound to help him get inside if he played his cards right.

"I work for a prince of Sundland." He gave a conspiratorial wink. Sometimes the best lies were rooted in truth. If any of them bothered to look into his claims, they'd discover unsavory rumors about his time in Artria, or they'd assume he was working with his uncles who were far away from here and unable to prove his story either way.

"Aye?" said the older man.

His companion elbowed him in the ribs. "What is your patron seeking here in Basilia?"

"What any man in this city is seeking, to see the goddess' chosen. Between you and me, he's hoping to host a dinner that the goddess' avatar might attend. And, of course, we could only serve the best wine."

The older man laughed. "Your prince might be waiting a long time. The goddess' chosen doesn't entertain kings or princes. She's too important for that."

Erich shrugged as if to say, What can be done about rich fools?

"May I ride with you into the temple on your delivery?" He put his meager bag of geld into the man's hand.

The merchant laughed as he placed the sack into his pocket. "I like you. Come up here and tell me more about this prince you serve."

Erich did just that, chatting with them a while longer, as the line inched forward. Since he liked wine, he had plenty of insightful questions for the winemaker, and by the time they reached the gate, they were laughing and joking like old friends.

Erich tensed, gripping the hilt of his dagger. But the young Midnight Guard took the merchants' names before waving them on into the room beyond.

It appeared to be a large cave, retroactively fitted to be a sort of cellar and storeroom. At the back, there was a long hallway stacked with boxes, barrels, and crates. And at least half a dozen acolytes were milling about, counting items and checking inventory.

The wine merchant unloaded his cart as an acolyte counted the casks. Meanwhile, Erich loitered, looking for the best way past the acolytes for a way to enter the temple proper. But, as the casks dwindled and no opportunity presented itself, Erich feared he'd either have to try and use his allure on half a dozen veiled acolytes—an attempt that would surely fail—or retreat and try again another day.

Then he saw a familiar face enter the cellar. She was talking with one of the acolytes when she looked up, and her eyes widened in recognition. Erich's gaze darted to the exit. They'd met once in the tunnels beneath the palace of Artria. If she sounded the alarm, this would all be for nothing.

To his relief, she stepped away from the acolyte and went off to a deserted corner, where she pretended to be interested in a barrel of pickled vegetables. Erich sidled over. "Do you recognize me?"

"Yes. Though I think you're crazy to be here." She didn't look around as if she were frightened but kept her eyes forward as if there wasn't anything more compelling than fermenting cabbage.

"I need to get a message to Liane. Can you do that for me?"

"What could you possibly have to say to her?" she asked.

"Something urgent. I wouldn't be risking my life if it wasn't."

"Say I deliver your message—how could I convey her reply? Are you going to sneak into the temple? You're a wanted man, you know."

"I'll wait outside that door, in the alley beyond. Ask her to meet me there."

She chewed on her lower lip and wouldn't look directly at him. "I don't know..."

"Please. I'm begging you."

She sighed. "You're as bad as her."

"Is that a yes?"

"I'll pass on the message to her. But I don't know what good it will do you. I'm not even sure she wants to see you."

"I have to try at least."

"Meet me outside the service gate later tonight. I'll pass along her reply." She turned and walked away.

At the same time, the wine merchants were wrapping up their business. Though he wanted to get into the temple proper and find Liane himself, he knew it was best he didn't press his luck.

As he retreated, his chest swelled with something that felt like hope. Perhaps he'd get Liane out of the temple and find a cure faster and more easily than he'd imagined.

6

Rather than claw at the walls waiting for the Avatheos to begin her lessons, Liane buried herself in the books Sylvie had recommended. Most of the texts were rather dry and boring, however, and she found that her focus drifted more often than not. If she'd thought she'd find some firsthand account of what it meant to be the goddess' chosen or how one might navigate having a holy blade in their back, she'd been sorely mistaken.

The only way she was going to figure out how to use and control her power was via the Avatheos, but he was slow to act and even slower to dole out information. He'd promised to teach her about her powers once she'd recovered. But he'd sent no word, nor made any indication he planned to teach her at all. She was starting to fear she'd been lied to again and she'd waste away in the temple waiting for lessons that would never come.

But just as she was about to resign herself to a life as a hermit, there was a knock on the door. Luzie was out on an errand, so Liane went to answer it.

When she opened the door, the acolyte who'd been knocking recoiled.

Liane touched her face. Was there something about her that was shocking? "Yes?" Liane asked.

"Your divinity, I wasn't expecting to see you uncovered." The acolyte lowered their head.

Ludwig was back at his post guarding her door, and he gave her a helpless shrug.

"Am I supposed to be covered up even in the privacy of my own chambers?" Liane asked.

They cleared their throat. "Of course not. Ah. As it was..."

Liane waited for them to collect their thoughts.

"I was sent with a message from the Avatheos—The stars are favorable tonight, and you shall begin your training this evening."

Liane's chest fluttered. This was it, the moment she'd been waiting for. But she couldn't go as rumpled as she was.

"Give me a few moments to prepare. My, er—maid stepped out for a moment," Liane said, and before they could question her, she closed the door and ran around the room.

Liane pumped her fist in excitement, hardly containing her delighted squeals as she made a victory lap around the room. She was in the middle of her celebration when Luzie returned. Her cheeks were flushed as if she'd run the whole way there. Liane rushed over and grabbed Luzie by the shoulders.

"I've had the most wonderful news!" Liane exclaimed.

"You know already?" Luzie gasped.

"Yes. They've just come and told me."

"I wasn't sure you'd want to see him. I was dallying in the hall, debating if I should tell you or not."

Liane frowned. "Why wouldn't I want to hear from the Avatheos? I've been waiting for word from him for days."

Luzie flushed. "Oh, the Avatheos. Of course... Bit drafty, isn't it?" she asked as she went over to fuss with the window.

It was actually quite warm given that it was late summer, and the meager breeze coming through her window was hardly sufficient to cool her down even with the sun setting.

"You were talking about the Avatheos, weren't you?" Liane prodded her.

Luzie kept her back to her and continued to struggle with closing the window. She was hiding something from Liane. Luzie was a terrible liar. The guilt of it ate her up, and she wouldn't look Liane straight in the eye.

"What are you keeping from me? Spill," Liane said with her arms crossed.

Luzie sighed heavily and turned to look at her. "While I was out, I ran into someone we both know."

Liane's brows rose. She wasn't sure who Luzie could possibly know in Basilia, other than Ludwig, and then it hit her. Erich had come to find her.

"Go on," Liane said, struggling to keep her voice steady.

Luzie shook her head. "I shouldn't mention this. Really, it's nothing. Forget it actually." She paced away, and Liane stalked after her.

"Tell me." She grabbed Luzie's arm and tugged until she was forced to face her.

"Prince Erich wants to meet you."

Liane's heart raced, and she tried to keep her expression neutral, but Luzie knew her too well.

"Have you been in contact with him? Liane, he's a corrupted..." Luzie whispered the last word, eyes glancing furtively around the room, as if the very mention of corruption would bring the Midnight Guard down upon their heads. She'd confessed everything to Luzie not long after Erich had vanished from Artria. She thought she'd never see him again. And the thought of keeping the knowledge of her and Erich to herself made her want to explode.

"What did he say to you?" Liane asked, heart in her throat.

Luzie bit her lip as if debating, and Liane had to hold herself back from shaking the information out of her. It surprised her how desperate she was for news of him. To see him again. She'd tried to forget him. She'd thought once they'd slept together, she'd forget him, like sweating out a fever. But if anything, she only wanted more.

"He wouldn't tell me much, just asked to arrange a meeting," Luzie said.

"I need to see him," Liane said.

Luzie looked skeptical, and she was kind enough to not remind Liane of the mob likely waiting outside to tear her apart or the fact that the Midnight Guard wouldn't let Erich into the temple to see her. But she had to see him. If only to say goodbye properly. Because certainly once she did, she would be able to focus on her studies.

"Stars above, but what do I do about the Avatheos? I'm supposed to go to my training…"

Liane paced around the room, weighing the two options against one another. "Perhaps I could go to my lessons and sneak away after they're done and talk with Erich?"

"Are you sure? I could take a message to him and let him know you're busy."

"No. I can do both. I'm sure of it."

Luzie looked skeptical, but there was no time to argue. Liane had to dress and prepare for her lesson. The churning anxiety in her gut had transformed into a buzzing excitement. The waiting had been worth it. She'd see Erich and begin her lessons. Everything was moving forward as it should.

Liane and Luzie opened the door and found the acolyte was

still waiting with an awkward Ludwig, who gave her a pleading look.

"Ready," Liane said.

The acolyte's lips were drawn in a thin line. "The veil, your divinity," they said.

Liane waved away their concern. "I prefer not to wear it."

They looked as if they might protest but said nothing. The veil would get in her way, and Liane wanted to see and hear everything without a fabric barrier in between her and the Avatheos. The acolyte guided Liane to the Avatheos' personal chambers at the top of one of the temple's towers.

Liane had learned from Sylvie that most priests and priestesses lived in shared rooms, depending on rank. The lower your rank, the more roommates you had. Only the elite members of the church were afforded the luxury of a private space.

When they arrived, the acolyte knocked on the door, and a voice called from within for them to enter. The anterior room was spacious, with a large domed roof and an arched window, which looked out onto the starry sky. There was a desk before the window with a small model of planets suspended by metal rings, and tools for measuring the star maps were strewn across the desk. Up until this moment, the Avatheos had seemed much more mythic figure than man. But seeing the small touches of lived-in elements in his room made him feel more real. There was a plate of half-eaten food teetering on a pile of old books.

"Welcome," the Avatheos said, greeting her and drawing her attention to where he stood at the back of the room. There was another doorway, which she presumed led to his personal bedchamber. The room was crowded with books, more tools, and small globes. The globes didn't have any continents on them, but rather constellations painted in thin black lines.

The Avatheos approached her, and atingle of power swept over her. She'd sensed it the few times they'd been alone before, but not once on the ship, and she'd been starting to think she'd imagined it.

"You may leave us," the Avatheos said, gesturing to the acolyte and Ludwig. She looked at him as he walked out, and he gave her an encouraging smile. Her escort and Ludwig filed out until it was her and the Avatheos alone, staring at one another across the table.

All her confident bravado of asking him to allow her to leave the temple wilted upon seeing him face-to-face, or as close to it as they'd get. Like all members of the priesthood, he wore his veil, which obscured the top half of his face, at all times.

"I see you chose not to wear your veil again, your divinity," he said, gesturing for her to sit in the chair in front of her, and she sank into it staring at him from across his large oak desk.

"As I said, I'm not a priestess." Liane smiled as she sat across from him and folded her hands in her lap in a way her mother would have approved of. But the urge to fidget crawled over her skin, and it took all her concentration to keep still. She was trying to maintain her composure beneath the unseen stare of the Avatheos, and even though she couldn't see his eyes, she felt them boring into her just the same.

"I see. Well, I thought we'd start today's lesson with a demonstration."

"You're going to show me magic?" Liane asked, leaning forward eagerly in her seat.

The Avatheos smiled; before now, she would have sworn he was incapable of it.

"Of a kind." He placed one hand on a velvet bag and the other on a round, smooth ball. "Normally those who show an aptitude for magic have their training started at a much younger age. We test children to see what route suits them best —light magic or the sword. Had you come to us at the appropriate age, you would have gone through both schools of magical discipline to make you the perfect avatar. As it is, time is short, and we must truncate your training."

She deflated a little further. If there was magic to learn, she would have liked to know it all. The church guarded their secrets closely, and somehow, she thought being the chosen one meant they'd divulge it all to her.

"Don't be too disappointed. You are her sword born into flesh, and the magic will come more easily to you. I have foreseen it."

"What is it that I should be able to do? Apart from glow and maybe burn things?"

"Oh, but you can do so much more." The Avatheos opened the velvet bag and out clattered runes. They were used in death augury and carved from bones. With a wave of his hand, they floated up into the air in front of him. They circled around his head like constellations, spinning around and around faster and faster until they were merely a blur. Then one came flying at her, and she was too slow to dodge it. It had a sharp edge that she hadn't noticed before, and it sliced into her cheek. Blood trickled down to her chin.

The Avatheos leaned forward and pressed the tip of his finger against the cut, and a warmth suffused her body as pulsing began in her back. It eased the tension she'd been holding in her body for days. In fact, she couldn't remember the last time she'd felt this light and uninhibited by pain.

"You took away my pain," Liane said in an awed whisper.

The runes floated to him and neatly placed themselves back in the bag. "You have the power to do that and more. You could heal corrupted once you're fully awakened."

"Tell me how!" Liane said.

"Magic courses through you. Can you feel it? Traveling through you like golden light?" he asked.

Liane leaned back in her chair. She had been trying to

summon her magic ever since the incident, but it was easier when she was under duress. And other than the odd spark of light, she couldn't do much. Whenever she did magic, it left her with a pounding headache, so she'd stopped trying until the Avatheos could guide her.

"Not really. I was feeling pain, but you took that away…"

He was silent for a long moment, and she got the distinct impression he was disappointed.

"I feared as much." He stood up, the smooth metal ball gripped in his hands.

He approached her from around the desk, and when the ball got closer, she realized it wasn't plain metal but covered in unfamiliar writing. It seemed to be alive as the markings zipped around the ball, like a thousand flickering fireflies.

"Take hold of the rune catcher. And concentrate on making the light."

She took hold of the ball, and as soon as her fingers brushed against it, she felt a zing race up her arm. Then it settled into a tingling sensation, as if the ball were vibrating very slightly. She concentrated on summoning light. She imagined sunbeams, a flickering candle. Her back throbbed with the effort, and after several minutes of hard concentration, all she was able to conjure was a faint shimmer along the ball. And almost as soon as she'd summoned it, it disappeared.

"Interesting," the Avatheos said, more to himself than to her. And she felt an ashamed blush rush over her.

"Am I doing something wrong? Should I say an incantation or something?"

His tutting and muttering were making her feel exceedingly self-conscious. "You certainly have the sparks of power, but something seems to be blocking your magic."

"What?"

"We'll need to find out. Perhaps your power has been too long suppressed and needs something to help draw it out."

He stood up and walked over to a cabinet at the back of the room that she hadn't noticed before. He opened its double doors. It was filled with all sorts of strange oddities, odds and ends of various types. He ran his hands along the shelves before he stopped, selecting one. Then, he turned and walked toward Liane with a jagged black blade in his hand.

The blood in her veins quickened, and the closer he got to her, the more her heart pounded. She felt a spark along her skin, and perhaps even a faint shimmer.

"What is that?" Liane asked, fear making her recoil.

"This is a dagger carved from a revealing stone. We use it to uncover hidden magic."

Liane licked her suddenly dry lips. Her heart was pounding. Surely the Avatheos wouldn't do anything that would hurt her, would he?

"Hold out your hand, Liane," he said.

Her hand trembled as she held it up—from fear or excitement, she wasn't sure. But the moment he placed the tip of the blade against her palm, all she felt was flames, white-hot surging through her veins and threatening to consume her from within. Red filled her vision, and even when she tried to close her eyes, it was still there. It felt like the first time she'd illuminated, but so much worse.

The pain stung like a burn that ran through her flesh and down her back, a searing, splitting pain that felt as if her back was being broken open and the Avatheos was reaching in to yank the sword out of her back or crack open her rib cage and rip the sword out through her chest. She cried out and tried to pull away from the dagger, but the Avatheos grabbed hold of her hand, forcing the blade to pierce her palm deeper.

"The sword, I can see it!" he shouted, free hand outstretched as if he'd grip hold of it.

Tears were streaming down her face. Was it really supposed to hurt this badly? The edges of her vision were clouding, and the pain was becoming unbearable. Then she saw wings beating at the edge of her vision. There was a monstrously large crow sitting in the corner of the room, watching her with its head cocked, mocking her.

"Run," it cawed. Liane lurched back, pulling her hand away, and the dagger fell to the ground between her and the Avatheos, shattering into a thousand pieces. The raven had disappeared, and she wasn't sure if it had been a fevered delusion or a vision.

The Avatheos stumbled backward, clutching the hand that he'd reached out with to grab the sword, and it was red and inflamed. Or, at least, she thought it was because every candle and light blew out in that moment, and they were both plunged into darkness. Panting and cradling her injured hand, Liane stood, her instincts telling her to run, but her devotion to finding the truth kept her in place. The candles reignited, and the Avatheos, also breathing hard, stood back from her as if he was terrified of her, though she couldn't imagine why.

"The revealing stone is harder than diamond. It shouldn't have shattered so easily," he said. He rubbed the bottom of his chin. "But I saw it, the Golden Blade fused with your back. We'll need something stronger to draw it out, I believe."

It seemed he was talking more to himself than her, but she was too tired to care. The pain in her hand was fading, and the shock of what had happened was starting to settle, and in its place, her stomach was roiling.

"I think I'm going to be sick," she announced a moment before leaning forward and vomiting her dinner onto the Avatheos' polished floors.

"Perhaps I pushed you too hard for your first time. Return to your room and rest. We will resume your training another day, after I have consulted the stars on what to do next."

Liane nodded and stood on wobbling feet. The Avatheos must have called for Ludwig because the next thing she knew, he was there, his arm around her waist, half dragging her out the door.

"What happened?" he asked.

Liane shook her head, not wanting to talk about it and preferring the temptation of sleeping for a thousand years or more.

Without his assistance, she would never have made it to her room, where she collapsed onto her mattress and decided sleeping for a thousand years sounded like a very good idea, not realizing she'd completely forgotten her meeting with Erich.

7

T he dragon was much too restless for a waning crescent night. Erich had nearly been crawling out of his skin in anticipation of seeing Liane again and spent most of the day prowling the city, fighting the impulse to loiter for fear of raising suspicion from the Midnight Guard. But when the sun set, he returned to the rendezvous point. The dragon's hunger was concerning. He'd seen it take interest before, when it'd taken a man's life, but back then, it hadn't been possessive; it'd been bloodlust, a desire so deep to devour and maim he'd lost control and killed like a wild animal. He'd been trying to ignore the gnawing hunger of the dragon for weeks. But it'd been swelling inside him, crowding out all other thoughts besides Liane, especially at night. It'd only gotten worse since he'd saved her on the dock—pressed his fingers into her flesh, smelled the rosewater in her hair, and let her slip through his fingers once again. This was the dangerous game he was playing. He danced upon the knife's edge, both her savior and her destruction. How long before the hunger turned to bloodshed?

A pair of Midnight Guards strolled past where Erich

loitered, and he slunk back into the shadows, praying he hadn't been seen. A bell tower chimed the first curfew warning.

He'd hoped she'd have come out by now; the closer to curfew, the more Midnight Guards there'd be wandering the streets.

He knew the risks of waiting for a reply that might never come, and he was willing to accept them. But there was a wrongness about the stillness of this night. His skin prickled and twitched, just days before the change. Although this didn't seem to be coming from within, even the dragon had gone quiet. There was a faintly sweet scent in the air— magic.

Erich surveyed the shadows that surrounded him. What if she'd betrayed him and he was walking into an ambush? He gripped the hilt of his dagger, pushed the sheath down with his thumb, and revealed the inscription along the blade. He dragged his thumb along the inscription there. His maternal uncle who'd gifted him the blade would have teased him for being so suspicious. Liane had helped Erich escape once, even knowing what beast lived inside his skin. She wouldn't turn on him. But that didn't mean her maid could be trusted. He'd been blinded by his decision to trust her. Should he turn back? But he waited.

The second of three alarm bells rang, and the streets were empty. Erich tapped his fingers against his dagger and continued to wait.

A man walked up and gave Erich a crooked smile, the sort of look he'd seen on plenty of common criminals. He reached for his dagger and whistled, pretending not to notice him, hoping he'd pass him by. But he wasn't so fortunate.

"You're still here?" the man said.

He'd never seen the man before, but presumably, he'd noticed Erich earlier.

"Just on my way back," Erich replied and turned to walk away. He'd circle the street and come back, praying to the Trinity that Liane didn't choose that moment to come meet him.

The man fell into step with Erich, walking down the street with him.

"I heard your master has ambitions to meet the goddess' chosen."

"Don't know what you're talking about," Erich said.

"Filbert. I'm a dealer." The man thrust his hand out, offering it to Erich to shake. But the gleam in his eye made the hairs rise on the back of Erich's neck.

"What sort of dealer?" Erich asked, though he had a good idea of what the man was after.

"Information." He smiled, revealing his one golden tooth.

Erich eyed him up and down. He was well-dressed in the gaudy, sort of flashy way of men of his kind—golden chains dangling from his neck, a pearl-encrusted walking stick.

"What sort of information?"

"In this city, there's plenty to be found. But in your case, I can tell you how to get in contact with the avatar directly."

"Can you now?" Erich said with an uninterested and skeptical tone. With this many in the city desperate to get in contact with the avatar, he sincerely doubted this man could help.

"For the right price," the man said with a wink.

"No thanks," Erich said.

"It'll be worth it, I can assure you."

Erich didn't reply as he lengthened his stride and turned two corners in an attempt to get away from the man. He took a winding path down a few city streets before returning to the alleyway where he'd been waiting. There was no sign of Liane as the third, and final, warning bell rang. If he didn't retreat and leave for the inn, the Midnight Guard would arrest him. And if he were caught, there was no Ivar to rescue him. But he remained glued in place.

His eyes bored into the back gate, closed tight, not even the faintest glow of candlelight beyond it. This was a fool's errand. He should have known it was too easy to try and reach her this way. What should he do next? Storm the temple and kidnap her? Risk his life and perhaps hers in a desperate attempt to remove her from the church's clutches? He'd never been one to rush in, but something about Liane made him reckless.

Someone had snuck up behind him and pressed a knife to his kidney. He tried to draw his dagger, but they put a hand over his wrist.

"Don't move too quickly, if you want to keep your insides... in," the dealer said.

"What do you want? Money?" Erich asked, tensing his muscles, readying to land a blow into the man's gut with an elbow, but before he could, the man stepped back, and Erich spun around to face him.

His assailant swung his cane, and the strike burned, as if the cane had been coated in hot embers. Erich caught a quick glimpse of the runes circling around the shaft. This wasn't some dealer in secrets. But a hunter undercover. Erich hit him with an uppercut, and he stumbled backward, clutching his bleeding nose. Which gave Erich a chance to run, but as soon as he reached the end of the alleyway, his path was blocked by two hulking figures—a man with a scar across his face who was wielding an axe, and the other man who was missing his thumb and pointer finger. These were the same hunters who'd cornered him before. Erich sized them up and rushed the short one, whom he assumed was their leader, catching his arm and twisting it behind his back before pressing his dagger against his throat.

"You're rather quick on your feet." He laughed.

"Do you find this funny?" Erich replied.

"Extremely. You think my associates over there give a damn if you slit my throat?"

The hunters laughed, and Erich hesitated. If they were merely out to kill him, they could have done it already. But they'd hesitated. Why?

"What do you want?" Erich repeated.

"I have a business proposition for you." He gestured away down the alley.

"What if I said I'm not interested?" Erich snarled.

"Then we do this the hard way," the man said, his tone shifting.

The two hulking figures approached, and Erich scored a line along their leader's neck, and even as blood rolled down, they didn't slow their pursuit. Erich shoved him to the ground and made a run for it. The dragon rose to defend him, but he fought the urge to use its power. It would have been fruitless anyway. They tossed something onto him—a net or something similar —that knocked him to the ground, and Erich crumpled, limp as a doll. His arms and legs were too heavy to lift, and he saw the binding marks twirling around the fibers of the net they'd used to capture him. There must have been a sleeping spell woven in as well because his eyelids were growing heavy despite the rush of adrenaline in his veins. He had to fight it, but he couldn't resist its pull.

His captors stalked closer to him, the man he'd cut holding a handkerchief to his wound.

"Bring him—" The second half of his sentence was lost to the fog of Erich's fading mind. The last thing he saw before they put a bag over his head was the gold-toothed smile smirking down at him.

"You should have come quietly."

Erich woke with his face pressed against a very plush carpet and his hands and feet bound. The runes in the ropes burned against his skin, pulsing like an infection. It was unusual for hunters to leave their targets alive. Not that it boded well for Erich's chance of survival. Maybe he wasn't as valuable in human form, and they planned to torture and kill him until he transformed or simply hold him captive until the full moon, when he'd have no choice but to transform. He'd been too consumed with reaching Liane to watch out for hunters. They were mercenaries of a secret order, which hunted and harvested corrupted like himself for profit.

A door out of view creaked as it opened, and heavy footsteps approached. Erich twisted in his bindings to face a man. He was tall and lean, with a neatly cropped goatee and shrewd eyes. His sleeves were rolled up and revealed a hunter's tattoo on his forearm, with dozens of hash marks. Each one represented a dead corrupted. It was a dangerous profession. Most didn't make it to middle age, and this man had survived more encounters than most. He leaned over, studying Erich as if he were some curios on a shelf.

"I apologize for this indelicate meeting. I've never met a dragonborn before, and as such, we had to take every precaution."

He'd never heard his curse referred to that way. His uncle merely called it his affliction. But whatever he called him didn't matter. Erich tested the ropes tying his arms behind his back and his feet together, and felt the sting of binding runes. It muted his connection with the dragon and sapped his strength. Meaning he had the strength of an ordinary man, leaving him helpless and at this hunter's mercy.

"Are you saying you don't usually knock guests over and tie them up?" Erich remarked.

"It used to be I killed your kind on sight. Too risky." He leaned back against a desk, crossing his arms, as they glared at one another. After their brief staring contest, the man exhaled out his nose and turned his back on Erich to reach for a bottle of wine. He poured two glasses of dark-red Sundland wine, and then he raised one toward Erich as if he could take it from the man's hand. It felt like a targeted insult. Either this man knew who Erich was and was using his favorite thing to mock him, or this was a cruel twist of fate even Fritz couldn't have foretold. The hunter lifted his glass to his lips and sipped at it slowly. After making Erich watch him take his time enjoying his drink, the hunter set down his glass.

"Now, we can either speak to one another as civilized men, or I can turn you over to the Midnight Guard to do with you as they wish." He picked up a piece of parchment from the desk and showed it to Erich.

The artist's depiction of him wasn't perfect, but was close enough that anyone who saw him near the poster might give him a second glance.

"If we are going to speak like men or boys, why are we playing games?" Erich asked.

"As my associate tried to explain before, I have a business proposition for you."

Erich wanted to spit on the man's shiny boots, but he had enough sense of self-preservation to say, "Alright, let's hear your proposition."

The man dragged out the moment by picking up the second glass and swirling its contents.

"First, let me introduce myself. I am Leonhard Harnisch, head of the Hunters' Guild here in Basilia and a collector of rare and powerful creatures, such as yourself."

Erich ground his teeth so hard his jaw ached. He knew this man by reputation only. The Basilia hunters were rumored to be backed by the church and had grown wealthy and powerful. And their leader entertained the city's elite with his illegal chimera-fighting pits, where he put beasts, and sometimes men, up against one another in death matches. He knew why this man had sought him out now. Why they'd captured him rather than killed him. He wanted Erich for his spectacle. Erich supposed there were worse fates. He could have his guts cut out and dried into jerky as some strange remedy for the foolish.

The man crouched down in front of him. "Can you control your shift, Prince Erich? Or is the blood too thin for that?"

"I'm corrupted, not dragonborn or whatever you think I am."

The man waved his hand. "Corruption, curse, dark magic. I've heard it called many things, but it's not what your kind were always called. Not before." He picked up an old book from his desk, thumbed through it, and held an open page to Erich. There was a drawing of a man, a man-dragon with scales and small wings, as if he were halfway through transforming.

The book didn't interest Erich. It didn't matter if there were others. All he knew was the curse was killing him. "So you've seen creatures like me in books. And you want me to transform, what, for you?"

"No, I want you to fight in the arena. I think it would be spectacular." There was a greedy glint in the man's eyes that made Erich's mouth turn to ash.

His dagger lay on the desk, the handle toward him, perhaps another mockery. Erich's hand ached to take hold of it and drive it into this man's throat. But he had to bide his time instead.

"You'd have me choose between death in a pit or death by execution?"

The man crossed his arms and studied Erich for a moment.

"I'm a businessman. I don't make investments that I don't expect to pay off. If the legends are true, you'll perform well against whatever I throw at you."

"And then what? I keep fighting until my untimely demise?"

"I do treat my champions well."

"And is there some sort of reward for winning?" He was taking a big gamble. But if he'd learned anything from spending time in the underbelly of the continent for close to six years, it was that big risks were the ones worth taking.

A smile spread across Leonhard's features. "Rather bold to be making deals, given your position. But yes, I reward those who please me. Tell me, what would you like should you survive?"

"When I win your match... help me get into the temple."

"Who says I have that sort of sway?"

"You're organizing pit fights with corrupted under the nose of the Avatheos. You've got to have someone in your pocket, or many someones. There's no way the Midnight Guard hasn't caught wind of your operation."

"You have my measure, it seems. Fair enough. You win, and I'll give you access." He shrugged. Then he looked past Erich, toward what Erich assumed was the door, and called, "Come in."

The door creaked open. Erich assumed he'd be dragged to a holding cell or something, but instead, someone came in and yanked him onto his knees. They pulled back the collar of his shirt, and Erich fought the urge to struggle against them. Once they had his neck exposed, he felt something hot against his shoulder. That was when he did try to thrash, but whoever was behind him had an iron grip on him, and he couldn't move.

He felt the mark burning into his skin, searing his flesh and making the dragon inside him roar with dissatisfaction. But he could do nothing to stop it. He'd heard of these sorts of marks before. A hunter's mark—one that could allow a hunter to track their quarry.

"A bit of insurance. You understand. Can't have you escape and get away before you've performed." Then, to the person who'd branded him, he said, "Take him away."

8

ristea's carriage came to a halt outside Duke Mattison's rented town house, but she didn't move to exit. She shouldn't be out during her grieving period. Any connections she might make would be sullied by conflicting with the practiced traditions. But how could she possibly strengthen relationships without speaking to them? A year was too long to wait. She had to attend events like this, no matter the scandal. But it wasn't just the mourning veil troubling her. Aristea hadn't realized how serious Mother was about her courting the duke until she'd brought it up at dinner last night. Of all the petty things that bothered Aristea, the worst infraction was his age. He was at least twenty years her senior. Aristea wasn't young anymore. Approaching thirty and reputed to be barren, even as heir to an empire, marriage candidates were always going to be slim.

Because you cannot rule on your own. Heinrich's words taunted her.

Delaying her exit was holding up the line of gilded carriages behind her. Duke Mattison hadn't lied. She recognized many family crests of the city's elite as her carriage circled the block.

Anyone with eyes knew what he was after. Aristea was just so tired of this game. She was much too old for it now. She watched young girls, in their best brocades and silks, giggling behind their decorative fans as they climbed the steps of the town house. Had she ever been so young and naive? Maybe not quite that naive. She'd been engaged young, and apart from a short daydream about Jonathan, she'd never held delusions of her life being hers to choose. Which she'd preferred at first.

But ever since Heinrich died, questions long buried had started creeping up, chipping away at the foundation of her carefully crafted life.

The rules said she shouldn't be out. But her goals superseded propriety. Aristea rubbed her temples as she felt a headache coming on. No point in delaying any further. And yet she still hadn't moved.

Maybe it wouldn't be so bad. Half the court cheered his death, many of them his supposed allies. He wasn't well-liked, even by those closest to him. It was what he'd represented—the legitimacy of a man's claim was stronger than a woman's. But she knew she could change their minds, as Mother had. She'd changed the rules being the first empress, and with the church's backing, she'd carved out a new empire. But now the church was too preoccupied with Liane to support her rule. Aristea shook her head. She couldn't begrudge Liane; she hadn't chosen this fate. They all had their roles to play, Liane within the Church of Sol, Aristea as head of the empire, and Mathias, their younger brother... he was risking life and limb to uncover the elven plot. She could withstand a little embarrassment to help secure the empire's position. If the elves were planning an attack, they needed allies like Sundland. Mother was right to send her.

The coachman rapped on the door. "Your majesty, do you wish to exit, or shall I drive around one more time?"

He was being exceedingly kind, even though they'd already circled the street several times. She was beyond fashionably late and starting to border on rude.

"That won't be necessary," she called.

Through the gap in her curtains, she could see the footman waiting to open the door and the coachman standing back, rubbing his neck. Aristea straightened her black veil and smoothed out her dress before pulling back the curtain to nod that they could proceed. The door swung open, and those few courtiers lingering on the steps turned as if their heads were on swivels. Aristea stepped out of her carriage, back held ramrod straight, and descended the steps. Courtiers bowed as she passed by, dipping their heads low in respect. But as soon as her back was turned, the buzz of whispers followed. It was fine. Let them talk. The fate of the empire mattered more than petty gossip. Aristea gritted her teeth as she passed through the crowded foyer, sailing past the lined-up courtiers waiting to be announced.

In the seconds before she was announced, Aristea scanned the ballroom. For having only been in Artria for a little over a month, Duke Mattison had amassed quite a network. She noticed the Sundland ambassador and his daughter squabbling in the corner. And apart from the ambassador, she saw many more of the largest and most powerful families in Neolyra, some of whom she hadn't even realized were in Artria for the summer. There were a few unfamiliar faces in the crowd as well, perhaps merchants or guild masters. The music paused to proclaim her arrival. And though she'd stepped into a hundred rooms before with all eyes on her, it still made her stomach flutter. The specter of Heinrich's taunts rang in her ear. *Don't linger too long. They'll think you're vain. Don't walk so stiffly. You look cold and unapproachable.* Even through a shroud of black lace and Heinrich's past criticisms ringing in her ears, she smiled as she entered the ballroom.

Several dukes, leaders of the principalities that made up the empire, were in attendance. There were two factions among them—those who'd supported her mother during the rebellion and those who'd sided with the rebels. Outside of official royal functions, high holidays, and council meetings, they didn't mingle. But there were representatives from both sides in attendance tonight, which was shocking. They stood on opposite sides of the room, glaring at one another over their brandy glasses. But no knives had been drawn, which felt like a miracle in itself. Since Heinrich died, she'd been trying to appease his faction, but none had come calling. She decided to favor a trio of Heinrich's former favorites first. Among them was their quasi-leader, Duke Krantz. An ancient man with a long scruffy mustache and a gruff temperament, he wasn't one she could approach directly, as he was a stickler for tradition. Normally, she would have spoken with his wife, the duchess, but Aristea didn't see her in attendance.

Aristea approached, and they greeted her with a bow.

"Your majesty," they murmured.

"My lords." She nodded, then turned to their wives, one of whom she'd matched with one of Heinrich's allies in an attempt to heal the rift. "Duchess Baumstein, it looks as if marriage is treating you well."

"Thank you, your majesty." She dipped her head, accepting her compliment. But she did not engage Aristea in conversation as she normally would have.

A long lull in conversation followed, and Aristea felt the strain of it as if it were a weight upon her chest.

"A lovely night, is it not? And Duke Mattison is a gracious host," Aristea remarked.

"It is, your majesty," said the woman's companion, a lady

Aristea had seen around court but never been introduced to. Perhaps her sister or cousin?

No one else spoke. And the tense silence hung in the air. The dukes continued their conversation as if she weren't there at all. The way they had done it when Heinrich had been alive. She hadn't thought about how much she relied on him until he was gone.

"And how is your husband, Lady Herberger?" Aristea said, trying to press on with making small talk, no matter how painful, looking sidelong at said husband, who'd turned his back on her.

"Well," Lady Herberger replied.

Aristea wasn't the type to fidget. She had trained herself to keep perfectly still and poised. But uncertainty pricked her, and she wished she could tap her foot or wring her hands in this moment. The awkward silence was painful. This went beyond the impropriety of her being out while in mourning black. She expected gossip and private condemnation, but not this cold shoulder she was receiving. She was the future empress. Were they really so bold as to ice her out? Unless they didn't think she'd become empress. Did they know something she didn't? Aristea tried to push away those thoughts and pressed onward.

"It's been a while since we've talked. I would love to have you visit for a luncheon and hear more about your life as a wife," Aristea said.

"Thank you, your majesty," Lady Herberger replied.

Aristea knew a dismissal, and rather than prolong her suffering, she made up an excuse to get away. She was glad for the veil, which hid her face from view, because her cheeks burned with embarrassment.

None of them ever liked you. They all thought you were a stuck-up snob. Remember? Heinrich's ghost whispered in her ear.

Aristea kept the smile and moved to the next group, those

who supported her mother. They were younger dukes who'd never fought in the war but had inherited titles and loyalties from their fathers.

"My lords," Aristea greeted them.

They, too, exchanged brief pleasantries before they drifted away with thin excuses. Her stomach sank. If even her mother's allies wouldn't speak to her, then she had made a grave mistake coming out. Or was the wind of change blowing and rebellion stirring? The thought made her heart race, and rather than stand and allow the storm cloud of thoughts to gather, she kept moving, weaving through the crowd, greeting guests, with no destination in mind until her path dead-ended at the buffet table, but she had no appetite. Everyone seemed to be standing away from her—perhaps deterred by the veil obscuring her face, or perhaps by nefarious plots to remove her and her mother from the throne. She couldn't breathe. Her chest felt tight in the way it had when she and Heinrich would fight, and he'd call her hysterical.

She couldn't have an episode here in front of everyone. The shame would be too much to bear.

It's because without me, you have nothing. Do you think they'll let you rule, over your brother? the Heinrich in her mind mocked her. She shook off the specter of her deceased husband and turned from the banquet table, searching for the exit, but the room blurred around her. She couldn't seem to catch her breath, and she feared she might faint here in front of all these people. Aristea gripped the banquet table behind her, bracing herself to catch her breath.

"Your majesty?" A soft voice cut through the buzzing noise in her ears. Jonathan looked at her with a calm, sympathetic gaze. Before she could speak, he grasped her gently by the shoulders and guided her from the crowded ballroom into an adjoining sitting room. By some miracle, it was empty. He turned her so her back was to the door and locked eyes with her. Her breaths were a wheezing mess, and she wished very much to run but found her legs were leaden.

"Take a couple of deep breaths; you're going to be okay."

She did as he instructed, breathing in and out slowly until her breaths resumed a normal cadence. The knot in her chest loosened, though the trembling in her hands had worsened.

"There, you're okay." His soothing voice calmed her. "Will you be alright if I leave for a moment to get you a drink?"

All she could manage was a nod, and he walked away, his cane thudding with each step he took. Aristea's knees buckled beneath her, and she collapsed onto the nearby sofa. The buzzing had stopped, and she was feeling more herself once again.

Jonathan returned a few minutes later and offered Aristea a glass of wine. "Here, take a couple sips. It might help."

His hands brushed against hers as he handed her the glass, and her stomach did a somersault. Her attack must have affected her more than she'd realized if she was feeling queasy. Jonathan's smiling face filled her vision.

"Thank you," she said.

"No need. I'm always happy to help a lady in distress," he said.

"I don't remember you being this gallant," Aristea said as she sipped her wine.

"I'm not usually. But you make me want to be chivalrous."

Her cheeks burned as her eyes darted around the room. She'd already mucked things up tonight. If Duke Mattison saw them together, he might get the wrong impression. Not that she should care. She didn't want to marry him, but she wanted him to think she might. The thought made her chest squeeze tighter.

She stood up to leave, but her head spun, and her knees

threatened to give out again. Jonathan grasped her by the elbow, and they stood frozen in time, looking at one another. Heat coiled in her stomach, and it had nothing to do with her panic attack. They couldn't keep running into one another like this. She might start wanting things she couldn't have.

Someone cleared their throat, and they stepped apart.

"There is our guest of honor. I've been looking all over for you," Duke Mattison boomed as he approached her, bowing low.

"Forgive me. I was feeling a bit overheated and stepped away for a moment. Lord Sommerfeld was kind enough to bring me some wine."

"A kind gesture indeed." Duke Mattison's eyes barely skimmed over Jonathan before coming to rest on her. His lips curled into a smile. "Come, I want to make a toast to you."

Aristea flapped her hands, trying to dissuade him, but Duke Mattison pressed his hand into her lower back and was guiding her out of the room and back into the crowded ballroom before she could protest. It was much too familiar for such a casual acquaintance, but the words to protest froze on her tongue. He was a foreign guest and had foreign customs, and she didn't want to upset him. They took to the stage at the front of the room, and he called everyone to attention with a clink of his glass. Another glass of sparkling wine was thrust into her hands as the crowd turned to look at them.

"A toast to our gracious Princess Aristea and continued harmony between our two countries." Duke Mattison raised his glass, and the guests thrust theirs up in agreement.

Aristea looked at Duke Mattison, who smiled at her with malicious delight. The implication of such a toast was that they were courting. When her husband was a mere month in the grave. Even if she weren't trying to court her traitorous husband's allies, it was audacious to imply it publicly without discussing it with her first. But she couldn't say anything on stage without making a scene, and so she smiled and turned from the crowd to lift up her veil enough to take a sip. The sparkling wine fizzed on her tongue and burned all the way down, turning her stomach sour. Though she feared his reaction, she couldn't help but seek out Jonathan in the crowd. He was watching her from the back of the room, his brows drawn together.

His kindness meant nothing. He was a good person. She had to keep reminding herself of that, but she still felt the need to explain herself.

"You are a gracious host and a good friend, Duke Mattison." She held up her glass to make a second toast.

His smile turned down slightly at the corners, but he made no comment. Everyone toasted to their collective good health, and then Duke Mattison insisted on Aristea sharing a dance with him.

She couldn't decline after his overture of marriage, so she let him lead her onto the floor. When they were dancing close together, he whispered, "You look beautiful tonight, your majesty," he said, his words dripping with honey. It reminded her, with a twist of her gut, of the way Heinrich would pour on sweet words after upsetting her.

"You're too generous with your praise, with your words, and your toast," Aristea remarked.

"What else could I do? You are a vision and the future of Artria. I heard rumors that you seek to finish what your grandfather started. You want to destroy the elves," he said.

Aristea looked around them out of the corner of her eye. If anyone were eavesdropping, they gave no indication of it. How he'd learned of their elvish problem, she could only guess. Either way, she had to tread carefully with him. Heinrich had been collaborating with the elves who'd supplied him with stardust. And she feared more co-conspirators remained lurking in the shadows.

"Perhaps," she said, trying to remain coy.

"It is a problem both our nations share, and when I have the army of Sundland behind me, I could make your dreams come true."

Her attention snapped to Duke Mattison. "Is that so?" She had to admit it was a tempting proposition. Rather than try to win over Heinrich's fickle lackeys, she could marry Mattison and use his army to force anyone who might stand against her to their knees. But it also meant giving up power to another man who reminded her too much of Heinrich.

"The elves have grown restless and bloodthirsty. We captured one who spoke of a great calamity, one that might destroy all of humanity."

Her chest tightened. "That is worrying."

"I think we can find a solution together." He reached out to cup her cheek, and she had to fight the wave of revulsion that threatened to overcome her.

She gently stepped away. "I'll consider your offer."

"Don't think too long. The elves won't wait."

Her heart thumped in her chest. He was right, of course. But would she have to give up her own happiness a second time for her country? How much more would she have to sacrifice to get what she was owed?

9

E rich's prison stank of urine and fear. They'd locked him in overnight, or at least he assumed a night had passed. There were no windows in his cell, and this far underground, no light came through the doors. Guards had changed and three meals had been brought at regular intervals. Each meal was a thick gruel, with a side of salted meat. His guards never opened the door but watched him from a distance as if he were a mad creature willing to pounce at the slightest provocation. And they were right to do so. Once the rune ropes had been removed, he'd felt the dragon just beneath the surface of his consciousness, testing its barriers, trying to break free like a caged animal. When the guards had come to deliver a ration for dinner or breakfast, it'd lunged within him, and it'd taken all of his concentration to prevent himself from transforming. He was accustomed to feeling as if he were split in two, man and monster. Most of the month, the man was in control, and the beast within gave its input, which he ignored. When its obsession took hold, however, it was as if it were gnawing on the back of his skull, like a rat biting a hole in a grain cellar door. The longer he spent in the cell, the more of his willpower it'd taken, until eventually the dragon was an ever-present monster, lurking in the shadows of his mind, poised for attack.

Though Erich couldn't see much beyond the bars of his cell, he heard plenty. Creatures growled. A dying man moaned in agony. Another pleaded in a high-pitched, whining voice, promising to pay back his debts for hours at a time before, presumably, exhaustion overtook him, and he'd sleep only to wake and resume his pleading. Erich couldn't sleep, though common sense said it would be wise. He feared that the moment he lost consciousness, the dragon would take hold, as it had the last time he'd given in to the dragon's obsession. He'd fallen asleep without proper control of the dragon and woken in a murder scene, a dead man in front of him, and himself covered in blood. He'd run away from Sundland the same day. His shame was too great to bear. How could a monster like him become a king? His search for a cure for this dragon curse had led him to Liane, and now here.

His arm rested on his bent knee, and he curled his hand into a fist. Erich had been in dire situations before. Though he was hard-pressed to think of much worse. This gamble he was taking with the hunters, it all hinged on them keeping their word. He hadn't tangled face-to-face with many hunters, but they had every reason to betray him. But if Erich played their game, and if he survived, he might have his best chance of reaching Liane. This might be the route that Fritz's visions couldn't see. He wouldn't linger too long on the thought of what he might face in the ring later. It could be a chimera, or worse, something with a human face. Whatever it was, he'd cut them down with his bare hands if he had to. Whatever it took to get to Liane. The thought seemed to settle the dragon, and it eased back a bit, though it remained dangerously close to the surface.

Erich tilted his head back and looked at the black, grimy

ceiling. Had Liane come to meet him after he was captured, or her maid with a message? It was a setback he couldn't afford. There was still so much unsaid between them. She must think he was a liar and a con artist. If Duke Mattison had been spreading rumors to ruin his reputation and paint him as a fraud, then he already had two strikes against him. If he got out of here and fumbled their meeting, would that be his last chance? Erich shook off the thought—better to focus on what lay ahead of him.

Another guard change happened, and they took away the moaner and then the pleader. In the absence of the cries of his dungeon mates, he could hear the roaring of creatures clearly; they were somewhere deeper in the dungeon. Men shouted as the guards presumably transported them to the arena, and Erich retreated deeper into his mind, a sort of self-preservation tactic his uncle had taught him that was meant to keep the dragon under control but, in this instance, helped calm his mind from racing at the thought of what he'd face in that ring.

Then they came for him—two hulking hunters with a dozen hash marks between them. His muscles tensed on impulse as the door swung open, and the dragon hissed in his ear, ready to slash at them with claws he didn't have. Erich stood with his hands clenched as they tied them back with the same rune rope they'd used when they'd captured him, and he allowed himself to be led through the dingy halls of the dungeon. The ropes had long leads, and one guard stood in front and the other behind. Each carried a long spear, which they'd probe him with if he slowed his pace even a little. They treated him more like a beast than a man, and maybe that was what he was to them.

At the end of the hall, glowing yellow light came from holes in scarred wooden double doors. A buzzing sound increased in intensity as they approached, and it wasn't until they were nearly upon it that he realized the sound wasn't a buzz but a roaring crowd. They removed his ropes and pushed him through the double doors and then barricaded them behind him. The space was small, perhaps ten square feet, and on the opposite end were bars, which could be raised by a pulley system. Someone in the arena released a bloodcurdling scream that was followed by a collective gasp and cheer from the crowd. An announcer was saying something, but their voice was too muffled for him to make out. He smelled blood and terror, and it made his stomach roil. The dragon was thrashing at its bindings now. Its sense of self-preservation fighting against Erich's need to hold back his transformation. He wouldn't fight and die like a monster.

The gate rattled open to reveal a sandy arena, and the crowd roared with approval. The holes in the door were for the guards to push their spears through and force him out if he resisted, but Erich strolled out into the arena, blinded by the bright spotlights pointed down at him. Guards were dragging out the body of his predecessor, leaving a bloody smear in the sand. The chimera Erich was meant to fight paced along the perimeter of the pit, preoccupied for the moment by the keepers who were luring it toward the wall to the delight and terror of the crowd. Though it was an impressively sized creature, it couldn't have scaled the walls if it tried. The walls were old—cracked and patched a hundred times over—and three times Erich's height. The chimera was a concern, but the attendance was more alarming. This wasn't a secret underground fighting ring; it was a citywide spectacle. He looked at the crowd above him, and their faces were indistinguishable from one another. But he heard the bloodlust in their voices as they chanted for his death.

When he'd agreed to this battle, he'd assumed it would be

in some small warehouse out of the way, an underground pit fight. This was something from the history books. Organized and professional. This coliseum had to be hundreds of years old, built before the Corruption. Blood sports had been banned by the Church of Sol a century ago, or so he'd thought. This shouldn't be happening. The dragon roiled around in his mind, fighting against the chains that bound it, eager to break free. His heart was hammering in his chest as his opponent turned to face him. It'd caught his scent, and the keepers were no longer of interest to it.

It watched him with narrow red eyes. It had rows of sharp teeth in a skeletal, lizard-like head with deer antlers, dripping with blood, and the long, spindly legs were those of a deer but split open with spines protruding from them. The chimera looked more like a monster wearing a deer skin than any deer he'd seen. Black crystal formations were clustered at its joints. It was an old chimera, held together by the corruption magic that'd created it, rot held off by perhaps some magic to keep it fighting in the arena.

They'd taken Erich's dagger and other weapons. But before he could properly assess his next move, the creature came barreling toward him. Erich dodged by rolling out of the way. And as he did, he spotted a half-broken spear between him and the beast. The chimera turned, pawing at the ground, and lowered its antlers before racing toward him. Erich lunged for the spear, grabbed it, and blocked the antlers inches from impaling him. They wrestled for a moment, the lizard's snout snapping and biting at him. Erich twisted and shoved the chimera back, and it pivoted to kick him hard in the stomach, knocking him to the ground. It stalked closer, and the dragon, sensing he was in dire straits, pushed even closer to the forefront.

It had claws that could tear and jaws that could rend the

chimera's flesh. Erich ignored the temptation and rolled over, grasping a handful of sand, which he threw in the monster's eyes, giving him enough time to scramble toward a glint of metal he saw a few yards away. He grabbed hold of a hilt and pulled out the rusted end of a sword. He circled behind the chimera, but the beast merely spun and charged again. He dodged and managed a deep cut into one of its hindquarters. It stumbled for a moment but kept moving even as the leg dragged behind it. With preternatural speed, it was on top of him, its antlers piercing his shoulder and shoving him up against the wall.

Erich grabbed onto its ankles, trying to shove it off, and felt the delicate bones beneath his hands. He couldn't win without a weapon, and the broken blade lay several feet away. With the dragon's strength, he could snap its legs and then its neck. The dragon roared with delight, and he gave in to the power, but without the moon, he only half transformed. His arms were covered in scales; his hands were clawed and reptilian. He squeezed, snapping the leg of the deer. It reeled back with a guttural cry. And he grasped hold of its neck to snap it and end the fight, but as he did, the chimera bit into his shoulder, drawing blood.

Erich roared, his voice raw and animalistic. His blood pounded, and he felt his back ache as if wings would burst from his skin. But he held back, not wanting to give in fully to the dragon. Instead, he channeled his rage into wringing the neck of the monster, ending their fight, as they held onto one another like a lover's embrace.

He felt its grip weaken as it died before it slumped into his arms. Erich's knees gave out beneath him, and he sank down into the sand. The crowd came back to him in a rush as if his ears had been muffled before.

The announcer was shouting, "The dragonborn wins!"

Erich looked down at his scaled hands, equally horrified and amazed at his partial transformation. He'd never willfully done it before. Then he looked at the crowd, taking them in for the first time now that his life wasn't in danger. The man who'd put him there was sitting in a box in the stands, a smirk upon his face. Erich bowed his head to him—their deal struck. He'd won his fight. Would he let him go as promised?

The gate rattled open, and Erich stood up on shaking legs and headed out. This time, he wasn't slapped in chains the moment he passed through the door. In fact, he was greeted with a towel, and a glass of wine was thrust into his hands. He chugged it down, feeling impossibly thirsty and not caring if it was sour and bad. He was escorted to another room, where he was offered food and a bath. On top of his thirst, he was ravenous, and he gorged himself on cheese, meat pies, and bread until his stomach felt as if it might burst. It was awkward eating with clawed hands, but he learned to manage without accidentally scratching his face. Then, when his stomach was full, he soaked in a hot bath and washed off the ichor and blood from his skin. As he sank into the hot water, his muscles relaxing, the scales began to fade, and his skin returned, pink and new like a scar.

He turned over his palms, half in disbelief he'd managed a partial transformation without losing himself to madness. When he was dry and given fresh clothes, he was escorted to Leonhard's personal box. Another fight was happening down below; two chimeras were circling one another and tearing at each other's throats. The uncanny growls and screams of the crowd didn't seem to faze Leonhard, who opened his arms wide to greet Erich.

"Quite the performance. You could become one of my best acts," he said.

"I have no intentions of becoming your act," Erich said. "We had a deal."

Leonhard raised a brow. "Pity. Yes, I suppose we did. Here's the payment I promised." He held out a gilt invitation to a party a few days away.

"And a chance to talk with her? That was the other part."

"It will all be arranged."

Leonhard tossed a brass token to Erich, which he caught in the air. It had Cyra's star engraved on one side and the Hunters' Guild symbol of crossed daggers on the other. Even though he'd just fought and nearly died, it felt too easy. As if he'd turn around and they'd lock him back in the cell again. He reached for his dagger, which he didn't have.

"And my weapons, I came with?" Erich asked.

"They'll be returned to you at the exit. Can't have you turning on me, now, can we?" He winked as if he hadn't just thrown Erich in a death pit. The men looming behind Leonhard's shoulders were his bodyguards, and they'd be difficult to fight, depleted as Erich was. And while he was angry at the fact that he'd been locked up and nearly killed, he didn't want revenge. He wanted to forget it'd happened.

"What about the mark on my shoulder?"

"That's a bit of insurance, you see. The Avatheos' orders; any humanoid who walks the city must be... maintained."

And there was the catch he'd been looking for.

Erich bristled at this. "Then you're not really letting me go."

"I'm giving you my protection. Which is worth more than a single night's entertainment. The Midnight Guard won't let a wanted man walk into their midst without that. You should be thanking me, honestly."

"And what's the cost of this protection?"

"I think you know." He smiled.

Erich could have argued or tried to fight it, but he knew a good arrangement when he saw one. He'd fought in the pit and won, and now he was free to enter the temple and speak to Liane. Once he got inside, he'd just need to get her out. The rest he'd figure out later...

IO

Liane dressed in the early dawn light and prayed to Cyra that Erich would come back, after she failed to send a message or meet him. It was a foolish hope. But she figured prayers couldn't hurt. Though Cyra never seemed to answer hers. Luzie was sleeping on her cot, snoring lightly, as Liane tiptoed across the room. If she were back at the Golden Palace, she'd have slipped out through a hidden passageway, but despite a thorough investigation of her room, she'd found no convenient escape routes.

Eyes on the doorknob, Liane held her breath as she reached for it. Luzie moaned slightly, and Liane froze as Luzie rolled over and pulled the blanket tighter. Then Liane turned the knob slowly, praying Ludwig was sleeping rather than guarding her door.

But Cyra was not on her side that morning. The door swung open, and Ludwig was waiting with crossed arms.

"Absolutely not," he said.

"I won't be gone long!"

"And where is it you're going exactly?"

"Out…" She waved in the general direction of the door.

Ludwig raised a skeptical brow. "Liane, last time you went 'out,' you were mobbed. Do you think it's safe for you to leave the temple?"

"It's early. People won't be out yet."

"There's already a line outside the temple of people waiting for a chance to get in and meet you."

"There is?" She'd been locked in her room most of the time, and when they'd toured the temple, there'd hardly been a soul around. If there was a line outside, why weren't they letting them inside?

He shook his head. "Is this about Erich? You said you were done with him."

"I am. We are. He wanted to talk. To end things." A blush was burning on her cheeks. She sounded ridiculous. Ludwig might not know everything about Erich, but he knew enough to want to stop her.

"Silence is answer enough."

"Either you let me go, or I jump out the window." Liane backed up toward the window. She'd make good on that threat. She needed closure with Erich to squash out this ember of hope she kept kindling in her stomach. The goddess' chosen and the corrupted didn't end up together. That was not how their story went. But he deserved the courtesy of her thanking him to his face for saving her at the dock.

"You're supposed to be the goddess' chosen, and yet he's reducing you to using emotional manipulation?" Ludwig asked. The look of disdain on his face was something she'd never seen before. It felt like a dagger to the gut. Was that how he really felt?

The heat from her face spread to her neck and chest as her anger rose.

"You're acting rather high and mighty. Where have you been sneaking off to? Have you started using stardust again?"

Ludwig flinched as if he'd been slapped, his arms hanging at his sides. And she wished she could take the words back. She'd forgiven him. She knew that he'd done it partially under the compulsion of Heinrich's power. But apparently, despite them both trying to make amends, there were wounds left festering for both of them.

Ludwig looked away and ran his hands through his hair. "No. I'm not."

She hated this. Ludwig used to be the one person she could trust above all others, and now she didn't know.

Liane reached out to him as a sort of olive branch, but before she could make contact, a priestess came up behind Ludwig's shoulder.

"I hope I'm not interrupting?" they said.

"Not at all." Ludwig walked down the hall, and she watched him go until he disappeared around a corner.

"The Avatheos wishes to present you to the temple today. Prepare yourself. The veil is required."

Luzie sprang up, apparently having been lying there listening to her and Ludwig argue all that time.

"She'll be ready in a moment," Luzie said, then slammed the door.

When they were alone again, she wrapped her arms around Liane, pulling her into a tight embrace. Liane rested her head against her friend's shoulder.

"I keep hurting him," Liane muttered.

"I know."

"I'm the worst friend imaginable."

"He did betray you. It takes time to rebuild trust."

Liane sighed heavily as Luzie patted her back comfortingly.

After a few more minutes of dawdling, Luzie said, "We better get you ready." She turned to gather up Liane's things, including the dreaded veil. Liane eyed it dubiously.

"I don't know how I could have forgotten the meeting. Do you think you could…?" Liane asked.

"I'll go out to look for him, but no promises. Ludwig isn't wrong; silence is an answer."

Liane had been afraid she'd say that. It wasn't as if she didn't feel bad enough as it was, but she had to see him one more time. When her duties were done for the day, she'd fight her way out of the temple if she must.

THE REST of the day was long and grueling. Wearing the veil was cumbersome and suffocating; it trapped her breath near her face and made everything wet and unpleasant. On top of that, she'd been paraded around the temple to greet the rich and powerful of the city, who'd groveled and tried pressing bribes into her hand for miracles she couldn't perform. It reminded her of the same sycophants who'd followed her around in the Golden Palace to get closer to her mother and sister. Thankfully, the priestess escorting her kept the worst of them at bay. But, to Liane's horror, she was informed she'd have to greet the crowds again tomorrow. The people were getting restless, and they wanted to see the goddess' avatar. The thought of being near crowds made her stomach turn, but she'd been persuaded when they'd told her she'd see them from a balcony no one could reach.

BY THE TIME she got back to her room, her feet and her back were aching. But she was determined to get out of the temple and go meet Erich. She tore off the veil the moment she was alone.

"Any luck?" she asked Luzie.

Luzie shook her head slowly. "I'm sorry. He wasn't there, and it's a large city."

Liane deflated. Ludwig was right; perhaps Erich had assumed she didn't want to speak with him again.

She turned to the window; it was a moonless night. Had she lost her chance? It wasn't like Liane to give up so easily, but they were also worlds apart from one another. Maybe it was simpler to let go of him and focus on the destiny in front of her.

A sudden knock at the door startled them both.

Clutching the front of her gown, Luzie opened the door and discovered a group of veiled priestesses standing there.

"The hour is upon us. The oracles have summoned the avatar. She must be prepared for the ceremony." They spoke in unison, their voices carrying a hollow, eerie tone that sent a shiver down Liane's spine.

"The hour for what?" Luzie asked.

But they didn't answer and pushed their way into the room. "The avatar must be purified before being presented to the oracles," the leader said.

Ludwig followed them, an apologetic expression on his face.

"Can someone please explain what's going on?" Liane asked.

"Some sort of ritual, I think," Ludwig said.

The priestesses surrounded her, and this many bodies around her caused the bile in her throat to rise. "You must bathe before you enter the sanctum."

They pulled at her clothes until Liane pushed them away, covering her body with her arm.

"I'll bathe, but you can't just paw at me like this."

They stepped back, their faces impassive. They reminded her of the porcelain dolls she'd had as a child that she and Mathias would line up as their audience for their childhood plays. When it became apparent they weren't going to leave, she turned around to strip out of her clothes. Luzie held up a sheet for privacy and wrapped it around her.

They brought in a bronze tub and buckets of steaming water, which they poured into it as one priestess stood over it, whispering prayers and sprinkling fragrant oils into the water.

Liane stepped into the scalding water and flinched, but the threat of them forcing her into the water made her sink in, little by little. The scar on her back pulsed, and her head pounded. Luzie hovered out of reach, blocked from approaching by the priestesses who'd created a barrier between her and Liane.

Two priestesses took up positions on either side of Liane and roughly scrubbed at her arms and hands before moving to her back and then legs. They were not as gentle as Luzie would have been. In fact, they seemed to be using the roughest cloth and were determined to take off layers of her skin.

"Is this necessary?" Liane asked while flinching.

"It is essential that you are scrubbed of all impurities before entering the holy sanctum."

"What holy sanctum? Why wasn't I warned about any of this?"

"Because they did not know the hour was upon us until the constellation of the ox entered the house of the raven in the sky tonight."

They might as well have been speaking another language to her. Liane knew that the Avatheos and the oracles divined prophecy from reading the stars, but she couldn't imagine what those things meant. She was curious to find out and endured their rough ministrations.

Once they were satisfied and her skin was pink, Liane got out of the bath. The priestesses rubbed her skin with fragrant oils, as well as her hair, which they then braided into a coronet. The robes they presented were heavy, gilt, and glittering with semi-precious stones. And what was worse, they placed a gilded headpiece on top of the veil. It was reminiscent of her mother's crown—a series of sunbeams across her brow, three gold chains on either side of her head hanging down below her ears, and star pendants and pearls. She wasn't sure she'd seen her mother wear this much wealth at one time.

Like her other veils, this one was sheer enough to see through, but the weight of the headpiece made her neck compress painfully. And she imagined if she wore it for too long, she'd have a roaring headache. Her back was already aching, and she was starting to regret playing along.

"You are ready. Let us head to the inner sanctum."

She gestured for Liane to lead the way, as if she had any idea where this inner sanctum was. It hadn't even been on her tour.

"Where is that, exactly?"

"Within the temple. You'll know it when you see it."

Liane waited for further explanation, but when there was none forthcoming, she reasoned she'd figure it out on the way. She walked out the door, but when Ludwig and Luzie attempted to follow them, the priestesses blocked their path.

"She must go on her own, and even then, only those of the inner sanctum may view the ceremony."

"I'm her guard," Ludwig protested.

"And we are the goddess' chosen. No harm will come to her in our care."

"I'll be alright," Liane told him.

There was still too much left unsaid between them, but now wasn't the time to argue. Ludwig let them go, and as she looked at Ludwig and Luzie one last time over her shoulder, she saw Luzie leaning against him. Last night and today hadn't gone as she'd planned, to be certain, but this was what she'd come for, to unlock the temple's mysteries and her own. She turned her eyes to the path ahead. Maybe tonight's ceremony was Cyra's way of sending her a sign that she'd draw the sword out at last. Liane had come here to learn how to use her power, and the oracles were the most powerful figures in the country, apart from the Avatheos. Perhaps. Together, they could help her draw the sword out of her back. They headed toward the shrine room, where Sylvie had begun the tour days before. And the halls were lined with acolytes and priests. They held candles in their hands, which flickered as she walked past and cast strange shadows over their features, making the exposed lower half of their faces appear ghoulish. They hummed under their breaths, and the sound of it made her skin prickle and her scar throb.

After passing through the priests, she stepped into the temple room where Cyra's statue stood. A window in the ceiling had been opened, and moonlight bathed Cyra and gave her statue a heavenly glow. Thirteen figures stood in a half circle, flanking both sides of the statue like the wings of a great bird. The Avatheos stood in the center.

The priestesses who escorted her departed, and the doors to the room were closed. No one spoke for several long minutes, and Liane felt as if her breathing were too loud in the hushed space.

Then the statue began to groan and shake. She stumbled back a step as the statue slid aside on invisible tracks, revealing a passageway down into the darkness. The discovery of a hidden passageway in the temple was dampened by the crowd watching. The group turned as one and marched down the stairs. And without other instructions, Liane assumed she must go down as well. Liane licked her suddenly dry lips.

It shouldn't have surprised her that there was a secret passageway in the temple. She'd spent most of her childhood underground in catacombs and crumbling tunnels. But the air in here had a sweet odor that faintly reminded her of stardust and made her uneasy. The stairs descended into a wide vaulted room, circled by large pillars, which seemed to be carved from stone. In the center of the room was a raised dais with a bleating sable goat tethered to it. There was a channel in the floor, circling the dais and then spreading outward in a pattern she could not discern.

The Avatheos stood behind the goat and beckoned Liane closer without a word. She stood before him and felt the strange sizzling of his magic sweep over her. She was awkward and out of her depth, having no clue what her role was in this bizarre ceremony.

"Liane Starweber." The thirteen spoke together with one voice, and it echoed around the room, seeping into her bones, making her body feel heavier.

"Yes?" Her voice trembled as she spoke.

"You come before the oracles to be initiated into the Church of Sol as one of our priestesses and our avatar. Your magic shall be tested, and should you be found worthy, you will be welcomed into the fold of the church. Should you fail, you shall be cast out from this place and your name erased from the records."

A cold hand seemed to have grasped at her nape, and Liane had to fight the urge to shiver.

"Do you understand?" they asked.

"I—Uh—Yes?" she said.

"Begin."

The Avatheos broke rank to approach the goat. He grasped its nape, and its eyes rolled. Though it bleated, it did not move as he sliced the neck with the ease of long practice. Its blood spilled out onto the dais, rolling down into the channels carved into it. Then he cut open its belly, drawing out its steaming entrails and studying them as its blood dripped off his wrists and splattered onto the stones.

Something fizzled on her skin, and as much as she was horrified by the display, she also couldn't look away.

"A temptation lies ahead; darkness closes in. You must guard your heart and your purity to prevent the end of all things," the Avatheos said.

"You saw that?" Liane swallowed past the lump in her throat as her thoughts leapt to Erich. Was he the temptation the Avatheos warned her about?

"You are the goddess' chosen; I can see it here." He held up a section of entrails. "The end begins, and we who guard the light must protect it."

Suddenly, the room was plunged into darkness. Liane felt her heart pounding in her chest as she waited for what would happen next. This was all theater, surely. Not some ill omen.

"The time has come. The darkness shall evade. The time has come. The darkness shall evade," someone started to chant.

Then a second and a third picked it up, until their voices were surrounding her on all sides, and a strange sensation was creeping over her body. Their words seemed to cast a spell upon her. Liane couldn't move, couldn't breathe. The air felt as if it'd frozen in her chest. Her skin prickled, and the hair on her arms stood on end. Then she felt the glow building in her gut, burning deep within her. It flowed outward. It started like a faint illumination, before it got brighter and brighter. It coursed through her, thrumming in her veins, and cast shadows on the walls around her.

The priests stopped chanting, but their voices echoed inside her head as the murals on the walls seemed to come alive— deer leapt, farmers plowed, and women harvested wheat. The stars on the ceiling began to spin; they circled around and around, faster and faster, until she started to feel dizzy from it and feared she might vomit if she didn't look away. But she couldn't look away. No matter how hard she tried.

And then the stars formed together to make a face. A woman. Her lips curled in a mischievous smile. She spoke words that Liane didn't know the language of, but she felt their meaning at her very core.

"I've been waiting a very long time for you. A destiny written in your blood. The one who will cleave the dark and free me at last."

She had no way of knowing for sure, but it must be the Nameless Goddess—the sister of Cyra, who'd betrayed her and brought corruption into the world. She felt the woman reach out toward her through the dark, but when her hands brushed against the light, she hissed and recoiled. The light grew brighter, burning hot enough that Liane had to close her eyes, as if she were staring into the sun. Then she felt the warm brush of a hand against her face, and she opened her eyes and thought she was seeing Cyra, but when she blinked, the face was gone.

It was all too much. And then Liane's knees buckled under her, and she fell to the ground. The light faded from around her, and the silence that fell was deafening. The priests and priestesses swarmed her, but none dared to touch her. She lay immobile for what could have been minutes or hours—she wasn't entirely sure. Then she saw the Avatheos standing over her, offering her a hand.

She stood up on shaking feet and turned to face the oracles. They were no longer standing but kneeling before her, as was the Avatheos.

"She has come, the goddess' chosen, at last," the Avatheos said.

The oracles cried out in excitement.

"What did you see? What vision did the goddess grant?" the Avatheos asked.

Liane's tongue felt thick, but she was compelled to answer. But if they knew she had seen the dark goddess, what would they think? Would they cast her out and leave her cursed to a life of pain and suffering, of utter obscurity and exile? Though it felt wrong to lie to a priest, she said, "I saw Cyra. She embraced me."

The Avatheos smiled, and it made her stomach churn with guilt. She'd seen darkness as well, and darkness embraced her. What if she wasn't the chosen but the world's damnation? She spoke none of these fears aloud.

"As I told you, she is pure and goddess-touched. She shall destroy the darkness at last."

II

Aristea kept herself busy after Duke Mattison's ball. When she had a spare moment between meetings, she picked up her current embroidery project and sat in stifling silence amongst her lady's maids. It was her favorite tactic to keep unpleasant thoughts at bay. Like the idea of marrying a man her father's age, or her bubbling feelings of resentment as she was faced with making yet another sacrifice for the good of the empire. How much more did they need before they would be satisfied? They'd taken her youth, her womb, her everything. Even now, she was still paying the costs of Heinrich's sins. No matter how hard he'd tried to father a bastard, he couldn't. Maybe it was his seed that wouldn't quicken, yet she was branded barren. She stabbed her needle too hard into the fabric and pricked her thumb.

She hissed as she stared at the bloom of crimson on her digit. Then Yvette handed her a handkerchief to stanch the bleeding. Aristea took it and waited for it to stop. It was a small prick, nothing serious. And that was what she should think of Duke Mattison's proposal, a small prick. She snorted.

Her lady's maids looked at her sidelong but made no comment.

If she stopped to recount all the injustices of her life, nothing would get done. It was better to use that energy toward her plans. For instance, she had a meeting scheduled with Captain Rosen. Captain Rosen had been in charge of the stardust-smuggling case. Liane had been able to uncover Heinrich's plot in part thanks to Captain Rosen's help. If anyone knew who Heinrich's co-conspirators might be, then it would be her. Aristea needed to find them and either bring them to heel, or remove them from power. Whichever fit Aristea's ends.

Liane might have helped her, if she hadn't sailed off to Basilia to become the beloved avatar. Before she'd left, her great miracles had already been growing in exaggeration. Last Aristea had heard, Liane had cured a dozen sick with a single touch of her hand. It was religious propaganda, Aristea was certain. She knew because she'd seen how it shaped Mother's power and influence. The people believed she ruled with the goddess' blessing and by the Golden Blade she used to hold at her side. With it gone, Aristea feared their positions were weakened.

She wished the blade had chosen her instead. Maybe then she wouldn't have to plot and scheme to keep her throne. For weeks since Heinrich's death, she'd been sifting through his ledgers and documents, looking for shreds of evidence as to his accomplices and connections. All she'd managed to find was a tangle of incoherent notes and boastful letters to friends. It was becoming increasingly clear Heinrich wasn't the mastermind they'd thought he was, but perhaps a figurehead to a broader operation.

When he'd been alive, she'd thought he was rather clever because he often painted himself as such. Heinrich walked with the air of someone born to rule. Men had flocked to him, throwing themselves at his feet to do his bidding. While she had to work hard for every scrap of recognition she got. No matter how hard she studied or worked to be a worthy successor, even his ghost overshadowed her.

Since he'd died, many of his closest allies had fled to their country homes. Though knowing the fools he surrounded himself with, she doubted they were of much concern. It was the dukes behind Heinrich who were the problem.

Aristea laid down her embroidery. She hadn't made any stitches in several minutes, and there was no point in pretending it was distracting her now. She stood up and her lady's maids rose as well, but she waved them down and headed back to her writing desk, where a pile of Heinrich's correspondence was waiting for her. Before her meeting with Captain Rosen, she'd prepared a list of suspects. She'd scribbled down a few names, but she wanted to cross-reference them once more before heading out. She flipped through the sheets of parchment, but nothing stood out to her. The same names she'd written on her list were signed at the bottom of the letters. The usual suspects. Save one. Duke Krantz. She'd seen him at Duke Mattison's ball. And before Heinrich died, they used to visit him often. She'd never paid much attention to their conversations, because the man hardly spoke in her presence, and his wife was severe and cold. She tapped her paper. Why hadn't she considered him before? Most of the other dukes of their faction listened and respected him. Could he be the true mastermind behind the stardust operation?

Aristea had asked once or twice about him, but Heinrich had always dismissed her inquiries and said he was clever and that was it. Duke Krantz wasn't among those who'd left the capital when Heinrich had died, but that didn't mean he wasn't guilty. Maybe he had business to attend to. Chasing him down might lead to nothing at all. But it was something.

Aristea gathered up her notes and returned to the drawing

room, where her ladies were still chatting and working on their embroidery projects. She dismissed them for the day before heading out to her meeting, with her head of guard shadowing her. She greeted courtiers as she went, but no one stopped her to chat. The veil had other advantages in that it kept idle chitchat to a minimum. Captain Rosen's office was in the Midnight Tower, the church's foothold within the Golden Palace. Officially, they were there to protect the capital from corruption. Though Aristea had never seen any evidence of that. Guards stood sentry at the entrance. They bowed, moving aside to allow her entry. The interior was sparse stone, with a single spiral staircase upward to the next floor, where the captain's office was. Aristea left her guard at the foot of the stairs and climbed with her guard escort, who opened the door to the captain's empty office.

"Where is the captain? We had an appointment," Aristea said.

"She's running late, but she'll join you shortly. Would you like refreshments while you wait? It's nearly lunchtime, your majesty."

"No, thank you," Aristea said stiffly. Was the captain against her as well? Officially, the church was neutral, but Aristea knew that wasn't entirely true.

She bit her tongue and resigned herself to wait. The guard left her, and Aristea stood still for a few minutes, but as they ticked past, she grew restless and cast about the room. It was rather spartan, all things considered. Captain Rosen was a formidable woman, a few years older than Aristea and one of the only women who'd risen to a position of power within the Midnight Guard, which was primarily a male-dominated sect of the Church of Sol's military branch. Before Mother became empress, women were banned from joining altogether. Aristea admired her. Whenever they met, she was efficient and straight to the point, which Aristea appreciated. But Liane idolized her, and most of what she knew of her illustrious career, she'd learned from her sister. And maybe her loyalties were with Liane and the church, and that was why she was making her wait...

Time was ticking by, and the captain still hadn't returned. It wasn't like her to be late, and after this appointment, Aristea had council meetings to attend and dinner with a duchess. She was about to leave and reschedule when she heard whispers coming from the tower steps.

The voice was a low, feminine voice, different from the captain's gruff, clipped tones. And she wondered if someone else was coming up the stairs. She listened harder, but as the seconds stretched on, the voice grew stronger, but there were no footsteps.

"Aristea, pretending you're strong again."

She felt a chill curl down her spine. The voice seemed to be coming from the room she was standing in. She pulled back the curtains on the window and checked under the desk. But there was no one in the room but her. Was someone pulling a trick on her, perhaps hiding from a hidden passage?

"You'd dare insult your princess?" Aristea asked.

The voice merely chuckled. "Do you think they'll take you seriously? Do you really think they'll make you empress? Why choose you? Isn't that what Heinrich always said? Your brother lives, ripe for rulership and on his way to becoming a hero just like the beloved emperor he's named after. He will do as his grandfather promised and rid the empire of elves at last. No one will want you after that."

Aristea wrapped her arms around her torso, as if she could block out the voice's cruel words.

"Show yourself."

"Poor, fragile, Aristea. Crying again. You always were

emotional." It wasn't Heinrich's voice, but those were his words, whispered to her by a stranger. He'd always been careful to save his insults for when they were in private. But someone must have heard, and now they were taunting her with them.

"Who are you? Show yourself," she demanded.

"I am everywhere and nowhere. If you want to see me, come below, into the dark..." The last word was hissed out.

She reached for the door and yanked it open, but when she did, the hallway was empty. She stood there, panting for breath, waiting for the voice to mock her again, but she heard nothing. She closed the door again and paced to the other end of the room, massaging her temples. She'd been working herself too hard, and she was hearing things. That was all. Then the door opened, and Aristea nearly jumped out of her skin to see the captain standing in the doorway with a frown.

"Forgive my lateness, your majesty," Captain Rosen said with a scooped bow.

Aristea pressed a hand to her chest as she tried to catch her breath. "It's fine. I thought I heard someone speaking in the halls. Are you alone?"

Captain Rosen raised a skeptical brow. "I was..."

She opened her mouth to reply and then closed it again. The captain's voice was deeper and gruffer than the melodic taunting voice she'd heard. It couldn't have been her. But admitting out loud that she was hearing voices would make her look insane. Something that didn't exactly instill confidence in a future ruler. On top of that, she was here to tease out information about Heinrich's co-conspirators.

"I must have been hearing the wind."

Captain Rosen looked concerned, but she didn't press the issue. She walked over to her desk and offered Aristea a seat, which she took gratefully.

"Forgive my tardiness. We uncovered a new stardust den, and we were interrogating the men we captured."

Then her hunch was right. Someone was still supplying the city.

"Did you find anything?" Aristea asked.

"I wish I had good news to share. But it feels as if we're cutting the heads off a hydra." Captain Rosen sighed. "Every time I take out a den, two more pop up. Is that why you came to see me?"

Aristea shook her head. The captain was direct and to the point. She wasn't one for wordplay and subterfuge. It was a risk to play her cards, but Aristea reasoned it was better to be blunt. "I've come to the conclusion that Heinrich wasn't the mastermind behind the stardust plot. I think either he might have been leaning on one of his friends, or they were pulling the strings." She offered up her list, and Captain Rosen leaned forward to take it from her.

She silently scanned the list of names before setting it down again. "These are powerful men. I cannot simply arrest them without cause. It would incite unrest."

"Believe me, I'm well aware. Is there anyone on this list who stands out among the rest?" Aristea asked as she studied Captain Rosen's expression.

Captain Rosen tapped her fingers on the top of her desk as she considered the list.

"I cannot recall any connections to the names listed here. But I shall keep these names under advisement, and should any new developments emerge, I shall inform you straight away."

It wasn't what she'd hoped for, but Aristea tried not to show her disappointment on her face. "I thank you for your time, then." Aristea began to stand.

"Though one name has come up that isn't on your list," Captain Rosen said.

Aristea turned to look at her. "Oh?"

Upon seeing the captain's somber expression, Aristea sank back in her seat, and Captain Rosen folded her hands on top of her desk.

"As you're aware, the men we've captured report receiving the stardust through an elven supplier. We were fortunate enough to catch one of these elves. And while he gave away little, Prince Mathias' name did come up."

Her stomach clenched. "Is my brother hurt or captured?"

"No."

"Then that's good news..."

"We don't know much, but we learned he is no longer in the feral lands, and it appears he's working with the elves. We have since received reports of him in the northern provinces. When members of the army tried to approach him, he fled and—"

Her stomach sank. "Surely it was a mistake or some plot to sow discord?"

"He was seen by a former squad member of his who confirmed his identity. And he was also spotted in the home on the border of Duke Wagner's territory."

She didn't add on the part that Duke Wagner's father had famously introduced Heinrich's father to elven mages who'd aided in his rebellion. The former duke had been executed, and his then-infant son had been spared and warded by the rival faction. But he might have sought revenge. She could see it all, but not Mathias. Sweet Mathias wouldn't rally a rebellion. He was the family peacemaker. He wouldn't attempt to rise against her. Unless the elves had gotten hold of him, put him under a spell...

"There must be an explanation..." Aristea trailed off, her heart in her throat. She knew her brother; he wouldn't betray the empire.

"We won't know until we speak with him. But I've been

keeping track of the dukes closest to the deceased Prince Heinrich, at your mother's behest, and they are restless. Now that he's gone, we're hearing more and more of them calling for Mathias to be made heir."

"But Mathias would never agree to that. He has no ambitions for power." The voice had known. Before Captain Rosen had told her. How was such a thing possible?

"What else is in the dungeons?"

Captain Rosen seemed surprised by the change of subject. "Nothing as of now. Are you sure you're alright, your majesty? You look pale."

Aristea swallowed past the lump in her throat. It was madness. All of it.

Captain Rosen leaned forward across her desk. "I know he's your brother, and it's impossible to imagine a family member would betray us. But I think we need to be prepared for a possible attempted coup."

Aristea wrung her hands together and then dropped them to her sides. She couldn't show weakness. Even to the captain. But she was right. Aristea couldn't know her brother's heart. And even though she trusted him and couldn't imagine he would turn against her, she also could not, as future empress, pretend the threat wasn't very real.

"Thank you for telling me. I shall inform my mother straight away."

"I'm sorry for giving you such troubling news, princess."

Aristea waved away her concern. "You're merely doing your duty. And I thank you for it."

She excused herself and exited the tower as fast as her feet could carry her. But with each step she took toward her mother, she felt as if she were walking to her own funeral. She refused to believe Mathias would willingly betray them. But the voice's whispered taunts had her second-guessing.

"If only you were strong enough to claim the throne with your own power," the voice whispered. "But you aren't, are you? The power is in your blood. You simply need something to awaken it. I can help you...".

She turned, seeking its source. But she was alone, and she was afraid she was starting to jump at shadows. A few passing courtiers saw her spinning around like a madwoman, and Aristea laughed too high and falsely as she blamed her erratic behavior on an insect under her veil. She walked away as fast as she could, on the verge of a run. All the way to her mother's chambers. The guards stepped aside and let her in. Mother was speaking with her steward, but when Aristea entered, she sent them away.

"What's happened?" Mother asked.

Aristea unraveled all that Captain Rosen had told her. Mother looked pale by the end of it, and her hands were white-knuckled even while folded on the table in front of her. "We'll keep this quiet. I agree with you. Mathias wouldn't turn on our family this way. But we must move with caution. If some foreign entity has taken hold of him, if the elves have him... we are all in danger."

Aristea felt the weight of it all landing on her shoulders. She felt powerless. Forces beyond her control were closing in, and what could she do? Maybe Heinrich was right, and she was useless.

"What about the duke's dinner party? Any progress there?" Mother asked.

Aristea picked her thumbnail below the lip of the desk to keep her fidgeting out of sight. "The duke seems amiable to an alliance."

"Marriage?" Mother asked bluntly.

Aristea nodded. "He implied as much in his toast. But isn't it unseemly? I'm not even two months widowed..."

"I would not have you jump into another marriage so soon after the death of Heinrich. But we cannot dismiss important allies when our enemies are closing in."

"Of course." Aristea's head sank down to her chest.

Mother stood and came around to kneel in front of her, the way she had when Aristea was small. She cupped each of Aristea's cheeks. "I wish I did not have to lay this burden at your feet. Even though you're older than I was when I inherited an empire, I still fear you're too young. You've made so many sacrifices. If you do not wish this marriage, tell me now and I will find another way."

The refusal was on the tip of her tongue. Mother would be good to her word, she knew. But asking for it, knowing that her claim was shaky as it was, felt too selfish.

"I'm willing to give my all for the empire. Don't worry."

12

Even with his healing ability, Erich was sore from his fight. But despite Fritz's suggestion that he rest before attempting to use Leonhard's token, he'd risen early to join the queue outside the temple. Fritz had insisted on coming with him, which felt dangerous, but the elf had the ability to shift his appearance and had previously infiltrated the temple in Artria, so he didn't argue. Despite the guild master's assurances they'd be granted entrance without problem, Erich was still skeptical, and his grip on the handle of his dagger hadn't loosened once. Days ago, he'd been a wanted man. Now he could play the role of visiting prince as much as it repulsed him to slip on his shed identity, it was useful. Like previous days, there was a long line snaking its way down the street. They passed them by, token clenched in Erich's fist. Midnight Guards blocked the entrance, and with sweating palms, Erich raised his head to meet the guard's gaze. He donned the prince's mask once again, pulling it on like a second skin. Gaining entrance required the confidence of someone who belonged there. He let go of his dagger, and kept his hands loose at his sides, and a smile in place.

The Midnight Guard looked him up and down. Did they recognize him from his wanted poster? And would they swarm him to take him into custody for his audacity to show up here, a monster parading around as a man? He resisted the urge to reach for his dagger, though the impulse was great. Fritz stood beside him, looking around at the crowd and the temple, as if he were the wide-eyed servant he was pretending to be.

"I'm Prince Erich of Sundland," he said, thrusting his signet ring toward the guard. The token the pit master gave him was clutched in Erich's palm.

The guard reached out, palm up, waiting for Erich to deposit the token in his hand as he pretended to look at the ring, though he couldn't have given it more than a cursory glance.

"Prince Erich?" the guard asked, rolling the coin in his hand.

Erich nodded. "I've come to see the avatar I've heard so much about."

"I was told to expect you. And who's with you?" He jutted his chin toward Fritz.

"My valet," Erich said. "I don't go anywhere without him.

"It's rather full inside. Not sure I can make room." He scratched his chin.

Erich knew this game and pulled out a sack of geld and pressed it into the guard's hand.

He was pushing his luck, he feared. But Fritz insisted that he join Erich on their mission. Chances were they'd reject his bribe and toss them both out onto the street, or worse. The guards paused for a moment to study Erich, and Fritz looked at them serenely. Erich wasn't sure if he was good at hiding his fear or if he'd had some vision that made him fearless. Erich was about to piss his pants. These were the same people who'd run him through if they knew the truth.

But the guards stepped aside, allowing them entrance into

the crescent-shaped anterior room. A small mural of Cyra greeted them. She was standing in a sunny field, farmers working the soil around her, backs bent as they harvested golden wheat.

A part of him still couldn't believe it had worked, even as he was shuffled along with the crowd down the hall toward the first ring of the temple. They didn't even try pressing a revealing stone on either of them as they did with the regular pilgrims who came to visit. This ploy shouldn't have worked. Knowing the right people shouldn't have allowed him to gain entrance over the devoted who waited days outside just to be turned away. He clenched his hand in a fist, shoved down his guilty feelings, and followed the shuffling crowd through the corridors of the temple. This was for Liane; he had to talk to her and explain himself. Getting inside was the first hurdle, finding Liane was the next. Given the zealous crowds, he doubted she'd be accessible to the public. This first trip into the temple was likely to be more reconnaissance than rescue mission. But even though he knew that logically, the dragon still protested. He had to be patient. He'd bought them a chance with the guild's protection, but it would only last until the next time he was summoned to fight, he was certain of it.

The hallway emptied out into a sanctuary where a gilded statue of Cyra greeted supplicants. It was unlike others he'd seen in Artria. This one did not hold a sword, but rather stood, hands cupped in front of her, and large white marble wings spread out behind her as if she might take flight. The ceiling was covered in clear glass, and light shone down on Cyra's statue, illuminating her in an unearthly glow. He'd never seen her depicted with wings before, but he had to admit he didn't know much of the church's lore. The room was stiflingly hot because of the glass ceiling, and sweat trickled down his neck. Pilgrims left offerings in her cupped hands, which overflowed with flowers, baked goods, and fruits. Even more offerings had been left at her sandaled feet. Nestled amongst candles, burnt down to nothing but pools of wax, were smaller offerings of glass beads and other small trinkets. It reminded him of a crow's nest.

"They made the raven into Cyra. Interesting," Fritz muttered. "I knew they'd erased the ancients from their history, but I hadn't considered them repurposing the old statues in this way."

Erich looked around them to make sure no one had heard him. But if they had, they gave no indication of it. They were all focused on their offerings and prayers.

"Now isn't the time to be spouting heretical nonsense," Erich hissed under his breath.

"Did you know, in the legend of the two sisters, the raven took the Golden Blade from Cyra's cult when they turned on her sister and her followers?" Fritz continued, as if not hearing Erich's whispered warning.

Erich grasped him by the elbow and yanked him away from the crowd before he got them both killed.

Fritz didn't take the hint and instead kept talking about the architecture of the hall they were walking through. "This temple used to be dedicated to both goddesses. It was a rarity even before the fall. See how they've altered the crescent mosaics, but they couldn't change the crescent hallway. That's her symbol. And these paintings are adaptations of the myth of her raising the dead. It's been altered, obviously. Look at the way Cyra overlaps here. The mortar is thicker and—"

Erich had to stop him by clamping a hand over his mouth. "Would you shut up? Now isn't the time to share."

Fritz stared at him wide-eyed, and worshippers a few feet away gave them strange sideways looks. Erich bobbed his head and pulled Fritz out of the hall and into a central garden with a fountain. It was mostly empty but for a priestess tending to the bushes, but even more importantly, it had no murals or other religious depictions on which Fritz might commentate.

"You're going to get us both killed," Erich said in a low tone.

"Forgive me. I've read about this temple since I was a child. It's a religious site my people thought was lost for good. It was one of the largest temples to dual moon and sun worship. It's fascinating and horrifying to see how they've retroactively erased the Moon Goddess from the art and architecture."

"Don't you fear they'll discover you when you talk like that?"

Fritz frowned. "They're too absorbed in their own pursuits. You saw the type of people they let in here, the rich and self-important..." There was a hint of bitterness in his tone.

Erich stared at him, gobsmacked. He was right, but still...

"You're right. I lost myself. I was a priest once, and seeing this place, feeling the magic here, however faint... I spoke out of turn. It won't happen again."

Further conversation was diverted when a loud announcement rang out through the halls. "Make way for the avatar; make way, the avatar comes!"

The halls flowed with bodies as the crowd surged toward the direction the call had come from. Erich and Fritz shared a wordless look before following. The crowd gathered in a crescent-shaped courtyard and stared up at a marble balcony twenty feet in the air. The pilgrims stood at the foot of it, their hands upturned as if to catch something. The crier he'd heard was standing on the balcony, a veiled figure.

"Behold the goddess' chosen," he said, and the crowd surged forward, pushing bodies against the stone, crushing people in their desperation to reach a figure they could never touch. Erich held his breath, waiting for her to appear. The curtain was pulled back, and two figures stepped out. He knew the veiled woman the moment his eyes fell upon her, as if some invisible thread around his heart pulled taut. The second figure was the Avatheos in his full raiment.

The people screamed and shouted for them, raising their hands up to reach for her as if they could catch onto her from a far distance. Liane flinched away at the sound of their voices, and it made the dragon uneasy.

"You who've come in search of light and healing, look upon the goddess' chosen avatar and be blessed." The Avatheos' voice boomed around the courtyard, and the people screamed.

She shrank back another step, but the Avatheos urged her forward, and seeing him lay his hands upon her made Erich's insides boil. He couldn't see her expression, but he saw her discomfort in every line of her body. She gripped the railing of the balcony on which she stood and then slowly raised her hands. As she did, a golden light glowed. Not from her but from the curtain behind her. At the right angle, or if you were determined to believe, it looked like she was casting sunlight down on the crowd. But Erich could see it for the farce it was. He'd seen Liane glow before; this wasn't her power.

The people wept and cried, thanking her profusely.

"Leave your offerings of thanks, and spread the word of the goddess' chosen's healing light, that the entire continent be healed," the Avatheos said.

The people shouted as Liane was escorted from view, and they tried climbing the walls to get to her.

Erich couldn't stand to watch a moment longer, broke away from the crowd, and rushed down a nearby hallway. The entrance to that balcony had to be around here somewhere. He tried a few locked doors to no avail. Then he rounded a corner and came face-to-face with Liane's guard, Ludwig. His instincts had been right; she must be nearby.

"What are you doing here?" Ludwig hissed.

Erich shrugged. "I'm here to learn about the Church of Sol. Is that a crime?"

"I heard a rumor you were in Basilia. Perhaps it's best if you leave," he ground out.

Erich leaned closer to Ludwig. "Is she mad that I missed our meeting?"

Ludwig crossed his arms as he glowered. "She doesn't want to speak to you."

"I'd like to hear it from her."

"I won't act as a messenger like Luzie would. I think Liane's made her intentions clear. She's dedicated to the church."

The possessive part of him was rankled by the idea of this man trying to stand between him and Liane. But he had to rein in those impulses. They would get him nowhere. "I would never hurt her. You have to believe that."

Ludwig narrowed his eyes at him. "Because I won't let you."

The church wasn't the only thing standing in his way of getting Liane out. He couldn't imagine why Liane kept Ludwig around after he'd betrayed her. Or what his motives were.

They simply glared at one another until Fritz intervened.

"Your hands are shaking," Fritz remarked.

With Ludwig's arms crossed, Erich almost hadn't noticed the slight tremor in his hands. Ludwig dropped his hands to his sides and balled them into fists instead.

"What of it?" Ludwig snapped.

"You've had stardust before," Fritz replied.

Ludwig didn't answer, just glared.

"The church isn't what you think it is. They're the piece you've been missing in your search. Seek out the Midnight Guards, and you'll uncover what you're hoping to find," Fritz said.

Ludwig's nostrils flared, and his eyes dilated slightly. "What do you know about what I'm seeking?"

"You want to know where stardust comes from and how to rid yourself of that craving you still can't shake. Am I wrong?"

Ludwig looked around the room as if fearing they'd been overheard. But there was no one else around. Ludwig shook his head as if he could shake off Fritz's words.

"I saved your life once," Erich said. "I won't ask you to pay the debt, but let me see her. Just this once."

Ludwig glared at them a moment longer before sighing heavily. "Don't ask me again. This will be the last time." He turned, and they followed him down another passageway and through a locked door into a hidden ornamental garden with rows of low bushes and several trees that provided shade from the day.

Erich recognized the maid keeping watch at the end of the pathway, who waved them over as they approached.

"I can't believe you brought him," she said to Ludwig.

"Believe me, I didn't want to." Ludwig sighed.

The dragon raised a curious head as they approached, and Erich felt the invisible tethers that bound them together pulling him closer to her. Liane was waiting for him. Had she seen him in the crowd? Her elaborate veil was pulled back, and her face was glowing. She looked like a goddess. The golden light seemed to illuminate her from within.

"I didn't believe it when I saw you in the crowd. You really came. Do you have no respect for your own life?" she scolded him.

Erich approached her before falling onto his knees in front of her. Her eyes widened, and her mouth hung open as she looked at her companions. Erich inhaled raggedly.

"I lied to you about myself and my intentions when we first met. I'm a monster who doesn't deserve to be standing in front of you."

She shook her head, hands hovering as if she were

debating grabbing hold of him. And if he was honest, if she touched him, he might unravel. He was barely controlling the dragon around her as it was. And he hated how much her scent intoxicated him, how desperately he wanted to be close to her, and each day chipped away at his already threadbare control.

"Don't say that—"

"Please," he croaked.

Her lips pulled into a thin line, and she nodded for him to continue.

"I came looking for a cure for this dragon curse, and to do that, I intended to steal the sword I now know is in your back."

She inhaled sharply. "I see."

"My reasons don't justify my actions, but you could be my salvation or my damnation."

She grabbed hold of her robe, bunching it in front of her. "What makes you so certain?"

"I saw it in a vision," Fritz said as he stepped forward.

Liane noticed him, and her eyes grew wide. "You were there that night... You're an elf." The last word she whispered.

Ludwig's and Luzie's heads swiveled in Fritz's direction, who, for his part, didn't seem scared, despite being very vulnerable in that moment. Either one of them could call the Midnight Guards and have them both thrown into the dungeon. No one moved. In fact, everyone seemed to be poised and ready but frozen in time.

"I am, and I came here with an important message for you. Do not let them seal the sword's power within you."

Liane looked at Fritz as if he'd spoken in another tongue. "What does that mean?"

"It means exactly as it sounds. The Avatheos has plans to bring about the apocalypse and with it another cataclysm, the likes of which we haven't seen in centuries. And to begin that, he needs to ensure the power the goddess has entrusted in you never reaches its full potential."

Liane wrapped her arms around her torso and took a step back. "You're wrong. He's trying to draw the sword from me."

"He's trying to control your power. Tell me, did he try to draw the sword from you himself, or did he guide you on how to?"

Liane's eyes widened as she looked at Fritz, but she didn't answer. Erich knew he'd struck a chord.

Erich stood. "Did he hurt you? I'll—"

She placed a hand against his chest, and the dragon purred.

She smiled at it, and it took all his self-control not to pull her into his arms.

"No one can draw the sword but the avatar. Only you can pull it from your flesh. What the Avatheos is trying to do is take the blade for himself. Ask him about the Dark Blade. And if he will not answer, find the books about it. I think you'll learn more from that than you will from me."

She looked at Fritz and then at Erich and took a step back.

"I appreciate everything you've done for me. More than you could ever know. But I've made my choice. I am dedicated to the church. And I will not be swayed by the dark."

She turned her back on Erich, and on impulse, he reached for her, grasping onto the hem of her robe.

"Liane, don't. I came here to rescue you."

She smiled softly. "I don't need rescuing. I'm where I'm meant to be. And for us, this is the end." She grasped a fistful of his tunic and placed a quick, light kiss on his lips. At least that's what she'd intended until he wrapped his hand around her waist and pulled her flush against his body. Her eyes widened as he kissed her. Her lips parted, and the taste of her, was agonizing, the feel of her soft mouth, her tongue brushing against his. Erich groaned against her as his hand snaked up her back to hold her by the nape of her neck. He could get drunk on the taste of her, the feeling of her breasts against him, the way her body shifted slightly to fit more firmly against him.

Then, much too soon, she pulled back, eyes wide and lips swollen.

"Goodbye, Erich," she said hoarsely, and this time, when he tried to chase her, Ludwig stepped between them. And either he chose to fight him, or he let her go, for now. They both knew that once was not enough. It would never be enough.

13

Liane went straight to the Avatheos' study after the farce of a ceremony and the knee-buckling kiss she'd shared with Erich. Questions burned on her tongue, and she couldn't wait for another cryptic summons to get answers. His study was empty, and the priest who let her in told her the Avatheos would come and find her once his meeting was finished.

She stood poised on the threshold, eyes roving over the clutter, fascinated and terrified of the magic it represented that she didn't fully understand. The minutes ticked by, and he didn't return, and Liane reasoned she was safe to take a seat at least. She folded her hands in her lap, poised, still as a statue of Cyra in front of his desk, trying not to re-examine the thoughts tumbling around in her mind.

What Erich had proposed was blasphemous to even consider. Kissing Erich had been dangerous and borderline heretical. The Avatheos had warned her she'd be tempted, and surely Erich was the temptation he'd foretold. Doubts had lingered in her mind about her worthiness to become the avatar since the night of her initiation. If she was destined to save the world from darkness, then she certainly shouldn't be frater-nizing with elves. But the elf's words continued to ring in her mind. The Avatheos was trying to draw the sword from her, to use it for himself. She recalled the hungry desperation on the Avatheos' face, the uneasy crawling sensation she sometimes got around him. Was he trying to use her or take the sword from her? Or was the elf projecting his own wicked motives onto him?

Then, if the elf was wrong and Erich was corrupted, she needed to find a way to cure him of it. Hadn't the Avatheos told her she could when she mastered her powers? But she didn't really know what her powers were—healing perhaps, glowing for sure, and a sword that was infused within her body. Maybe the Avatheos knew a way to help him, and she could free him of his dragon curse. She desperately hoped that was possible. If he weren't corrupted, it would make these lustful feelings for him acceptable at least.

Liane stood up. Priestess or avatar, or whatever she was, they didn't have lovers. They were stripped of identity and indi-viduality and lived simple monastic lives. That was what she was destined for. Cyra willed it, and who was she to deny the goddess?

She paced the room to distract herself from the thought of Erich's large hand on her neck, the feel of his stubble on her chin. Something golden glimmered in the shaft of light coming from the room's window. It was a quadrant and a celestial globe lying on the table beside a journal with dates from the year she'd been born, with constellations beside a series of numbers. The Avatheos had circled one of the constellations multiple times and written a note—dragon star and the day of her birth. A prickle raced up her spine.

The months were marked by the constellation that was most visible in the night sky—boar, rabbit, ox, deer, etc. Every thirteen years, a thirteenth month was added to the calendar, and that month was a dragon, and that year was called a dragon year. Liane had been born in a dragon year, a few days before dragon month. Maybe it was a coincidence. If she'd been born under a dragon star, someone would have told her surely? But then she thought of the sword in her back and realized there were many things her family didn't tell her. A thought occurred, something the raven had said when her powers first manifested. This year was another dragon year. She found an almanac on the table and flipped through to her birth month and day. There was another dragon star predicted on the winter solstice. The calendar had a small star map too, and when she peered at it, she swore she saw the shape of a sword in the dragon's mouth. But surely she was imagining that...

She backed away and tried to push it from her thoughts. She was seeing things. Erich's dragon curse couldn't possibly have anything to do with the sword in her back.

Liane paced the perimeter of the room to distract herself. The room was full of strange objects; she could only guess at their use. Replicas of planets hung suspended all in a row, delicately threaded together by wire. When she tapped one, it sent them all swaying back and forth so fast she feared the entire display would break, and she struggled to still them once more.

When she was certain she hadn't broken them, she stepped away and moved across the room to where the Avatheos had left an illuminated book out on a podium. As she gazed at the picture of the tree and the pools of golden light, she realized it was almost an exact replica of the one she'd seen in the book back in Artria. But here, there was no raven, no two-toned stag, and certainly no dragon. There was simply Cyra drawing a sword from a magic pool at the base of the tree. Liane frowned as she looked at the page, then flipped a few more. She recognized other illuminated passages from the book. But there were no signs of the raven, stag, or dragon anywhere. If anything, Cyra was more present. She seemed to invade every page.

A few pages later, there was a map of Neolyra unlike any she'd seen before. Rather than marking cities, mountains, or other landmarks, there were dozens and dozens of tiny lakes, with thin, jagged rivers connecting them. But they were not in places she knew lakes to be, like the one near the royal hunting lodge.

"You wished to speak with me, your Divinity?" the Avatheos said, startling her from her snooping.

Liane spun around, caught looking at things she shouldn't have. And she felt like a child caught swiping sweets from the kitchen.

"Forgive me. I got bored—" she started to say, but that seemed improper. "I was curious about these lakes. I've never seen them before."

He walked over to pick up the book and showed her the map with the strange golden lakes and rivers. "They are the veins of magic—the lifeblood of creation and Cyra's gift to humanity."

Liane's eyes widened. "The ones that were corrupted in the Corruption?" Everyone knew about them. That's why magic was so rare and so precious now, because the Corruption had polluted the veins, and from the taint came the chimeras, who plagued cities and villages.

"Yes. Is that what you came to ask about? I thought Sylvie had given you plenty of books on the history of magic."

Liane flushed. Sylvie must have reported back to the Avatheos. But what was worse was she'd hardly skimmed those books. If she'd taken her studies seriously, she'd know this already.

The Avatheos motioned for her to sit across from him before he answered her. And she felt compelled to do his bidding; he set the book out in front of her hand, sweeping across the illuminated vellum pages.

"Before the Corruption, the magic ran wild and aided much of humanity's day-to-day life. Every common man, woman, and child could access its power. But The Corruption made the magic turn against us. Now, accessing its power often turns on the user, spreading corruption and disease or, in worse cases, transforming everything it touches irrevocably. That is why it is the charge of the church to keep what veins remain pure."

"And what happens if the church doesn't find someone who can access this magic?" Liane prompted.

"Magic corrupts without an outlet, and they start to wither," he said and steepled his fingers. "You are fortunate that your form of corruption merely came in the form of fevers and pain. Had it gone on much longer, it would have begun to decay your body. It was reckless of the Vice Premier to hide your powers. You should have come to us."

If it were true, that was a dire fate indeed. But Mother must have known, and for all her faults, and as angry as Liane was at her for not telling her the truth, she wouldn't have sentenced her to death to keep a secret.

"And why would my mother do this? What was she so afraid of that she'd risk me dying of the withering?"

"Motherhood is complex." He stood up and walked around the table to grasp her by the shoulders. "I have known your mother a long time, and though I do not doubt her love for you, she desires control. And the Golden Blade inside your back is what won her the war. If she loses it to you, then she risks losing her kingdom."

"I would never rise up against my own mother!" The thought made her stomach turn. Her mother was far from perfect, but Liane couldn't imagine she'd kept it a secret out of greed or a lust for power.

"Even if it were for the good of Neolyra?"

Liane stood up and backed away from the Avatheos. "My mother is what's best for the empire. We've had peace and prosperity for over three decades."

"And yet the elves are growing restless. They've struck at the heart of the kingdom. They slew the opera singer playing Cyra. Do you think your mother has the strength to protect the kingdom when they make their next move?"

"Of course," Liane said. And she felt it with certainty.

The Avatheos shook his head slowly. "I have seen a vision. It has been coming to me in bits and pieces for a long time, but I saw it all the night you were born. A golden blade, charging into battle against a rising army of the undead. Do you know who I saw at the head of that army of darkness?"

Liane's throat was tight. It was her, surely.

"It was your mother. Golden hair streaming in the morning light, she sent wave after wave of corrupt chimeras and monsters, to devour fields, livestock, and innocents. Anyone who stood in their way was turned to ash."

"My mother wouldn't..."

"But the Nameless would. Now that the sword has returned, the seal that keeps her in place is cracking. She will grasp onto power by any means necessary and use it to bring about her dark reign of terror. Unless you can stop it." His voice rang with such assurance and certainty that Liane could almost see his dire vision in her mind.

"What do I need to do?" she asked.

"Follow me, trust me, implicitly."

Liane felt his gaze boring into her. Once again, she had that strange sensation that he could see through her, into her very soul, and was ready to bring forth all her sins for examination.

"I do," she said.

He did not reply but walked to the far end of the room and

picked up a piece of cloth. Beneath it was a cage and a small, round bird.

"Time is running short; the last crack in the seal will break the night of the winter solstice. Before that happens, we must draw the sword from your back at the fall equinox in order to prepare you. Your mother robbed you by not giving you a temple education, but there are things I can teach you to make this process easier." He set the bird and the cage between them.

The bird was fluttering inside the cage, beating its tiny wings against the bars of its prison. The Avatheos reached into the cage and grasped hold of the bird, cupping it gently in his hands. Liane thought for a moment he would let it fly free, out of an open window. Then he clenched his fist, and the bird stopped moving.

"Hold out your hand," he said.

"Why did you kill it?"

"Your divinity, you trust me, don't you?"

Liane swallowed past the lump in her throat. "Yes." She held her cupped, shaking hands open. The Avatheos placed the lifeless bird into them. It weighed nothing at all, and its little wings were bent at an odd angle.

"Heal the bird."

"I can't heal it. The bird is dead."

"The vessel is damaged, but the bird is not dead—not yet," he said. "Pull upon the threads of life and mend its broken body."

Liane looked down at the bird, feeling helpless. She wasn't sure what she was supposed to do. But she desperately wanted to help. When she looked closer, she could see the very shallow breaths it was taking. Its tiny black eye seemed to be pleading with her to save it. *Please. Let me save it.*

Then her hands started to glow faintly, a shimmering golden light that surrounded the bird, wrapping it in a sphere of luminescence, growing brighter and brighter by the second. Then, as quickly as it started, it stopped. The bird sat up on her palm, unharmed. It tilted its head side to side, examining, as if it were thanking her. Then it fluttered up and took flight out of the open window. Liane stared after it in a daze. She'd healed the bird with her own two hands. Could this power be harnessed to save Erich as well?

Liane sat up straighter. "Could this power heal corrupted? Is that what I'm meant to do?"

The Avatheos narrowed his eyes. Did he suspect? Had rumors of Erich reached him? "Did you know before the Nameless Goddess betrayed the light, there were cults in her honor, and they were the first who turned corrupted when the rivers of magic turned?" He motioned to the map on the table. "Our magic comes from these veins of the goddess. Her blood and tears filled them, and those who drank from those magic springs were granted her power. Similarly, those the Nameless Goddess birthed, like elves and dragons, were born corrupted, and the black ichor in their veins cannot be reversed, because they are the antithesis of the light."

"But chimeras are born from the corruption. How do we know that dragons and elves can't be saved?"

"You have a generous heart, but you cannot save the damned."

Her stomach twisted into knots. She wanted to save Erich, and she wanted to believe there was a way to do it. "What about the sword? Surely that gives me some power. Maybe it can reverse the darkness."

"The sword in your back is a weapon of light. If it were to be drawn against those sworn to the shadows, it would turn them to dust. That is why we must draw it out, to use it in the coming battle. Forget these dreams of salvation. They will not be as kind to you when they come to destroy your kin."

"And what about my mother? Can't we stop this corruption from happening?" she asked.

"Fate cannot be undone." He sighed. "Perhaps it is best if I show you." He motioned for Liane to follow him out the door. They went down the spiraling staircase, down the steps, and into the hall. Those they passed along the way moved aside.

He took her to the inner sanctum, which was emptied of worshippers. And he walked toward the statue of Cyra. She looked much as she did the night of the rite. But the moon was filling and illuminated her face. The Avatheos approached and pressed a button near her sandaled feet. Something clicked, and then a grinding sound rattled through the room as the statue moved aside, revealing the stairwell she'd used to get into the inner chamber below. The Avatheos went first, and Liane followed close behind. The room where they'd performed the rite felt cold and creepy without the oracles to fill it.

She feared he'd perform another strange ritual on her, but instead, he walked toward the back of the room to a door that she hadn't noticed before now. He swung it open and revealed yet another set of stairs. They descended into the dark, led only by the torch the Avatheos carried. As they approached, she heard a sound like rushing water, and then her skin started to glow, followed by a rhythmic throbbing in her back.

"Do you feel it calling to you?" the Avatheos asked. There was a strange rapture to his voice.

"What is it?"

"The source of light, the origin of light magic," the Avatheos replied.

The stairs ended at a door covered in markings she'd never seen before. The Avatheos pressed the markings in an order that she couldn't follow, and then the door swung open. It revealed a vaulted room with smooth walls that glimmered faintly in the golden light emanating from the river that ran from the room. It was nothing like she'd seen before. It made her scar throb and her stomach churn.

"What is a source?"

"When Cyra wept for her sister who betrayed her, it was here that her tears gathered, and from here, all light magic flows. All those who serve the light as her priests and priestesses enter the water and are purified of what darkness might linger in them. And, as a result, they are given her visions, her healing, her strength. During the fall equinox, you shall enter the water and awaken the sealed power within you, becoming a holy warrior, her divine justice." He stared at the vein with a sort of rapt awe.

Liane nodded, half in a trance. It seemed to be calling out to her in the way the dark pool in the ruins had. The sword in her back was throbbing, aching to be freed from her flesh.

She took a half step toward it, but the Avatheos caught her wrist and held her back. "Do not give in to its pull. Though I know the temptation is great. Entering it now might cause irrevocable damage to you. The ceremony must be completed at a time when darkness and light are in balance. In the same way it fused the sword with your back, a premature entry could kill you or, worse, allow the Nameless Goddess to use you as her wicked vessel. She will continue to tempt you until the ceremony is complete."

Liane took a step back, and she saw at the fringes of the pool black spiderweb tendrils, nearly absorbed by the light but spreading like cracks over the glittering surface.

He reached out as if to touch her face, and Liane fought the urge to recoil. When he touched her, she felt a wave of revulsion come over her. Every instinct was telling her to run.

"You've experienced too many worldly indulgences. And I fear it has made your destiny harder. But I can fix you, if necessary. Because I know it is you who will save us."

"I'll do my best," Liane croaked, and that seemed to snap him out of whatever trance he'd been caught in.

He stepped back from her, and his shoulders bunched. "That's enough for today. Return to your room and meditate on what we've spoken about. Tomorrow you will meet more of your supplicants, whose support is vital to our future endeavors."

She felt her mind swirling with everything the Avatheos had told her. She couldn't save Erich; her mother would lead the realm's destruction. How could any of it be true? She wanted desperately to believe the Avatheos that she was the goddess' chosen. But what if he'd gotten it wrong and she was the destruction he'd foretold instead?

14

For the first time, Liane was leaving the temple, and she wasn't sure what was worse: the prospect of facing fanatical crowds at the ball or the idea of finishing the letter she'd started to her mother about the Avatheos' prophecy. She'd attended thousands of balls without incident before, but the shadow of her attack on the dock lingered, and her nightmares of it had taken on a more sinister twist—the people who attacked her were now her family, rotted and putrid with chunks of skin peeled back to reveal the bone.

As was usually the case, obligation won out. Luzie suggested that she act as Liane's body double during the event. Luzie and her were of similar height and build, and should the situation get tense, they could swap places. While she didn't love the idea of putting Luzie in danger, Luzie didn't seem frightened at all. When Liane had protested, Luzie countered with, "We'll be among our peers. They won't dare swarm you. It'd look improper. Besides, it's been ages since we've been out to any sort of soiree."

With Luzie's reassurances, they prepared for the ball. She had to admit it was the first time she'd been glad to wear the veil. This time, the level of anonymity would be welcomed. Luzie helped her get ready, excitedly chattering about who might be in attendance, what waltz they might dance, and on and on. Liane let their conversation flow over her like water as she tried to forget her concerns for Luzie's sake. But the dark thoughts continued to swirl.

"Ready," the head priestess declared as she pinned the sash of Liane's robe just so.

Luzie held up a mirror for Liane to admire her reflection, and through the gauze of her veil, Liane saw a complete stranger. She was draped in gilt fabric. The crown on her head and the chains around her waist reminded her of statues of Cyra. In fact, if she weren't looking in a mirror, she would have thought she was looking at Cyra herself. It made the small hairs on the back of her neck rise. She felt like a fraud.

There was no time for self-reflection, as their priestess entourage arrived. The priestesses and Ludwig escorted them through the temple. They descended down a flight of rough-hewn stairs that reminded her of the tunnels beneath the Golden Palace and into a storage room, where stacks of crates and barrels were crowded together. The doors opened onto a city street, and Liane braced for a mob. But it was empty except for an unmarked carriage. Luzie giggled as they climbed in. Ludwig took a seat next to the driver.

Then the driver took them through the city. It was an open and bright place with people drinking wine on balconies overlooking the street, who waved to them as they passed. If she weren't terrified of being attacked, she would have loved to explore the city more. Their destination was in one of the richer neighborhoods, where the villas loomed. Their courtyards were filled with citrus trees and fragrant flowering vines.

Their host's villa was surrounded by high walls, and Midnight Guards were posted at the entrance. A few commoners were lingering outside the gates, and at the sight of them, her chest clenched. But they passed them by without issue. Unlike her usual arrival at events, she was let out of the carriage at the back servants' entrance.

The Avatheos arrived separately, in his private carriage, and when he stepped out, he offered his bent arm for her to take. They climbed the narrow servants' staircase and entered an unfinished hallway. This was how the Avatheos seemed to materialize into rooms. The priestess in charge informed them that Luzie would wait in the servants' passage until she was needed. For now, Liane and the Avatheos would take their seats and wait for guests to arrive.

The guards and Ludwig did a sweep of the perimeter before declaring it safe, and guests were allowed to enter.

There were two gilt chairs at the head of the room, somewhat akin to thrones. It felt wrong to sit there after what the Avatheos had said to her. She'd never try to usurp her mother, or Aristea, for that matter. Liane had seen the pressure being a ruler put on them both and had no desire to share their fate. Whatever the Avatheos' vision might have been, there must be another way around it.

Liane twisted her hands as she watched guests pour in. They lined up to greet her, giving her a bow and making the sign of the star against their foreheads, before filing off to mingle and pick at the banquet table. She'd eaten before she arrived, at the Avatheos' insistence. The divine didn't need to sustain himself on something as mundane as food.

Ludwig leaned in from behind her and whispered in her ear, "If you need a break, just say the word."

"I'm fine," she said.

Ludwig stepped back without another word, and she felt the sweat gathering on her neck. She was sweltering beneath layers of fabric, and her back was starting to throb. Was a fever brewing? Stars above, she hoped not. More people filed by; their faces ablur. And she took a few deep, calming breaths. She could do this. The goddess wouldn't have chosen her if she weren't capable. Visions could be misinterpreted, even by the Avatheos.

When the ballroom was sufficiently full, the Avatheos stood. And she thought she would be able to hear a pin drop as the crowd turned to face her, their attention hungry.

The Avatheos held the silence for a few heartbeats before he said, "Thank you all for coming tonight. We are pleased to present the goddess' chosen vessel, the holy warrior who will conquer the darkness."

A cheer erupted from the crowd. Glasses clinked in a toast, but the fire burning up her back was becoming unbearable. More people lined up to greet her, but their faces melted into one another. And each new wave of people that came up to her felt like waves crashing against the shore. Some wished her well, others offered prayers or subtle bribes for miracles she couldn't perform. It was a strange out-of-body experience.

She felt like she was choking. She grasped hold of the arm of her chair, nails biting in hard enough to bend them back, her breathing ragged. She stood, and they fell silent, waiting for her to say something profound.

"I need a moment to catch my breath," she said.

Ludwig was at her elbow, guiding her out into the secret passageway. Luzie had been slouching in the hall but perked up when they entered.

"I need a few minutes. Mind taking over?" Liane asked.

"Take all the time you need."

Liane squeezed Luzie's shoulder and hurried down the hall and out the servants' entrance. She'd really mucked it up. If it weren't for Luzie, she might have made an even bigger mess.

She needed air and a second to think. To clear her thoughts with something that wasn't destiny or doom.

The villa had a back garden, with tall hedges that she could get lost in. The air was humid and sticky, and she pulled back her veil to uncover her face, but it got caught on the golden spikes of her headpiece. She wanted to rip it off her head, strip down to her underclothes, and splash in the fountain that she could hear somewhere in the garden. The weight of her veil and gilded crown made her head throb. The fountain she'd heard was mounted against the garden wall, and a stream of water trickled from it. She cupped some cold water in her hands and then splashed it against her face. It did little to soothe her.

The coiled trapped feeling she'd been ignoring for days was ready to snap. She wasn't suited for life within temple walls, shrouded in silk, and meant to act mysteriously divine. Maybe she should confess her vision and be free of this role as avatar before someone really got hurt. But then what became of his vision of doom, and the sword in her back? The fate of the kingdom was on her shoulders, and she couldn't stand it. She wanted her life back.

A jasmine bush climbed up over an archway leading to a shadowed part of the garden. Liane glanced at Ludwig for a second before running into it. Her feet pounded on pavement, and his armor rattled as he pursued her. She ran through the garden until the fear that spiked her veins subsided, and she was doubled over.

"What are you doing here?" Ludwig asked.

She popped her head up to answer, but he wasn't talking to her. Her breath caught in her throat to see Erich haloed by moonlight. Her stomach swooped. Was this a hallucination, or was he really there?

"I just want to talk to her."

"You have no right—" Ludwig started to say, but Erich ignored him and looked at her.

When their eyes met, she felt as if his gaze set her skin ablaze as she remembered their last kiss. The garden, the party, and everything else fell away. She thought giving him up would be easy, but nothing about him was ever simple. He took a step toward her, and Ludwig inserted himself between them. Erich's eyes flashed gold for a second before he extinguished whatever fire had burned in his gaze and looked at Ludwig.

"Let me talk to him. Alone," Liane said in a commanding voice.

"Liane." Ludwig suddenly sounded very tired.

She crossed her arms and stared him down. After a few minutes, he ran his hands through his hair, a sure sign of defeat, and said, "This better be the last time." And then he left them alone at last.

Erich stood back from her, his eyes roving over her body. Tingles shot down her arms as she remembered the way he'd touched her. The feel of him so near and yet outside her reach was torture.

She needed to say goodbye. Whether he was a dragon or a man. A prince or a corrupted. The goddess had chosen Liane's path, and her destiny couldn't be entangled with his. But stars above, she wanted him more than she'd wanted anything in her entire life. She'd thought saying goodbye would have closed this chapter, that she would have been able to set him aside, as if the memory of him wasn't consuming her day and night.

"Erich. How are you here?" she gasped. Something between a question and a desperate plea.

"Do you want an answer, or do you want to kiss me?" He closed the distance between them but didn't touch her. She kept her hands firmly at her sides, though she was desperate to feel him, to run her hands over the hard planes of his chest and arms.

"A little of both."

"I know the host, Leonhard. He invited me and said I would want to be here, and now I know why."

His gaze burned into her, set her aflame, made her want to burn with him if only to turn them both into ash and be freed of this torture. Hand trembling, she reached out to touch his face, to see if he was truly there, and he wasn't some delusion. His stubbled chin brushed against her palm, and turned to kiss it. His lips moved up to her wrist, along her arm, up to her shoulder. Liane leaned into him, hands draped around his neck, melting into him as his mouth lapped at water droplets along her throat.

He took his time kissing up her neck, nibbling on her ear before moving to her lips. Soft and gentle at first, as she opened up to him, his tongue thrust into her mouth, invading her like a conquering general.

She moaned against him, and his hands balled into fists at her waist, as if it was taking all his self-control not to run his hands along her body.

"I've missed you," he groaned against her mouth.

The words shot through her, and any questions or thoughts of saying goodbye were chased away by the feeling of his hands along her hips, gripping her so she could feel his hardness against her belly. Warmth pooled at the apex of her thighs, and she rubbed them together, fighting the urge to wrap her legs around his waist and climb him.

She broke apart their kiss, chest heaving as she stared at his dumbfounded expression.

"What spell have you put over me?" she said. His forehead was pressed to hers, his lips parted, his hands splayed against her hips.

"I was about to ask you the very same. Liane, no one has ever consumed my thoughts in the way you do. I cannot stop—"

She silenced him with another kiss. If she heard his next words, she'd give up anything and everything for him if he asked it of her. Her hands tangled in his hair, and as his tongue swirled around hers, their teeth clashed together as if neither of them could get close enough.

His hand moved down over the swell of her hip, gathering up the fabric of her skirt, hiking it up to draw his hand along her thigh. She quivered beneath his touch as he slipped closer to her sex, pulling back her undergarments as he rubbed against her mound. Her breath hitched as she pressed against him, desperate for more as he teased her, building the anticipation. With her leg hooked behind his leg, she ground against his hand and bit down on his shoulder to stifle her moan.

"You like that?" he growled in her ear as he slid a finger to part her folds and pressed his thumb against the bundle of nerves there. Her eyes widened as he made slow circles, building in speed. She kissed him, biting at his lower lip, as she rode against his hand amongst growing waves of ecstasy, bringing her nearly to the brink before he pulled away. Liane shamelessly whimpered as he did. Then he popped his finger into his mouth and sucked the juices off it.

If she had been wet before, she was drenched now. He looked at her as he swirled his tongue around his finger, eyes hooded.

"Ever since that night, all I've wanted to do is taste you. Can I?" His voice was husky and sent a lustful shiver down Liane's spine.

If he didn't, she might burst apart at the seams.

"Please."

He picked her up, carrying her over to the garden bench

before sitting her down. Then he knelt before her like a suppliant, his hands on her thighs as he pushed back her skirt, and then parted her thighs and rested them on his shoulders. Liane squirmed in anticipation, bucking up toward his mouth. He chuckled against her, his warm breath fanning her and building the anticipation for what was to come. He breathed her in, his eyes flashing gold in the dark as he looked up at her. Was this the dragon or Erich? She wasn't sure she cared in this moment. He ran his thumb across her sensitive nub once more before he parted her folds with his finger and moved in and out of her slick opening. She arched, begging him to go deeper, and then he grasped hold of her rear, bringing her up to his mouth, and swirled his tongue as he thrust with his finger.

Stars reeled overhead as she bit down on her hand to dampen her moans of pleasure. With her free hand, she grasped hold of his hair, forcing him down as she ground against his face.

"You taste incredible. Do you know you drive me insane?" he murmured.

"Yes," she gasped. It was the only word she could utter in her lust filled haze.

He inserted a second finger, and all she could think about was him, the feel of his tongue as he matched her rhythm. She rose higher and higher until she was pulsing with ecstasy and losing herself in him as she climaxed.

By the time it was over, she felt limp and wrung out. Erich lowered her legs and pulled down her skirt, before sitting back on his heels.

She could see his erection straining against his breaches, and she attempted to grasp his waistband, but his hot hand on her wrist stopped her.

"Let me—"

"Come away with me, Liane," he said at the same time.

The post-orgasm haze must be confusing her. She sat up straighter.

"Where? Your room?" She laughed.

"No. Leave the church, Liane. I came to Basilia to save you from the Avatheos."

She bristled and pulled away from him. She thought of the Avatheos' menacing presence and the twist in her gut that she couldn't seem to quite ignore.

"I don't need to be saved. I'm destined to save the realm."

"He wants to use you, Liane. Don't you see it? He's hurting you. You said so yourself."

Silence followed, a yawning, strangling silence that threatened to consume her. She wanted to fill it, but found her tongue too thick to properly form words.

"That's insane. He needs me to save the world."

He shook his head. "I'm not explaining it right. Please just trust me."

She stood up. "Is that why you did this? Was this some form of manipulation to get me to go with you and the elf? They're plotting to overthrow my kingdom. You know that, don't you?"

"It's not like that. If you'd talk to Fritz, you'd understand."

"And let him put me under his spell? Maybe you're the one who's been deceived."

"Trust me, it's not safe. Look, I can explain more once we're away." He reached to grab hold of her wrist, but she pulled away before he could touch her.

"Why would I go anywhere with you, Erich? You're corrupted." The verbal blow landed, and he winced. She remembered the last night they'd spent together.

"Perhaps what we did just now was a mistake," he said.

She laughed bitterly. "You cannot be serious." She crossed her arms. "You come in here, bury your face in me, and then have regrets? Typical. I never should have given you another chance." She turned to walk away, but he grabbed her arm.

"I shouldn't have said that," he said. His eyes darkened again, and she felt as if he were trying to control himself. "Which is why it should be the last time. I can't control the dragon when I'm around you. It wants you."

Those words sent a chill down her spine, and she hated how much it aroused her to think of his claws and scales coupled with his dexterous human hands. But it was good that he was drawing a line in the sand. She couldn't keep doing this, not as the avatar, not as a woman. She had some self-respect. She knew men, and he would only hurt her in the end, and her life was meant for the church. Eventually, he'd grow tired of her and move on.

"Well, good, because you and your dragon can't have me." Then she turned and walked away without a second glance because she feared that if she did look back, the doubts would continue to creep in.

15

Erich had been reckless, thinking with his cock rather than using this rare opportunity. He could have whisked her out of there with ease. He was a fool. It was taking all his restraint to stand back and watch her walk away. If he followed her, forced her to come with him as he'd planned when he'd followed her into the garden, he wouldn't be teetering on the edge of the dragon's obsession anymore—he'd be diving headfirst into it. For now, its tastes were lewd, but it could turn bloodthirsty in an instant. And despite his disappointment in himself, his cock was straining, and the dragon was desperate to bury himself in her to the hilt.

All Erich could do was tighten the chains around it in a futile attempt to subdue this suffocating desire he had for her. The dragon wouldn't go quietly. It scratched and clawed at his insides until he was trembling with the exertion.

If the moon were fuller, he might have lost, but after several minutes of wrestling with his inner dragon, Erich collapsed onto his knees, panting for breath but back in full control of his impulses. From the moment he'd arrived in Basilia, he'd felt this faint aching in his bones. No, it was before that, in Artria.

The first moment he saw her, he felt the ache in his chest, a desperate longing for something he couldn't put into words. And it was Liane. It had always been her. The dragon's desires were unfathomable at times and often blurred with his own. He tried to keep that part of him separate, the monster under his skin and the man fighting for control. But every time he was around Liane, those lines started to blur.

He'd known from the start that convincing Liane to leave the church would be a monumental task. Asking her to abandon her faith, which formed the foundation of her kingdom and supported her mother's rule, was a big ask. What he hadn't expected was her rejection to pierce him down to his soft, vulnerable core. He wasn't a stranger to rejection, to the fear and revulsion in people's eyes when they learned the truth, from his father to the strangers he'd met on the way while seeking a cure. He'd thought Liane was different, but maybe that'd been wishful thinking on his part.

The hour was late, and curfew loomed, but each step back to the inn felt as if he were dragging his feet through the mud. He needed to recoup, to think up a new approach. Perhaps one where he wasn't left alone with Liane. He wasn't sure he could trust himself otherwise. Before tonight, he'd thought he had it under control, but maybe it was the dragon who'd had him under its claw all along. This was a new facet to the dragon's curse he hadn't experienced before. Perhaps the advancement of his condition was spiraling him closer to his inevitable demise.

He needed to keep it in check long enough for Fritz to get her away. Then he'd succumb and pay his debt to Leonhard by fighting in the ring, a miserable monster too afraid to die. Erich couldn't fathom why he'd given him an invitation to the ball, but his gut had told him he had to go. Then he'd seen Liane and knew what game he was playing. Like the Sundland wine and the dagger, he was using her to taunt him and remind him of his debt yet to be paid. The mark Leonhard had left upon him burned, and after tonight, he was likely expecting Erich to come to him, but he'd ignore the summons. And would continue to do so until he had no other choice.

Pilgrims and laborers seeking an evening's entertainment before the curfew bells rang crowded around the tables in the common room of the Raven's Wing Inn. The innkeeper rushed between tables, arms laden with pewter mugs of ale, and the scent of stew filled the space. Erich was ravenous, but the thought of sitting amongst a crowd attempting to eat seemed ill-advised. He trudged up the stairs to his room, ready to collapse onto his bed and sleep until sunrise.

He swung open his door and was greeted by a warm fire and the smell of freshly baked bread, cheese, sausage, and meat pies. Fritz poured wine into two glasses before greeting Erich.

"I couldn't find Sundland wine, but I hope this will suit you." He raised a glass toward Erich.

Erich stared slack-jawed at the spread. Fritz gestured for him to take a seat, and without proper words to express his thanks, Erich sank into a chair, ripped open a piece of bread, spread warm butter over it, and tore into it. The last time he'd eaten this well was back at Ivar's town house. He'd eaten plenty of inn food. This wasn't the usual bowl of stew, hard bread, and nearly rancid sausage he'd become accustomed to at the Raven's Wing.

Rather than thank Fritz for the food as he should, he asked, "Where'd you get this?'

"Isabella isn't Bertha, but she is a good cook when properly motivated."

Erich bit a sausage in half and chewed slowly, contemplating the elf across from him. He assumed Bertha was the innkeeper who owned the inn Fritz had spent the better part of a year living out of in Artria. It shocked him, given the history between their kind, that Fritz cared for humans. If Erich had to guess, Fritz had buttered up Isabella to make him this feast. Fritz ate a few bites of cheese and meat and smirked at Erich.

"How are your balls?" Fritz asked.

Erich nearly spit out the wine he was drinking and set down his glass as he swallowed hard.

"I meant to say the ball," Fritz said, hiding his smile in his glass.

He didn't want to know if he'd seen what happened in a vision or not.

Erich leaned back in his chair and tried to appear nonchalant, but feared he was failing miserably. "She won't hear anything I have to say. The Avatheos has dug his claws in deep."

"She can fight it all she wants, but your destinies are too entwined to be untangled. It would be like asking the moon not to rise as the sun sets."

"But the moon doesn't always rise." Erich rubbed his stubbled chin.

He'd eaten a feast after the fight, and yet his hunger still gnawed at him. He wondered if he'd ever feel satiated again. Liane's flushed face and parted lips flashed through his mind, and his manhood stirred once more. He'd need to take himself in hand later to calm that particular beast. Not that he was certain it would really cool his desires.

"Just because you cannot see her, doesn't mean she's not there," Fritz said cryptically.

He was going to assume he was waxing poetic about the moon and couldn't tell where Erich's thoughts had strayed.

"Speaking of the moon, the full moon is less than two weeks away. We should make plans for when I need to leave the city and transform."

"Yes, I suppose we will," Fritz said distractedly, as he pushed the crust of bread around his plate.

"Leonhard knows where we are, and he's close to the Avatheos. I think for both our safety, it's best if we pull up roots."

"Do you know what really caused the Corruption?" Fritz asked.

"Are you trying to change the subject?" Erich asked with an arched brow.

Fritz didn't look up from his plate. "What humans call the Corruption, we call the flood of tears. It's what started our genocide. The sun cult, now known as the Church of Sol, burned the moon temples and places like here, where dual worship protected the source. They murdered those of us with ties to the moon—the elves, the dragonborn, and the others. Our blood seeped into the ground and created a chain reaction that swept through the veins of magic, polluting and weakening them. The Nameless Goddess tried to stop them, but Cyra's cult had grown too strong, and they sealed her inside the veins, locking her power and cementing their own." Fritz recited this all, staring out into the distance, haunted and terrified. As if he were reliving those moments himself.

"Why are you telling me this now?" Erich asked.

Fritz turned to look at him, his vision clearing. "Because you need to understand light cannot exist without dark. Everything requires balance. It may seem that your warnings to Liane have gone unheeded, but you've planted a seed of doubt in her mind, and if it is cultivated, it shall bloom. If she didn't want to believe you, why would she have spoken with you tonight?"

Erich didn't have an answer for him. Not one that was decent for polite company. But suppose Fritz was right, and Liane could be convinced, how much longer did he have before Leonhard got bored with this game of cat and mouse and decided to call in Erich's debt? Or before the Avatheos caught wind of a dragon loose in their mist and had him executed?

"Let's find another inn after I return from my transformation. And perhaps consider splitting up." Erich stood.

"You're not alone anymore. I know you're itching to rescue her, but we can do this together. If you give me more time..." Fritz said. He reached across the table, then recoiled at the last moment.

Erich had spent so long alone that it felt wrong to lean on anyone. Besides, the longer they spent together, the higher the chance he'd get Fritz killed.

"Don't worry about me. But if you find a way to get Liane out of the temple, I'm all ears."

Erich took a few steps toward his bed and turned around once more. "And thanks for dinner."

Fritz smiled softly. "Anytime."

16

Aristea picked at an apricot on her plate. She hadn't touched her bread or sausage. Yvette and the other lady's maids had finished their breakfast long ago, and they kept glancing in her direction as they waited patiently at the table for her to rise. The silence was oppressive, and her gaze kept sliding to the door, half expecting Liane to come bounding in, cheeks flushed and a mischievous smile on her lips. But her sister was miles away in Basilia while Aristea was trapped here in the mausoleum of her own making.

Aristea pushed aside her plate. She had no more appetite, and her lady's maid, Jana, glanced up.

"My lady, are you finished?" she asked.

"Yes, thank you."

Jana took her plate and handed it off to a kitchen servant. Aristea's other ladies rose without a word, filing into the dressing room to prepare her next black gown. They worked with silent efficiency as Aristea reflected on how this cold silence hadn't always been the norm. Before she and Heinrich had combined their households, she'd been surrounded by maidens she'd called friends; they'd laughed and teased one another and whispered about courtiers they fancied. But Heinrich didn't like them and arranged for their marriages and replaced them with daughters and sisters of his favorites. She tried making friends with them, but they were quiet and cold. And over time, she'd become used to the silence and the distance that grew between her and those who served her. "It was the way of things," Heinrich had told her when she'd complained to him. The household you kept was said to reflect its mistress, and Aristea wanted to be respected, and the ladies were demure and obedient as she should be. But now she wished they'd giggle or gossip or do anything other than sit around her like dolls she'd placed in a playroom.

The silence hadn't been quite so stifling with Liane around, but with her gone, Aristea felt deeply lonely.

She wanted to talk to someone besides Mother about Mathias. Someone who understood him as well as she'd thought she did. Aristea didn't want to believe Mathias would plot against the throne, not her charming, funny baby brother. But the evidence was damning. Heinrich never trusted Mathias and often whispered in her ear about how, until Aristea had a son, the council would demand that Mother name Mathias her heir. As much as she didn't want to believe, the truth didn't matter. The rumor was enough to destabilize everything Mother had built. If the elves chose to attack in the midst of another civil war, the empire couldn't survive. Aristea could see the fissures in the empire, like cracks in a vase; one wrong movement and it would shatter into pieces. They needed to squash the rumors, and Aristea needed to strengthen her alliances now more than ever. That was why, rather than continue dancing around him, Aristea decided to talk to the wife of one of the most powerful men of Heinrich's faction, Duke Krantz.

Her lady's maids finished dressing her, and she didn't even bother looking at herself in the mirror. She hated the veil, hated the color black. It made her look pale and sickly. But mourning clothes weren't meant to be flattering. And the alternative was removing the veil and presenting herself to be available for marriage, and the thought of that was equally distressing.

Normally, these sorts of meetings would be hosted at the palace. But Aristea was desperate enough to go directly to Duke Krantz's town house. She'd sent notice that morning, asking to visit. But it wasn't as if they could deny her. When the carriage pulled up to the town house, their servants were lined up on the steps to greet her. And, on the topmost step, was Duchess Krantz, an austere woman with thin, wrinkled lips and iron-gray hair. Aristea was disappointed, but not surprised, to see that Duke Krantz wasn't with her. The duchess bowed stiffly to Aristea as she exited. Yvette, who'd ridden with her, followed her out of the carriage door. Duke Krantz had been one of Heinrich's closest allies and was the head of his faction. Duke Krantz's personal army had been the bulk of Heinrich's father's forces during the rebellion. Duke Krantz had often hosted her and Heinrich at their town house parties over the years. The men would drink and talk politics while Aristea endured small talk with the ladies in the drawing room. Despite a long acquaintance, the duchess had never warmed to Aristea.

"Your highness, thank you for honoring us with a visit," Duchess Krantz said dryly.

"I appreciate you welcoming me on such short notice," Aristea replied.

"Did I have a choice, your majesty?" the woman said with a raised brow.

Aristea just smiled at her jab, glad for the veil that would hide any of the frustration on her face, and gestured for her to show the way.

The duchess leaned heavily on her own maid, shuffling her way into the drawing room. Aristea took a seat and dismissed

Yvette to wait outside while the duchess' silent servant prepared a tray of finger sandwiches and wine. Then, when the duchess gave the signal, they retreated as well. The duchess' shrewd gaze was piercing. She had a reputation for being rather blunt but cunning, and Aristea was under no illusion that the duchess didn't know exactly why she was there. Which would either make her task easier or harder.

It was rude to jump straight to the point, and Aristea attempted a few lines of small talk, all of which fell flat. The duchess gave one-word answers that killed any attempts to start a conversation before sipping from her wine and staring down Aristea as if she'd asked the wrong question.

Aristea was feeling increasingly uncomfortable when the servant returned to refresh her wine. After she left, Aristea started another line of polite inquiry.

"Your husband is well, I hope…"

The duchess set her glass down heavily on the table beside her. "Your majesty, perhaps we could do away with the pleasantries and cut to the heart of your visit. I grow weary of this vapid talk."

Aristea sat up a bit straighter and cleared her throat. "I didn't mean to cause offense." She attempted to act demure.

"No, I expected not. But you wouldn't be visiting me unless you needed something, would you?"

Aristea curled her hand into a fist on her lap and said, "I've come to see where Duke Krantz's loyalties lie now that my husband is dead."

It was a gamble to speak bluntly. For all she knew, they were plotting against her and would turn on her the moment she walked out the door. But she, too, was growing tired of games.

Duchess Krantz smiled. Aristea thought it might be the first time she'd ever seen her do such a thing.

"I knew you had some of your mother's backbone." She rang the bell on the desk next to her, and the servant re-entered the room.

"Bring the princess another cup of wine."

"No, thank—" She hadn't even finished the first glass, but the older woman cut her a look, and Aristea slammed her mouth shut.

The servant began to fill her already full cup, but frowned as Duchess Krantz scoffed.

"Not that bottle. Get a fresh one from the cellar—something old and dusty from Sundland. Their wine is the best."

The servant nodded before backing out of the room.

"It's not necessary. This is perfectly adequate," Aristea said, gesturing to her full cup.

"Have something against Sundland?" Duchess Krantz asked with an arched brow.

Aristea coughed and turned to cover it.

The old woman cackled. "Nice to see you're not made of stone. No, I sent her off on an errand to make sure she doesn't eavesdrop. Never know who's paying whom to listen in on important conversations."

Aristea felt foolish for not considering it sooner, but of course, she should have. It was reckless to speak without being certain they weren't overheard.

"Pardon?" Aristea said, trying to make sure she understood her meaning.

"I never liked Heinrich," Duchess Krantz confessed. "He was a self-important fool, but he was a man of royal blood and in line to the crown, which is why fools flocked to him. Including my husband."

Aristea took a moment to process everything the duchess had said. She'd never heard her speak more than a few words at a time, and now she was practically eviscerating her husband and Heinrich.

"I wouldn't—" Aristea couldn't think of something diplomatic to say. Heinrich had been terrible. He'd been cruel and vain, and when he'd died, she'd been relieved. But despite how awful he'd been to her, she felt guilty for letting someone speak ill of him. As if she should still defend him.

Duchess Krantz held up her hand. "Don't make excuses for him. I know you're only wearing black to keep his father's followers happy and to keep that slobbering Duke Mattison away from you."

Aristea was too stunned to speak and instead took a few gulps of her wine to wet her suddenly dry mouth.

"Now that we've got that out of the way. What are you planning to offer the dukes to win their loyalty? I'll admit even your mother had better incentives, with the elves growing restless at the borders and the idiot dukes grumbling about succession, as if it weren't settled long ago."

"I, well..." No one had asked about her plans. And she had plenty. Getting her sister's endorsement as Cyra's chosen, consolidating the Midnight Guard's power to fight the elves, finding the mastermind behind the stardust distribution, and so much more. But that wasn't what she was asking, was it? Those were the obvious answers. What any future ruler might say.

"Surely you have a plan," Duchess Krantz pressed.

"I want to be the most powerful and feared ruler that ever was," Aristea said

The old woman didn't show her feelings on her face. "You don't start small, do you? I have to say I'm impressed."

"The question is which side will you be on when I ascend?"

The old woman threw her head back and cackled. "I know where I will be. My position has never wavered."

"And your husband, would he help me uncover who was really pulling my deceased husband's strings?"

Her expression sobered. "This goes deeper than you think, your highness."

"Do you think that will deter me?"

"Don't be a cheeky fool. This has been a fight going on longer than you've been alive, girl."

Aristea recoiled. She thought they'd reached a certain rapport. But maybe she'd been wrong?

"Are you saying Duke Krantz is involved?" Aristea asked.

Duchess Krantz sighed and pinched the bridge of her nose. "I'll speak with him on your behalf, but it'll be up to him how much he's willing to divulge."

"Does his loyalty remain to Heinrich's line?" Aristea asked.

The old woman laughed. "His loyalty has been, and always will be, to his own ends. He backed Prince Heinrich's father in the war because he was convinced that it would enrich him. And he stayed close to Heinrich for the same reason. He's an opportunist through and through. But I have to warn you that he likely won't see you. He doesn't trust the Starwebers."

This verged on treason, but Aristea was willing to take a gamble if it meant having a powerful man on her side.

"And when I win him over, will that bring his allies?"

"Don't get ahead of yourself; you'll need to win him over first."

Duke Krantz wasn't the sort of man you wanted by your side, too fickle and selfishly motivated. A man like that with a small personal army was even more dangerous. But fortunately, she was desperate enough to overlook his faults if it got her what she wanted.

"What do I need to do?" Aristea asked.

She cackled. "You really are nothing like I thought you were."

"Thank you," Aristea said. "And might I be so bold as to say you're not how I imagined?"

"Thought I was nothing but a senile old woman?"

Aristea blushed and stammered an apology, but the duchess waved it away.

"Don't apologize. Your mother knows that rule. You're going to be empress someday. You have to make decisions and stick to them no matter what."

Aristea nodded; it was sage advice.

"I know the world is changing, but while old men like my husband remain in power, it will not be as simple as wanting to change minds. You can't buy his loyalty, I can tell you that. But win his heart instead."

"Thank you for all your help."

She shook her head. "I don't do it out of the goodness of my heart. Just make sure you remember my kin when it comes down to giving out titles and positions."

"I will keep it in mind." She bowed her head to her.

Again, a dismissive wave of her hand. "I cannot guarantee I can get you what you want, of course, but hopefully, it will be better than nothing."

"Certainty," Aristea said.

They talked a few minutes longer before Duchess Krantz declared she was tired. Aristea got up to leave, and on their way out, they were greeted by the servant.

"My lady. Lord Sommerfeld is here..." He trailed off. Or perhaps Aristea had stopped listening.

Jonathan was standing in the parlor of the Krantz's town house.

"What are you doing here?" she asked.

Jonathan's eyes bounced between her and Duchess Krantz.

"And how do you know my son-in-law, Lord Sommerfeld?" the duchess mused, seemingly intrigued by their attachment.

A flush burned across Aristea's face, and she was even more thankful for the disguise.

"The prince consort facilitated my marriage to the duchess' late daughter, Ida," Jonathan said, his eyes barely moving from Aristea to acknowledge his mother-in-law. She knew Heinrich had arranged the marriage, but she'd forgotten it was Duke Krantz's daughter. And his late wife? Why hadn't she heard? Had it been recent? Her mind swirled with the implications.

"Ah," Duchess Krantz said, as if that explained it all.

But Aristea couldn't be more mortified by her outburst. "Forgive me, Lord Sommerfeld. That was rude of me."

He smiled at her. "Think nothing of it. Your highness."

"If you have business with me, see to it later. I'm too tired for you today," Duchess Krantz said and started to walk up the stairs. "But see Her Highness to her carriage for me, will you?"

There was no pause for him to answer. Just an expectation to be obeyed.

Jonathan shrugged as if to say he had no choice. And he offered his bent arm to her. As if she needed escorting the few feet to her awaiting carriage outside.

She should have politely declined, but the reckless and greedy part of her took his offered arm and walked with him outside the house.

"I hope she wasn't too rude to you. She can be cold, but she means well," Jonathan said.

"Not at all. She was very helpful."

"I'm glad we ran into one another, actually," he replied.

"Oh." A small thrill ran up her spine, thinking of another accidental meeting. She'd sworn she'd stay away, but it seemed that fate kept thrusting them together.

"I thought you might want an introduction to Duke Krantz. He's rather biased against your family, I'm afraid. But he's got one weakness."

Aristea looked up at him, wide-eyed. "How did you know?"

"I saw the way you looked when Duke Mattison implied he was courting you. It's presumptuous of me, but I came here to ask the duchess to intercede with my former father-in-law for you. But I suppose you did that yourself." He rubbed the back of his neck.

"Jonathan," Aristea said in an awed whisper.

"Once a week, he strolls through the park. If you happened to run into him, he'd have no choice but to greet you or give great offense."

But would it be wise to just walk around the park by herself? Wouldn't that be exceedingly suspicious?

"I'll escort you if you like."

That offer again. Another chance to see him. To talk to him. She knew she should say no, but the next words were out of her mouth before she could stop herself. "I'd love that."

"And I'll bring our secret weapon," he said as he opened the carriage door for her, and she stepped in.

"I'll see you in a few days then." Aristea nodded and closed the door. She couldn't help but peek out the window one more time as they drove away. Her stomach fluttered with butterflies.

She was going to see him again, soon.

17

Back home, Liane had loved discovering hidden passages and forgotten corners of the ancient structures. She'd enjoyed unraveling a mystery. But rather than examine what Erich had told her, she spent her days exploring the temple grounds—the halls, towers, and sanctuaries—three times, seeking distraction from her storm cloud of thoughts. Could she trust the Avatheos' intentions? The best way to get answers would be to ask the Avatheos himself. But during their increasingly frequent meetings, he'd evaded her questions until he started snapping at her to study the text and meditate to better understand Cyra's will. Liane tried to accept the church's truth. But her doubts were piling up.

Those questions drove her to the library, where she pulled down a multitude of books. They kept records of almost everything. They charted the stars' movements, deaths, and births of the nobility and royal family, but records of the past lives of priests and priestesses were murky at best. Oracles' prophecies were almost never recorded, but in a few cases, she found old journals belonging to priests long dead. If the Avatheos had seen a dire prophecy for the kingdom, surely, he must have told someone. Or recorded it somewhere. Or someone else had seen as he had. But she could find no evidence of it. That didn't necessarily mean he was lying, but it didn't prove his intentions either.

~

AFTER DAYS OF FRUITLESS SEARCH, she was back in the library again. Words were swirling around in her mind, and she wondered if she'd ever be without questions lingering at the back of her mind. There were only three archivists working, while dozens of other desks lay empty. The archivists recorded all the portent star movements and sent out messages to the regional dukes and vice premiers with instructions or warnings. The ceilings were high and vaulted, and the bookcases that lined the room reached from floor to ceiling. Ladders leaned against them, and a few late-night working priests pushed carts, returning tomes to their places on the shelves.

She strolled along the aisles, and the familiar scent of ink and paper comforted her. Liane ran her hands down the spines, surveying titles. They were mostly theological texts debating the intricacies of religious dogma—the types of books the goddess' chosen should gravitate toward. But she was sure that if she even attempted to read them, she'd be snoring in minutes. She turned a corner and found an aisle of books with dates printed on the spines. When she pulled down a book at random, she discovered it was a history of Neolyra from a few years after the Corruption.

So much had been lost after the Corruption, but perhaps not everything. The Nameless had caused it, and according to the Avatheos, she was trying again. But maybe it hadn't been the first time. And if that were true, there'd be some record of it, surely. Perhaps there even were other avatars before her who'd fought back the darkness. Maybe that would assure her the Avatheos wasn't using her, that she was destined for something greater and not a pawn in a political game. Liane went to the desk where an archivist was scribbling on a piece of paper. They looked up as she approached.

"Are there any books I might read on past avatars?" Liane asked.

The archivist paused a moment. "I can look. But I'm not sure I've heard of another one before you?"

"Nothing? What about the rise of the Nameless?" she asked.

They frowned at her and said, "Why would you want to read about that?"

It would be blasphemous to say she wanted to prove the Avatheos' prophecy was true and not an elaborate manipulation meant to entrap her. Plus, she doubted there were books like that. "What about books on Neolyra's history?"

They sighed. "What era?"

"All of them since the Corruption?" she asked, tone rising with uncertainty.

"Take a seat, and I'll bring you what I have." They waved her away impatiently.

Liane thanked them and wandered over to sit down at one of the desks. The last rays of light from the day were falling through the window, and she had a view of the city beyond. Golden-red light warmed her skin and made her back tingle pleasantly.

A few minutes after she'd sat down, three priests and an acolyte brought over towering stacks of books. They set them down on the table around her with loud thumps. She looked up at them all realizing what a daunting task she'd set out to accomplish. But she needed to prove to herself that Erich was wrong. She picked up a book at random and started reading, but it quickly became apparent that this book was a dry account of wars fought and won after the Corruption. There was nothing about the church. No problem. She skimmed over the titles, searching for books that mentioned the church's history. She pulled out three more books from the stack, only to be met with the same problem. None of the books gave an unbiased history, but were rather full of theological allegory—the same stories she'd been hearing her entire life.

She sighed and closed the last book, setting it atop her teetering pile of rejects. She was ready to give up when she noticed a book at the bottom of the pile. It was titled *Lyra: Before the Creation of Neolyra and the History of the Ancients.* It was much older than the others, and the author's name had nearly faded away.

Touching the book gave her pause. It sent a jolt up her arm. On the cover were illustrations of the two-toned stag and the black raven she'd seen in her visions. She remembered a similar book she'd read back in Artria and was immediately intrigued.

She cracked it open, and the pages were brittle. This didn't seem like the sort of book she should be reading. It felt more like a book that should be locked in some scholar's private study and only looked at and never touched.

She glanced around the room at the archivists who'd delivered the books and saw they were preoccupied. She was turning the pages when she saw a page with a golden sword crossed with a black blade.

Two swords for two sisters. Divided, they fight. Together, they strike. Liane frowned.

She turned the page, expecting to find more, but instead discovered a drawing of Cyra standing in front of the blazing sun, a black raven on her shoulder. On the next page was a woman veiled in black, her pose the mirror of Cyra's, and coiled around her shoulders was a white dragon.

Liane's fingers traced over the dragon.

She flipped a few more pages. *The dragonborn, beloved of the Moon Goddess' and protector of her temples.* She recoiled. Then the Avatheos was right. Erich was an agent of the darkness, just like the elves...

With it written on the page in front of her, the truth was apparent. Erich was the antithesis to her. She turned a few more pages, but they were illegible. She could only pick up a word in three beneath the scorch marks. She scanned the rest of the book, hoping to find something different, something that didn't confirm her worst suspicions.

Liane rubbed her temples, shaken by what she'd learned. She knew she shouldn't be surprised. She'd known being drawn to him was wrong, and yet a small part of her held onto the hope that he could be redeemed, but this book proved otherwise.

One of the priests who'd delivered the books came back over.

"Forgive me, your divinity. I think I misplaced one of my books in your stack." He reached for the book she'd been reading.

She handed it back reluctantly. "It looks interesting. I've never seen mention of Moon Goddess before."

"It's a heretical book that belongs to the moon cult, one of the few that survived the fires that burned the library during the Corruption. It's very fragile and not meant for anyone to read."

The sword in her back throbbed as if asking her to give it a second look. But she'd gotten her answers, hadn't she? He belonged to the Nameless, she to Cyra.

With nothing left to learn, Liane began to retreat from the library, but her skin was prickling with anxiety. She watched as the priest carried the book to the back of the library, toward a metal cage that bisected the library. The temple in Artria had one similar. She turned to leave and nearly collided with Ludwig.

"You're plotting something," he said.

"I was reading in the library."

"And eyeing that locked cage."

She shrugged.

"What are you trying to find out?"

"Nothing. I got my answers." She headed out of the library, but as she did, a hooded priestess stepped into her path.

"Your grace, did you see the book I left you?" Sylvie asked.

The hairs on the back of her neck stood on end.

"Which book?" Liane asked.

She lowered her head guiltily. "I heard you've been asking questions about the church's history. And I thought you'd appreciate reading something that hasn't been heavily censored."

"That was kind of you." Liane tried to muster a smile. Sylvie was innocent and couldn't have known that she'd closed the door on Liane and Erich's relationship for good.

Liane began to walk past her when Sylvie grasped hold of her sleeve. She turned to look at her.

"If I might be so bold, your divinity. I have a favor to ask of you."

People wanted blessings from her, or begged for miracles, but she always turned them down. Apart from the spectacles the Avatheos made her participate in, Liane couldn't do much for the people who were seeking a miracle.

"If I can help, I will," Liane said.

Sylvie rolled up her sleeve and revealed black veins spreading over her arm, crawling up toward her shoulder. "I'm corrupted. Technically, all initiates are until we've been puri-fied. But they don't think I'll last until the equinox. It's why I wanted to meet you so badly. I thought maybe you'd be able to help me."

Liane grabbed her by her elbow, pulling her into an empty alcove. Ludwig turned his back to them, watching the hall to make sure they wouldn't be overheard.

"How long have you been withering? We should take you to see the Avatheos and have him heal you," Liane said.

Sylvie shook her head. "I was born with it. We all are, those of us with magic. He can't heal me, no one here knows how. Maybe a long time ago, before the corruption. But no one has the power now. We know medicinal herbs and small magics, but nothing for this. Only going into the water can save me, or so they say. But some don't make it out of there either. They drown or who knows what." She wrapped her arms around herself.

"By 'the water,' you mean the source?"

Sylvie nodded.

"Then why not go into the water?"

"I haven't been found worthy enough yet. We are all like this. Most don't progress this far before they take their final test. I guess I'm one of the unfortunate ones."

Liane's head was spinning. "If everyone is corrupted before they're purified..." She didn't know how to wrap her head around this information.

"That's how we're selected for service. Some mark or indication that we've got magic in our veins. We're trained in how best to use it. Some excel and others, like me, well, the marks start forming, and we don't always survive..."

Liane thought she was going to be sick. Her head was spinning, and Erich's words were echoing in her head. But he was the enemy, wasn't he?

"Maybe my unwillingness to die proves how unworthy I am, but I just can't..."

"You cannot die, Sylvie. I won't let you. What can I do?"

Sylvie wrung her hands and shifted from foot to foot. "I know it's presumptuous to ask the goddess' chosen, but I found an old spell with a ritual that could cure me. I'm not strong enough. But you might be." She held out a weathered old book.

Liane took it in trembling hands. She still didn't know how to use her magic. But if she were the goddess' chosen, then it should be possible, shouldn't it? The Avatheos had said so, and she'd revived that bird. Sylvie was a lot bigger than a bird, though. There was no choice, really; she had to try.

"I'll help you."

18

The morning Aristea was scheduled to meet Jonathan, she spent too long debating between her black gowns. It was a frivolous waste of time, and yet as Jana held up two options, she couldn't choose. There was no real difference; one was a brocade with lace trims at the sleeves, the other a silk overskirt with a panel of brocade down the center. But she wanted to make a good impression on Duke Krantz, and only him. Seeing Jonathan after finding out he was a widower had nothing to do with her indecision. He was the facilitator of her plans, and future empresses didn't marry widowers, especially those of low rank. The Dukes' Council wouldn't sanction another marriage for her unless it were with someone like Duke Mattison, a man of royal blood whose ties to another royal house could strengthen the empire. Princesses didn't marry for love; Aristea knew that better than anyone. But despite all logic, she fussed over her appearance, having Yvette redo her hair coronet half a dozen times before she was satisfied.

They headed out for the palace gardens. Many of the nobility strolled through the gardens in the warmer months. There was plenty of shade here and fountains to relax by. She often walked the garden paths between appointments, her entourage of guards and attendants following behind her. Nothing about what she was doing was out of character; the courtiers she passed nodded politely, and no one gave her any strange sideways glances. And yet she couldn't shake the feeling she was doing something scandalous.

The plan was to meet somewhere inconspicuous, as if they happened to run into one another while both strolling through the garden. No one would suspect anything untoward about it. And if they lingered to talk in a public place, who would question it? And if they happened to run into his former father-in-law, that was innocent enough. And yet her heart raced the closer she got to their meeting place. It was the same rendezvous location where she'd "accidentally" bumped into him during their brief teenage romance. Back then, it was never planned. She just kept going there, and he kept showing up. They'd hardly talked; it had been for a chance to see him. Maybe it was the memories that made her heart race. The nostalgia of their long-gone past was making her silly and girlish.

She reached their destination and wiped her sweaty palms on her gown. A fountain with a depiction of Cyra pouring water from a jug splashed. Mother had commissioned it for the five-year anniversary of the end of the civil war. Low hedges surrounded it, and there were marble benches facing it, where people might lounge. Aristea hadn't been to this spot in years, as the memories were too painful. She'd imagined it often, though, turning the corner and finding Jonathan there. The thought of visiting their secret spot and him not being there made her heart ache. But as she turned the corner, she saw him seated on the bench, his bad leg stretched out in front of him and his cane resting against the bench as he massaged his leg.

When he saw her, his face lit up and he rose to greet her.

A few nobles were strolling along the other side of the

hedges. They didn't turn to look, but if they had, they'd have seen how he looked at her, and rumors would swirl. Her chest tightened. That smile and that light in his eyes—could she mistake it for anything else? Could she delude herself into thinking his intentions were merely friendly? She considered turning around and heading back to her room. There must be another way to win over Duke Krantz. But her traitorous feet remained glued to the spot as Jonathan ambled over to her. She noticed how he winced as he walked and leaned heavily on his cane, As a teen sometimes his foot pained him and she felt a stab of guilt for making him walk out here to meet her on one of his bad days.

"Are you in pain—" she asked as he said, "Your Highness, lucky running into you here."

They both lapsed into silence, staring at one another awkwardly.

The group she'd noticed on the other side of the hedges turned and entered the fountain area. They must have caught at least part of the exchange because their heads swiveled in Aristea's direction.

"Your highness." They curtsied to her.

One of the women said to Jonathan, "Hope you're not too stiff after last night's party."

"Nothing I can't handle."

The woman trilled a laugh at his comment, and the group fluttered away. The women wore bright pastels, and the men had flourishes of color in their clothes as well. Aristea felt suddenly self-conscious of her black, as if she were lurking about in the bright garden like an ominous raven. It'd been many years since she'd longed for an average life. One where she could be a girl in a pretty dress, flirting with other courtiers.

The courtiers passed them by, and when she and Jonathan were relatively alone—apart from her entourage, who lingered behind her—he moved closer. The swarm of butterflies in her stomach took flight. This close, she could see the shadow of stubble on his face and the dusting of freckles across his nose. And she was transported for a moment to the naive young woman she'd been, wanting to run her fingers across those same freckles.

"There's someone I wanted you to meet before we go and find my father-in-law," he said.

"Oh?" she asked.

He turned and gestured behind him. A little girl screeched and ran from behind the bushes, her golden pigtails tied up in ribbons bouncing as she ran. Behind her, a tired-looking nurse gave pursuit. The kid's precocious nature reminded her of Liane as a child. She'd given their nurses trouble, constantly climbing and scraping her knees, getting into mischief.

Then reality came crashing in as the girl reached for Jonathan. He knelt with one hand braced on his cane to match her height. He smiled at her and smoothed her curls with familiar affection. The child couldn't be more than six years old.

"Darling, this is Papa's friend I told you about. Will you greet Her Highness?" Jonathan asked her.

She nodded her head enthusiastically and unwrapped her arms from around Jonathan to perform a childlike curtsey.

"A pleasure to meet you, your majesty." Her voice was high and sweet, with the barest hint of a lisp.

Jonathan had been married nearly as long as you, Heinrich's voice whispered into her ear. *And had a daughter. Maybe even a son. But your worthless, barren womb couldn't do that. If only you'd had a son, or two, there wouldn't be any talk of sedition. They'd gladly let you be empress until he came of age. But you couldn't even do that. You couldn't do the one thing a woman is good for.*

Aristea didn't respond. She was frozen in place for too long, and the girl looked at Jonathan as if she'd done something wrong. That's when Aristea plastered on her porcelain smile.

"It's lovely to meet you. May I know your name?" Aristea asked, the words catching in her throat.

The girl beamed, revealing a gap-toothed smile. "Elisa!" she declared proudly.

The longer she looked at this blue-eyed child, the more she saw the resemblances to Jonathan, the upturned nose, the sprinkle of freckles on her face. And though it hurt her heart to admit, she looked as Aristea imagined her and Jonathan's children might have looked. Or would she have robbed Jonathan of fatherhood as well? Her hand drifted to her flat stomach.

"Why are you wearing all black?" Elisa asked.

"Because my husband died."

"But Granpa says he was a wicked man, and the empire is better with him dead." She placed her hands on her hips and declared this with all the seriousness a small child could muster.

Aristea choked back a laugh. It was a relief to hear it spoken so plainly by a child who saw the world in black and white.

Jonathan tugged Elisa to look at him. He still hadn't stood up from his kneeling position. "I asked you not to speak of that. Remember? We talked about it. Sadness is a big feeling, and we all feel it in our own way, especially when it's someone we care about."

Aristea bit her tongue to keep from correcting him. Did he think she grieved for Heinrich? That couldn't be further from the truth. But saying something now felt inappropriate.

"Did you wear a black veil when Mama died?" the girl asked, tilting her head.

Jonathan smiled as he pushed back her hair from her face. "No, I didn't. Women wear veils. But I did wear black for a long time."

"Mama died so I could live," Elisa explained for Aristea's benefit.

Aristea couldn't think of anything to say other than, "I'm sorry."

"It's ok. Papa, Gran, and Granpa love me extra in her place." She shrugged, but there was sadness in her expression.

"Now, why don't you go and play with the nurse while we wait for Granpa, hmm?"

"Ok," she said and took the hand of the nurse, nearly dragging her toward the fountain.

Jonathan watched her as she climbed up onto the lip of the fountain, his face one of utter love and devotion. Aristea had so many questions. Did he come to love Elisa's mother, or did he wear black out of duty like her?

"What do you think of my secret weapon? Duke Krantz can never say no to his granddaughter." Jonathan looked rather proud of himself for his plot.

Aristea shook her head. "You didn't have to do this for me. I would have found another way."

He turned to face her fully. "But I wanted to."

The air felt charged as they stared at one another for several beats.

They were interrupted, however, by a sudden splash. They turned to see Elisa, one foot in the fountain, being bodily dragged back from the edge.

Jonathan rushed over and then winced in pain. Aristea beat him there, and Elisa stood with crossed arms.

"Nurse never lets me have any fun." She pouted.

"You shouldn't do dangerous things like that; I'm sure Nurse told you not to?"

"I did," the nurse said wearily.

Elisa looked dejected.

"If you're bored, you and I can play together while we wait to see your granpa."

Her eyes lit up. "Really?"

"You don't have to," Jonathan started to say, but she waved him away. It was the least she could do for him, helping her.

"But I want to," she said, repeating his words back to her.

He smiled and gestured for her to continue. Elisa led her in a game of hide-and-seek, where they took turns hiding amongst the bushes. And for a few short moments, Aristea felt like a girl again as she crouched down behind bushes, lying in wait to spring out and catch Elisa, who giggled. She was so preoccupied with their game that she didn't notice the two figures who had approached until Elisa squealed with delight and rushed toward Duke Krantz.

He was a severe-looking man with bushy gray brows and a thick white beard. Duchess Krantz spotted Aristea crouching in the dirt and arched a brow. She stood quickly, but the damage had been done. She looked terribly improper.

"Your Highness?" Duke Krantz asked.

Elisa practically threw herself into her grandfather's arms. And his expression changed from austere to soft and gentle as he rested her against his hip.

"Granpa, Princess Aristea, and I were playing specters and spirits," Elisa said.

"I can see that," the duke said. "Your highness, what a strange meeting this is."

"I don't think it's that strange. I may not have any of my own, but I delight in children, Duke Krantz."

Duke Krantz arched his brow, and the duchess covered a laugh with a cough.

"The princess kindly paid me a visit recently, and I thought we might have her around for a dinner party," the duchess said, looking at Aristea with a sly smile.

"Oh, could we all have dinner? I want to show her my favorite hiding spots at your home, Granpa," Elisa begged.

"I suppose I have no choice," Duke Krantz said. But he didn't seem displeased at the notion. If anything, there was a wary curiosity on his face.

Aristea bowed to him in thanks for the invitation, and after a few more minutes of inconsequential small talk, they parted ways. Elisa went with her grandparents, who'd promised her sweets, and Aristea and Jonathan were alone once more. When she turned to look, he was smiling.

"You seem rather proud of yourself that your plot worked," Aristea said and brushed the dirt from her skirt. She couldn't believe she'd knelt on the ground. But it had felt good too. She'd seen mothers playing with their children and always felt a sense of envy. It was as fun as she'd imagined it would be.

"I told you he couldn't tell her no."

Aristea laughed. "She's a clever accomplice and looks just like you."

"You're the first to say so. Her grandparents are convinced she's the spitting image of her mother." His gaze turned wistful at the mention of his late wife.

"She was their only daughter, wasn't she?" Aristea said. She'd looked up the royal lineage archives after their last meeting. "I suppose having her daughter helps them with their grief. And for you, too."

He nodded. "She deserved a husband who would have grieved the way you're grieving for Heinrich. She knew I could never love her, and then she died trying to give me a son..."

It was an ugly fact, and a truth she secretly delighted in. And it compelled her to say, "I'm not sure I ever loved Heinrich. It was more that I felt obligated to. Even now, this veil and these blacks are more for his allies than me."

"He didn't deserve you," Jonathan said with more anger and conviction than she expected of him.

The words hung between them. And she wanted to reach out and take hold of them. Grasp them so tight they couldn't slip through her fingers. Or simply ask, when you said you could never love your wife, was it because you loved me? Was it greed that made her hope that he'd held onto the flickering flame of love for her? Or was she simply deluding herself into seeing something there that wasn't?

"Maybe if the fates were kinder—" Aristea started to say, but she couldn't finish the thought.

"We could have been together." He reached out to grasp her hand.

A jolt seemed to go down her and pool in her stomach. She felt hot all over. And it felt as if her heart might beat out of her chest. She'd thought the way he'd made her feel when they were young would have faded, but now it felt more primal and raw. It melted some of the ice around her heart that had formed during her marriage to Heinrich, and that terrified her. She pulled her hand out of his.

"I have other meetings to attend to. Thank you again for your help."

And before he could say another word, she made her retreat, regretting each step she took.

19

L iane agreed to meet Sylvie a few nights later. It gave Liane time to make preparations and study the book Sylvie had found. There were many spells written in the book with detailed notes in the margin of strange markings that the author called runes. Each page listed the necessary runes and items for each spell.

The healing spell wasn't necessarily for reversing a withering like Sylvie had, but a general one. It said it would purge the body of corruption. Liane gave the long list of items that were needed for the healing ceremony to Luzie to acquire. Ludwig was even helping without complaint. Having a task to focus on was a boon, as it reminded her of the old days when the three of them had worked toward the common goal of eradicating stardust in Artria.

Liane paced the length of her room, wringing her hands, as the appointed hour arrived. Ludwig was the lookout, and Luzie held a caged chicken, which quietly clucked. The pure-gold dagger lying on the table next to the cage was the hardest to procure. Luzie had had to commission a jeweler to make it for them. The thought of what must be done with it made Liane's stomach heave. But one chicken's life was a small price to pay to save Sylvie. This was the destiny the goddess had set before her. To be a healer, and maybe a warrior, against darkness. Erich was wrong. She kept chanting it over and over in her mind, as if repetition would convince her.

Someone knocked at the door, and Liane's yelp startled the chicken. It squawked indignantly as Luzie set down the cage to answer the door. Sylvie stood in the doorway, head bowed, and Ludwig was looming behind her shoulder.

"Come in," Luzie said.

Liane walked over to greet Sylvie and tried to think of something comforting and reassuring, but she was scared out of her mind. The goddess had chosen her for this task. She knew healing was possible.

Sylvie glanced around the room nervously.

"Would you like something to drink?" Luzie asked Sylvie.

"No, thank you. I don't think I could keep anything down." She was wringing her hands together.

There was no use in waiting any longer. Liane cleared her throat. "Shall we get started?"

"Yes. I see you got the necessary items." Sylvie glanced around at the items they'd gathered—a white chicken, a golden dagger, several candles, and more.

Liane nodded as she swallowed past the lump in her throat. She reached for the dog-eared book, as if it were a touchstone that might give her the guidance and knowledge she needed to perform this task. She opened it up to a marked page and read it one more time. She'd read it perhaps a dozen times since Sylvie had given it to her. As she ran her fingers over the now-familiar words and pictures, she inhaled and exhaled. She could do this.

First, she needed to define the space in which the ritual would be held. A circle must be drawn and marked by specific runes. Luzie rolled back the carpet in her room, and they pushed the furniture to the walls to make space for the draw-ing. Then Liane took a piece of chalk and drew the circle before standing back to study its shape. The book said it needed to be perfectly symmetrical. By her eye, it looked even. She hoped it was perfect. Then she walked the circle, writing down runes that overlapped with the circle. Those had to be written first. The book emphasized how important the order was. As she scratched them onto the wooden floorboards, she felt a jolt of something spark through her fingertips. As if some deeper part of her knew and understood what she was about to do.

Once the circle runes were drawn, she moved on to draw the outer circle. And she felt the power building under her skin like a light buzzing sound. But what she was doing felt right. Even if her back was throbbing by the time she got to the inner-most circle of runes, and her hands were shaking, and she felt a headache pulsing behind her eyes. She was probably about to come down with a fever, but some voice in her head told her that this was the right path, that she was doing as she was meant to.

Liane stood back and studied her work; the runes had been placed in an exact replica of what she'd seen in the book. And everything was prepared. Sylvie stood off to one side, hands folded in front of her as if in prayer. Liane could see that the tips of her fingers had blackened and were starting to shrivel. The withering was progressing quickly. Liane would save her and countless others who were similarly afflicted. She'd find a way to save them all; there'd never be another Elias or Sylvie again.

"I think we're ready." Luzie brought over the cage, and Sylvie stepped into the middle, careful not to smudge any of the markings Liane had made.

Liane's heart was in her throat as Luzie handed her the chicken. It had large, dark eyes and pristine white feathers. If Liane looked at it too long, the guilt would start to gnaw at her.

"Should I or...?" Liane asked Sylvie. The book wasn't clear on the order of this part.

Sylvie reached for the chicken. "It's me who is being healed, and the sacrifice is for my sake. It should be me, I think." Her throat bobbed as she held the chicken.

It was being incredibly docile as if it knew what its fate entailed and had accepted it. Luzie handed Sylvie the dagger, and she took a deep breath, then brought it to its neck and sliced. The chicken died soundlessly, and then she laid it on the ground, letting its lifeblood pump out onto the runic markings. As soon as it touched the markings, Liane felt the prickle of power across her skin and watched as the runes illuminated one by one the same way they'd done in the chamber under the temple. The blood spread to the edge of the circle but no further, as if it were held in place by an invisible barrier.

Sylvie knelt down and pulled back her hood. She had mousy-brown hair and large brown eyes that stared up at Liane with both terror and hope.

"I'm in your hands now." She turned her withered hands palm up toward Liane.

Luzie handed Liane a dish of white ash, and she dipped her fingers in it to draw the sign of the star on her brow and the pulse points on her throat and wrists, mimicking the drawing in the book. Then she stepped into the ring of runes and blood to do the same to Sylvie. As soon as her foot touched the ring, she felt a jolt run up her spine that pinned her in place. It felt as it had the time the Avatheos had tried to draw the sword out of her, as if someone had their hands on her spine and was trying to rip it out of her. Liane gasped, shoulders clenched, as she tried to breathe through the pain. After a few moments, it subsided, but sweat was trickling down her brow, and her skin was glowing enough to illuminate the space.

Sylvie stared up at her, and the light coming from Liane's

skin was illuminated on her face as she leaned forward and placed the same markings on Sylvie's brow, throat, and wrists. As she finished the final mark, she felt a tug, like a rope being pulled taut between them. Her vision blurred for a moment, and all she could see was golden light. As her vision adjusted, however, she saw ribbons of light, flowing like the many rivers and pools that the Avatheos had shown her. But these weren't rivers but blood, a network of magic flowing through Sylvie and her. Along her arms and hands, darkness swirled. Those same golden veins were muddied and black, moving like sludge, changing the golden rivers.

She'd never seen anything like it before, but instinct told her she had to reach out and purify it. And so, she touched the golden threads within Sylvie's body, tracing down to where it met the dark sludge that was destroying her body. Golden light enveloped them both, and the darkness started to recede.

"It's working," Sylvie said tearfully. And Liane, encouraged by her enthusiasm, pushed forward, reaching into the darkest, most tainted parts of her body. The golden light from Liane's body encompassed the darkness and snuffed it out. For a moment. But just as she thought she'd conquered it, the darkness showed up on Sylvie's other hand. Liane reached for it and snuffed it out, only for it to start to spread.

The darkness was growing, as if fed by her magic. It moved faster, spreading across Sylvie's body, and she cried out in fear and pain, her back arching. Liane tried to grasp onto more of the darkness, but no matter how much she poured into Sylvie, it made no difference. The darkness was consuming the light, growing bigger and more powerful. She tried pulling away, but Sylvie screamed, a heart-wrenching sound of pure agony.

Luzie was shouting, and Liane was trying her best to detach, but she couldn't let go. It was as if, beyond her control, she were drawing all the light out of Sylvie and into her.

It took Ludwig physically pulling her out of the circle for the connection between them to break and the light to dim. The runes were smudged, and blood was smeared on the ground. Even with their ritual over, the damage didn't stop. Sylvie was convulsing on the ground, as black corruption had crept over her fingertips and covered half her face, shriveling the skin until it clung to her skull and hollowed out her eye sockets.

Liane could do nothing but stare, powerless, as her weak knees trembled and collapsed beneath her. She felt a fever coming over her, burning her eyes and mouth as if she'd been similarly left out in the sun to bake. While Sylvie clawed at her face, the tips of her fingers curled inward, turning into shriveled husks. She'd done this. Liane wasn't goddess blessed but cursed. She'd doomed this poor girl to a horrific death for her pride.

"We have to do something," Luzie shrieked.

"Go find the Avatheos," Ludwig shouted, and Luzie ran to do just that.

Ludwig knelt beside Liane and grasped her by the shoulders, shaking her until she came back to herself.

"You need to pull it together for her sake," he said.

Liane nodded numbly, crawled over to Sylvie, and pulled her into her arms. She was terribly young. And small, and the withering made her feel even lighter. As brittle as burnt bones. One-half of her face remained youthful and pure, while the other was sunken and dead. Was there any hope of coming back from this? Surely the Avatheos could do something. A single tear rolled down Sylvie's cheek.

"I don't want to die," Sylvie said.

"You're not going to die. I promise. I swear," Liane said, even though there was no truth to her words. She'd caused this with her hubris. With her desire to prove her worthiness, she'd doomed an innocent girl.

But Sylvie's breaths were a death rattle, and Liane remembered how Elias had looked in his final moments—so much like this. She thought she could save someone for once, but apparently, she wasn't strong enough.

The door to her room burst open, and several people rushed in. They carried Sylvie out, ripping her from Liane's arms, and held her back from reaching out for Sylvie.

"You cannot follow, your divinity. You'll risk corruption," the priest who blocked her way said.

She was too weak to do anything and instead collapsed against Ludwig once more. Then the Avatheos entered. He swept into the room, golden and terrifying. She felt the holy wrath of his stare beyond the veil and knew she'd been wrong to try it alone. To ever doubt the church or his words.

He walked over to her and cupped her face, turning it upward toward him.

"Do you have something to confess?" he asked.

"Will she survive? Tell me you can save her," Liane said.

"That depends on you, Liane."

The guilt was too much. Her vision swam; the fever was going to overwhelm her. She was fighting to stay conscious. And she desperately wanted to sink down into that blissful oblivion.

"Tell me what's happened," he said, more a command than a question. His hands held her in a vise-like grip, cold to the touch, and yet she felt that electric pulse of his magic coursing through her, keeping her awake long enough to answer his question.

"I tried to draw out the corruption from her. But I only made it worse. Surely you..."

He shook his head slowly. "If you were pure, she would have been saved. This was a test, and you failed."

A sob crept up her throat, and Liane wanted to curl in on herself, but the Avatheos' grip held her in place.

"What do you have to confess?"

She wanted to throw up; she wanted to shout, but she felt transfixed by his touch and his words, and suddenly words were spilling out of her. "I was with a man the night of the party. I've held thoughts of him in my mind since that night, and I have doubted the church and Cyra's gift to me. And I…"

"Go on."

"I saw the Nameless Goddess. She beckoned to me."

He let her go, and Liane collapsed onto her hands and knees. Ludwig stepped forward to help her up, but when he did, the Avatheos waved him back.

"Your pride and your vice have doomed this poor girl. You can never heal the people with darkness lurking in the corners of your heart. The world has tainted you, as you've been raised by it. And if you do not turn away from it fully, you will never reach your full potential."

In this moment, she was so desperate to please him, to be the being of pure goodness he wanted her to be, that she would have done anything, said anything to reverse the damage she had done.

"What must I do?"

"For this sin of the pleasures of the flesh, you must go into confinement. Time in isolation and thoughtful prayer can save you, but only if you're willing to give up everything for the church."

Tears were rolling down her cheeks. "I'll do anything to fix this," she said.

"Then let us bring you to the tower. There you can reflect and purify yourself in isolation."

"Anything," she whispered.

Anything.

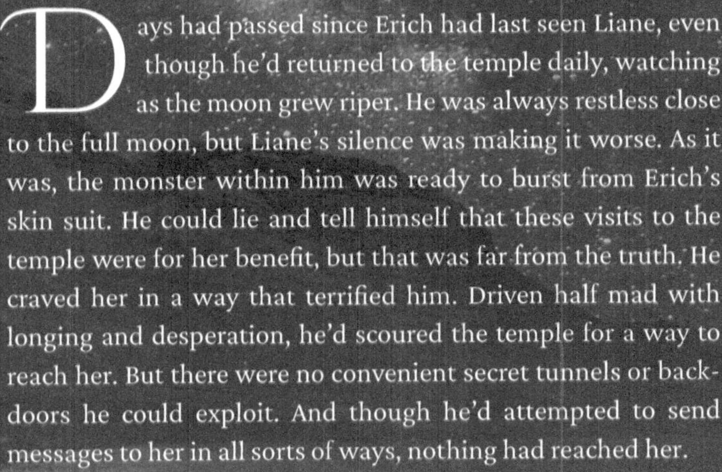

20

Days had passed since Erich had last seen Liane, even though he'd returned to the temple daily, watching as the moon grew riper. He was always restless close to the full moon, but Liane's silence was making it worse. As it was, the monster within him was ready to burst from Erich's skin suit. He could lie and tell himself that these visits to the temple were for her benefit, but that was far from the truth. He craved her in a way that terrified him. Driven half mad with longing and desperation, he'd scoured the temple for a way to reach her. But there were no convenient secret tunnels or back-doors he could exploit. And though he'd attempted to send messages to her in all sorts of ways, nothing had reached her.

If he wanted to rescue her, he'd have to resort to kidnapping her. And once he'd freed her from the church's clutches, would he be able to quietly walk away and act as if she hadn't engraved herself onto his heart?

He knew the answer, but he dared not speak it aloud.

The sun was sinking below the horizon by the time he reached the temple. The line of worshippers attempting to get in had dwindled down to almost nothing. They stopped letting people in at sunset. But the token burned into his palm, a free pass in that set him above the masses. He stalked closer, no longer timid or fearful. The approaching full moon, or the dragon's growing obsession, had emboldened him. He walked up to the guards, like a raptor swooping in for a kill, and thrust his token toward them.

The guards didn't question his presence. His wanted posters had been wiped from the city, and he was another rich eccentric desperate to meet the avatar. The cost was high, but he was grateful for this chance—another opportunity to glimpse Liane, to convince her to leave the church behind. He passed through the outer halls, where a few worshippers still lingered, and with each ring, he felt his proximity to Liane like a coil pulled tight in his gut. His hand flexed as he grasped the handle of his dagger, trying to draw from it some of his uncle's calming assurances.

His uncle had been the one who had helped him through his first change and had guided him through his rocky adolescence. His uncle made him believe he could live with this accursed dragon within him. Until he'd killed a man the dragon had become obsessed with. The moment had spit in the face of his uncle and everything he'd taught him. The more he indulged the dragon, the more of his humanity would be stripped away until nothing was left but a monster wearing human skin. No matter what his uncle said. And each month's transformation proved that. He'd lied to himself and said that once he had the sword, he'd be healed. Then, once Liane could heal him. But the dragon was commandeering more and more of his thoughts, slowly consuming him, and soon he'd have to choose a life as a monster or die a man.

He shouldn't have come tonight, but rather gone straight out of the city gates, as he'd told Fritz he was planning to do, and sequestered himself in the woods to wait out his transformation, where his mind would become wholly the dragon for a night and sate his hunger on deer and boar. Erich tipped his head back to stare into the face of the nearly full moon. One more night before the change took him. And he was hiding in a garden, waiting for a glimpse of Liane from afar.

Midnight Guards watched the doors to the inner sanctum where Liane resided, preventing outsiders from intruding. It took all his self-control to not attempt using his allure on them. It might not work, and they'd arrest him, or it might, and he'd tip too far into damnation. He kept staring at the moon and felt the guards' eyes on him. He'd felt the moon ripening for days, like a bright juicy apple, its fragrance that of forbidden fruit. It reminded him of the story his uncle had told him about the first dragon cursed, their family's ancestors. The long-time past ancestor was the head of a small village, and one day, they were visited by the Trinity, the three-faced goddess. But they didn't know it was her, as her outward appearance was shrouded and garbed as a crone. The head of the clan welcomed her into his long house and offered her a place to sleep by his fire, and in payment, she offered him a strange silver fruit and urged him to share it with his people. From his first bite, he was consumed by hunger so great that nothing else would sate it but the fruit. He planted the seeds and hired the best farmers and cultivators to grow him an orchard. The next year, when it bore fruit, he urged his wife and children to partake of it as well. Soon they could eat nothing but fruit, think of nothing but it, because nothing was as delicious as it. But apart from with his family, he did not share the fruit.

Years passed, and the head clansman had begun to neglect his duties. Famine took over the land, and diseases spread. The village was on the brink of ruin until the crone returned and revealed herself to be the Trinity. She condemned the clansman and his family for their greed and cursed their line to transform into a hungry dragon on each full moon.

This was his legacy. Greed and hunger. This curse that stalked his lineage for generations. It'd been decades since someone had been born with it, but his mother had hidden that secret from his father and married him anyway. A hidden seed that eventually bore fruit in Erich. An abomination who killed his own mother during his birth. And was rejected by his father until he saw use in him. If he could tear this part of himself out, he would. Rather than continue to suffer, slowly descending into madness month by month, chipped away by each turning of the moon. He'd prayed to the Trinity. Begged them to free him of this torture, but his prayers fell on deaf ears. The gods did not care for the plight of mortals. And those who ran their churches would only continue to exploit the gods in the name of those gods. That was what he knew. It was why he'd known Fritz was right when he'd said the church would only use her.

A shadow crossed over the moon's surface. A black-winged bird swooped down and landed on a nearby bush and tilted its head to look at Erich quizzically.

"We must go to her," the raven said in his mind.

Erich was startled to hear its voice spoken so clearly within his thoughts.

"Easy for a bird to say," Erich said under his breath, praying the guards didn't see him talking to it and think he was insane.

"You want to take her away from this place, don't you?" The bird preened as it taunted him.

It was madness to even entertain this conversation.

"More than anything," he admitted aloud. Perhaps a bit too loudly because the guards were glancing in his direction.

If the guards noticed, they might interrogate him, and then he'd lose his access to even this much of her. Erich forced his feet to move before the guards decided to question him. But each step was like walking through mud. Normally, he'd expect the dragon to protest. Whenever he left the temple, it thrashed and roiled. Now he felt it poised, waiting, almost cognizant. Was it listening to the raven too?

"Your destiny is to protect her. And yet you're afraid of her." The raven followed him, hopping along the bushes.

He wanted to see her. Ever since their encounter in the garden, his desire for her had only grown more intense. His awareness of her more keen. But he couldn't squander his chance. Leonhard had been lenient with him—one fight in the ring had given him unlimited access to her, and Leonhard hadn't called in that debt yet. If Erich ruined this, he feared what the price would be.

"I will be her destruction," Erich said.

"That is what you fear; it is not the truth."

Erich felt the dragon stretch its wings within him as if he truly were a puppet and the dragon were the puppeteer. It forced his feet to turn around and take a few steps back toward the guards before he regained control, and he tipped forward, fingers digging into the mortar of the nearby wall. Erich rested his head against it, felt the rapidly cooling night air against his fevered skin, and noticed the guards approaching. The dragon and raven were conspiring against him, forcing his hand.

"Enough," he gasped.

"Time is running short. She needs to draw the sword. Go to her."

Erich curled his hand into a fist. Hadn't he come here to save her? Either he convinced her to join him, or he gave in to the monster he was becoming; those were his choices.

"I will not force her. She must come to me willingly."

"Then change her mind. She has been locked in the tower. Go to her," the raven urged.

One of the guards grabbed Erich's shoulder, and he spun, muscles tense and poised for action.

"Is something the matter?" the Midnight Guard asked him.

Erich felt his power coiling inside him like a snake about to strike.

"Please, I've come from Sundland. My father is sick, and I need the avatar to cure him." He wrapped each word with power, tugging at the threads of his sympathy. Erich watched as the guard's eyes glazed over.

"She's not seeing pilgrims today."

"Just let me through the door," Erich said, resting a hand on the guard's shoulder. He found physical contact strengthened the bonds of his persuasion.

"I don't know..." But Erich could see the power overcoming the guard, molding him into submission.

"I will go willingly into exile if you let me gaze upon her once," he pleaded.

The guard rubbed the back of his neck and said, "Go quick, and don't get caught or else..." He wasn't able to finish the thought before Erich was racing past him and into the hall beyond the guard. Thankfully, it was empty, and he wouldn't have to exert more of his power. This was madness. If he were caught, he'd likely be arrested, and yet his feet did not slow as he ascended the stairs, guided by the raven, who flew ahead of him.

"Stay to the shadows," it instructed.

Erich did as he was told and pressed his back against the wall. In the same way Fritz could slip in and out of the shadows, so too could Erich blend in with the darkness. Cloaked as he was by the night, he slipped past priests walking down the hall. The raven landed on a windowsill beside the door he presumed was her chamber. There were no guards outside her door, which felt like another stroke of luck. Perhaps the Trinity was on his side after all. He didn't want to have to deal with Ludwig.

When he entered, the room was empty. Her bed was made, and the space smelled like her. This did not please the dragon, who pulled and fought against its bindings as Erich considered his next steps. Then the door at the far side of the room opened, and her maid, Luzie, walked in carrying a bundle that she dropped upon seeing him.

"Where is Liane?" Erich asked, not bothering to disguise the desperation in his voice.

She swallowed past a lump in her throat. "In the tower, in isolation."

"Take me there," he commanded.

"She's meant to be purifying her soul. I don't think..." she stammered.

Erich grabbed her shoulders, forcing her to look at him. He felt the hooks of his allure grasping onto her, forcing her to do his bidding. "Take me."

She swallowed hard and nodded slowly. She had no choice. Erich felt as if he were careening out of control, drunk on his own power and the dragon's and urgent whispers in his ear from the raven. There was no more room for reason or control. He had to see her. They passed through the halls and went up a long spiral staircase.

The dragon was just beneath his skin, near ready to explode out of him. Erich grasped the doorknob, but it was locked. The dragon wanted him to break the door down, but he held onto that last tether of humanity to ask Luzie, "The key?"

"The Avatheos has it."

"Who's there?" Liane called out.

Her breath caught, and he felt it echo in his veins.

"It's me," he said, pressing his eye to the slot in the door that acted as a window. It was barely big enough to slip his hand through. Liane sat on a cot, with nothing but a stack of religious texts, a single candle, and a pitcher. She was wearing a thin cotton sheath that hugged her body in ways that made his imagination run away with itself.

"Erich? What are you doing here?" She padded across her cell, coming closer to peer at him through the bars.

This is what he'd come to prevent. They'd made her a prisoner. Maybe now she'd realize how wrong the church was.

"I came to rescue you," he confessed.

She inhaled a ragged breath. "You shouldn't have." She turned her back on him.

But he thrust his hand through the hole in the door; his hand was covered in scales. The dragon was taking over. He recoiled, but she grasped onto his hand, cupping his rough and scaled flesh in her soft, pale hands. She wasn't repulsed by him as she should have been.

"Have they hurt you?" he gasped. He was fighting every single urge he had to rip the door from its hinges. But on closer inspection, he saw runes moving through the wood. Any attempt to break her free would result in an alarm at the least, but he wouldn't be surprised if there were reinforcements on the hinges and wood that made them impossible to destroy. He couldn't get her out even if she asked him to.

"I belong here; I killed a girl because I am impure."

"You're perfect." And he meant it. She was radiant. Even these dim and dreary surroundings hadn't dimmed her luminousness. He couldn't fathom the circumstances in which she'd take a life. It couldn't have been intentional. But he also knew the weight of that might crush her, and more than anything, he wished he could hold on to her, provide her comfort for the shadows in her eyes.

She squeezed his hand. "You're saying that because you're corrupted and want me to join your side," she said, but there was no conviction in her tone. He could hear the doubt ringing between them.

His hand flexed. The dragon wanted to tear down the door with his teeth, but he held him back from doing that. He wouldn't take her against her will, not in this condition. He feared what he'd do if this door weren't between them.

"You have to leave this place, Liane. They'll destroy you if you let them. They're already stripping away your humanity. You weren't one to be caged before."

"I'm doing this for the good of the empire. I have to let go of you and all vices in order to become pure." She released his hand, and he felt cold in the absence of her touch.

The tone of her voice, the shame in it, it felt as if they'd dimmed all the light from her. And that was what they wanted, wasn't it? To strip her of her humanity, to make her another faceless creature of their own design.

His anger and helplessness, and the closeness of the full moon, were having an effect on him. He felt the tethers on the dragon snapping one by one. His muscles strained, fighting back the change. It wasn't the full moon yet, but time was running out just the same. He couldn't save her, not yet. But he would come back for her.

"Liane, when you are ready, I will come for you."

"Forget about me. Please, Erich, for your sake."

His claws curled against the door, leaving deep gashes. He needed to get far, far away, so far that he could never reach her again, for both their sakes. And so he fled.

21

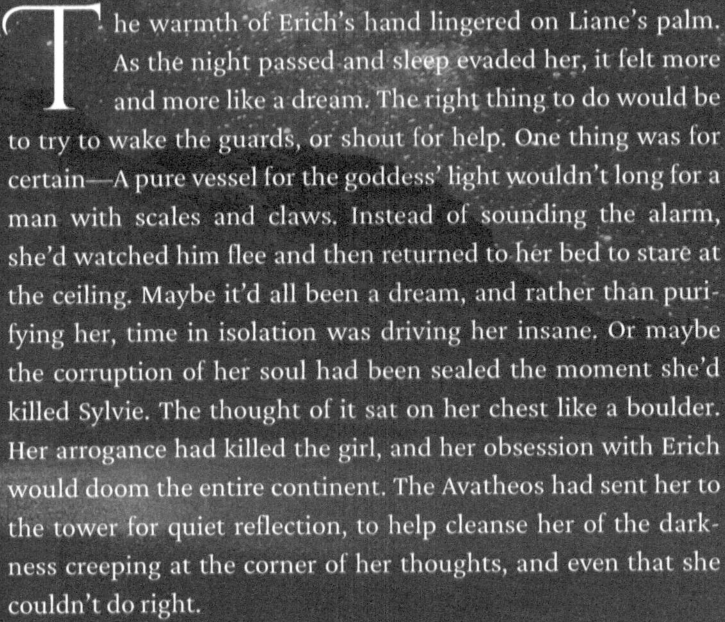

The warmth of Erich's hand lingered on Liane's palm. As the night passed and sleep evaded her, it felt more and more like a dream. The right thing to do would be to try to wake the guards, or shout for help. One thing was for certain—A pure vessel for the goddess' light wouldn't long for a man with scales and claws. Instead of sounding the alarm, she'd watched him flee and then returned to her bed to stare at the ceiling. Maybe it'd all been a dream, and rather than purifying her, time in isolation was driving her insane. Or maybe the corruption of her soul had been sealed the moment she'd killed Sylvie. The thought of it sat on her chest like a boulder. Her arrogance had killed the girl, and her obsession with Erich would doom the entire continent. The Avatheos had sent her to the tower for quiet reflection, to help cleanse her of the darkness creeping at the corner of her thoughts, and even that she couldn't do right.

She bunched up her bedding into a fist and then pulled. Why had Cyra chosen her? Why not someone beautiful and good like Aristea or brave like her brother, Mathias? Why her? She was selfish and arrogant and refused to obey authority. Rather than chase her circling thoughts, perhaps she should ask Cyra directly. She was her chosen after all, and the Avatheos had said she was the closest to Cyra of them all. She knelt down beside her bed. Resting her elbows on the edge, she upturned her hands in prayer. She never prayed, apart from during religious ceremonies and sun rites rituals. She hadn't seen much purpose in it. But maybe that was the missing piece. Maybe she'd been so determined to carve her own path, she hadn't stopped long enough to hear Cyra's voice.

But where did she begin? Should she confess her sins to the goddess? Was she listening? If Liane was the vessel, she supposed she was.

"Ah. Hello, Cyra," Liane started awkwardly. Talking aloud to the empty room felt silly, so she continued in her head, which felt just as ridiculous, but at least no one could overhear it. "If you're omnipotent as they say, you probably know what I've done... but I have my doubts about your divine plan... What do you want from me?"

There was no answer, of course. Maybe she wasn't praying right. Or as the Avatheos had said, she wasn't pure enough. Maybe once she cleansed herself spiritually, Cyra would speak to her, but how, through visions? Or a voice? She wasn't sure. No one told her anything. They only pointed out what she was doing wrong. She'd been in Basilia for nearly a month, and she felt no closer to mastering her powers than when she'd gotten here. The church had always been cloaked in mystery to her, and its mysticism was something that she hadn't cared to wonder about. And even now, when she was at its very heart, she had more questions than answers. When they'd first met, Sylvie had mentioned to her how the church was meant to save her. If she had been suffering from corruption all along, were they all suffering in some way? Was it her destiny to save them all? What if she couldn't?

The corruption was starting to take over Erich, too. He'd half transformed before the full moon; shouldn't that be proof enough that she was better without him in her life? But why couldn't she convince herself that was the truth? As guilty as she felt, when he'd told her she was perfect, she'd wanted to believe it was true—that there wasn't something wrong with her but the systems in which she was bound.

"Tell me what I'm doing wrong. How can I be good enough? How can I be pure enough? How can I prevent another Sylvie..." Tears rolled down her cheeks as she pressed her head against the mattress. She sat there until her back ached and her knees trembled from kneeling on the cold stone ground. But there was no answer from Cyra.

Sylvie's death couldn't be cleansed by ritual, prayer, or isolation. It would remain like a stain upon her soul forever.

Liane sat back on her heels and gave up the pretense of prayer. There were stacks of holy books in her room. She'd been trying and failing to read them for days. Every time she opened one, she thought of Sylvie writhing in agony, screaming as Liane killed her. Reading religious texts wouldn't change anything, and reading about the Nameless Goddess' great betrayal only made her feel as if she were cast in the wrong part of the opera of the betrayal myth. She picked a book at random from the stack and flipped it open. It landed on a page about the end of times prophecy.

"A pure life is one without temptation. You should become as the goddess made you, nameless, unattached to this world, and a living vessel for her divine works."

The words sent a stab of guilt to Liane's gut, and she shook herself as she set the book aside. Reading wouldn't help. Instead, she walked over to her open window. It wasn't much wider than her arm, but it allowed a stream of light in.

The light of the waxing gibbous moon poured in through

her open window, and she stared out at the moon. She hoped Erich was safe and he hadn't been caught by the Midnight Guard half transformed. But it'd been quiet across the temple since he'd left, and she hoped that meant he'd left unscathed. She might have prayed for his safe escape, but it felt like sacrilege to pray that a corrupted intent on warping her mind escape.

The city was quiet. Curfew was in effect, and all the houses had their lights out. The moon cast silvery light over the landscape, giving it an eerie glow. In fact, the play of shadows, the light and dark, reminded her of the two-toned stag. She thought of how it'd lured her through the forest to the pool. It, too, must have been corrupted and trying to lure her down the wrong path. The Avatheos and the Church of Sol were meant to be the defenders of light. Anything that stood against them was evil, wasn't it?

If only life were as simple, as black and white. Erich and the stag seemed to think there was some other destiny she was meant for. But who did she trust? The church and the way of light, or potential corruption and damnation? It seemed like an obvious answer. If a friend had asked her that question, she would have called them a fool.

But everything about the temple felt wrong. As if she'd put on a shoe made for a different foot. What if the Avatheos had misinterpreted his prophecy? Hadn't scholars and priests argued about the meanings of the holy books for centuries? She'd read that prophecies were often vague and obfuscated in rhyme. It was up to the receiver of said prophecy to decide the truth.

If only Liane could discern what that truth was.

She sighed and leaned onto the windowsill in front of her. She wasn't a religious scholar. She heaved another heavy sigh just as she noticed a shadow pass overhead.

Liane looked up, expecting to see a dragon, but instead, she saw a giant raven, twenty times the size of a normal one. Its piercing golden eyes sent a chill down her spine as it swooped toward her.

She leapt back as it dove, even though it was much too large to pass through the window. As it approached, it shrank down and swooped in to land on her bed. Liane pressed her back against the wall and considered shouting for help. Though she likely wouldn't be heard from the top floor of this tower. She'd seen this raven before—the moment her powers had first flared in the temple and through various visions. It let out a long, low caw, and as it did, the door to her room swung open. She rubbed at her eyes. She must be dreaming. There was no way a shape-changing raven and Erich had visited her on the same night.

When she tried pinching herself, it hurt. Not a dream, then.

"Come. The hour grows late. We've not much time," it cawed before flying down the stairs.

Ludicrous as this was, she felt compelled to follow it. The raven waited for her at the foot of the stairs, cawing before swooping down the hall, headed for the inner ring of the temple. The halls were empty, strangely so. Even when the curfew was in effect in the city, many priests and acolytes worked late into the night tracking the stars. But it was as if she'd stepped into a liminal space between worlds, the light like twilight. Rather than question it, Liane followed the raven into the inner sanctum.

The high-domed glass ceiling was filled with moonlight, and when she gazed upon the statue of Cyra, she noticed her appearance had changed. Her golden visage, which sparkled in the daylight, was shadowed and contorted. Her once-golden hair looked onyx in the moonlight, and her cloak was blanketed in stars. Liane stared at it for a long moment before it dawned upon her. This wasn't Cyra but the Nameless Goddess. Not as she'd been depicted, shrouded and sinister, but pearlescent and sparkling like the moon and the stars.

"This is Yneas' true form," said the raven. She'd never heard the Nameless Goddess' name spoken before, but the word sent a ripple through her, as if the name itself evoked her presence. The hairs on the back of her neck stood on end as she turned to face the raven, half expecting to see the veiled goddess beckoning her beyond the veil as she had in her vision. The raven had grown again and was nearly five times Liane's height, its head close to brushing against the domed ceiling. As it moved, its massive talons clacked on the lacquered floor.

"Does your presence here mean I am damned?" Liane asked tremulously.

"You are not."

"Then why do you keep haunting my visions?"

"Because I am the guardian of the sword that resides in your back," the raven said.

Her heart was hammering. This all must have been a dream. It had to be. But she felt the sting of her pinch throbbing on her hand, felt the cold breeze produced by the ruffling of the raven's wings.

"I've seen you in the books. You were on Cyra's shoulder."

"You're right. I have been there since the beginning of all things. I watched the sisters turn on one another and have seen their followers bring this world to the brink of destruction."

"And are we on another such precipice?"

"Yes."

A cold chill slithered down her spine. "The sword is in my back, but I fear I am not worthy of it."

"When I gave your mother the sword, I told her the price would be owed. And you are one-half of that price, the wielder who was promised, who can set the world's balance back in order."

"That's what the Avatheos told me. I am doing everything, but I still don't hear her voice."

"It is not her voice you need to hear."

"Then whose? Are you trying to corrupt me, to lead me astray, to unleash the Nameless Goddess?"

"What has been set in motion cannot be undone. You can prevent nothing, but you must end it."

"How can you say that? I killed a girl. She came to me for help, and I cut her life short."

"The church killed that girl. She was doomed to death before she ever met you. They filled her head with promises that could not be fulfilled. The sun cult is killing magic. The more they try to control it, the more it withers. When they severed the two magics from one another, they created a rift that grows larger and larger and will swallow the world if you cannot stop its spread."

"I just want to be good, to follow the light."

"To magic, there is no good or evil. There is no light without the dark. The doubt that lingers in your mind will be your destruction if you do not accept the path. You know what must be done. You know the answers. Either let magic die and, with it, let the world wither and fade to nothing, or take your first step on the path of your destiny."

"Then I choose the church and the Avatheos," Liane declared.

The raven opened its wings and squawked at her. Liane stumbled back a step, catching herself from falling by grabbing onto a nearby pew.

"No! They will bind your power to theirs. To let them draw your sword is not why you were chosen. You do not bend the knee; you do not back down. Why let them cow you?"

She looked at her shaking hands and thought about what Erich had said. The feeling of wrongness that wouldn't leave her. The lingering doubts in her mind. She'd become someone she didn't recognize.

"How do I draw the sword?" she asked.

"You know the answer."

"The pool, back in Artria? I can't go back there. It's too far."

"There is another closer by. Call on your shield to bring you; finish the ceremony that was interrupted." The raven was starting to fade away; she could see the walls behind it.

"You can't leave it there. Tell me more. Take me out of this place."

But it didn't provide any answers. The shaft of moonlight that had illuminated it moved, and the raven burst into a cloud of mist and disappeared, leaving Liane standing, shivering in her nightdress, back in the tower.

22

Erich didn't usually remember the change. Typically, he woke crusted in dry blood and a foul taste of meat in his mouth. Since the change happened at the same time every month, he removed himself from populated areas, stripped down before sunset, and let it overcome him. The next morning, he'd wake, dress, and resume his normal life. After he'd left Liane in the tower, the change swept through him, two days before the change should have taken him. He barely made it out of the city before the scales had covered his entire body, and his muscles were tearing, reforming, and bones were breaking as they elongated. He was usually spared the agony of transformation, but this time, he was aware of each inch of his body becoming the dragon. The walls of the city were out of sight when the wings burst from his back and the compulsion to take to the sky overcame him. He'd be visible to farmers or late-night travelers on their way to the gates, but exposure was the least of his worries. Within the walls of Basilia, the Midnight Guard would hunt him down and kill him. He flew up, toward the swelling moon that hung high in the sky, fully transformed into a dragon.

Rather than slip into oblivion as he normally would, he watched through the dragon's eyes as it stalked a fat boar rooting in the forest. As he crunched through bones and devoured entrails, he wasn't repulsed, but neither was he satisfied, and he took to the sky once more, searching for more prey. The feeling of the wind over his scales was rather refreshing. Why hadn't the dragon taken over his mind? Had the moment come where he'd lost himself to the curse for good? And would he spend eternity suspended in this state, a man within the monster?

Thoughts like these slipped through his fingers as the animalistic impulses overcame him. He spotted a deer and plunged toward the ground to clutch it in his talons before carrying it off to enjoy his meal perched atop a hillside. He spent the rest of the night hunting in the rolling hills and forests. No matter how many creatures he devoured, he never felt satisfied. When the wildlife wasn't enough, he strayed toward a field of sheep and felt the impulse to burn them. Before the human part of his brain could stop him, Erich unleashed fire from his gut, burning them to a crisp, and gorged himself on their charred corpses.

When the sun rose, he retreated to a cave, but did not return to human form. Rather, he curled up and slept through the daylight hours. The next night, he was even further from the man he'd been, lost somewhere in a waking dream. A part of him had forgotten that he'd ever been a human. He hunted; he flew across the countryside, killing wildlife and livestock indiscriminately. For the second day, he slept, but his sleep was restless, and yet his dragon mind couldn't understand why. The full moon was when the dragon was at peak strength, and the human part of his mind was becoming a distant memory. But there was something tugging at his lizard brain, trying to draw him back somewhere he couldn't quite recall.

The night of the full moon, the hunting was good. He ate until his stomach might have burst. Over the three nights flying across the countryside, he'd gotten closer to civilization. Not much in nature could harm a dragon, so he did not fear the humans, even when they flung their useless weapons against him, but as he saw the yellow glow of the city on the horizon, he felt an instinct to draw closer.

Which was a mistake because these humans near the walled city were armed with magic that could penetrate his hide. They shot something toward him that tore a hole in his wing. The dragon pulled back and unleashed its fire, scorching the ground and the bodies below, but rather than fear him, they pressed forward, shooting nets that he twisted midair to avoid. A thought was screaming at the back of his mind. *Run*, it said. But the dragon saw a woman's face. Liane. A wistful gasp at the back of his thoughts. He had to return to her.

But when he tried flying back toward the city, their cannons and their magic repelled him. The desire to see her was overcome by the desire to survive, and he retreated into the wilderness. Erich, buried in the dreaming thoughts of the dragon, swam back to the surface, gasping for air as he steered his stolen body. He didn't have a full grasp on the damage he'd done or the chaos he'd brought upon himself or the city, but he knew enough to know even as he was entangled in the monster, he'd made a terrible mistake.

He felt the dragon's hunger for Liane like the keen edge of a knife, and its obsession had almost gotten him killed. The sky was lightening as the full moon set, and Erich untangled his thoughts from the dragon, like unraveling a ball of yarn. When morning came, he'd have full control again, but he wasn't sure how much longer he could hold back these urges. He flew as far as he could before dawn and collapsed into a forested area miles from the city. Even on horseback, the

Midnight Guards wouldn't have been able to keep up with his retreat, but they'd be on alert, looking for him. How could he possibly get back into the city and rescue Liane from the church now?

By the time the sun rose, and he'd shed his dragon form as a lizard sheds its skin, he was exhausted. And though he rarely remembered changing back into a human after the full moon, Erich felt every bone break and regrow as the scales and flesh fell away before burning up like steam in the morning light. The pain was so intense that the edges of his vision were turning black, and he nearly lost consciousness by the time dawn rose. The pain was subsiding, and he lay naked beneath a canopy of trees.

His body demanded he rest and recuperate, but there was no time for that. The Midnight Guard would be looking for a dragon, and if they found him lying naked in the forest, they'd make the connection. Despite the protest of his aching bones, he got up and went through the long-held ritual of post-transition. He washed the dried blood from his mouth and neck before searching for a cottage or farmstead where he could procure clothes. What he'd been wearing when he'd transformed was nothing but tattered ribbons now. He found a farmer's cottage, and his gamble paid off when he found clothes drying on the line. He stole them and dressed before retreating once more into the forest to plan his next moves.

Three days he'd been the dragon, and he'd attacked the Midnight Guard. He'd never spent that long in that form before, and it was likely his grip on humanity was slipping. Which meant he had to finish what he'd started before the next full moon. He didn't know how many more transformations he had left before he would become a monster for good. He shoved that thought aside and focused on returning to Basilia. But he wasn't sure if he'd be able to get back in. After a dragon attack, the Midnight Guard might lock down the city to prevent anyone from coming or going.

And maybe that was for the best. Maybe it'd been arrogance that made him think he could be the one to save her. This could be the Trinity telling him that it was time to move on, before he hurt someone. There was no cure. He might as well disappear into the wilderness and live a life as the monster he was, stealing sheep and terrorizing farmers until the Midnight Guard inevitably caught up and killed him.

As if sensing his thoughts, Leonhard's brand on his shoulder started to burn, reminding him of the unpaid debt. He might not make it long enough for the Midnight Guard to kill him; the Hunters' Guild might get him first. Was there already a bounty on his head?

Who was he kidding? He knew he couldn't leave Liane to the church's mercy. Not after he'd seen her locked up in the tower. Erich clenched his hand into a fist and started his long march back to the city. He reached a crossroads and followed the signs for Basilia. When the roads got rougher and signs scarcer, he stopped to ask a farmer tilling his field for directions, and he confirmed what he'd feared—It would take most of the day on foot to reach the city.

It was about midday, and miles from where he'd stolen the clothes, when he waved down a farmer and his wife on their way to the market, asking for a ride. The farmer was a stoic but agreeable man who allowed him to sit in the back with the chickens.

It stank, and the chickens were noisy, but it was faster than walking. They were far down the country road, and night was setting in.

"Lord Arcaro has a visitor," the wife remarked.

"A fine piece of horse flesh he's riding and dressed too good even for the likes of Lord Arcaro," the farmer mused.

"Why else would a nobleman be riding through here then?" the wife snipped.

"I couldn't tell you. None of my business."

"We should ask," the wife insisted.

"Bah, none of our business," he replied.

By then, Erich's interest had been piqued, and he looked past the driver's seat to see a specter from his past. His uncle Endland. The man who'd raised him and taught him how to control the dragon curse. What he couldn't understand was what he was doing on a country road on the outskirts of Basilia, hundreds of miles from Sundland. He had two options—He could either pretend he hadn't seen his uncle, or he could confront him.

Before he could decide, his uncle rode up, waving down the cart, and called out to the driver. "Hello, stranger," his uncle said. "I'm searching for a young man. Have you seen any strangers heading toward the city?"

As soon as he said this, Erich jumped down from the cart. Then it wasn't a coincidence; his uncle had come looking for him. Which meant it was better to get it over with, rather than let him chase him all around Basilia.

"Uncle," Erich said in Neolyrian for the farmer and his wife's benefit.

His uncle did a double take, as if he couldn't quite believe his eyes. Erich stood, fists clenched at his sides, feeling very much like the boy he'd been when he left his uncle's home for court at his father's summons. Uncle had begged him not to go, and when Erich had then escaped court, he had done so in the middle of the night, never to be seen again. His uncle dismounted, the smiling face Erich remembered blank. Erich braced for the tongue-lashing he knew was coming or the demands to return home. Instead, his uncle crossed the distance between them and enclosed him in a crushing hug. A small part of him wanted to return his uncle's embrace, but doing so felt like giving in to the demands he knew would follow, and he'd never return home... He didn't deserve compassion from this man he'd betrayed. He was a monster. Best they make that clear.

His uncle pulled back and studied him for a moment. Then, without another word to Erich, he turned to the farmer and his wife, who were watching their exchange with interest. "Is there an inn nearby where we might get a meal and a drink of ale?"

The farmer nodded. "Over the next bend, there's a good inn."

His uncle thanked them, and Erich was pretty sure money exchanged hands. Before he could protest, he was being whisked away to a crowded inn full of happy chatter, and a young doe-eyed innkeeper's daughter was fluttering her long lashes at them as she delivered steaming hot soup to both of them.

"Anything else I can get you?" she asked, her gaze lingering on Erich with interest. He hadn't spoken since they'd arrived and stared into the bowl of soup as if it had insulted him personally.

"No, that's all for now, thank you," his uncle said, and she scurried away.

His uncle didn't touch his soup or his ale but watched Erich expectantly. The awkward silence stretched for what felt like an eternity, and Erich looked anywhere but at his uncle. If he hadn't eaten an entire herd of sheep over the last few days, he might have busied himself with eating, but the thought of consuming anything in that moment made his stomach turn. The chatter of happy farmers and villagers was starting to grate on him, and he knew if he didn't speak soon, they'd spend all night in this silent stalemate.

"What do you want?" Erich asked, again in Neolyrian,

partly out of habit and partly to distance himself from his motherland.

"You left for six years, Erich, without a word. We're family. Did you think I would accept that loss without explanation?" his uncle replied in Sundish, Erich's mother tongue. He'd not felt homesick over the past six years, not once. But hearing his uncle scold him in his native language, he felt a brief pang of longing for Sundland.

He didn't respond, too overcome by guilt and longing to form a proper explanation.

"I won't accept silence, you're too old for these childish rebellions, Erich."

Erich felt the comment slice him down to the core. Even now, as a grown man, seeing disappointment on his uncle's face hurt worse than a mortal wound. There had been a time in his life when he'd have done anything to make this man proud. But the boy he'd been was dead, and it was time his uncle realized that.

Erich gripped the handle of his mug tight enough to crack it.

"This isn't about rebellion. I left for your safety as well as others. I'm a monster," he replied in Sundish.

"Even if I were to believe that, what part of your plan to spare us your monstrous nature included swindling royalty and entering fighting rings before terrorizing the countryside in dragon form? Was all that for my benefit, too?"

"Ivar wrote to you?" Erich guessed. As for the rest, he knew he'd been reckless, but he'd come too far to give up. He'd retrieve Liane and disappear once more before he became a danger to her and himself.

"And thank the Trinity he did. I've been chasing ghosts until he sent me in your general direction. Finding you in the fighting ring in Basilia was a Trinity-guided moment as well. Then you slipped away again, back into the shadows. I assumed with the coming full moon, you'd have removed yourself to change. Then I heard from locals about burnt sheep, and I connected the dots."

Erich sighed as he pinched his brow. "I know you've come all this way, but I'm not going home."

"Your father is dying."

"Good."

"Duke Mattison is attempting a marital alliance with Neolyra."

"Good for him."

"He's cruel, if not crueler than your father, and with the might of the Neolyrian empire behind him, he'll be unstoppable."

"What's worse, a man who is like a monster or a monster who wears a man's face? I killed Hallbjorn Geirsson and his family." Erich said this part while meeting his uncle's gaze directly. He hadn't spoken the name aloud since the incident that drove him from the palace and in search of a cure.

His uncle swallowed. "It was your father; he forced you to do his dirty work..."

"My father is a monster, just like me. But I have magic and claws. And I killed Geirsson because the dragon became obsessed with him. Father asked me to torture him for information, but I couldn't stop. I lost control and slayed him, then I killed his family in my insane bloodlust. Do you think someone like that will be a good king for Sundland?"

"I know your heart, Erich. And you're not bloodthirsty like your uncles. Or willing to consult dark magics to your own ends, like Duke Mattison is rumored to be involved in."

"And when the dragon within me consumes me, will the kingdom be safe? I just spent three days as a dragon. I'm losing control." Erich's mouth suddenly felt dry, and he took a large swig of ale, but it was bitter on his tongue.

"I've told you that the dragon is not something to fear. It is a part of you, not a monster to be tamed. If you are willing to fight, you could make a real change for Sundland. Have you no sympathy for the innocents who will suffer? This could lead to war or famine. Your uncles' civil war could destroy Sundland or lose it to the greed of the empire's expansion."

Erich leaned back. He wasn't completely coldhearted; he did feel for the people. But his uncle's and Ivar's assumption that he would somehow be better was preposterous. He'd killed a man when the dragon had taken over. His sanity was slipping. And he was on the verge of doing the same to Liane if he couldn't keep threading this delicate balance.

"I appreciate you coming to find me, Uncle. But I cannot be the king you want me to be. Consider me dead." Erich stood up from the table, but before he could walk away, his uncle grasped him by the upper arm.

"At least think about it. I brought a ship, the *Snow Dragon*. If you change your mind, find me at the port; we can sail back to Sundland together. We can make a change, Erich."

Erich's lips twisted at the ship's name. Endland's family crest was a white dragon; no one would think twice about that name. But he hated his uncle for naming his ship that. As if their dragon-cursed blood was something to celebrate.

Erich shook him off. "Go back to your estate, Uncle. And leave me to my wicked ways."

23

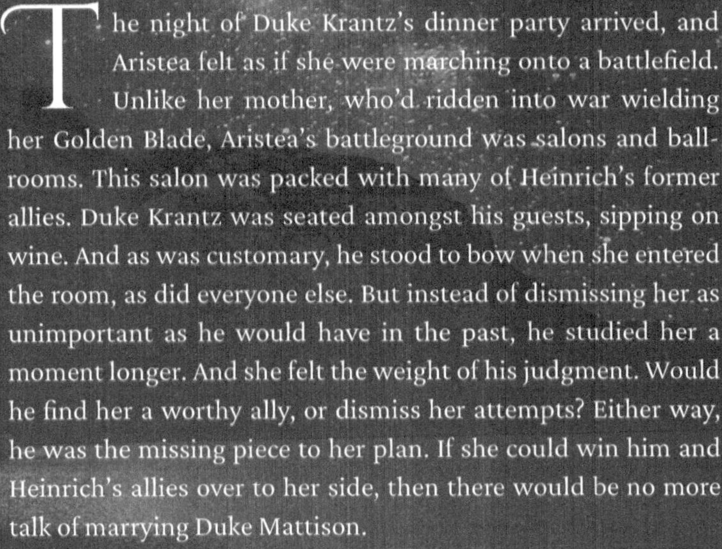

The night of Duke Krantz's dinner party arrived, and Aristea felt as if she were marching onto a battlefield. Unlike her mother, who'd ridden into war wielding her Golden Blade, Aristea's battleground was salons and ballrooms. This salon was packed with many of Heinrich's former allies. Duke Krantz was seated amongst his guests, sipping on wine. And as was customary, he stood to bow when she entered the room, as did everyone else. But instead of dismissing her as unimportant as he would have in the past, he studied her a moment longer. And she felt the weight of his judgment. Would he find her a worthy ally, or dismiss her attempts? Either way, he was the missing piece to her plan. If she could win him and Heinrich's allies over to her side, then there would be no more talk of marrying Duke Mattison.

She studied the rest of the crowd. Her gaze snagged on Jonathan, and her chest thumped traitorously. He smiled, and unlike the others who'd given her the perfunctory greetings that were necessary for a monarch, his smile was warm and inviting. And much too familiar for people of their different positions. She looked away as fast as she dared, but she felt that magnetic pull toward him, even as she drifted over to the corner where the wives and daughters of the powerful men sat assembled. She'd mingled with this group before and knew their proclivities for gossip, but she had to put as much distance between herself and Jonathan as possible. The ladies greeted her formally, and even those she'd had an easy rapport with in the past were distant with her. Though she tried to make small talk with them, she felt as if she were standing on an island, looking at them on a distant shore. They floated away one by one, leaving her feeling naked and exposed. She'd never realized how many people hated her until Heinrich had died, how much her influence had been impacted by him standing at her side.

He was right; she was nothing without him. A servant came around offering aperitifs, and Aristea snatched at a glass, desperate for something to do with her hands. She felt Jonathan's eyes on her, and her gaze slid traitorously in his direction. Just a quick peek, she told herself, but then she caught his stare and held it.

She felt everyone's eyes on them as he walked over to her. Each strike of his cane on the parquet floor had her heartbeat speeding up. If they were seen chatting for a third time in public, people were bound to talk. She should find a distraction, another person to talk to. But even as she rationalized her plan, her feet remained planted on the ground. She wasn't sure if she should be excited or terrified.

"Your majesty. It is lovely to see you this evening," he said.

A pair of women by the fireplace surveyed her up and down before whispering behind their hands and giggling. Everyone gave her nothing more than passing glances and shallow bows.

Aristea's stomach swooped. She felt as if her feelings were

written plainly on her face for all to see. She couldn't seem to come up with a greeting. What did one say when meeting an old friend? She couldn't remember.

She was saved from trying to make small talk when Duchess Krantz called for her.

"Your majesty, I would be honored if you would sit beside an old woman and entertain her."

Aristea latched onto the greeting and gave a hurried excuse to Jonathan before joining the duchess on her sofa. She was holding court among a few of the other duchesses and ladies. And Aristea was spared from having to say anything at all. She could simply sit serenely by her side while she cast sidelong looks in Jonathan's direction.

He was watching her too, and the attention he put upon her made her face flame. He was bolder than when they were young. He'd been shy and awkward, careful to not cross the line. And it thrilled her to be the subject of his attention, but it was doomed from the start. No matter how bold he was, the dukes and Mother ultimately decided her marital fates, and they'd never agreed to such an unequal match.

"Is there something wrong, your majesty?" the duchess asked.

Aristea shook herself out of her thoughts. "No, nothing at all."

The duchess harrumphed but did not press her. Aristea let conversations flow around her, sitting like a living statue. She'd come here on a mission, to win Duke Krantz's favor and the flow of money and power that came from him. If she won his approval, the rest would follow suit, she hoped. But propriety dictated that she sit and chat with the women while the men discussed business. That was how it had always been. She might address them as men in the council meetings with her mother at her back, but here, she was another widow, whom they suffered to have in their company.

A few of the ladies ventured to engage her in conversation, and she may as well not have been there at all. She couldn't focus on discussions of marriage and births, embroidery, and weaving. If Jonathan were bold enough to make his intentions known and buck tradition, why couldn't she be? She'd get nothing accomplished sitting in the corner with the ladies, talking about embroidery floss colors.

Duke Krantz was standing off to one side, talking with Duke Licht, a horrid man whom Aristea despised. He was another one of Heinrich's old hangers-on who'd often traipsed about with Heinrich on drinking trips. He'd also attempted to woo Liane, but she'd been courageous enough to turn him down straight away. Liane wouldn't have even entertained the idea of Duke Mattison. She'd have refused him and carved her own path. Aristea should approach Duke Krantz; let her ambitions be made clear. Aristea stood and was preparing to approach the two men when a servant came in and announced dinner was served.

Everyone rose and filtered into the dining room and shuffled over to their assigned seats. Aristea was given a seat of honor near the head of the table. To her dual delight and dismay, she was seated across from Jonathan. He noted their placement across from one another and said not a word, but a crooked grin broke out across his face. On her right was Duchess Krantz, and at the head of the table, Duke Krantz.

The first course, appetizers, was served, and servants entered with silver cloches and placed morsels on their plates while a second set of servants filled their goblets with Sundland wine. Dinner conversation was light due to mixed company. Aristea spoke with the duke about his granddaughter, which seemed to be a favorite topic of his. He regaled Aristea with tales of Elisa's antics. It was a lovely distraction from Jonathan, who her gaze kept straying to throughout the meal.

After dessert was served, the ladies rose from the table, and out of habit, Aristea stood as well. It was normal for the men to linger in the dining room and discuss politics and manly topics while the women drifted off to the salon for private chats amongst themselves. As the other women filtered out, Aristea hesitated and, on instinct, looked at Jonathan, who gave her a nod of encouragement. She'd come here to find a seat at the table with the men, to declare herself their equal. But would they accept her? Did she have the audacity to insist?

"I thought you might stay and discuss kingdom matters, your majesty," Duke Krantz said, helping aid her decision.

Duchess Krantz was one of the last women to leave, and as she exited, she gave Aristea a nod of approval, which helped to settle the flutter of uncomfortable butterflies in her stomach. This was her destiny. If she wanted to fill her mother's shoes as future empress, she needed to be strong. The men moved closer, filling the gaps the women had left behind. It was the same group of men she'd sat at a council table with countless times before. But this felt more intimate than a Dukes' Council.

She gazed at the men around the table—some looked indifferent, others looked ready to protest, but dared not speak out against Duke Krantz. She smiled back at them, displaying a level of confidence she did not feel. Mother said a smile was her power; it could disarm her enemies and keep them guessing before her next move. But she didn't think they were disarmed at all. If anything, she felt like a fool. She sat back down. Jonathan gave her a comforting smile from across the table, and she was grateful to have him there with her.

Mother regularly worked with these men. They respected her, to some degree. And when Aristea became empress, they'd have to respect her too. This was why she'd come after all, to win their devotion and loyalty. But when she looked at them, she felt the lack of Heinrich in their midst. He'd been close to all of them. Scheming, cavorting. She shook off the specter of him from her thoughts. She didn't need him or Duke Mattison or any man behind her to rule this country; she was strong enough on her own.

The discussion wasn't much different from any she'd experienced in a women's salon. They discussed banal things: their investments, their land, their horses, and their hunting dogs. One man started to mention his mistress but was cut off by a strong glare from Duke Krantz, then teased by his compatriots. Aristea mostly listened, and as the whiskey flowed, they became more relaxed in her presence, as if they'd forgotten she was there at all. Nothing they could say was too shocking; she'd heard Heinrich say more and worse.

Then, when she felt the moment was right, she struck. "I'm glad we had a moment to talk. You were all my husband's friends, once."

But it was as if a hound had seen a rabbit. The room tensed as they all looked at her. Aristea suddenly felt as if she were sitting on a stage, lights burning into her eyes.

"A good man," Lord Northangel said. He took a long swig of his drink, draining the glass of its amber liquid.

"You used to do a lot of business for my husband, I heard. Perhaps you could tell me more about it?" Aristea said, testing the waters.

There were furtive glances around the room. And Aristea felt as if she were walking along a blade's edge once more.

"I don't know if now's the right time for such a discussion, your majesty."

"Duke Spiess was just discussing the sale of his sheep. What's wrong with discussing business?" Aristea said, playing coy.

Duke Krantz cleared his throat—a warning for her or Lord Northangel, she couldn't be sure.

Aristea had two choices at that moment—Either she played dumb and lost any chance of their respect, or she grasped this chance while she had it.

She decided to barrel forward. "Is it because you're still dealing in stardust?" It was a wild guess, but whether he was involved or not, she wanted it out in the open to break the seal and let them know she was willing to overlook it to join hands for a common goal.

The silence was deafening. The men shifted uneasily in their seats and refused to look at Aristea directly.

"You don't need to pretend it doesn't exist on my account. I knew what my husband was working on creating soldiers for his own personal army."

Northangel leaned across the table. "We're allowed men-at-arms, are we not? As leaders of the sovereign nations of the empire, it's only fair we arm ourselves against the growing threats from the north and beyond..."

"Of course. And I am not opposed to your business ventures, as long as our goals are aligned."

"What if our goals don't align with the church?" Duke Krantz asked.

Aristea raised a brow, but a chill was running up her spine. The church was the backbone of the empire. It was the Avatheos' support that had helped Mother claim her throne. They couldn't be implying that the church was the problem.

"My sister is the avatar; you need not worry about the church."

"But the Starwebers' involvement in the church is the problem, isn't it?"

They looked back and forth between one another.

Aristea's mouth felt dry, and sweat was drenching her

palms. She wanted to wipe it off on her gown, but she feared the slightest twitch from her would reveal her feelings about these blasphemous thoughts.

"The church and the empire are intertwined. They have been since our founding."

"But is that what's best for the empire?" Duke Krantz set down his glass heavily. "Heinrich was leading an investigation into stardust's properties and its effect in awakening dormant magic. The church has been keeping secrets about magic in the realm. Careful administration of stardust on the right bloodlines has yielded impressive results. It makes soldiers stronger, and we're close to uncovering a way to bring magic back to the people. So it's not just under the thumb of the church."

"To what end?" Aristea asked, her chest constricting. Were they plotting sedition?

The men around the table shared a look as if they were silently deciding whether to speak with her or not.

"You must feel how the tide has turned. Your mother became empress thanks in part to the support of the Avatheos. But now he has your sister, the goddess' chosen, he's named her. And he's made your brother into a holy warrior when a faction is already rallying behind him. None of us wants civil war, but we fear it is inevitable. The church has gained too much power and influence over the governance of this country. It's time we arm ourselves."

It was sacrilege to speak thusly, but Aristea feared speaking out would silence them, so she waited as he continued, "If we regained control of magic, think of the implications. In defense against other countries or battles from within. We'd be able to expand our borders and grow the empire in ways that haven't been possible in centuries."

"But the stardust is killing people."

Lord Northangel waved his hand. "It's a necessary cost of

learning what it is capable of. Once the elves realized they could sell it to anyone, the distribution grew out of control. But a strong army..."

Aristea's heart was hammering in her chest. Her head swam with the information relayed. Then it was as she'd suspected; they were building an army. And if she didn't play her cards right, then they'd use that army against her.

"Then I'm glad to have you on my side, Duke Krantz," Aristea said, trying to keep her tone light.

Jonathan, seated across from her, gave her an encouraging smile.

"All of us here wish to see the empire thrive. There is one concern, however. The continuation of the royal line," Duke Krantz said and glanced over at Jonathan.

Aristea looked between the two of them. They couldn't be implying...

"Meaning my heir?" Aristea prompted.

"Yes, and while we admire your dedication to your deceased husband, time isn't on our side," Duke Krantz continued.

She was used to these sorts of criticisms, but having Jonathan there, seemingly part of a discussion about her womb behind her back, stung. She'd thought he was different, but maybe all men were the same.

"We would not want you beholden to another man or kingdom. Heinrich was a tyrant, all of us knew it. But with the right consort, we could create a new era with you as an empress."

Her mouth had gone dry, and she could not properly form a sentence.

"I take it you have someone in mind?" She looked around the room at the drunk, lecherous old men around her. Half were married or widowed. None would be her choice of a partner. But she'd known this sort of negotiation would be expected of her. And she might pretend to consider their offer, at least until she could secure their loyalty some other way.

"I do. The father of my grandchild, in fact. Lord Sommerfeld."

Jonathan smiled at her from across the table, but Aristea felt as if the world had stopped.

When she didn't return his smile, his slowly faded while Duke Krantz continued on, "And should your union not bear fruit, you could name my granddaughter, Elisa, heir to the throne. I think it is a rather tidy solution to our problem."

Aristea's ears were ringing, and she felt as if her stomach might heave up her dinner. She'd thought Jonathan had come to her out of true affection for her. That he'd desired to rekindle the sparks of a love that'd never borne fruit. But this entire time, he'd been plotting with Duke Krantz to position himself as her consort. To give Duke Krantz access to the throne.

She stood up, and as she did, half a dozen chairs scraped to follow her. "You've given me much to consider. But the hour is late, and I should go."

Aristea turned and stormed out of the room. She was halfway to the foyer when she heard Jonathan call out to her.

"Aristea, wait!"

She wanted to ignore him, but she seemed to be tethered to him by invisible strings. She turned to face him. "Did you know what they were planning?"

He twisted his cane in his hand, avoiding her gaze. "Yes. But I'm not like Heinrich. I did it for you…"

She shook her head. "You tricked me and used my feelings against me. Was Elisa part of your scheme as well? Show your precious daughter to a barren widow to convince her to make the girl her heir."

Tears pricked the back of her eyes, but she dared not let them fall.

"Would you be happier marrying a man your mother chooses again? To rule as a puppet in a man's shadow?"

"Better him than a liar. At least I know what I'm getting into with him."

Aristea swallowed down the bitterness in her throat and turned to walk out. She wasn't sure what she'd been expecting, but she feared all her plans were in ruins.

24

As her confinement stretched onward, Liane found no greater clarity, peace, or acceptance of Cyra's divine plan. In fact, the more time she spent alone, the angrier she became. Her rage felt like a slow-building fire, and each passing day was another twig fed into it, slowly smoldering, waiting for fuel to ignite. All told, she spent nearly a week in isolation, turning over the things the raven had said to her like a stone in a river until she'd worn it smooth. She laid out everything that had happened since she'd arrived in Basilia like marble pieces on a chessboard. The attack on the dock, performing for the masses, dancing to the entertainment of the rich and powerful, Sylvie's death. Every step maneuvering her to bend to the Avatheos' will.

She understood why her mother had hidden the truth, because to reveal it meant getting caught in his greedy grasp for power. Liane had known and hadn't heeded her mother's warnings. Now that she was in his trap, how did she break free? The first step was getting out of the tower. She had to convince the Avatheos that he'd broken her spirit and she was his to mold.

She wore her veil constantly, and whenever the caretakers were near, she pretended to pray. And when the Avatheos came to visit, she was meek and obedient, on her knees, begging for his guidance and blessing. She quoted the holy text and played her role as a dutiful and compliant avatar.

Though it made her stomach churn to pretend, her efforts paid off, and she was released from the tower. On the day of her release, an entourage of priestesses arrived with a tub and buckets of steaming water. She limply let them wash her with scalding water, scrubbing the last of the impurity from her body. She saw the fingerprints of humiliation and control in the ritual. It reminded her of the pure-white goat they'd sacrificed during her initiation. Liane was meant to be like that goat, livestock passively led to slaughter. She'd let them think her broken if they'd release her.

They needed to plan their escape. Walking out of the temple wasn't an option. The Midnight Guard wouldn't let them, and if she tried, she feared the fervor of the pilgrims. Whether the attack on the dock had been intentional or orchestrated, she feared for her own safety out in the open. Ludwig wouldn't be enough to protect her. She'd need Erich, but she wasn't sure where to find him.

If anyone could find him, Luzie and Ludwig could. They were her right and left arms. Without them, she felt cut off and adrift.

The priestesses pulled Liane out of the bath, and the goose-flesh on her arms rose. The fall equinox was fast approaching, and at sunset, the air was starting to have a touch of chill. They braided her hair and brought a pure-white robe and veil for her to wear. She let them dress her, sitting as still as a doll. Though her fingers twitched in agitation.

She had to show restraint. Rushing in was what had killed Sylvie, arrogance over her own ability. She was surrounded by enemies, and she had to be strategic about her next moves. She still wasn't sure what they were preparing her for, but she suspected it would be public, when they placed the ceremonial headpiece on her head, with its many chains and radiant beam crown.

It felt heavier than the last time she'd worn it, but maybe it was the weight of the church's plans for her that made each step heavier. The equinox was still two weeks away, so they wouldn't be attempting to seal her power, not yet.

They led her to the balcony, where she'd greeted pilgrims and performed with her light power numerous times before. She didn't ask questions but let their flow be her guide.

As she climbed the steps, she heard the soft hum of suppressed conversation. They'd gathered a large crowd. And she felt their expectations like a buzz against her spine. In the same way as when the Avatheos had insisted she be purified in the tower, something felt discordant about their expectations, and she felt a cold hand grasping the nape of her neck.

When they reached the anterior staging room, the Avatheos was waiting for her.

Seeing him made her stomach clench, and that feeling of wrongness washed over her, as if she were going to be sick.

"You've proven your faithfulness and endured your isolation. Now it's time you displayed your power to heal the people," the Avatheos said as he approached her, palms upright.

Liane's mouth fell open. This must be a cruel joke. "But I can't heal anyone."

"They merely need to believe you can. Word got out about poor Sylvie's untimely death; doubt has crept into their hearts. And with a dragon attacking the city, they need assurances that Cyra is with us, that she has chosen her vessel, who will purify the darkness." He placed his hands on her shoulders, and she felt as if a boulder weighed her down.

Erich had attacked the city. Had he survived? If he had fallen... was there any hope?

"Are we in danger?" she asked, the real questions caught in her throat.

"Everything is happening according to her plan. You've been tempted as Cyra was, but you are still a part of the light, aren't you?"

That familiar smoldering rage that had gotten her through confinement threatened to consume her. Liane bit down on her words and nodded.

The Avatheos let go of her, but she still felt the fizzle of his hands on her, as if a film clung to her that she couldn't shed.

A priestess came forward and thrust a gold-plated blade into her hand. It was the same replica her mother had used at ceremonies and official functions.

"Play your part," the Avatheos warned before stepping out to greet the crowd. And her stomach churned. Did he see through her facade? She swallowed past the lump in her throat. She had to get through this and speak with Luzie and Ludwig to make a plan.

The curtains parted, and the Avatheos exited first to the sound of a roaring crowd. Liane held her breath for a few beats before following him.

An excited murmur rippled through the crowd as she stepped out to stand beside the Avatheos.

The Avatheos raised his hands, silencing them. When they'd settled, he said, "The avatar has finished her time in isolation and purified her body. I have read the bones and runes and determined that she shall fully ascend during the fall equinox. And she shall unleash the healing power of Cyra across the city, ending the scourge of corruption that plagues our great empire!"

"Hold it up and glow," the Avatheos instructed under his breath.

She did as she was commanded, like a puppet on strings, and the crowd roared their approval. To them, she was holding out the true Golden Blade. Liane's stomach was in knots. They didn't know the sword was in her back. They didn't know she couldn't do much more than glow. Her back ached from holding up the false sword, and the light coming from her burned. This was wrong.

As she looked out at the starved and dirty faces of the masses, she thought of Sylvie, who'd put her faith in her. This wasn't right—giving these people false hope. It was cruel. Liane couldn't be what they wanted from her. And maybe she was never meant to be.

The Avatheos saved her from further torture by raising his hand, and she lowered her sword. The crowd fell silent.

"Today, you shall witness a miracle. Watch as she heals the corruption of this withered man."

He gestured to his right, and the curtain pulled back. Liane could see the black lines of paint snaking over his body. To the crowd below, it'd look like he was withering. But she'd seen the effects on a person up close when it'd consumed Elias and Sylvie. This man wasn't sick. But leaning heavily on his cane and with enough stage makeup, he was a convincing fraud. Just like the sword clutched in her hand, this was another part of this play, and Liane was the star.

Guilt stabbed at her, but at least no one else had to die from her lack of power. If he wanted a show, she'd give him one. Liane sheathed the golden blade in her belt and knelt before the pretender, cupping his face. He looked up at her, eyes wide, as he trembled slightly. What had the Avatheos threatened him with to make him play a role in this farce? She'd probably never know.

As it was, she did the only thing she could do; she flashed a bright light, and in that moment, the man swiped away at the black paint on his arms. And when the light had faded and everyone's vision had cleared, he appeared healthy. Liane stepped back, her stomach churning as the Avatheos grasped the man's arm and brought him to the edge of the balcony.

"He has been healed! Cyra be praised, hail the goddess' chosen!" the people shouted in an exuberant cheer.

The ceremony continued on, but a veiled priestess came forward to escort her away, and Liane followed them out into the interior holding room. When she entered, she felt as if her legs were made of jelly, and she nearly collapsed, but she was caught by strong arms. And when she glanced up, it was to see Ludwig looking down at her.

"Ludwig?" Liane gasped. Stars above, it was good to see a friendly face.

He squeezed her hand to reassure her. But she knew from the lines bracketing his mouth that something had gone very wrong.

He escorted her back to her old rooms, and she never thought she'd be eager to return there.

"Luzie!" she called out as she entered, but there was no reply.

She turned to Ludwig and noticed for the first time the rising sun emblazoned on the front of his uniform. The sigil of the Midnight Guard.

"You joined the guard?" she asked and felt an odd sense of betrayal.

"I had no choice. Either I joined the Midnight Guard, or I would be dismissed from the temple. Like Luzie."

Her stomach sank. "Why was Luzie dismissed?"

"Officially? Lewd acts," Ludwig said.

"That can't be true. Luzie..." Liane bit off the rest of her sentence. Why hadn't she seen it sooner? This was all part of their plan. They'd taken Liane away from her family and her home, brought her into the temple, locked her in isolation, but even that hadn't been enough. While she had been locked in the tower, they'd quietly removed her allies. She felt as if a snare was tightening around her neck, strangling out her breaths. Every instinct in her mind was telling her to run, to grab Ludwig and make their escape. But where could she go that the church wouldn't follow when she had the thing they wanted most of all embedded in her spine?

"I don't understand. How could you join the Midnight Guard?" Liane asked him.

Ludwig rubbed the back of his neck and looked around the room guiltily. "You were right. I've been keeping secrets."

Her stomach clenched. Not again.

He waved his hands in front of him. "Not in that way. When I didn't die from stardust withdrawal, I knew something wasn't right. I started looking into the reasons, and then that elf helped the final piece of the puzzle fall into place for me. Stardust awakened the power in me. I don't know how or why. But I took the test, and they've accepted me as their own. I had the training in arms, though I'm a probationary officer for now... I did it to protect you. I couldn't leave you alone here in the temple."

Liane felt a wave of relief wash through her. She knew she'd been unfair to Ludwig by not trusting him, but now she needed him more than ever.

"I wanted to explain myself to you a thousand times. But there never seemed to be the right time or place. I've had my doubts about the church for a while now. And they were sealed when they locked you up and dismissed Luzie."

She grabbed his hands in hers and squeezed. There was still more healing to be done, but for the first time in a long while, she felt as if they were seeing eye to eye.

"I was wrong to trust the Avatheos. I should never have come to Basilia. I should have left when Erich offered to take me away."

Ludwig scoffed. "I don't know about that..."

She grabbed Ludwig's arm as a drowning woman might a piece of flotsam. "I need you to find Erich. He knew all along, and he promised to save me."

Ludwig looked at her for a long moment, and she feared he'd refuse, but he nodded slowly.

"I'll find him, and we'll get you out of here," Ludwig said.

25

rich felt like a philandering husband slinking home after curfew. He thought he was used to walking away. But seeing the disappointment on his uncle's face in person felt as if Uncle Endland had driven Erich's dagger into his gut. He had no choice other than to walk away. He couldn't be king. Not with the dragon curse slowly consuming him. If he was lucky, he'd get Liane out before he lost all control. There was no future for Erich.

When he reached the city on foot, the sun was rising on a new day. Four days had passed since he'd last seen Liane. Two, since he'd attacked the city walls in dragon form.

Large swaths of the wall were scorched black, chunks were missing from the parapet, and the crumbled remains were scattered at the base of the wall. A line had formed at the gate that wound down the road, a mix of pilgrims and merchants coming into town to sell. Erich joined the queue behind two men whom he presumed to be father and son. They were perched on the back of a cart piled high with squash and root vegetables. The father was speaking with an old woman with a large bag strapped to her back, overladen with cabbages.

"Is it true she can heal the withering?" the woman asked with a furtive glance toward her companion, who was clutching his arm, which was concealed in his sleeve.

"If you can reach her. Though not many can," the older man in the cart replied.

"This is the first bit of good news we've had in a long time," she said, hoisting her pack up higher.

"Don't know how lucky we are. There's also a rumor going around that a dragon attacked the city," the man with the pack said, nodding toward the scorched walls.

"I heard! My stars, what is the Midnight Guard doing, sitting on their hands while the corrupted run mad? I saw a man on the road from Hutthausen, said his entire flock was devoured and he's come to the city asking for compensation from the church."

Erich flinched at this. If he had the means, he would have found a way to compensate those who were terrorized while he was in dragon form. But he not only lacked the geld, he would incriminate himself. *But if he were king, he'd have geld a plenty to send*, a voice whispered at the back of his mind. A thought he quickly dismissed. He wasn't going back.

"The church is protecting the goddess' chosen, as they should. If the forces of darkness are attacking, I'd say the church is doing right. We all should return to our villages and not trouble her with our small worries," said the man with the withered arm.

"Hush now. She'll heal you," the woman with the pack chided.

"Should have left me behind to die in peace. If they catch me..."

Then the line lurched forward as more people were let in through the gate. And Erich noticed the space around them had grown, and the others eyed the man skeptically. Typically, those with the withering were treated as social pariahs, borne of the belief that it was contagious. The man in the cart and his son shifted uncomfortably. Erich felt for the man; he'd been subject to similar scorn and hatred from people once they'd realized what he was. This world wasn't kind to those who were blighted. It wasn't fair and it wasn't right.

The line moved forward, and Erich noticed the guards were checking everyone who was attempting to pass through the gates, and as the man in the sling reached them, they turned him away. He and the woman with the cabbages retreated, dejected. By the time it was Erich's turn, he was a jumble of nerves. The pit master's token was lost, and after his performance last night at the gate, he wouldn't be surprised if they turned him away or arrested him on sight. He intended to use the allure to convince the guards to let him through. And if that didn't work, then he'd fight his way in if he must. Whatever it took to get back to Liane.

A guard waved him forward, and Erich held his breath as he attempted to school his features into indifference.

"Reason for entry?"

"I'm here on business," Erich said, infusing his words with persuasion, glamouring the guard to see what he wanted them to see: another merchant coming in from the countryside. The clothes he was wearing, hopefully, helped sell the illusion.

His luck had run out, it seemed. The guard's gaze snagged on him as he surveyed him up and down, and then he signaled for his nearby companion. Erich shifted from foot to foot, clenched his fist, and reached for his dagger, but he'd lost it when he'd shifted early. It was probably lying in a gutter somewhere in the city, along with the tattered remains of his clothes.

"Can you step aside for a moment?" they said.

Erich's hand flexed, prepared for a fight, but he lacked weapons. He wasn't even certain if he could transform and fight, even if he wanted to. Days of transformation had depleted him. The guard turned his back to him, presenting an opening for him to attack, but before he could strike, a heavy hand landed on his shoulder. Erich looked up to see one of Leonhard's goons—the one with the scar across his face—grinning at him.

"He's with me. Leonhard vouches for him."

The guards looked annoyed but waved Erich to leave with the goon, who steered him down a street with a firm, beefy hand on his shoulder. They headed toward a nearby alleyway, where he half expected to get jumped by more of Leonhard's men.

"Went on a little journey outside the city, I see," the grunt commented.

"Thought I'd get some fresh air," Erich remarked.

"Well, good thing you came back; I was about to hunt you down through the countryside."

"Wouldn't want that," Erich replied, and maybe it was just his imagination, but the brand they'd put into his skin started to burn. Out of one trap and into another. He supposed he ought to be grateful that they hadn't assassinated him straight away. Leonhard would throw him in the pit first, he was certain. Better to get a show and make some extra coin from Erich's death to repay his debt.

As he'd suspected, three more armed hunters emerged from the shadow of the alleyway.

"I suggest you come along quietly," the hunter said.

"I was hoping to meet with Leonhard. You've saved me fishing for an invitation," Erich said.

Erich let them lead him to a carriage and throw him inside. Sandwiched between two of Leonhard's hunters and with two more sitting in the carriage seat, there was no point in trying to escape.

They rode in tense silence until they reached Leonhard's town house. As he was escorted up the steps, Erich had a sinking feeling. He'd almost prefer being taken to the coliseum. A servant answered the door and silently led Erich to Leonhard's study. The same room where they'd first met. But this time, his face wasn't pressed to the carpet, and he could see the dark oak shelves lining the walls and the old books. His desk was strewn with documents, and a half-drank bottle of port sat open next to his hand. Leonhard looked up as he entered, as if they had an appointment.

"There's our wayward prince," he said. So close to seeing his uncle, the comment stung.

Leonhard was taunting him. He was certain of it. Would this be the end of their cat-and-mouse game at last? Had he come to call in his debts?

"You wanted to meet with me?" Erich asked.

"I wanted to make sure you weren't stepping out on our deal. You got rather far away during the full moon."

"I had business to attend to."

"Indeed. Well, I think it's time this little game of ours came to an end. I can't keep wasting the resources on keeping track of you. Especially if you're going to wander so far afield."

"Pity. Does this mean you'll kill me?" Erich doubted it. They hadn't even properly bound his hands or feet as they'd done the first time they'd brought him in. Leonhard didn't seem like the type for pointless violence.

"No, that wouldn't serve either of our ends, I'm afraid. But I do have an offer to make you."

"And what's that?"

"There's someone I need to extract. A friend of mine is in the dungeons beneath the Church of Sol. You've spent a lot of time within those walls over the last few weeks, and I can think of no one better equipped."

"That's why you gave me the token?"

"And to win the favor of a prince. Can never have too many favors." He winked.

"You've got power and influence. The Avatheos brought the avatar to your townhouse. Why involve me at all?" Erich couldn't help but ask.

Leonhard rubbed his chin. "The Avatheos and I have an arrangement. The hunters are an old order. You could say we were the mold from which the Midnight Guard was formed. But we worship different goddesses. He's willing to look the other way as long as I'm willing to supply him with test subjects. At times, our arrangement is even mutually beneficial. I keep money and power flowing into his city. And I have what I need to complete my research." He gestured to the books lining the room.

"That doesn't explain where I come in."

"I've tried bargaining to get my friend out. I've pulled every lever I can to free her. But the Avatheos won't budge. She was one of his, you see. And he doesn't like giving up what he thinks belongs to him. So I've been forced to subvert my methods a bit to keep the wheel turning."

"That's a long way of saying you want me to do your dirty work."

Leonhard shrugged. "Call it what you want. But we're working toward the same goal, you and I." He gestured between the two of them. "The hunters have been restoring things to the way they were for centuries before the corruption. But while the church consolidates magic in its control, we can only make so much progress."

"Let's say I knew how to get into the dungeons, which I don't. How do I enter them? I don't think your token will work this time."

"For that, I do have an answer. Go to this location, and your contact will explain the rest." He handed Erich a card with the name of a butcher and a time.

"Then that's it? I get this person out for you, and we part ways? What about this brand?"

"Oh, nearly forgot that." He stood up, strolled around the desk, and grasped Erich by the arm where the brand was burned into his flesh. Up close, he could see the rune marks moving over his skin, sliding up his neck and down to his palm. Leonhard grasped hold of Erich's shoulder, and Erich felt a slight pinprick as the marks moved from his flesh and back onto Leonhard.

"There you go, a bit of an advanced payment."

"You're rather trusting, considering," Erich remarked as he rubbed the spot where the brand had been.

"I know you'll want to help because the person I need you to get out of the dungeons is an oracle, and she's seen that she'll guide Liane on how to draw the sword from her back."

Erich felt as if a cold chill had washed over him. What else had the oracle seen? Was all this preordained, and he'd merely been Leonhard's puppet all along?

"Who are you, really?" Erich asked him.

"Just a man." Leonhard winked. "It was nice meeting you, Prince Erich. Maybe someday I'll call in that favor."

And with that, Erich was dismissed. He exited the town house and onto the empty street—brandless and with a location and name written on a piece of paper. He shoved the paper in his pocket and started walking toward his and Fritz's new rendezvous. They'd changed inns to escape Leonhard's attention, but that seemed to have been pointless now.

Everything was coming to a head, and he felt as if his skin were still too tight, like when the dragon was close to the surface. But it wasn't the dragon who'd receded to the furthest reaches of his mind. It was his fear that set his teeth on edge. He was getting what he wanted. His plan had worked. Why then did he have this feeling of dread looming over him?

Erich reached their new hideout, asked after Fritz, and was directed to a smaller inn room than they'd had before. Fritz stood up as he entered, relief on his face.

"I was worried you wouldn't come back," he said.

Erich slammed the door behind him and proceeded to tell Fritz everything that'd transpired since they'd last seen one another as he paced the length of their tiny room.

"You'll wear a hole in the floor before long," Fritz remarked when Erich was finished telling him.

"I don't suppose you've had some convenient vision that might give us the answers we need?"

"Unfortunately, no. This seems to be our only option."

Erich growled and ran his hand through his hair in frustration. There would be no second chances. Entering the dungeon and extracting two prisoners left little room for error. And the thought of that was paralyzing him.

Erich growled again, and then there was a knock on their door. Both Erich and Fritz froze, staring at their door.

Erich reached for his dagger before inching toward the door and signaling for Fritz to stand back. The elf didn't need to be told twice and stepped behind him. Erich eased open the door and was surprised to find both Liane's maid and her guard, Ludwig, standing outside his door. He lowered his weapon slightly.

She was pale, and dark circles stood out beneath her eyes. And Ludwig looked no better.

"Thank the stars, it's you," she said.

"How did you find me?"

"It wasn't easy. May we come in?" she asked. "I promise we won't bite."

But judging from the glower on Ludwig's face, that sentiment wasn't mutual.

Erich looked back at Fritz, who nodded slightly, and Erich stepped aside to let them into the room. They entered and stood in an awkward standoff. Fritz offered them wine, which they both declined.

"What brings you here?" Fritz asked.

"Liane wants you to help her escape," Luzie explained.

This was the stroke of luck they needed. Insiders close to Liane could make their plans much easier to pull off.

"Can you help us from the inside of the temple?"

Luzie's face fell. "I can't. I was dismissed. Ludwig can, though."

"Are you truly willing to work together?"

"I don't like it, but protecting Liane is more important."

They stared at one another for a few moments, in a prolonged standoff, and then Erich nodded.

"How do we get them in and close to Liane?" Ludwig asked. "The Avatheos is trying to keep her away from everyone."

"I may have a plan for that. Though there are risks involved," Erich said.

"I'm listening," Ludwig replied.

And for the second time, Erich explained what Leonhard had told him and showed them the card with the address on it.

Ludwig looked at it thoughtfully for a few moments. "That explains where the tunnel leads."

"Care to elaborate?"

"There's a tunnel guarded beneath the temple. I only got a glimpse of it when I was touring the Midnight Guard's domain beneath the temple. I saw empty carts near there, but I'm not sure what was being delivered."

"Well, it's nearly time. Why don't we go find out together?"

They headed out into the city, one by one, so as to not draw suspicion, with plans to meet up at the address on the card. Erich made his way through the tangled rows of streets that made up the holy city, looking over his shoulder every few blocks. He made half a dozen turns, and he was certain Ludwig led him past the same street at different intervals several times, as if he were making sure they weren't being followed before he'd take them to their destination.

Eventually, they ended up in the butcher's district. The smell of blood and rot made his stomach roil. The streets were stained red-brown, and the walls were speckled black by flies, which burst into flight the moment you walked by, then settled back down again. The address Leonhard gave him led him to an unassuming butcher shop. A man in a bloody apron came to the door, looked him up and down, and then nodded.

"Another one? Are you the last of them?"

"I believe so."

"Go back around with the others." His eyes lingered on Erich a moment, which made a prickle run down his spine.

Erich went around the back as instructed, past a pile of rotting castoffs. There was a cellar door propped open, and Erich could hear Fritz, Ludwig, and Luzie talking in low tones. He walked down the bloodstained steps into the cellar. A half-carved pig was laid out on the block, and a cleaver stabbed into the wood.

The butcher joined them, wiping his hands on his stained apron as he closed the cellar door, leaving them in the dim gloom of candlelight. Erich hated being in enclosed spaces in general, and the stench of meat, blood, and fear clung to the place and made the hairs on the back of his neck stand on end.

"Leonhard didn't say he'd be sending four of you. I was expecting two." He looked them up and down.

Then Leonhard had found out that Erich wasn't working

alone. The thought unsettled him, but he pushed it aside for the time being.

"They're working with me," Erich said. "And you're paying off your debt. Does it really matter?" Erich was taking a stab in the dark. He had no idea if the man had a debt or not, but knowing Leonhard, he probably did.

The man shrugged as if it didn't matter to him one way or another. "Either I pay off my lost winnings, or die. Not sure it's worth dying at the hands of the Midnight Guard if one of you squeals, though."

Luzie yelped when the butcher's eyes narrowed on her.

"None of us is going to reveal your secrets," Fritz assured him.

The butcher shook his head and gestured for them to follow as he stomped over to a cabinet at the back of the room. When he threw open the doors, another set of stairs going down was revealed. He headed down, without glancing back to see if they were following. Ludwig went after him. Then Fritz. Luzie lingered a moment, eyeing the stairs dubiously.

"I'll take up the rear," Erich assured her.

She nodded and followed Fritz and Ludwig down. Erich held his breath before joining them. It was colder down in the tunnel, and he felt the faint echoes of faded magic. Another vein that had dried up, he'd guess. The stairs ended in a tunnel filled with large blocks of ice that dripped from the baskets that held them.

"This is where we keep the bodies until the church retrieves them," the man said.

Erich walked over to one of the said bodies. It was what appeared to be an elk, but disfigured and transformed, with scaled protrusions along its body and a serpentine tail along its back.

Erich recoiled at the sight of its lolling tongue.

"You're delivering chimeras to the church?" Erich asked.

"That's how they make it. Stardust, or something very like it, is extracted from the chimeras caught in and around the capital," Ludwig said. "They give stardust to the Midnight Guard and priests to awaken their powers."

Erich felt a chill run down his spine. "How did you learn this?"

Ludwig nodded toward Fritz. "He helped me put it together. I told the guards that I had been a user once and recovered. They tested me, and I was found worthy." There was a wry twist to his mouth. "I thought the Midnight Guard and the church were meant to protect the people. But for every person who can withstand the magic, another three wither away. It's unspeakably cruel."

Erich looked at the chimera on the table. This was why Leonhard was allowed to continue his coliseum and operate in the city. If it gave the church the means to keep producing stardust, they could continue to control the flow of magic—who had it and who didn't...

Erich turned to the butcher. "And what can you reveal about Leonhard's grand plan?"

"I'm your transport, so to speak." He gestured to a cart, piled with corpses, along a track that disappeared into a dark tunnel.

Erich already felt sick to his stomach at the thought. "You want me to pretend to be a body?"

"For a short time. There's only room for two, though. You'll have to draw straws, I suspect." He rubbed his nose and sniffled.

Delightful. As horrid as the prospect was, Erich knew he'd have to go through with it.

"I can meet you on the inside," Ludwig suggested.

"And I'll wait at the rendezvous point with a carriage," Luzie said.

Which left Fritz, who was staring at the pile of bodies, his face the color of fresh milk.

"Are you sure you're up for this?" Erich asked him.

"We have no other choice. I need to be with you in the dungeon. I don't know why. I just know I do," Fritz said. His voice had taken on that eerie prophetic tone.

Everyone turned to look at him. His breaths were rising in clouds of vapor, as the temperature of the room seemed to drop. They all looked at one another, bound together by their desire to protect Liane. There was no turning back now. The only way out was forward.

26

A veiled figure beckoned to Aristea, its withered hand outstretched and a knobbed finger crooked.

"Come to me, Aristea," it crooned. "Together we will achieve greatness."

Though every instinct within her was telling her to run, she felt compelled forward, as if invisible hands were pushing her toward the veiled woman. She was standing before Aristea; the veiled woman's blackened nails were long and rotted as if they belonged to a corpse.

"Without me, you'll never be strong enough. Together, we can reshape the empire to make it greater than ever before."

It showed Aristea crowned, carrying her mother's Golden Blade, not the fake one, but the one from inside Liane's back. She stood on the palace balcony; the masses were bowing before her, including the dukes. And at her side, in ermine robes, was Jonathan, her emperor consort. It was everything she'd ever dreamed about and more.

"Come to the depths. Free me, and I shall give it all to you." The creature held out its hands as if to embrace her. Aristea was leaning forward, tipping toward it, when she was startled from her sleep.

In her waking haze, she thought Heinrich had returned home drunk and agitated. He'd often woken her in the middle of the night to rant at her about petty disputes that had nothing to do with her. It didn't matter if it hadn't been her fault; it was she who'd borne the brunt of his anger. Then she remembered, Heinrich was dead.

She sat up in bed, body still tensed, awaiting the verbal barrage, but it wasn't Heinrich sitting at the edge of her bed, but her Mathias, looking scraggly and thin. His beard was much longer than when she'd last seen him, and there were smears of dirt on his face and hands.

"Mathias?" she asked, reaching out to touch his face and make sure he was real, and this wasn't part of her strange dream.

She brushed a hand against his cheek and felt him smile.

"It's really me."

Relief and anxiety swept through her. He'd returned safely and without an army at his back. But she felt the weight of the unresolved tensions settle on her. She glanced around the room, expecting to see her lady's maid sleeping on her cot nearby, but she was awake, and a strange woman had her hands over her mouth to prevent her from screaming. The woman had attempted to disguise her long elven ears, but Aristea could see the tips of them pointing out from her jet-black hair. And there was no hiding the angular shape of her face and the unnatural way she stood perfectly still.

Alarm bells were ringing in Aristea's head.

The rumors were true; he was working with an elf. Her eyes darted to the sword at his hip, and she scooted back in the bed, away from him.

"Let Jana go," Aristea said slowly. Eyes darting between her brother and the elf.

Jana's eyes were wide and terrified as she trembled in the elf's grip.

"She's innocent," Aristea said.

Mathias looked confused for a moment and then glanced over at the elven woman. "Sorry, I know this is a bit of an abrupt greeting. But we couldn't have her alerting the guards, and I didn't know how else to approach you, given the circumstances." He shrugged. As if he hadn't snuck into her room, past her guards, and wasn't holding her maid hostage. Had he gone mad?

"Mathias, does she have you under her spell? Can I help you break free somehow?" she whispered, eyes darting toward the elf.

Mathias glanced back at her with a smile. "Katya? She won't hurt you. She and I... Well, it's a long story. Which is why I came to talk to you first. Actually, I went looking for Liane but found out she's gone. Mother won't hear reason, but she listens to you, so..."

What should she do—try to call for help? But if she did, they might slit Jana's throat. She had to be careful. Think things through.

"What is it you needed to ask me?" she asked in her best older-sister tone, even while her heart was thumping wildly in her chest. And hoped it could reach him behind this spell that the elf had cast over him. Her brother wouldn't betray her to the elves. It must be a spell, even if he didn't realize it.

"I need you to help me convince Mother to partner with the elves. They're not like we thought they were. And they're not this source of corruption the church led us to believe."

She pulled her blankets closer to her and tried to act as if this were a normal interaction between siblings. But her eyes kept darting toward the door, then to the elf, who was glaring at her, hand grasping tighter onto Jana. What if she pretended to drop something by accident? Would it be loud enough to alert the guards? No, that elf was watching her like a hawk; one wrong move and she'd follow through on the threat in her gaze.

"Even if that were true, they are still our enemies. They've been attacking the borders and killing our people," she said.

"You're the ones who committed genocide against us and forced us into the frigid north," the elf snarled.

Mathias held up his hand toward the elf. "Katya, please."

She narrowed her eyes but pulled Jana into the tunnel and out of sight. Aristea's eyes widened. She could only imagine what she was doing to Jana. But what was worse, Mathias didn't seem to be under her control. She'd listened to him. How much more was true? Was he gathering a coalition like Captain Rosen had claimed?

"You're seriously working with her?" Aristea asked.

He exhaled heavily. "I went to the feral lands, as you know. And I was intending to find out what they were planning. What sort of invasion... but when I got there, I discovered they aren't plotting anything at all. They don't have the means to scale any sort of attack. They're struggling for survival. They're not the organized threat we make them out to be."

"You're lying."

"Why would I lie?"

"Tell me this, have you been in contact with Duke Wagner?"

He looked away from her and tugged on his beard hairs. "I don't know why that matters."

"Answer me." Her voice shook.

Mathias turned to look at her. "He's sympathetic to elves, and I needed a way safely into the city. I know what you're thinking. I'm not plotting to overthrow you."

She laughed bitterly. "I'm just supposed to take your word for it as you plot to stab a dagger into my back?"

"It's not like that. I have no aspirations for power."

"Of course you do. You've been pretending to be the martyr all this time, and for a while, I believed you. But now you came in here, threatened me, and my maid. You're not the brother I knew," Aristea said, pointing an accusatory finger toward him.

Mathias reeled backward, as if he'd been slapped. "I was going to die for the empire and get out of your way, but when I found out the truth, I knew dying was the coward's way out."

Her blood ran cold. Duke Krantz would join Mathias' side with his magical soldiers, and then with the elves, she'd never stand a chance. She'd be forced to give up her place or fight an embittered civil war for succession.

And even if she won, she'd likely end up married to some awful man, like Duke Mattison.

"Don't be like that, Aristea. You weren't like this before. Remember when you talked about how you were going to change Artria for the better?"

She bit her lower lip. "That was childish hope on my part."

"You don't have to hope. You have the power now. Mother listens to you. I need your support; the elves aren't our enemies."

She felt as if someone had a vise-like grip around her heart and was squeezing it. "But you are. We're rivals now, don't you see? Without a husband, I cannot become empress while you're alive. Not with my current strength."

"It doesn't have to be this way," he protested.

"It was always this way. From the moment you were born, Mathias, my position as heir has been destabilized. We've been pretending to get along, but I can't continue. Not anymore."

Aristea stood up. Mathias jumped up, throwing out his arms to block the door.

"What are you doing, Aristea?"

"I should be calling the Midnight Guard to arrest you and end your claim. But…" She took a shaking breath. He was still her brother. She loved him dearly. Even if he didn't intend to usurp her, that was how this plan played out. Knowing that, she should turn him over and secure her claim, but she loved him despite how much she hated him.

They faced one another. In her heart, she knew it might be the last time.

"Do you hear yourself? I'm your brother."

"I know, and that's why I'm giving you a fair chance. Leave now. I'll give you a head start. Take Jana with you if you must. But don't come back here, because I'm going to fight to keep what's mine."

He stared at her for a long minute before shaking his head and turning to walk away without a word. He exited through the secret passageway, and she waited to alert the guards. The time stretched out for an eternity, but she wanted to be certain he would be clear of the castle walls before the alarm sounded. She didn't want to do this, but she didn't want to give up on the one thing that made her something. Without the crown, she was just another body, another forgotten vessel, discarded and unloved.

When she was certain he wouldn't be caught, she screamed for her guards. They rushed into the room.

"Mathias, he came into my room and threatened me with a sword. He took my lady's maid and escaped through the secret passage." She pointed a shaking finger toward the door.

The guards rushed into the secret passage, though Aristea was certain that they wouldn't find him. She prayed Jana had been spared. One guard was left behind to watch over her.

"I need to speak with my parents."

He bowed to her command and escorted her to her parents'

room. The palace was ringing with alarms, and the few nobles in residence wandered out into the halls in their nightclothes, muttering to one another about the commotion. The palace guards urged them back to bed as Aristea strode past them.

Mother met her in the drawing room in her nightgown, her evening coat wrapped around her. Father followed, looking rumpled and half asleep as he rubbed his eyes.

"Aristea, tell me it's not true. Mathias threatened you?"

She swallowed down the partial lie. "Yes. I'm afraid our worst fears have been confirmed. He confessed to me that he is working with Duke Wagner to usurp me."

"Perhaps it was a misunderstanding," Mother said.

"I can't believe Mathias would do this," Father murmured, rubbing circles on Mother's back.

She hated them both suddenly. Even when she told him her life was in danger, they sided with their son. In addition to that, they had something so rare among royal arranged marriages. They'd fallen in love and genuinely cared for one another. Aristea had hoped for the same, once. With Heinrich. And a small part of her had hoped she'd have a second chance with Jonathan, but even he had betrayed her. She was deluding herself, holding onto the dream of love.

"Would you rather he be the heir? Tell me now so I can stop struggling."

Mother turned, her eyes wide. "That's not what we meant at all."

"Then trust me when I tell you that civil war is coming unless we take a strong approach. We need to make a public example of his enemies and cut his power off at the knees," Aristea said.

There was that look again; Mother and Father shared something without words.

Mother took a step toward her. "Believe me, I have lived

through unrest before, and I do not wish to return to it. We've built peace over these long years, and I won't see the kingdom thrown into chaos over my children's squabble."

"Then you'd hand the kingdom over to the elves? He sided with them. He came to me asking me to intercede with you on their behalf. Your father, my grandfather, drove the last of them beyond the borders. Would you undo his work? Your own work?"

Aristea's head suddenly throbbed. She felt Heinrich whispering in her ear. *You were always the consolation prize. Mathias is a man, one with ambition, power, and the respect of the people. What do you have? Your parents will ship you off to Duke Mattison and put your brother on the throne. They're all against you.*

"Perhaps I should call the Vice Premier," Mother said. "You've had a traumatic evening. Rest will help you." She moved to grab the bell rope to summon a servant. But Aristea couldn't stand the idea of someone laying their hands on her. They were treating her as they had when she was a child.

Aristea stood. "Don't bother. You're right. I should get some rest."

Before her parents could protest, she headed for the door. As she was on her way out of the room, her thoughts were an angry swirl. Had they forgotten the bloody display from the play a few months ago? The havoc the elves would wreak if they were left unchecked? Did her parents expect her to stand by and let the elves destroy this kingdom? For what? To give their son a chance?

You're right, you'd be better suited to rule, a voice whispered in her head.

It was the voice of the veiled woman from her dreams. Aristea froze and scanned the halls around her.

"Whose there?" she asked

"Your highness?" a guard asked.

Her face flamed; the guards hadn't heard it. She must look insane to them.

"I'm a friend," it whispered.

The hair on the back of her neck stood up. There was a doorway to one of the underground tunnels to her right. It led to their emergency shelter and also to the labyrinth of tunnels beneath the palace. Among them were the catacombs and abandoned passageways left by ancient peoples who'd died hundreds of years ago. Liane liked exploring them, but Aristea had never dared. She only ever went underground in absolute emergencies. But the voice drew her to those tunnels in a way she couldn't fully comprehend.

"They think you're weak, but I see the potential in you. I know how strong you are. You deserve to be empress above all others. You have earned it. Haven't you sacrificed enough?"

"Your highness?" The guard approached her, but they might as well have been a million miles away.

"Come down to me. Free me, and I will give you the power that you crave. One without the puppet strings of men to tie you down. We will remake this empire in the way it was supposed to be. As your mother should have. Join me."

Aristea reached out her hand, about to grasp the tapestry that covered the opening to the underground passageway, but before she could, her guard tapped her on the shoulder, and she spun around to face him.

He looked at her, bewildered, and she felt as if her surroundings came back to her with ringing in her ears. She'd been about to follow a strange voice into the dark. Had she gone mad?

She shook herself.

"I thought I heard something behind the curtain. Check it. Mathias might be lurking about."

"Your highness." Her guard leapt to do her bidding, running down the stairs.

The voice didn't speak again, but she remained in place, arms wrapped around her torso, as if it could keep out the horrors she sensed beyond that door. He returned a few minutes later with a shake of his head. There was nothing there, and no sign of Mathias. It had all been in her head. Or so she should have believed, but she couldn't shake the feeling of wrongness. She'd heard the voice in the tower, too. Something was trying to reach out to her. And it terrified her because it tempted her more than she would like to admit. She shoved the thoughts away. Now wasn't the time to worry about mysterious voices. She had work to do. If Mother wouldn't help her, then she prayed Captain Rosen would. She'd been the first to tell her about Mathias' betrayal. She at least believed Aristea. If no one else would, perhaps she'd help Aristea in the fight to come.

The guards greeted her politely, as if they'd been expecting her in the middle of the night. She went straight to Captain Rosen's office. She was seated at her desk, dressed and waiting. She'd known to expect Aristea. She hoped it was a good omen.

"Your highness, I've just heard the news."

Aristea inhaled sharply. "You were right. He is working with the elves. I think my mother's judgment is clouded, but I fear we must prepare ourselves to protect the empire from invasion."

Captain Rosen nodded. "I feared much the same. But going against your mother..."

"Do what you must. I'll take any measure to protect the empire and anyone who defends it."

"Understood."

<h1 style="text-align:center">27</h1>

Erich couldn't think of a worse place to be than trapped under a pile of rotting corpses. Thick black blood dripped down onto his face, and the dead weight evoked the sensation of being buried alive in a mass grave. A fear he hadn't realized he had. If it wasn't for Liane's sake, he wouldn't have gone to such extremes. But this was his only way into the temple dungeon with minimal bloodshed.

"Do we really need to ride the carts all the way from the butcher?" Erich asked, not really expecting an answer, but talking helped distract him from the clawed hand that was cupping his calf and the horn poking into his kidney and the black ichor soaking into his hair. The smell was enough to make him retch, and he feared it would take a thorough scrubbing to wash out the stench.

"It could be worse. You could be dead," was Fritz's muffled reply, as he too was buried beneath rotting corpses.

"Thanks," Erich replied sardonically, but wasn't sure if sarcasm translated from beneath dead chimera bodies.

"No more chatter, you two," the butcher chastised. "Unless you do want to end up dead. We're nearly there now."

Silence descended, and Erich heard nothing but the rattle of wheels on the track echoing on the stone walls and the butcher's heavy footsteps.

Erich disappeared deep within his own subconscious, a place that he'd often gone when his father would beat him or while Erich had used his powers to torture his father's political enemies. It was the same place the dragon resided, chained and silent for now. But Erich suspected it was just biding its time, waiting for a chance to break free. It helped a little until the cart shook and a deer or bear carcass would push into his ribs and he'd be brought unpleasantly back to the present, holding in his vomit. Being covered in his own sick would make this infinitely worse.

He had to focus on their plan. Keep a cool head until it was time to move. Fritz would find the oracle while Erich rendezvoused with Ludwig to help free Liane. Then they'd all meet Luzie in the escape carriage they'd hired and travel through countryside villages to their next destination. Ludwig knew of a vein the Midnight Guard was protecting. They'd take her there and help Liane draw the sword from her back by entering the pool. It was a straightforward plan ripe with the opportunity for everything to go horribly wrong. A prickle of warning raced up his body, and he felt the approach of some magic.

The feeling of it grew stronger the further down the hallway they went. Erich counted each breath as they got closer to their destination, his body tensed in preparation for their inevitable encounter. But as much as he wanted to spring into action, he had to be patient. They had a meticulous plan, one that required perfect execution to pull off. The tower had an alarm system that, once triggered, would alert the entire temple, and if they didn't disable the guards at the tunnel entrance quickly, it would bring the guards' collected force down upon them.

They couldn't fight their way free, not even if Erich transformed. They came to the end of a long hallway, and Erich felt the cold breeze of their new surroundings and waited.

They weren't supposed to pop out of their hiding spots until the butcher started unloading the carts. But minutes passed, and nothing happened. Erich felt a crick in his neck and a spasm in his back. If they didn't move soon, then he might pull a muscle trying to escape. After what felt like an eternity, yellow torchlight filtered in between the gaps in the bodies. This first phase of their plan was crucial. Erich held his breath and did his best to appear corpse-like.

"Who's there?" a Midnight Guard said with disinterest.

"I've got a double shipment," the butcher said.

A pause followed, and then the guard said, "Bring it through."

Erich clenched his borrowed dagger tightly. It felt wrong in his hands, but it was better than nothing. Large metal doors creaked open, and they were rolled into the Midnight Guard's dungeons. As they passed beneath the archway, a pulse of magic rippled over him, and Erich glimpsed the runes racing along the arch of the doors a second before the wards were tripped and something made a high-pitched screech.

"What was that?" the Midnight Guard asked.

They hadn't been counting on the runes. The dragon rushed to the surface of his consciousness, as if summoned by the scent of magic in the air. This wasn't the plan; they were going to wait in the carts until the guards were gone and then crawl out.

"I'm not sure. It is the usual delivery," the butcher stammered.

"Empty it. We might have a live one," the guard said. "Be ready to sound the secondary alarm, just in case."

They started unloading the carts. Erich heard the carcasses thump on the ground, then the wet sound of flesh hitting flesh.

The weight on his shoulders was becoming less and less. He clenched his hands and grasped the hilt of his dagger. The light came through, and he made eye contact with the guard unloading the bodies. And for a moment, the guard didn't seem to notice, then he recoiled. As he was about to shout a warning, Erich shot up, flinging gore and blood around the room. As he rolled out, he sprang up and slashed at the nearest guard, opening up his throat.

The second guard was reaching for the second alarm—runic markings carved into the wall, as Erich flung his dagger to knock his hand away. The guard rushed toward Erich and drew his blade, which was etched with binding runes. Dagger gone, Erich was defenseless, and if that blade cut him, he knew his wounds wouldn't heal. Erich felt the dragon's wings beating against his insides, begging to be unleashed. But before Erich could let go, a black sword thrust its way through the guard's gut from behind, and he slumped over onto the ground. His sword lay in the rot and blood on the ground.

Fritz stood there, hands shaking and face pale.

"First time killing a man?" Erich asked him.

Fritz looked up at him, eyes wide and pupils blown. "It shouldn't be that easy." He looked at his spotless, shaking hands.

Erich sympathized with him; the first time you took a life was the hardest. But they didn't have time for Fritz to tremble and second-guess his actions.

Erich clapped him on the shoulder. "You saved us both. If you hadn't intervened, he would have sounded the alarm, and we'd both be dead."

The screech that had first alerted them of their presence had died down. And they had a moment's reprieve to collect their weapons and head out. Fritz couldn't tear his eyes away from the corpse that was slowly bleeding out on the ground. While he did that, Erich went and retrieved his dagger. It wasn't weighted as well as his. And he mourned its loss. But it was better that he let the old one go. Just like his uncle should give up on bringing him back to Sundland.

Fritz seemed to have collected himself enough to move on, and they exited the room. It opened onto a long hallway. On the outside of the door, there was no one around. But by the lack of windows, Erich surmised they were deep underground. With his weapon drawn, he motioned for Fritz to follow, and they took the labyrinth of halls through the temple. The tunnel had an uncanny resemblance to the collapsed underground tunnels he'd encountered in Artria, and he was certain that if he asked Fritz about it, he'd learn of their rich and storied history. In fact, if Fritz wasn't rattled, he'd probably be telling Erich right now. But Fritz was walking like a ghost behind him, and Erich feared he wasn't going to be able to complete their mission.

They needed to find the oracle, and more importantly, Ludwig, and a way into the temple proper. He had a general idea of the interior of the tower, thanks to Ludwig's map. But even Ludwig's intel had gaps in it. He'd barely joined the Midnight Guard's ranks, and they'd yet to show him all the inner workings of the dungeon. Erich had stopped beneath a torch to consult his map when he heard voices approaching him.

He silently signaled to Fritz to stand down and then pressed his back against the wall, waiting as the footsteps drew closer. As soon as guards turned the corner, he sprang and stabbed one guard in the ribs between a gap in his armor and angled up to hit his heart for a swift, clean death. Then Erich caught the second as he turned to run and sound a runic alarm carved into the wall by cutting his throat from behind.

"Help me hide them," he said to Fritz, who was looking a bit green.

They dragged the bodies into an alcove, and Erich hoped that no one else would come down this way for a while. From what he'd gathered, these alarm runes were all over the tunnels. At any time, they might startle a guard and alert the entire dungeon.

Erich grasped hold of Fritz's shoulders and turned him to look at him as he shoved the map into Fritz's hands. "Go find the oracle, and we'll meet back in the tunnel once I have Liane."

Fritz still looked as if he were in a daze, and Erich shook him lightly.

"Tell me you can do this."

Fritz glanced up at him, his vision clearing. "I can do it."

Erich nodded. "Good."

They parted ways, and Erich jogged down the hallway as he opened his dragon sight and saw the paths revealed to him. It was a tangled thread of interconnecting lines, but amidst it all, he spotted one golden thread. It was the same thread that he felt tugging him toward Liane whenever she was near. This was the path he had to take to get to her.

The dungeon was suspiciously empty, and he felt that same prickle of warning crawling up the back of his neck seconds before alarms started blaring. Erich brandished his weapon, waiting for an attack, but no one came in his direction. It wasn't Erich who'd set off the alarm but Fritz.

He felt his connection with Liane pull taut. He could use this distraction to reach her and remove her from the temple, but at the same time, he'd doom Fritz to death. Rather than push forward, he looped back and rushed down the stairs toward the dungeons, where the oracle was meant to be held. He saw the guards on the stairs, and with their backs to him and their attention focused on breaking down the door, Erich had made his way through half of them before they turned on him.

As their blood splattered on his face, Erich felt the dragon stir beneath his skin, felt it overcome him. He could reject it, or he could embrace it, and this time, Erich knew there was no point in turning away from the dragon within him. He unleashed the power and felt it ripple over his body, transforming his skin into something scaled and hard. He rushed toward the guards, knocking them down when they slashed at his body. Their attempts did not break the skin, and he tore through them like a creature through paper.

They were no match for him. And as his dragon eyes opened onto the world around him, he saw in brighter colors than he ever had before.

He pushed down the door and discovered Fritz and an old woman huddled together. There was blood on Fritz's face, and he was shaking.

"I got her out, but as soon as I did, the alarm..." He trembled.

"Don't worry. You did what we set out to do. Get her out of here, and I'll go get Liane."

"But the alarms..."

"Don't worry about me. Use your portal, or whatever you need."

Fritz looked stricken, but the oracle placed a hand on his shoulder. "It is what I have seen. We'll meet again at the vein." The old woman's eyes were glazed over and milky white. But even so, Erich felt as if she were seeing past him into a thousand branching futures.

The oracle's prediction seemed to embolden Fritz, and he nodded. He slashed at the air in front of him, creating a portal. He grasped hold of the oracle and stepped through, pulling her along. Erich remembered the last time he'd done that with Fritz and how much it had taken out of him. There would be no coming back for Erich. He was on his own.

More guards were rushing in from the tunnel, weapons drawn and murder in their gazes. And like he had done when he'd slipped into a darker part of himself when he had the bodies piled on him, Erich seemed to slip into the dragon's skin. Using teeth and claws to tear apart those who'd stand in his way, he rushed up the stairs, following that golden thread. All that mattered was reaching Liane. He'd lost his sense of self in that moment. He was nothing more than a creature of impulse.

Passing through the guards at the top of the stairs leading out of the dungeon and into the inner sanctum, Erich cut down anyone who stood to oppose him. Until he saw a familiar face standing in front of him, drawing a weapon but not attempting to strike.

"What have you done?" Ludwig said.

Erich came back from the red mist that'd fallen over him and looked at his gore-covered body.

"What needed to be done," he growled.

Ludwig looked appalled but made no further comment. "She's this way. Hurry, they're calling for reinforcement."

Erich followed Ludwig through the temple grounds and up the same winding staircase as when he'd come to visit Liane during her isolation. The guards were dead, likely Ludwig's doing. Liane was waiting in the tower room. She turned to him, her expression one of relief.

"Erich?" she said, her voice trembling. "You came back."

He held up his hands and saw the scales and the blood, and he recoiled in horror at it. This was exactly what he'd feared would happen. He'd killed too many people to count, lost control, all in his desire to protect her.

He moved as if to get away from her, but she grasped hold of him and wouldn't let him go.

They held one another for a moment, suspended in time. He smelled fear on her, and it made his blood boil.

"Get Liane out of here. I'll hold them off," Ludwig said.

"Ludwig, you can't," Liane started to protest.

But Erich saw the resolve in his gaze. And knew what he meant to do. There were no guarantees they could fight their way out and keep Liane safe. The fastest way was out of the window. He scooped Liane up in his arms. He felt his body reform as wings burst from his back, in a mix of agony and relief. His wingspan was large enough that he could carry his own weight and Liane's easily. She beat against his chest, trying to stop him, as the guards banged on the door, forcing their way in.

"He'll die. You can't let this happen. Please."

But Ludwig was right; the most important thing was keeping her alive.

Erich knew she'd be angry, but he had to do it, so he took the leap out the window.

28

Liane made the mistake of looking down as they flew over the city. The ground was nauseatingly far away and seemed to spin the longer she looked at it. Head swimming, she buried her face against Erich's chest as she let the wave of panicked nausea subside. His chest rumbled like a cat purring, and she was briefly amused by it until she remembered they'd left Ludwig to an uncertain fate.

She looked back at the window they'd just vacated. Even though she couldn't see Ludwig, she feared his odds against the entirety of the Midnight Guard's forces. He could leap out the window, but unless he also had wings he hadn't told her about, she wasn't sure how far he'd get.

"We have to go back for him. It's not too late," Liane protested.

"He made his choice," Erich grumbled. His voice was raspier in this half-dragon state.

"I'm not letting him die to save me." Liane slammed a fist against Erich's chest. His shirt had torn open, and her hand bounced ineffectively off the plate of scales. She could hit him a hundred times, and it'd do nothing. They were near the city walls, and they'd be passing one of the watchtowers with a balcony on its side. Liane eyed the distance. If she jumped and grabbed hold... She twisted in Erich's grip, muscles tensed to make the leap. Erich realized what she was trying to do, readjusted his grip, and she slid down his torso, scrambling to hold on to his hips, her face pressed into his ribs.

"Do you want to break your neck?" he growled.

She clung to the scraps of fabric that remained after he'd transformed.

"Maybe, or maybe you'll save me before I do and take me back to Ludwig to stop me from killing myself."

Fighting against the winged half-dragon man trying to carry her to safety wasn't the wisest idea.

She slid further down. Her feet kicked air, and she realized she did not want to test Erich's ability to save her should she make a suicidal jump. But she was running out of Erich to hold on to as her grip slipped along his slick thighs. Erich dipped down lower as he wrestled with her midair. He grabbed her by the waist, wrapped her legs around his midsection, and cupped her rear to keep her in place, face-to-face with him.

She felt his stiff cock pressed against the fabric of her undergarments, and her traitorous body responded with a tingle between her thighs. His golden eyes dilated, and his nostrils flared.

"I won't let anyone hurt you—not even yourself, Liane," Erich growled.

She slid down an inch, felt his member twitch, and tightened her grip with her thighs, which didn't make this any less erotic.

"You might impale me at this rate." She said it as a joke, but her voice was husky, and his fingers flexed against her butt as the muscles on his stomach tensed.

Now wasn't the time for aerial flirting. Think of Ludwig. Think of Ludwig.

"Don't tempt me," Erich said, with a possessive growl that sent another lightning bolt through her.

She felt as if there were a thread being pulled taut between them, and it made her desire for him more intense. She met his golden gaze and felt something sizzle through her. But she wasn't an animal, and neither was he, current appearance withstanding.

"He's my best friend, Erich. I can't turn my back on him."

"You have to trust he knows what he's doing. If we turn back around, this chance he gave us will be squandered. The fate of the continent rests on the sword inside your back." Erich bit out each syllable. Ludwig was the self-sacrificing type, and that was what terrified her, but he also wasn't the type to rush in without a plan. She had to believe they'd meet again.

They were beyond the city walls, and Erich was slowly losing altitude. Veins bulged in his neck as he fought to keep them both aloft. They were still in view of the cannons on the parapets, and they were turning them in their direction. They were going to shoot unless she did something. Liane concentrated her power into a glow, the only thing she was good at. If they knew he had her in his arms, then maybe they wouldn't shoot. Otherwise, she'd just made them a massive glowing target.

The light emanated around them, and Erich looked down at her glowing body, a crease forming between his brows, as she gestured behind them to the city watch who had signaled to stop. They'd stepped back from their weapons, seemingly afraid of catching Liane in the crossfire or sending her and Erich both crashing to the ground. The light, or the threat of immediate danger, seemed to give Erich a second wind, and he flapped his wings harder, flying higher up into the sky to hide beneath the cover of the clouds beyond the reach of any projectiles.

They flew a great distance above the clouds before Erich seemed to feel it was safe enough to dip down again. It was a clear night, and the waning moon provided ample light to illuminate the countryside. When she wasn't staring down death, it was rather breathtaking. Treetops swayed in the breeze, and in the distance, farmhouse windows glowed orange against the blue-black sky. They passed over ripening fields of yellow wheat and green rolling hills dotted with sheep and cattle. From this vantage point, she felt as if she'd been transported to another world entirely. She could have flown with Erich for an eternity through the night, her hands roaming over his rippling, scaled chest. But the further they got from the city, the more that tugging sensation grew. But, this time, it wasn't toward Erich but somewhere out there.

They were flying toward it, and she felt her chest tighten and her scar throb. The closer she got, the more she felt the sensation of water lapping over her. Like lying in a shallow stream as a child. It was the call of the magic vein; she'd felt it in the forest runes and beneath the temple. And she knew intuitively she was where she should be. Erich's strength was waning in earnest, and once more, they were losing altitude.

The pull of magic was no longer gentle. What had started as a prickle along her spine had grown to become a throbbing sensation as if the sword would cut its way out of her body. She was the sheath from which it longed to be drawn. Then Erich swooped down, gliding to a clearing amongst some trees.

Her head was spinning as they touched down, and it took a few moments to readjust from that weightless feeling flying had given her before she could unwrap her legs from around Erich and plant her feet on the ground. His hands lingered on her hips, stabilizing her. The tips of his claws lightly pressed into her. Erich's gaze was hooded as he met her eyes, and she felt a pleasant shiver rush over her body. She shouldn't want this, but she left her hand pressed against his chest and was excited by the rapid cadence of his breaths.

The memory of his tongue on her sex was enough to have her pressing her thighs together in anticipation.

He was the first to pull away, and he half turned his body from her as he clenched his fists at his sides.

"We'll wait here for the others, then decide our next move." His shoulders were tense and muscled. White opalescent scales led to his luminescent leathery wings. She reached out to stroke one of his wings, and it was smooth and soft, like fine riding leathers. He shuddered under her touch and pulled his wings tight to his body.

"Don't. If you keep going, I won't be able to control myself."

"I'm not afraid," she said and took a step toward him and placed her palm in the center of his back between his wings.

Erich spun and caught her wrist in a clawed hand. "But I am."

Her pulse jumped, but she didn't shrink away from him.

"Are you afraid of hurting me?" she guessed.

"Yes," he croaked. And she realized his hand was shaking. He let her go.

She stood back, wanting to give him space. Maybe she should be afraid, but she found this form as alluring as his full dragon form—the interplay of man and dragon, where scales faded into flesh. His face was human with white scales along his cheekbones and brow, and the wings were large enough to carry both their weights over large distances. How could she have thought something this beautiful was corruption?

"Did you hurt someone when you were like this?"

"No, this has never happened to me before." He held up his

hands, turning them over as if they were those of a stranger. And maybe they were.

"Why did it happen? Because of the moon?" she asked. She knew so little about his transformation and anything to do with creatures like him. But in the books that she'd read, it'd said those who served the Nameless were strengthened by moonlight. Dragons were said to have disappeared centuries ago. Maybe they were all living double lives like Erich.

"Part of it is the progression of my curse, and the other part is you..." He inclined his head toward her.

"Does it make you want to hurt me?"

"Not hurt you..." His eyes were heavy lidded, and Liane felt heat warming her cheeks.

"You mean... like in the garden?"

"Yes." His voice was husky.

Liane felt as if her entire body had been set ablaze. And it was taking all her self-control to not close the space between them. The thread or magic or whatever it was that was drawing them together felt pulled taut. They'd been dancing around with one another for weeks. And it was driving her mad, but it was a relief, in a way, to know it wasn't just her. Erich felt it too.

"I want you, so bad it hurts, Liane, but there's a fine line between a dragon's desire and obsession. If I give in, I may never be able to let you go."

Her stomach tightened, and she pressed her thighs together. "What if I don't want you to let me go?"

"You shouldn't want me. You should be terrified of me."

"But I want you too. Ever since that night, I can't stop thinking about you."

"The night in the garden?"

Liane's heart hammered so hard, she feared it'd beat out of her chest. She couldn't hold back anymore. She stepped closer to him and wrapped her arms around his neck.

"Before that," she said, tilting her head up to meet his golden eyes.

If the raven was right, there was light and dark in every-thing. Including her. Including Erich. Whatever magic dwelled in them seemed to fit together like puzzle pieces. She wanted to spend forever learning about him, and magic, and how it all fit into the goddess', and the ancients', plans.

Liane trailed a finger over his chest, pulling back the tattered remains of his shirt to circle his pectoral before closing in around his nipple. He shivered under her touch but didn't move to stop her. Liane leaned forward and licked his clavicle. His body trembled as if it were taking all his restraint not to move.

"You wouldn't hurt me—I know it," she said as she kissed a trail down his chest, her hands slowly roving down to his hips before hooking in the front of his pants. The pants were torn, exposing his thighs. She wanted to lick every inch of him in the way he'd done for her.

"I could." Erich's chest heaved.

She slid her hand down, inching her way toward his shaft, as he stared at her, eyes blazing. When she grasped hold of him, he was hard, twitching. She stroked it up and down a few times as she nibbled at his throat, gently grazing his scaled flesh with her teeth. He was nothing like any lover she'd had before. Most men would have crumbled by now, but she admired his restraint, and she'd tease him as long as he could last.

After one last tug, she let go, and she heard him moan in disappointment. Then she undid the last shreds of his pants and sank down onto her knees in front of him. His cock stood at attention before her.

"Liane." He said her name in the release of a ragged breath.

"I want to return the favor. May I?" she asked, looking up at him through her lashes.

"Please. Or I might explode."

She wrapped her hand tightly around his member and then licked him from base to tip, swirling her tongue at the end before taking him fully into her mouth. He bucked against her, hands balled into fists at his sides, as she sucked. Until she took one of his free hands and guided it to the back of her neck. His hand tangled in her hair gently, as if he feared putting too much pressure on her. She licked around the tip of his throbbing shaft, lapping up his dew. Seeing him hold on to this much control was a surprising turn-on. Feeling him tremble, his thigh muscles taut as if he were using all his restraint to keep from spilling his seed into her mouth.

But then he touched a clawed hand to her cheek. His scales brushing her soft skin sent sparks along her neck.

"Not yet. I need to be buried inside you when I finish."

He grasped her nape as he sank down to kneel before her, then he kissed her. His fangs pressed against her lips, and the grip on her neck held her close, as if to prevent her from escaping. His kiss was fierce and primal, fangs scraping her lip, as he gently bit and sucked, leaving her aching for more. She pressed her breasts against him, dying for friction, to remove the layers of fabric between them, but also, not wanting to rush things either.

Her hands explored his shoulders and his back, and she gently scratched downward as he put his hand on her waist, pressing her up against his hard length and letting her grind her sex against him with only a thin layer of cloth between them.

He kissed down her jawline, then her neck, raising goose-flesh along her body, as he pulled at her stays. He slowly stripped each layer, kissing her exposed skin—her shoulder, the top of her breasts. He swirled his tongue around her nipples one by one, before he lightly nipped at each of them, his fangs grazing against the taut peaks until she was grinding against him.

She rode him, feeling the buildup of pressure growing, growing, and she gasped with pleasure. Then he grasped each of her breasts in his hands, pinching her nipples between his fingers as she ground against him, her head thrown back in ecstasy.

Erich's hands roved down over her sides, over her skirts, then he hitched them up, tearing the fabric of her undergarments with a claw. With his knuckle, he pressed against her bundle of nerves until she was slick.

"Are you ready? I need to be inside you," he growled against her neck.

"Yes," she gasped.

Erich flipped her over onto all fours, pushed up her skirts, and parted her legs with his. He cupped her exposed ass, sending a shiver over her as she arched backward into him, pressing his shaft against her opening.

"I've been dreaming of this," he growled as he thrust into her, filling her, stretching her. They stayed like that a moment, breathing heavily.

Their first time had been hurried; this time, she wanted to experience him. To enjoy the touch of his skin as he pressed the pad of his thumb against the knot of nerves at the apex of her sex. He started to move slowly at first, letting her feel each inch of him slide in and out, then he thrust inward, hard. Gradually building momentum, and he'd do it again. She met him thrust for thrust, back arching, pressing her rear against his abdomen, feeling her climax building with each steady movement of his body until she was nearly ready to explode.

"I'm afraid if we go further, I'll never be able to let you go." He gasped, falling over her with his breath hot against her neck as he rammed his cock into her over and over.

"You can't stop," she gasped.

She would go mad if she didn't reach her release right this moment with him.

She arched her back as he stroked against her inner walls, her hands curled into the soft earth as her body throbbed around him. Her climax struck her suddenly, and she was trembling, body pulsing, crying out his name, the goddess', and a thousand other expletives.

Erich reached his climax moments after her, pulling out to spill onto the grass beside them. They both collapsed onto the ground next to one another, panting for breath.

Their limbs tangled together as he enclosed her in his embrace. She felt as if they'd always been meant to be this way. She'd never wanted to open up to someone or seen herself with anyone for the long-term, not when she'd been convinced they'd go on to hurt her. But Erich had come back, and he'd saved her. And, for the first time, she thought that maybe she'd found her forever.

29

Erich had felt the dragon's power as he climaxed. For now, its desires were satisfied. But the specter of its obsession still lingered at the back of his mind. When would pleasure turn to pain, when would devotion turn to destruction? For her sake, he never should have slept with her, but he couldn't say he regretted it. In fact, he relished the feeling of her body curled against his, and he took assurance in the steady rhythm of her heartbeat as she traced her fingers over the hairs on his chest.

"Your scales faded," she remarked.

"You're not repulsed by them?" he asked.

"I find them fascinating." She sighed, nuzzling closer to him.

Their legs were tangled up in one another, and she hooked her leg around him to half straddle his leg.

"Though I like you both in flesh and with claws." She brushed a hand against his stubbled chin.

Erich looked away from her. A monster like him didn't deserve her, and even if she were understanding, his time was limited. He couldn't give Liane forever, and wasn't it crueler to string her along for whatever weeks and months he had left, only to abandon her when he became a dragon entirely?

"Something wrong?" she asked.

This was the moment he should confess it all. End things before she got so entangled with him that she couldn't get away, but like the monster he was, he couldn't say the words out loud.

"Nothing. I was just thinking about how beautiful you look in the moonlight."

The silvery glow illuminated the lighter strands of her auburn hair that fell across her face. She giggled and pushed her hair behind her ears. Erich cupped her face, wanting to memorize her in this moment. If any part of him remained human when he became a dragon, he'd hold on to her.

Liane had a destiny to uphold, and he had a hard-to-contain monster inside him. Because once she'd drawn the sword and was free of the church, his role in her story would be over. But for tonight, until the sun rose, he wanted to pretend that things could be different before their interlude ended. She'd hate him for walking away again. Perhaps even curse his name. But eventually the novelty of him would wear off, and she'd find true love. The thought made his chest ache, but like he'd told her, he'd do anything to protect her. Even if it meant keeping her from him.

She lay her head back down on his chest, and they lay in the nest of tall grass they'd flattened with their copulation and stared up at the ancient oak tree above them. The night stretched on for a little while longer as they spoke of nothing of import. The words didn't matter; it was the magic of that moment, where they were both suspended in time. He was nearly dozing off when he heard a twig snap, and he sat upright.

Liane sat up as well and tugged her clothes back on. Most of his clothes were torn by the transformation, but shreds of his pants remained, and he covered himself as best he could, before drawing his weapon.

A couple of shadowy figures approached. They carried no lamps, which meant they were either guards doing a sneak attack or Fritz had found them.

When the figures got closer and Erich could make out their features in the moonlight, he lowered his weapon. Fritz and the oracle they'd rescued from the dungeon looked unharmed, and Fritz had a bundle under one arm.

"We would have been here sooner, but she insisted I find clothes for you," Fritz said. He cleared his throat as he thrust the clothes toward Erich and looked away from Erich's mostly naked body.

The oracle's glassy eyes scanned both him and Liane up and down, and he felt compelled to cover up Liane, even though he was less clothed than her.

"Believe me, if you're uncomfortable around a bit of exposed flesh, you wouldn't have wanted to be here when they were rutting like a couple of deer during mating season," the oracle said.

Liane yelped in surprise.

Erich had seen many frauds in his search for a cure, but his gut told him this woman was the real deal. He hadn't asked Leonhard why she was in the dungeon, but now he was curious.

"What about Ludwig or Luzie? Have you seen either of them?" she asked.

"I haven't seen anyone in many years, not in the flesh anyway," the oracle said with a bemused cackle.

Fritz shook his head. "We haven't seen them. But I'm sure they'll join us soon. Luzie was meant to take the carriage and flee to Artria if we didn't get to her in time."

Liane didn't look convinced. "And Ludwig?"

Erich grabbed her hand. "He'll come. Don't worry."

And she leaned against him.

"What now? Should we wait to see if Luzie and Ludwig come to find us?" Liane asked. "I don't want to leave Basilia without them."

She relaxed beneath Erich's touch, and guilt ate at his stomach. He'd fed her comforting lies to get her away from the temple, but he was skeptical of Ludwig's chances of survival. If Luzie were smart, she'd make a run for it. All that mattered to him was getting Liane to safety, and as long as she was within Neolyra's borders, he feared the church would keep pursuing her.

His uncle's offer of a boat to Sundland came to mind. But that was a ludicrous thought. There were other ways of escape.

Erich looked around at their surroundings. They were standing under a canopy of trees in a near-empty field filled with tall grasses, but as he looked closer, he saw remnants of the stone structures—a single column overgrown with vines, half-crumbled walls, and overgrown cobbled streets. Now that he wasn't thinking with his cock, he sensed the magic in the air and the half-faded runes carved into the stone.

"The old city," the oracle said.

"How do you know?" Erich asked.

"I wasn't always blind. I used to come here often. The magic called to me..."

"Then you're familiar with this place and the veins of magic?" Liane asked.

"Yes, it is one of the few uncorrupted veins of magic left. Which is why the church has tried so hard to keep people away," the oracle said.

"I think this is where the raven wanted me to come," Liane

said, staring off into the distance. Her gaze had that dreamy, farseeing quality he'd seen on Fritz's face before.

"You should have drawn the sword long ago," the oracle said.

"I've been trying."

The oracle shook her head. "When you were summoned during your thirteenth year. It should have been drawn out then."

"But that was when it fused with my back."

The oracle shook her head again, as if she were feeling impatient. "That's what the Avatheos thinks. You were born with the power within you. It comes from the blood. Like all magic, it is intrinsic to who we are. And why the Church of Sol's desire to take control of it is so dangerous. I tried to change the church from within, but in the end, that wasn't my role."

Liane's gaze sharpened as she looked the woman up and down. "And who are you?"

Erich was wondering the same. Leonhard had asked him to free her, but had left out instructions on what to do with her after. Was Leonhard going to come find them here in the wilderness?

The old woman folded her hands in front of her and glared at Liane for a moment. "The unfortunate soul whom the goddesses chose as their mouthpiece. I'm one of the last priestesses of the old religions. Though I didn't do much in my short time on this continent, I hope it's enough to return things to the way they were."

"I thought you were an oracle," Erich remarked. But his neck prickled as he sensed the tmagic in her. He'd heard whispers of the old religion. Most of what remained of it was worn-down ruins in villages, too small for the Church of Sol to care about. Or too remote to risk the priests to fully convert the people to the church's worship.

"I was one of the Church of Sol's chosen few. That inner circle privy to the machinations of the church. I thought we had a holy destiny. Until I saw a vision that led me to this place. I tried to undo the work the Avatheos did, in whatever way I could, until he discovered my plots and had me locked in a cell. I realized my calling too late, but it's not too late for you." She turned to Erich, and it felt as if her gaze might pierce him. "Every sword needs a shield."

He felt Fritz's and Liane's stare on him, and all of their expectations, but he couldn't be that for her. A shield was meant to protect, and he was capable of only harm.

"For her to have a shield, she needs to draw the sword first. Have your visions told you how she might do that?" Erich asked to draw attention away from himself.

The old woman stared at Erich as if she saw through all his fears and hesitations. And then she looked away. "Liane already knows. She can feel it calling to her."

They all turned toward Liane. She had her arms wrapped around her torso, as if she'd gone cold, but it was a warm night.

"I must enter the water of the vein. It's close to here. I can feel it."

"And swarming with Midnight Guards, unfortunately," the oracle said.

"You wouldn't happen to know how we could get close enough for Liane to enter, would you?" Erich asked the oracle.

"That's for you to figure out, shield. I'm just here to provide sage insights and spiritual wisdom," she said with a wry smile.

Three faces were staring back at him. He knew what must be done, though he wished he had Ludwig as backup still. Time was of the essence, and they couldn't wait to see if he'd made it out alive. They needed the cover of night to make this plan work.

"First, I'll do some reconnaissance, see what we're up against, and make a plan from there."

"Couldn't you fly me there?" Liane asked.

Erich shook his head. "Even if I had full control over the change, I doubt I'd have the strength. One transformation depletes most of my strength."

She nodded thoughtfully, then turned to Fritz. "How did you get here so fast?" Liane asked Fritz and the oracle.

"It was the elf." The oracle nodded toward him. "He took me through some dark doorway, and all of a sudden, we were here."

"Could you do it again, bring me close to the water's edge?" she asked, her gaze suddenly intensely upon Fritz.

Fritz was never flustered, but he looked flustered in that moment, stammering his reply. "I'm afraid I can't provide much help. The shadow travel drains me, I won't be able to use it for a while."

Erich had figured as much. He himself felt drained from his partial dragon transformation. The more he used the power, the more he felt limp and weak afterward.

"Fritz and I will search for a path together while you and the oracle wait for the others," Erich said.

Liane's eyebrows rose to her hairline as if she were considering protesting.

"It's for your safety," Erich assured her before she could voice any complaints.

"Besides, I have sage wisdom to impart, remember?" the oracle said.

Liane seemed assuaged, and they parted ways. It hurt him to walk away from her; the dragon, who'd been quiet, grew restless with every step he took. But this was a feeling he'd have to learn to live with. While she'd forget him, he knew he'd never forget her. He and Fritz walked along together in silence, and

Fritz, who normally had an easygoing nature, seemed on edge. His head was on a swivel as he surveyed their surroundings.

He spotted lanterns of their encampment off in the distance and tracks in the grass where they'd patrolled. They crouched down in the bushes to wait for a patrol to come by. They'd need to ambush them to clear a way to the pool, and even after that, time wouldn't be on their side. Erich sat poised, waiting for the sound of horse hooves.

"You flew, huh?" Fritz looked at him sidelong. "You're embracing your dragon more. That's good."

A flush burned across Erich's face. He wasn't sure how good that was, considering how close he'd come to losing control. He'd killed many people in the temple, and had he not gotten control when he did, he might have hurt Liane too.

He grunted to end the conversation there.

They waited a few moments longer, until he heard the soft patter of horse hooves. A single guard trotted by holding up a lantern to the shadows. He was young, perhaps a recruit, not expecting something to be lingering in the shadows. Erich lunged for him and pulled him from his horse. The animal nearly bolted, but Fritz grabbed its reins as Erich knocked the guard unconscious before tying him and his horse to the tree. He had enough blood on his hands, and without Liane's life in imminent danger, he didn't feel compelled to kill again.

"Liane doesn't seem to mind the dragon part of you either," Fritz said, picking up the thread of their conversation, as they made their way back to Liane and the oracle.

"Is there a point to this?" Erich asked.

"Mostly a distraction. I've had a bad feeling since we left the temple. Like a dark shroud is gathering, though I cannot see where it comes from."

Erich didn't like the sound of that. But without a concrete threat to prepare for, he decided to push forward. "Who knows?

We just need to focus on getting Liane into the water and the sword out of her back, and once we're out of Neolyra, we can go our separate ways."

Fritz stopped short. "What are you talking about?"

Erich turned to him. "My role is finished. I helped you get her out of the temple. The oracle will guide her through the transformation, or whatever would happen in the water. What else is there for me to do?"

"Getting her and the sword free of the temple is just the beginning. You have a destiny to fulfill to protect her. Didn't you hear the oracle? She called you her shield."

Erich faced him. "She isn't safe with me, Fritz. If anything, I'm putting her in danger. I'm losing to the curse; I was a dragon for three days straight, and now it comes out whenever it likes. Once this is done, it's better if I go."

"What do you mean 'go'?" Liane's voice sliced through him. Erich froze; he hadn't heard her approach, but now he felt as if the air had been taken from his lungs. This wasn't how he wanted her to find out. Not right before she was meant to step into the water.

Erich turned to see Liane standing beside the oracle. They must have heard him and Fritz coming, and he'd just been too absorbed to notice.

Erich fumbled to find the right words. He'd hoped to address this more tactfully. But it seemed the universe wanted to make a fool of him instead. Maybe it was better to just get it over with.

"Liane, you're destined for great things. I'm just a monster. I can't be your shield. I'll only hurt you," Erich said.

"So, you've fucked me and you're running away again? I shouldn't be surprised. This is what you do, isn't it?" she asked, hands planted on her hips.

He had no rebuttal because it was true. He kept everyone at

arm's length—Liane, Fritz, his uncle. No one he got close to was safe. And he did it for them, but Liane didn't understand that.

"You could have been honest with me. We didn't make any promises to one another. Instead, you were going to slink away like a bandit in the night. And that's what hurts most. But I should have expected that from you." She shook her head before stomping off.

He could only watch her walk away and feel like an absolute fool for it. But it was for the best, he told himself. She was better off without him.

30

Liane didn't have long-term romantic relationships for a reason, and this was it. Honestly, it was a relief to end things before they got complicated. She'd be living on the run, fighting the forces of evil. When would she have time for canoodling and hot, steamy sex? She and Erich had had their fun; she'd scratched that itch, and now it was time to move on. It was fine. She was glad, even. She'd never asked him to stay forever. They'd had a good time, a couple of good times, and that was all she'd wanted. Right? Sure, Erich had led her to believe he might want more from her, but there'd been plenty of other men who'd done the same. Besides, there were more important things to worry about. Like the fact that Ludwig still hadn't reached them and Luzie was nowhere to be seen, or how she needed to get a literal sword out of her back. What was some petty fling compared to the fact that she was the goddess' chosen, who had some undefined destiny to save the continent from darkness and destruction? Those were real problems.

She exhaled out of her nose and tried to untangle the snarled knot of emotions that tightened in her chest. The oracle had given her a brief rundown of what she should expect to face in the pool. The vein was a source of pure magic; this one was outside the control of the church. They'd been attempting to tame it for decades, but this pool was stubbornly untamable. A lot like Liane.

"It's been waiting for you," the oracle had said. "We all have our parts to play. I've done my best to keep this place wild, feeding it what little untamed magic I could, but my time is running out. It's time you claimed the power and completed the transformation."

She'd tried to conform to the church's rules and structures, but it'd never quite fit, like a mismatched shoe. Then she'd met the oracle, and even though she'd just met her, there was something comforting and familiar about her, like a wise grandmother.

A lot of what the oracle had told her mirrored what the Avatheos had told her. She'd step into the water and be imbued by pure magic. What happened within the water was where things differed.

"It won't be easy by any means," she had said to her. "Your body has grown accustomed to the sword within its flesh and won't give it up easily. You'll have to fight to take control. But the alternative is succumbing to it and the world losing that power forever."

Compared to the Avatheos' version of events, which had sounded like being wrapped in a warm blanket, the oracle's ritual seemed like a battle. They hadn't even reached the pool, and Liane was already bone-tired. And this was just the beginning; drawing the sword was the first step. She didn't want to think about what happened next.

She returned to Erich and Fritz, who were standing over the tied-up patrolman. The man was unconscious, and his horse was busying itself grazing on the long green grass. In the distance, guards' lanterns glowed, and a watchtower loomed over the horizon. She bet they could see all the ruins from there, those last crumbling remnants of a lost civilization. People whose day-to-day had been so intertwined with magic that pools of magic had been at the town center like a village well. She wondered what the veins had meant to them for them to build their cities and temples around them.

There wasn't much time to wonder as they heard horse hooves trotting in their direction.

"Hail!" a guard shouted.

They sank into the bushes.

"Hail, Armin. Answer if you can hear me," the voice called.

Liane's gaze slid to the man, who was unconscious no longer. His eyes were wide open and staring right at her. He opened his mouth to answer the call, and she lunged forward to cover his mouth.

Not before he got out a half grunt, "He—"

"Did you hear something?" a voice asked.

Erich knocked the guard over the head, rendering him unconscious once more, but the damage had been done. The glowing lanterns were drawing closer. They'd all get caught in a battle between guards on horseback. Liane didn't have a single weapon on her, and not a chance of standing up to the guards. She couldn't imagine small and slender Fritz the elf was much of a fighter, and she doubted the oracle was one for hand-to-hand combat either. Which meant they were greatly outnumbered. Erich had a grim expression on his face as he looked away from her and toward Fritz.

"They must have increased their patrol numbers," Erich said.

"What will we do? We're overpowered," Fritz replied, rubbing his face. There were dark circles under his eyes.

"We just need to keep them away from the pool long enough for her to enter," the oracle said.

They all looked at her. Had she seen this in a vision? Why not warn them so they could have come better prepared? But then again, that wasn't how visions worked. Any seeing might branch off in a thousand different directions.

"She's right; the plan remains," Erich said. There was a disturbing finality to his tone. As if he were resigned to death. Liane wanted to reach out and comfort him, but held back. He'd drawn the line on their relationship. She wasn't going to cross it now.

They retreated a few steps and strategized a plan.

"We'll lure them away from the ruins and send them on a chase. The longer we can keep them away, the more time Liane can use to get in and get out. Fritz, can you use any of your magic at all?"

"Yes, enough for illusions," he said, gesturing toward his face and rounded ears. She hadn't even considered he was maintaining a facade. Was that for her comfort? She'd never been close to elves. Three months ago, she wouldn't have even considered it. But in her few brief interactions with Fritz, she'd realized he was nothing like the elves she'd been warned about her entire life.

"Can you turn into Liane? If they think they see her, then maybe we can lead them away."

Fritz's face turned bright crimson. "I don't know if that's appropriate."

"I don't mind," Liane said.

He cleared his throat. "But still. It's frowned upon to take the visage of another person..."

"We need them to chase after me and Liane. I need you to do this," Erich emphasized as he met Fritz's gaze.

Fritz wouldn't look back at Liane as he wrestled with his own ethics. She didn't want him to break his rules of magic, but they were left with little choice.

She assured him once again, "Make yourself as close to me, without copying me exactly. It's dark and you'll be on the move."

Fritz looked up at her, gratitude in his gaze. "I like the way you think."

He placed his hand over his face, and like a sculptor working with clay, he reformed his features, softening his cheekbones, rounding his face. A more delicate nose and chin, fuller lips, and longer lashes. It was a surreal experience watching him change from a dark-haired elf to an auburn-haired woman, who shared a striking resemblance to her, though not identical. It was uncanny and made Liane feel a bit strange. It explained why the elves frowned upon exact copying.

"We'll draw them away, and you two run toward the vein," Erich said.

He turned to walk away, prepared to thrust himself into danger once again, for her sake. And this time, he might not make it back.

She could have let him go without a word, but even as angry as she was, she didn't want him to die.

"Take care," Liane said.

His gaze lingered on her for a moment. "I will make sure you escape unharmed. No matter what."

His words sent a shiver down her spine. "I'll hold you to that promise."

They stared at one another for a few beats, her heart in her throat. She hated herself for wanting more from him, but knew she had to let him go.

"Keep her safe," he said to the oracle.

"I will," the oracle replied.

And that was it. He turned and rushed toward the oncoming guards. The guards saw them and sounded the alarm before turning to chase after Erich and Fritz across a nearby field, leaving her behind with a sinking feeling and a dangerous destiny ahead of her.

The oracle placed a gentle hand on her shoulder. "Come. We should be ready."

They waited in the bushes as Erich and Fritz, masquerading as her, drew away the guards, then darted out from the undergrowth and into the crumbled ruins beyond.

They took a serpentine route through the ancient city, stepping carefully over vine-covered, crumbling walls and moss-covered cobbled streets, which had been almost entirely consumed by the encroaching forest. Liane felt the pool before they reached it. It seemed to call out to her, drawing her toward its center and making the scar on her back throb.

Then she got her first glimpse of it, filled to the stone brim with a shimmering void, which seemed to pulse through her, the same way that the other pool had called out to her. Liane stared at it as if mesmerized. Her eyes filled with stars.

"Careful stepping in. It's quite the drop," the oracle said.

"What if I'm not strong enough?" Liane asked, feeling less certain than ever before.

"You've got iron in your spine. Literally." The oracle cackled at her joke. "You were chosen for a reason. Don't doubt yourself now."

Liane felt the heat of the sword through her skin. She'd lived so long with the pain and the fevers—things she'd thought made her a burden, and undesirable. Instead, they were marks of her divine purpose. She could do this, because she was meant for it.

"I'm ready," Liane said.

"Then step into the water and prove it." The oracle gestured toward the pool.

Liane took that leap of faith and felt the water lap over her feet, and then she fell. Not the slow sink of water, but a free fall similar to what she'd experienced when she'd briefly slipped from Erich's grasp while they flew. She was tumbling through an endless void, stars reeling around her, zooming past her like comets. Panic bubbled up in her throat, and she tried to tamp down her fear, even as the burning in her back, which had started out as an itch, grew more and more intense.

She heard beating wings, and it felt as if something was clawing at her throat, forcing her mouth open. She was drowning. Water filled her lungs and made her choke. She kicked her legs, attempting to rise back up to the surface, but no matter how hard she kicked or flailed, she made no progress. There was no light from the surface. She was merely suspended in time, falling endlessly, while water poured into her mouth, but she never drowned.

Would she die here? Would the gods find her unworthy after all and leave her in this falling void?

No. The oracle had told her to fight. She had to resist the urge to panic. And though it challenged every screaming instinct inside her, she let go of her fear and breathed. There was no water rushing into her mouth. She wasn't drowning. She wasn't falling. She was suspended in a place, outside of time, and immersed in pure magic. She realized she'd been here before. The memories were hazy, but this was the place where the sword had first fused with her back.

Suddenly, she felt as if her feet were on solid ground, or at least as close to solid ground as she was going to get. Though the realm in which she found herself took shape and form, her mind knew it was all for her benefit. The magic was not material but merely thought. It was a disconcerting feeling. To be suspended in place—there, but not really.

"You came back," a voice said from within the void.

She tried to turn to see who was speaking. They were both young and old, genderless and ancient. Made of stars and sunlight, veiled as the person she'd mistaken for the Nameless Goddess.

"I have," she croaked.

"Then draw the sword."

"I can't. It's inside me. Aren't you going to show me how?"

"You do not need instructions. The power has been within you all this time."

"I don't know how. I've tried already. It's trapped within me."

"Draw it," the voice called.

Her insides churned, and she feared what would happen if she failed again. What if she was as powerless, useless, and terrified as she feared? She was no one's savior. She was that sick little girl bound to a bed, dreaming of being a hero. But she couldn't be one. No matter who she tried to pretend to be. How could she ever be considered worthy?

"Draw it now. The fate of the continent and the world rests upon your shoulders. Destruction will only continue to spread unless the sword returns to the world."

"And then what? What do you want me to do?"

"Return to the source of magic; join the two blades. End the rift."

"I don't understand."

"You will. Draw the sword."

The riddles were maddening, but they struck her with a sudden resolve. Liane reached to her back, which burned against her hand, flaming hot as if she would ignite. She clawed at her flesh, until she bled. The pain was unimaginable. It burned and it hurt, and tears were rolling down her face. But she had to do it. For Erich. For everyone she loved.

Then she felt a bulge beneath her skin pushing against her flesh, before it burst from her—a hilt. She pulled on it, and every second it was coming from her felt as if it would last an eternity, as if it were tearing her apart from the inside. Despite the pain, she kept pulling, even as the pain grew so intense the edges of her vision blurred, and her knees buckled, and she collapsed onto the ground.

All at once, it came free, and the pressure on her back lessened, but the weight of the blade in her hands was immense. She held the shining blade. It was so bright it might blind her. It was there in the flesh, and she felt it pulse in her grip, as if it were always meant to be there, and then she was flying upward, back toward the light.

31

Liane emerged from the water, the Golden Blade gripped tightly in her hand. It wasn't metal or bone or anything of the world, but seemed to be crafted of pure light given form. The magic pulsed against her palm, but the sword was also light and incorporeal, as if her fingers might pass through it, and it would disappear like mist. The light it cast illuminated her surroundings and the oracle's tearful expression. Liane's body felt lighter. She hadn't realized how much the pain had weighed down on her, and now the area between her shoulder blades was empty, as if a great weight had been lifted from it.

It had felt like an eternity had passed in the water, but on the surface, it was still night. The moon had barely moved from its position in the sky, and in the distance, she heard guards shouting to one another in their pursuit of Erich and Fritz. She had to go help them. Then she took a step over the lip of the pool, and her knees buckled beneath her, and she tilted forward. The oracle caught her before her face met the earth, and Liane felt guilty as she leaned against her frail frame.

The oracle guided her to sit on the ground as her vision swam. The weightless feeling was gone, and in its place, she felt a pressure building behind her eyes and her skin burning with a coming fever and the accompanying fatigue. Liane looked down at her trembling hands.

"I don't understand. I drew the sword. Why do I still feel sick?"

"You've looked into eternity, and you drew a sword forged for a goddess out of your flesh. Anyone would be feeling a bit peaky after that."

"But it was the sword that was making me sick, wasn't it?"

The oracle didn't answer and pressed a skin of wine into Liane's free hand and urged her to drink. She had no idea where she'd gotten it and didn't bother asking. She drank deeply. Her throat burned, and she felt as if she were suddenly ravenous. And as soon as the thought crossed her mind, the oracle handed her a hunk of very stale bread and old cheese wrapped in wax.

"Before they caught me, I stored some provisions. I knew you'd need it when you emerged. Magic takes much from us, but a full stomach can restore what was depleted faster. You'll learn the balance of it in time."

"What—" Liane tried to question her.

"Eat, eat," she said.

The bread was hard to chew, and the cheese was equally as tough. Liane needed the wine to soften it enough to bite through it and swallow. But she devoured it all in greedy mouthfuls, grateful for each morsel as it lessened the pressure building in her skull. Though she still felt the flush on her skin, it wasn't a full-blown fever.

"You can let go of the sword. It's not going anywhere now that you've drawn it out," the oracle said.

Liane maintained her death grip upon the hilt as she ate

and drank, which admittedly made it infinitely more cumbersome.

"You're safe. We have some talking to do first of all." The oracle patted her hand.

Slowly, Liane uncurled her fingers from around the hilt, and despite her fears, it didn't disappear when she let go. If anything, it became more corporeal, more like a real sword. On top of the pommel was a blazing sun; the leathers on the hilt were well-oiled, and the hilt gilded. But when it was out of her hands, it didn't glow. Yet she felt the magic inside it calling out to her.

Her back no longer ached, but the rest of her body did—as if the pain was no longer centralized but everywhere. She wanted to fight, but she wasn't even sure she could properly stand. She finished off her bread, cheese, and wine, then turned to the oracle.

"Why do I feel so weak?"

The oracle clucked her tongue. "Magic has a cost. Surely you learned as much in the temple? A pure-white goat to grant visions, carved bones to guide a spirit safely behind the veil. If an exchange cannot be made, the magic takes the price from the wielder's flesh."

Liane nodded. It had never been explained to her before, and she assumed that was intentional on the Avatheos' part. "You've fought a great battle today to take possession of the sword. You had to break the seal that fused it with your body and break past the chains that kept you tethered to who you were before. Add to that you are untrained... It will take time before using the sword doesn't deplete you completely, but there will never be a day when magic doesn't drain you. It is the double-edged sword all magic users must bear. If you'll pardon my pun."

Liane had hoped removing the sword would cure her. All

she'd longed for was a life free of pain and suffering. But with the weight of the world on her shoulders, she wasn't going to get that. And now that it was out, she still had to master its use? The goddess was cruel for this.

"I thought I was the chosen one," she grumbled.

"And the goddess doesn't make the path to greatness easy. If she did, then everyone would do it. You've got a long and windy road before you. But I think you've got the right person to guide you along that path." She looked past Liane, and Liane followed her gaze to see Erich striding over.

There was a cut taken out of his sleeve and a smear of blood, which may or may not be his own, on his cheek. Despite her exhaustion, she tried to stand again but swooned on her feet instead. He rushed forward to catch her. The feeling of his strong arms around her made her knees want to buckle for a different reason. And she fell against his chest, soothed by the steady beating of his heart. She'd gone into the water angry but stepped out with greater clarity. He was right; she had a destiny before her, one that she didn't even fully comprehend, and to ask him to tie his life to hers was unfair.

She pulled away from him to save her pride, though he had enough decency to look ashamed.

"Fritz is leading the Midnight Guards away, but his illusion won't last forever. We should get you out of this place before they realize he's a fake."

"Where do we go from here?" Liane asked.

The Avatheos had seen the rise of a dark army led by her mother. Should she head back to Artria and warn her? Try to stop it somehow?

"The dead will rise, led by the golden empress, and darkness will stretch far across the land. Only together can you defeat it," the oracle said, her voice ringing with prophecy.

"I don't understand why my mother would do such a thing," Liane said.

"Not your mother—your sister, Aristea," the oracle said, and her words sent a shiver down Liane's spine.

"Aristea?" She shook her head. "You must be mistaken; she's a good person. She wouldn't raise an army of the undead." The very thought was ludicrous.

"All things must be in balance; your destiny was written in your blood, from before your conception, when your mother first unsealed the sword. Magic must be healed, and this is the way it will be done."

"There must be a way to prevent this. I can't go to war against my sister!" Liane protested.

"I cannot tell you anything with certainty. The path ahead diverges, and there is darkness beyond my vision of this place. What I know is you both must go north, and Erich will be your shield."

Liane took a few steps toward the oracle, but her legs were too weak to carry her, and she stumbled over her own feet, colliding with Erich once more.

She was already mortified by her own weakness, but what was worse, Erich scooped her up into his arms.

"If the oracle says we go north, then I suggest we do that. You won't be safe in Neolyra. The church won't stop chasing you."

The oracle handed Liane the sword, which she laid across her lap. When it came in contact with her, it glowed, acting like a beacon to anyone nearby to spot them, and she had to put fabric between her and it to prevent it from giving them away.

"Prophecy is never straightforward, but many fragments of shattered pottery. You can put the pieces together and still not see the original vase. Trust the Divine Twin's wisdom, and you will find the way it must be done." The oracle looked at them both.

Liane felt a premonition prickle down her spine at the oracle's words. And Liane turned her gaze to Erich. She wouldn't ask him to stay. But if he chose her, she knew she'd feel more confident with him beside her.

"Let's get out of enemy territory before we start untangling ancient mysteries," Erich grumbled.

He was right; there wasn't time to discuss it then. An alarm bell rang, and guards shouted nearby. They needed to escape the ruins.

They retraced their steps and reached the perimeter unseen. Erich carried her the whole way, showing no signs of strain or fatigue, though she knew he must be exhausted after his transformation. She was impressed by his ability to run and carry her despite it. As equally impressed as she was with the oracle keeping pace with them.

They arrived at the original rendezvous location. The shouts had died down, and they waited with bated breath for Fritz to rejoin them. There was still no sign of Ludwig and Luzie, and Liane would soon be faced with the decision to either wait for them, or leave them behind. The thought made her stomach churn. She'd never been without one of them by her side.

But the night was fading into dawn, and they'd be exposed if they tried to escape by daylight.

Nearby, brush rustled, and Erich set Liane down so she could lean on the oracle as he drew a dagger from his waistband and approached the interloper.

A figure stumbled out. It took a moment for her to recognize the woman in the dark, with her face splattered in mud and her dress torn, but it was Luzie, her face streaked with tears as she rushed toward them. Liane pushed past Erich to embrace her. Luzie fell into Liane's arms, sobbing and muttering something unintelligible against Liane's shoulder. As relieved as she was to see her friend alive, Luzie finding them alone and without Ludwig made her blood run cold. Ludwig hadn't made it out.

"Luzie, what's wrong? Where's Ludwig?" Liane asked.

"Liane, you have to—"

And then her words were cut off by an arrow whizzing past. It went toward Erich, and he pivoted to avoid it a second too late, and a line of blood dripped down his cheek. The wound didn't last, as it healed over as soon as it appeared. Someone shot a second arrow, and Erich launched himself at Liane and Luzie, forcing them to hit the ground. It sailed over them and through the oracle's throat. She didn't seem surprised, and her expression was serene as she collapsed onto the ground.

Liane cried out something unintelligible.

Luzie grabbed Liane's arm. "Liane. Run. They forced me to bring them to you. They told me they had Ludwig and if I didn't comply, they'd kill him." Luzie sobbed.

Erich yanked them both to their feet, and they ran, but a wall of mounted Midnight Guards blocked their escape. They couldn't run, but that didn't mean they couldn't fight. The sword had come to her for a reason. The oracle had told her as much. Even though she was untrained, Liane knew she had to face them. They wouldn't hurt her, because the Avatheos wanted her back. Liane stepped in front of her friends, brandishing her sword. Its power blazed against her palm, flickering like a flame.

"Stand back," Liane shouted.

They pulled back on the reins of their horses, hesitating for a moment. A few made the sign of the star against their brows.

"It is the real avatar. Capture her!" the captain shouted, and the guards rushed her.

Erich pushed Liane behind him, claws out as he slashed at the flank of the nearest guard's horse. It reared back, throwing the guard from the saddle. Then another came up behind them, swinging to take Erich's head. He ducked under the sweep of their blade, and then he swiped at them, missing by an inch as they rode past.

Another guard was racing toward Liane, hand out to grab her. She raised her sword with shaking arms, and he looped away from her, before circling back, black sword drawn. Their swords crossed, and the blow of his strike flung Liane backward.

Erich was surrounded by four mounted guards, and they'd tossed a net over him. He threw his head back and roared, struggling to free himself from the net. Then they dismounted, and while one held him down, another pressed a stone against Erich. She tried to get up, but her body refused to listen. She felt as weak as a newborn and couldn't have raised her sword from the ground if she wanted to. All she could do was watch as two guards grabbed hold of Luzie, forcing her and Erich to their knees in front of Liane. She grasped onto the hilt of her sword, mustering the courage to fight, even as her vision swam. She climbed to her feet, swaying. Then they grabbed her, pinning her hands behind her back.

She tried to fight against them, but it was like dragging her limbs through mud.

"Come with us quietly, your divinity, and we'll spare your maid."

Luzie bowed her head, tears streaming down her face, while Erich thrashed against them, caught somewhere between man and wild beast. Then one of the guards kneed him in the back and ground his face into the dirt.

"Leave them both," Liane shouted. "I'll work with you, but only if you spare them."

The guard with a knee in Erich's back pressed the tip of his blade against the back of his neck. The man behind Luzie had a dagger to her throat.

"Choose one," the guard said.

"Liane, if I am your shield, let them break me to protect you," Erich snarled.

She couldn't possibly choose. Even if he wanted to part ways, she couldn't have his death on her hands. She lowered her weapon and shook her head.

"I can't."

Then Erich bucked backward, catching the guard by surprise. He reached for a dagger and threw it at the throat of his assailant. Before he whirled around to slash at the man holding onto Luzie.

Luzie got up and ran toward Liane as the guards unleashed a barrage of arrows onto Erich as he closed the distance between them. They caught him in the shoulder, and he staggered back, but kept on moving forward. Liane and Luzie clung to one another, helpless, as a line of a dozen guards closed ranks between them and Erich.

He managed to take out three of the twelve guards and had six arrows in his flesh before he collapsed onto the ground. A scream ripped from Liane's throat as he fell. She tried to run to him, but the guards caught her by the arm, and she was too weak to fight them.

She was numb with horror and disbelief as she watched the pool of blood spread out beneath him.

"Erich. Erich!" she screamed as they dragged her toward their horses.

"What do we do with the maid?" the guard who'd caught Luzie asked.

"Kill her," the masked leader said.

They didn't hesitate, slashing across her throat with their

sword. Luzie's eyes widened, and her mouth opened and closed as she gasped for air.

The sound that came out of Liane was animalistic. She curled into herself and felt for a moment like she had floated outside her body. This couldn't be happening. This all had to be a bad dream. They tossed Luzie's lifeless body onto the ground, as if she were nothing more than refuse.

Erich. Luzie. The oracle. Fritz. Ludwig.

All dead, and it was her fault.

32

Aristea's eyelids sagged as she fought off dozing while Duke Braun droned on about the fall equinox celebration preparations. She'd slept terribly the past few nights; she'd been tossing and turning, afraid to fall asleep in case Mathias or his elf friend came in to slit her throat. If she did manage to fall asleep, her dreams were haunted by the looming specter. She would run from it, only for it to appear in front of her once more, beckoning her with a skeletal hand. The sleepless nights were taking their toll on her. She couldn't hear anything the duke was saying. The room around her was starting to lose focus as her head dipped.

Then someone slammed their hand on the table, and Aristea shot up in her seat.

Duke Reiner was standing, hands splayed on the table in front of him.

"Why are we sitting around discussing festival preparations when a real threat is on our doorstep?"

Mother, at the opposite end of the table, sat up straighter. They'd agreed to keep "Mathias' little rebellion," as she had put it, under wraps and to try to keep it secret for now.

"What do you mean, Duke Reiner?" Mother said, her expression neutral, but Aristea saw the worry lines that creased her brow ever so slightly.

"The elves are growing more emboldened, and now our northern alliance is conspicuously absent." Missing council wasn't unheard of, especially during apparent times of peace, but Duke Wagner, whom Mathias had confirmed he was conspiring with, and the other northern dukes being absent, was rather suspicious.

Aristea blinked at his red face and around the room to gauge the mixed reactions of the men at the table. Since the Sun Ceremony, there hadn't been any new attacks or signs of the elves within the city. Officially, Mathias had gone into enemy territory to uncover their plot, but who knew how far rumors of his rebellion had traveled.

"I'm not sure what you're implying," Mother said coolly.

"I think rebellion is brewing, and your own son is plotting to usurp you with the strength of his paternal uncle and the north behind him."

"You're making baseless claims. Prince Mathias is loyal to the empire and would never dream of usurping me," Mother said.

"Then where is he?" Duke Reiner asked.

There was concerned muttering around the room. Mathias' original mission into the feral lands was a secret, and if Mother exposed it, she would reveal her fears of an elven attack. But if she didn't reveal it, it would only give more speculation to fuel the fires of discontent.

Aristea met her mother's gaze from across the table, arching a brow at her, wondering what she would choose.

"Prince Mathias is on a holy mission for the Avatheos, one that I am not at liberty to disclose."

"As the only legitimate male Starweber heir left, the prince should be here, learning state," Duke Hanz said, interjecting. "The Avatheos has Princess Liane. What more does he want from the Starweber line?"

"As Mathias is third in line, I don't see why that would be necessary. My heir is beside me." Mother gestured to Aristea across the table.

"And yet she has no husband. A man is necessary to keep a strong grip on the throne," Duke Reiner said, slamming his hand onto the table.

An uneasy shuffling of bodies filled the silence that stretched out. No one had dared to say anything even half as treasonous before. Aristea was the named and recognized heir.

Aristea's gaze slid over to Duke Krantz. He met her gaze and arched a single brow. Was this his doing? Or was he simply trying to mock her for not siding with him? If she were stronger, she'd stare the duke down until he looked away, to show she wasn't intimidated by him and was strong enough to be empress without a consort. She didn't need his support or his blasphemous schemes, but her eyes slid to the tabletop first, cowed by her own inadequacy.

A few dukes nodded in agreement with Duke Reiner. She noticed not all of them had been Heinrich's allies, as she might have assumed, but were dukes who'd fought and helped Mother become empress. A knot was forming in the pit of her stomach.

"Thank you, Duke Reiner, but we have no plans of changing the order of succession," Mother said, trying to steer the conversation away.

But Duke Reiner's words had emboldened dissenting voices.

"Even if Princess Aristea were to inherit, who would be her successor? Even if she were to marry and fall pregnant, she's past her prime to bear children. What if she died in the childbed?" Duke Beutler said.

Aristea's cheeks flamed, and she resisted the urge to duck her head. Instead, she balled her hands into fists until her nails embedded in her flesh.

"I am still healthy and young, as is my daughter, who isn't the withered husk you'd make her out to be. Are you so quick to replace me and her when my son-in-law is not even three months dead?" Mother said coldly.

Duke Reiner and the other dukes who'd spoken out lowered their heads, chastised. Even though she was a woman, Mother had command over the men. Because they thought of her as the goddess' chosen; the Golden Blade she had drawn marked her as such. That same devotion didn't transfer to Aristea. She knew this wouldn't be the last discussion around succession, and while Mathias' power was growing, Aristea could feel hers slipping.

The meeting ended, and the dukes filed out of the meeting room. They were still bickering over details of the fall equinox celebration amongst themselves as they exited. Mother sat at the head of the table; her eyes looked tired as she stared off into the middle distance. Aristea sat across from her quietly, waiting for her mother to acknowledge her presence.

"Am I a terrible mother for fearing my own son?" Mother asked.

Aristea felt a knot of guilt twist in her stomach because she felt the same. Had she done the right thing, letting him escape that night, or had she orchestrated her own demise? He was her brother, after all. She wanted to believe he wouldn't hurt her, but with the elves involved, she couldn't be certain.

"I'm worried too. But I equally fear the unrest that has simmered in the palace since Heinrich died," Aristea confessed.

Mother pinched her brow as she sighed. "Do you resent me for the burden I've laid upon you by naming you heir?"

"Never!" Aristea said. She crossed the room to sit beside Mother and reached out to squeeze her hand. "I was born first to continue your legacy, and I will do anything to keep hold of it."

Mother cupped Aristea's cheek, searching her face. "I wish I could have been more mother than empress for all three of you. It isn't fair what I've asked of you and will continue to ask of you..."

"I can only try to understand the burden you bear, and I share it with you willingly," Aristea assured her.

Mother gave her that look, the one when she didn't believe her but didn't want to argue.

"Duke Reiner's outburst today won't be the last," Mother said. "This kingdom is no stranger to civil war, and I fear we need to strengthen our position. We don't know what influence has taken over Mathias, and while I want to hope he can be saved, we must consider alternative paths..."

Her stomach churned. "You mean Duke Mattison," Aristea said flatly.

"He's shown interest in you, and it would be a beneficial match. But ultimately, the choice is yours."

Mother liked to paint it as a choice, but there was no choice at all. Sundland would bring a navy and a new realm positioned near Mathias' allies, should it come to war. Even if she were to entertain Jonathan and Duke Krantz's proposal, this was the superior match.

"I'll consider it," Aristea said diplomatically.

"This isn't the choice I'd have you make. Not after..."

Mother didn't like speaking Heinrich's name. And with good reason. He was a bad omen that hung over them. A sacrifice she'd endured for the family. And Duke Mattison, no matter how kind, would be another sacrifice she must bear for the empire.

"I know my place," Aristea said.

Mother sighed as if a great relief had been released and gestured for a servant to come closer. They presented her with a long, narrow box, which Mother set on the table and pushed toward Aristea. "Duke Mattison sent a present for you. I planned on having him around for a dinner party. I thought you could wear it and remove the veil to declare your intentions."

Aristea took the box with gritted teeth. Inside was a necklace with large rubies dripping like blood in a black metal working. She hated it and wished she could toss it on the ground to grind it beneath her slipper. But instead, she accepted it, calling over Yvette to take it to her room.

"I'll retire the veil then," Aristea said.

Mother squeezed her hand. "Thank you, Aristea. I know I can always count on you."

She felt a scream crawling up her throat, but she choked it back. With nothing left to be said, she excused herself and joined her guards, who were waiting in the hall to escort her to her next appointment. Mountains of paperwork were waiting for her in her apartment—petitions and reports. But thinking about sitting and shuffling through papers made her feel suddenly claustrophobic.

She needed fresh air, and so she headed out to the garden. She had no particular destination in mind and carelessly wandered toward her and Jonathan's secret spot. She shouldn't have been surprised to see him there, leaning against a tree, twisting his cane in his hand nervously. Her heart leapt traitorously. She was about to turn away when he called out to her.

"Aristea!"

She should walk away. With his limp, he couldn't catch up if she ran. Or she could tell the guards to keep him away. But rather than do either of those things, she let him march up to her.

"You cannot call me by my first name. What will people think?"

"The truth, that I care for you deeply."

A blush burned her cheeks. But she crossed her arms rather than acknowledge his flirting. She wasn't a fool; she recognized his agenda.

"Can we talk?" he asked. His expression was so earnest she couldn't tell him no.

"Are we not?"

"I lost you once, Aristea. I don't want to do it again." He grasped his cane tightly until his knuckles turned white.

"You never had me. I was destined to marry Heinrich, and now I'll likely marry Duke Mattison. Everything is as it should be."

"No, it isn't. You can't want this." He took a step toward her. The distance was closing, and her breath hitched.

"My lord." Her guard cleared his throat, and Jonathan halted his approach. He looked at the guards, then back at her, rubbing the back of his neck.

"I would rather we discuss this in private," Jonathan said.

"Whatever needs to be said can be said in front of my guard," Aristea replied coolly. She needed to widen the gap between them. She'd let him become too familiar and had opened her heart to a possibility that would never be. She'd marry Duke Mattison, as her mother had decreed, and become the empress. That was her destiny.

"Then I'll say it here. I don't care who knows. Aristea, I love you. I have since we were young, and I was too cowardly to say it back then. But I've lived every moment since in regret. Reject me if you must, but I had to let you know."

The words pierced her like an arrow through the heart. But her ambitions for the future would be shaken by a marriage to someone like Jonathan. She knew in her heart it was either Duke Mattison or no one at all.

She shook her head. "Jonathan—"

His face fell. "I can't bear to hear you say no, not when I know it's not what's in your heart. I don't want the throne. I want you. Run away with me. Denounce the throne. Whatever you must do. Haven't you given up enough for the empire? Must you bleed to satisfy the dukes and your mother?"

"It's not that simple. Mathias..."

"Could be a good emperor. It doesn't have to always be you, Aristea. You don't have to give up everything you want for some damned legacy."

"Is that what you want?" the voice whispered in Aristea's ear. "Will you give up everything you've worked for? All your sacrifices and heartache to become some country lord's wife?"

A cold chill ran over Aristea. This was the problem, wasn't it? Either he was part of some scheme of Duke Krantz's, or she gave up her goals. If she ran away with him into exile, she'd still be trapped. Not by duty to the crown, but beholden to him and his estate, as any other woman was. The life he offered seemed idyllic, built on a foundation of love, but it was a cage just as much as a marriage to Duke Mattison would be.

"Do you think I'll be happy as your wife? That I'd be satisfied in the country? This isn't just my mother's dream. It's mine too. I want this." And she meant it. She was sick of everyone else making the decisions for her. Letting men take the lead.

Jonathan recoiled as if she'd struck him, but she didn't care.

"Yes," the voice hissed. "Come to me. Let me fill you with power."

The voice granted Aristea a new vision. A realm under Aristea's command, no man in her shadow. Just her and the power she carved out for herself. She didn't need Jonathan or Duke Mattison.

"Goodbye, Jonathan." She strode away, not waiting for his reply.

33

Liane curled inward and brought her knees up to her chest. It wasn't enough; she wanted to collapse in on herself. Lying on her bed, she stared out her window at the waning moon, a mere sliver of light against the inky-black sky. Seeing the changing phases of the moon made her feel closer to Erich. A part of her was still in denial. She kept waiting for Luzie to come barging in with a smile and a bit of gossip. Or Ludwig to be standing silently in the corner. She wished she'd told Erich how she really felt and hadn't let their argument tinge her memories of him.

She felt empty, hollowed out like an old dried-up husk.

No matter what she wished, she couldn't change anything. The Midnight Guard had brought her back, hollow and sunken eyed, to the temple. She'd been locked in her room and there she'd remained, lying in her bed in a strange, suspended state, awake but not fully alive for days on end. They'd taken the Golden Blade away, but she couldn't find it in her to care.

Fighting was useless. Her friends had fought and died to protect her, and for what? Luzie would be alive if she hadn't followed Liane to Basilia. Ludwig would be safe, had he not given that vow to Elias. The oracle had foreseen her own death and embraced it, but that didn't absolve Liane of guilt. Fritz, they'd likely caught and killed him, and Erich... The thought of his body lying there with all those arrows piercing him made a lump rise in her throat. She wanted to scream, to retch, anything, but her body was too weak to move. She'd never felt more helpless in her entire life.

She thought the goddess had a destiny planned for her. But what was there left to save when everyone she cared about had been taken from her?

Priestesses brought her trays of food at regular intervals, but she'd refused to touch them. It would have been better if they'd let her die.

But they wouldn't even give her that. The priestesses had begged, wheedled, and then threatened her, trying to get her to eat or drink. But she'd merely rolled over to look out her window.

Then the Avatheos came.

She felt his power as it rolled into the room, like a slime sliding over her skin, as he pulled up a chair next to her bed.

"Liane, look at me," he said.

There was a command in his voice, one that turned her head despite her resistance. And she was shocked to see he'd pulled back his hood to reveal his face to her. She'd wondered more times than she could count what he looked like beneath his hood, and she was disappointed to see he was average. No villainous dark eyebrows or twisted malevolent features. He was just a man.

"I am coming to you not as the Avatheos, but as a citizen of this continent begging you to not give up."

She rolled away from him to face the wall. She didn't care what he wanted. He'd orchestrated it all, executed her friends, and wanted her as a tool for his own grasp at power.

But he kept on anyway. "I should have been honest with you from the start. I should have better explained what was at stake. Maybe then you wouldn't have made the choices you did."

"You mean I should have allowed you to seal my power, to take control of all magic?"

"I was trying to subvert the prophecy I saw. Sealing magic would have kept the darkness locked away. But now it is spilling out, and by the fall equinox, it will have taken control of your sister. Unless you work with me to stop it."

Perfect, beautiful Aristea. It was impossible to imagine her being swayed by dark magic. But the oracle had warned her of the same prophecy. Could it be true, and would she be destined to slay her own sister? That seemed an even crueler twist of fate. She laughed bitterly.

"This isn't a jest, Liane. This is real. I saw the face of the dark vessel clearly for the first time in a vision last night. I thought it was your mother, but now I see the true vision. You have unsheathed the Golden Blade, freeing the Nameless to consume Aristea and use her to wield the Dark Blade and raise an army of the undead to bring an end to all life on earth." His voice had a distant hollow sound, as if it weren't him speaking at all but something speaking through him. It sent a chill down her spine to hear it.

Liane didn't want this power or this terrible choice. Doom the continent or kill her sister? Why would the goddess do this to her? Hadn't she lost enough?

"You cannot make me kill her," Liane said, her throat raw and aching.

"It is not I who thrusts this decision upon you, but Cyra who chose you."

"You cannot sway me with your rhetoric. I'm not your puppet," she said, sitting up to face him.

"Then seal your power. The equinox is days away. It is not too late to bind your power to the church and subvert the prophecy."

There was no choice, not really, and perhaps there never was one. But there was freedom in letting go, in giving in to the currents that threatened to drown her.

"I'll do it. I'll let you seal my power."

When she thought of the sacrifices that her friends had made to get her here, she knew there was only one answer. She couldn't kill Aristea. She was no hero.

34

A red haze washed over Erich's vision, but despite the rage and the dragon thrashing within him, he couldn't move, even as Liane screamed his name, her voice growing distant as they took her away. The rune stones and enchanted nets had sapped his strength and destroyed his ability to heal. He was leaking blood from multiple wounds. Even if he was a monster on the inside, he was still mortal. Two guards stood over him, their faces shadowed as his vision went in and out of focus.

"Should we collect the body?" one guard asked another.

"We can't spare the men. The elf is still out there and so is Ludwig, that traitor." He spat on the ground. "Leave him and the women for the carrions."

They mounted their horses and rode away. Without even the courtesy of a clean death. This was it. The end. And he didn't even get to look up at the sky one last time. They'd left him face pressed into the dirt. The veiled face of the Trinity was reaching out to him with the promise of rest and peace in the endless night. He didn't have to fight anymore. There would be no more strife, no more fearing each full moon. He would be free of his curse at last. But as he was slipping into unconsciousness, and what might have been oblivion, someone yanked on the arrows embedded in his shoulders and back, and he returned to consciousness screaming.

Then they rolled him over and leaned over him to tend to his wounds. Their head was haloed by the rising sun, and shadows obscured their features. But his pain-addled mind saw Liane, though she couldn't be there with him. He'd watched her ride away.

"Liane, I'm sorry. I would have stayed with you forever." He reached out to touch her, but she shook her head. He didn't deserve forgiveness, not after leaving Ludwig to die and not being strong enough to protect her and her maid.

"You'll have to wait and tell her that yourself." Liane's face melted away, and there was Fritz instead. "I've removed the rune stones. You should heal some before he comes to find you. I wish—"

Fritz paused and looked into the distance. "I've searched for solutions a thousand different ways. And this is the only path that leads to your success. I know you'll think me cruel and coldhearted to let them die. But—" His voice was thick with emotion. "It had to be this way. We'll meet again soon, I promise. But there's something I have to do first."

And then he was gone, and the lightening sky above Erich and the slow healing dragged him inch by inch away from death. Time passed as he moved in and out of consciousness. Shadows moved around him, and he thought perhaps Fritz had come back because he remembered someone speaking to him, though he couldn't remember what was said. Over and over, his thoughts were consumed by Liane, seeing her terrified face as she'd shrunk in the distance. The rage and the despair. He had to heal, as Fritz had demanded, and get her back.

When he woke, fully, it was to the smell of smoke and

roasting meat. He was beyond ravenous. It felt as if his stomach were trying to eat itself. He jolted upright, lunging for one of the birds roasting over the fire, like a wild animal. He burnt his hand and pulled the skin around his freshly-closed wounds. But he didn't care. Erich tore into the juicy meat, grease and juice dripping down his chin. He'd nearly picked the bones clean before he noticed the bandages on his torso and the figure sitting across the fire from him, offering up another roasted bird.

Erich snatched the bird from Ludwig, who said nothing but turned over a third bird roasting above the fire. There was a flask of wine next to him, and Erich drank until his stomach felt fit to burst.

His hunger and thirst sated, Erich looked at Ludwig at last.

"Were you the one who treated my wounds?" he asked.

"They were mostly healed by the time I arrived. I'm sorry I came too late," he said, and his gaze trailed over two stone piles. He'd buried Luzie and the oracle while Erich had healed.

"I'm sorry I didn't save Luzie," Erich said.

Though he hadn't been the direct cause of Luzie's death, he still felt her blood on his hands.

"How did you get here?" Erich asked him.

"I walked. But I doubt that's the answer you're looking for."

"No, it isn't. When I left you in that tower, you had no means of escape. Either you're the most impressive swordsman in the world, or there's a secret you've been keeping."

Ludwig sighed as he ran his hands through his sandy-blond hair. "The stardust awakened me. That's what the Midnight Guard calls it, when the latent magic in your veins first starts to react with suppressed power. Most users die because it creates an imbalance within them. For me, it fed into me and made me... stronger. I thought that when I stopped taking it, when the cravings were gone, I would return to how I was, but I kept changing. I can move in the shadows, and I have strength no man should have. I told the Midnight Guard I'd awakened, but not what powers had manifested, and I was able to use that to my advantage to escape." He looked up to meet Erich's gaze as if he had the answers to this man's problems.

Erich had heard rumors, legends of the warriors of old. Leonhard would know more, he suspected, with his library of books on strange creatures. But that didn't matter right now. What Ludwig could do was more important. With the two of them working together, they might be able to get Liane out. Where they went after that was still a problem.

"Before we get Liane, we need an escape route, and I know someone who might be able to help," Erich said. Leonhard had the resources and, perhaps, the motive to help them. The oracle had died, but she seemed to have foreseen her own death. Maybe Leonhard was on their side.

If he could just get to the coliseum and speak with Leonhard, maybe he'd have an idea of how they could get into the temple and save Liane. The dragon's voice was quiet; perhaps the dragon was depleted by the trial of healing him. Without the dragon's power, Erich knew he couldn't have survived this ordeal. And he'd need that power to save Liane. Even if it sped up the consumption of his humanity, he'd use every last second to save her.

Erich stood and was glad to see he had enough strength for that. The birds he'd eaten and the wine he'd drunk had returned some of his strength, but not nearly enough. Not enough for a fight. And there was no way he was getting Liane out of the temple a second time without one.

Their journey there was slow and arduous, as his wounds hadn't healed entirely. But around the time night fell, he was starting to feel stronger. Being beneath the waning moon seemed to improve his stamina as well.

His hopes of getting help from Leonhard were dashed when they arrived at the coliseum and found it ablaze. He didn't have to see his town house to know it was in similar condition. They watched it burn from a hilltop several yards away. There were guards swarming it as they escorted Leonhard's goons away. Whatever goodwill he'd had with the Avatheos had been shattered.

There was only one avenue left. They'd have to take the temple by force. And find their own getaway by partnering with Erich's last resort. In all honesty, if his pride, his shame, and his fear, hadn't gotten in the way, he would have given up and sailed back to Sundland.

Erich needed to find his uncle's ship in the harbor and beg for him to help them escape once they'd rescued Liane. The cost would be returning to Sundland and facing the court he'd left behind, but whatever his uncle asked, Erich would give it up for her.

Getting into the city was a challenge in itself. There were no convenient secret tunnels to sneak into. So they had to go to the southern gate, which added another day to their travel. The going was slow, as he had to stop frequently to catch his breath. The healing and transformation had taken more out of him than he'd realized, and he needed the breaks to regain his footing. When they got to the city gates, Erich's magical persuasion, coupled with Ludwig's shadow power, got them through. But they had to keep a low profile on their way to the docks.

The city was buzzing with activity as the fall equinox was days away. By some miracle, they made it to the docks. Though by that time, Erich was swaying on his feet like a drunkard. How was he going to save Liane in this condition? He noticed the ship straight away. It was small and sleek, built for speed, reminiscent of the ones used in the raiding parties of his long-ago ancestors. The Trinity must favor him. It was the ideal vessel for a swift getaway when every other ship in the harbor was built for hauling cargo across the strait that separated the continent from Xi'an.

His uncle's banner fluttered from the mast, mocking him. Erich reached for his missing dagger, then let his hand fall to his side as he walked up the gangplank onto the deck. The crew was lazing about—some playing cards, others had their feet kicked up. His uncle sat easily among them, looking more like a sea-salted sailor than a country lord. His iron-gray hair was tied in a low ponytail, and his white shirt was open at the throat, exposing the golden chain he wore around his neck. He turned as they approached, and a smile cracked his somber face. Erich nearly turned around, overcome by guilt.

But then he thought of Liane alone in the temple, her fate uncertain, and he took the step toward him. His uncle opened his arms to him as if to embrace him. But Erich wasn't quite ready for a sentimental greeting.

"I've come to beg a favor, Uncle," Erich said, and he bowed low onto the ground in front of him. His uncle looked stricken and grabbed him by the shoulders.

"Please, whatever it is, there's no reason to beg. Stand up."

"I know you want me to become the king. And I'm still not sure I'm worthy," Erich continued, from his kneeling position. "But there's something greater than me and greater than Sundland at stake here. And that's why I've come to ask you for help."

The sailors had given up on their card game and turned their entire attention to Erich and his uncle. Uncle Endland, always pragmatic, looked around and said, "Maybe we should talk in private first."

There was some good-natured teasing from the sailors as

Erich stood and followed his uncle into the captain's quarters. It was a square room, with low, dark ceilings, a table big enough to seat six bolted to the floor, and a desk with a map and sextant laid out as if they merely awaited orders to sail onward to new adventures.

Ludwig guarded the door while Erich faced his uncle.

"Now tell me what is so important that you'd fall to your knees and beg me?" his uncle asked.

"It's a long story."

"Erich, when did I ever not love a good tale?" His uncle leaned back against the table, arms crossed.

Erich sighed and rubbed his stubbled chin. "Where do I start?" Erich wondered aloud.

"I've found the beginning is usually best."

And so, he told his uncle everything, from his and Liane's fake engagement, Fritz's prophecy, Liane drawing the sword, and his near-death experience. Uncle Endland listened patiently, not interrupting once. The sun was setting outside the window when he finished, and his throat was sore by the end of the telling. Erich's chest felt light, having unloaded the burdens he'd been carrying. Before Erich's self-imposed exile, Uncle Endland had been the one he'd talked to about his problems, and he'd held all his secrets.

"Then we must rescue her." His uncle clapped his hands together.

Erich blinked at him. Even though he knew his uncle was a generous man who'd do anything for family, he'd expected some resistance.

"Just like that?" Ludwig asked.

His uncle smiled. "Erich said the fate of the world is at stake. I know my nephew, and he wouldn't exaggerate such a thing. But I fear it's not my decision alone to make. My men on this ship have been traveling with me for a long time. They have a right to choose whether they'd be complicit in angering the Church of Sol along with us."

"I understand," Erich said. It was a reasonable request. Though the dragon was growing restless as night crept forward. He wouldn't be calm again until he knew Liane was safe.

His uncle rested his hand on his shoulder. "You have my support no matter what. I'm sorry I put so much pressure on you to become king. But you must realize the safest place for her, and you, will be in Sundland."

"I know."

His uncle nodded. "Good, as long as we both understand that. Come, let's talk to the crew."

They went above deck, and Erich was introduced to the crew of his uncle's ship. Though he'd be hard-pressed to recall their names if asked. His thoughts were consumed by Liane. Uncle Endland delivered an abbreviated version of events, and they were given a vote on whether to join or not.

When the vote was cast, the decision was unanimous. They wanted to help rescue Liane. A plan was made to ready the ship for a quick departure the moment they returned with her. Which left Erich with the task of figuring out how to extract Liane from the church a second time.

"There's one chance, I'm afraid," his uncle said. "The Church of Sol will present her on the outer temple balcony during the fall equinox ceremony. But the square and surrounding area will be swarming with Midnight Guards. We'll really have to thread the needle of your dragon's ability to pull it off."

Erich clenched a hand into a fist. Last time, he'd lost control and many people had died, but he couldn't worry about that. He'd slaughter every last Midnight Guard to get Liane back if he must. The dragon liked that idea, and he felt its bloodlust boil in his veins.

"Whatever it takes," Erich said.

"I thought you'd say something like that," Uncle Endland replied with a grim expression. "Well, if anyone can pull this off, it's you."

Erich just hoped he was right.

35

The morning of the fall equinox, the priestesses came to dress Liane. Before she stepped into the water and sealed her power, the Avatheos wanted to parade her around the city. It would inspire the faith of the people. They put on her ceremonial robe and headpiece, and she stood passively as they worked. There was no fight left in her but for one thing. If her power was to be stripped from her, she wanted the people to know the truth. As they dressed her, she ran through the plan in her head. They wouldn't return her sword to her until it was absolutely necessary. Before her procession through the city, she'd address the crowd on the temple steps, and she'd tell them the whole truth—The church was hoarding magic, to the continent's detriment, and she was going to seal her power to save them from the destructive tide of dark magic.

Either the people would rise up against the church and join her side, or the church would turn against her to silence her. It was a reckless plan, but there was no Ludwig or Luzie here to talk her out of it.

They passed through the halls of the temple and made their way to the outer ring. And then up the stairs to the balcony, where she would look down on the people of Basilia and address them before her procession. Her stomach was twisted up in knots, but she kept moving forward. The guards were outside the door that led to the balcony, and they opened it to let her through. A priest was waiting in the outer ring with the Avatheos, the sword in their hands.

The sun was high in the sky, and it nearly blinded her. Liane raised her hand to block it out.

This was the moment where she either rose to the occasion or failed spectacularly. And maybe this was the destiny she'd been designed for. Not all heroes had to fight epic battles or topple nations. Sometimes it took one person brave enough to stand and face evil. She wished Erich were here. She held the memory of him tight and took a deep breath before she stepped out onto the balcony. The sun warmed her face, and the crowd down below roared with approval. Their excitement and energy gave her courage and hope for a brighter future.

The priest holding the sword handed it to her. Liane's hands were slick with sweat as she reached for the sword. And she tightened her grip upon the hilt. Its weight felt right in her hands, and for a moment, she thought she heard the beating of wings in her ears, as if the raven were there with her.

The Avatheos addressed the crowd. "On this day of balance, we thank Cyra for her avatar, who will conquer darkness as the wielder of her holy blade."

He grasped hold of her wrist, a show of power and dominance, but rather than let him make her small, Liane stepped in front of him and raised the blade to the sky. A burst of light came from her and the sword.

"People of Basilia, I have drawn the Golden Blade. The goddess has given me a divine mission, one that will heal this empire," she cried.

They roared back at her, and she waited for it to die down

before continuing, "And I am here to tell you the church has lied to you. Magic is not dying, but has been systematically destroyed by the very church that swore they were protecting it."

There was a shout, and a confused murmurer moved through the crowd. The Avatheos tried to pull the sword from her hand, but she turned and pointed the blade at his neck. His throat bobbed.

"You are not worthy enough to touch me," she snarled, infusing all her power into her voice.

The Midnight Guard were hovering just out of sight of the crowd, poised to disarm her. But she felt the pulse of magic coursing through her and knew that if they tried, she would cut them down as if they were stalks of wheat. The Avatheos signaled for them to stand down, and all of them inched backward.

Then she turned to face the crowd once more.

"They are stealing your children, your family, your loved ones, and sealing their power so that it is under the church's control. But it ends with me. It ends now. Today, I will enter the source of magic and seal all magic to prevent the rise of a greater evil. And though I will sacrifice my power, it is you who must fight to break down the bricks of your oppressors and free the empire."

The words hung in the air, and Liane felt the threads of magic that carried her voice, and stopped the Avatheos from approaching her, begging to wear thin as the light around her began to dim. Pain bloomed behind her eyes and traveled down her back. She'd given it all for this moment, and she hoped it was enough.

A slow ripple moved through the crowd, a buzz of conversation that built into an unintelligible shout. Either they'd sensed the wrongness about the church, or they despised her for her blasphemy. Regardless, she'd thrown a match on kindling, and it had caught. The crowd rushed the guards at the foot of her balcony, pushing their way in. Panic ceased as she watched the chaos unfold. Scuffles were breaking out.

Liane threw her head back and laughed. Whether she was remembered as a saint or a devil, at least she had done something. She'd exhausted her power, and she collapsed onto her knees as the light faded for good. The Avatheos marched toward her and grasped hold of her neck and squeezed.

"I will delight in sealing your power. Why Cyra chose an insolent worm like you, I'll never understand. This display of yours will do nothing; you've sullied your reputation for nothing."

"Perhaps, but I'd rather be known as a heretic than a coward."

He squeezed harder as she clawed at his wrist, trying to break free. The edges of her vision were growing dark, and her grip on the blade was slipping. When suddenly he let go.

Liane gasped for air, and when she looked up, she was shocked to see Erich alive, straddling the Avatheos as he punched his face repeatedly.

"Erich?" she croaked, half crawling to reach him.

He turned from the Avatheos and strode toward her.

He cupped her face. "I told you I would never leave you."

Tears burned the back of her eyes, but there wasn't time for a tearful reunion when the Avatheos was getting back to his feet and raising one of the fallen Midnight Guard's swords over his head.

Liane screamed and held up her hand, shooting a burst of light from her palm, which knocked the sword from the Avatheos' grip. The Avatheos' hood had fallen back, and he stared dumbfounded at his empty hand, his mouth opening and closing like a fish. Ludwig rushed onto the balcony, his face splattered with blood.

And Liane started to cry. By some miracle, they'd both survived, and they'd come to save her. Erich stalked over to the Avatheos and lifted him off the ground by his neck. The Avatheos grabbed onto Erich's wrist as his feet kicked in the air.

"Your tyranny ends here," Erich said, before tossing him over the balcony.

Down below, someone screamed. She didn't want to see it. But she knew she had to confirm with her own eyes. She peered over the side and saw the spreading stain of blood on the marble floor; his limbs were turned at odd angles, and his skull fractured beyond repair. He was dead. The Avatheos was dead.

"We need to get out of here before the Midnight Guard organizes enough to get the crowd under control," Ludwig said.

Erich grabbed hold of Liane's right hand, and in her other hand, she held onto the sword. They ran down the balcony stairs and through the temple halls. All the while, her heart was in her throat. She grasped her Golden Blade tighter in her hand as they turned a corner, and a couple of Midnight Guards blocked their path.

Before she could react, Ludwig stepped in front of them and cut the guards down with a speed that seemed impossible for a human.

Liane stared at him wide-eyed. "Since when could you do that?"

"It's a long story. I'll explain later," he said.

They headed for the temple entrance. But the doors were locked, and people were banging on the other side. The crowd she'd incited was trying to knock down the temple doors.

"We'll go out through the service exit," Ludwig said.

They ran in the other direction, and passed through the chaos of the inner rings of the palace and into the kitchen, where acolytes had abandoned their work because of the commotion upstairs. They didn't try to stop them but merely cowered as they rushed past. From there, they passed through a tunnel, into a storage area, and out onto the empty city street.

Liane followed Erich's lead as he navigated them through the rioting city. Citizens and anarchists were throwing barrels, lighting torches, and causing chaos in the streets. Because it was so crowded, they took alleyways, climbing fences, and, at times, walking along low rooftops to avoid the worst of the mayhem.

Slowly, they made their way toward the docks. They were on another rooftop when Erich pointed to the harbor.

"That's our ship," Erich said, pointing to a small vessel a few yards away.

"Where did you get a ship?" Liane asked.

"My uncle. Long story."

"There seems to be a lot of those." She laughed in spite of the insanity of the situation.

She looked at the ship and then back at the city. Basilia was already further away than she'd ever traveled. And the oracle had told her to travel north. The prophecy that the Avatheos and the raven had spoken to her was still throbbing in her skull. She had to get to Aristea and warn her against the magic Liane had unleashed. But if the prophecy were true, it might already be too late.

Erich slid down from the rooftop and held out his arms to catch Liane. She jumped down into his arms. Their bodies pressed together as their gazes met. She wasn't sure where he intended to take her, but she knew she'd go anywhere with him.

A few yards remained between them and the ship, and they raced across the distance, past disgruntled yardmen carrying boxes and sailors playing cards across crates. The sailors on it were preparing to depart, rushing across the deck, tugging on ropes, and unfurling sails. As soon as they crossed the gangplank, they pulled it up and cast it off from the dock.

It was a small vessel and moved quickly through the bay. They were lucky to have gotten this far without pursuit, but their luck was running out. A ship flying the church's flag was bobbing in the harbor, near the twin oracle statues, and they were turning toward the signal tower to raise the chains and prevent them from escaping.

"Hold on, everyone. We're going to be making some quick maneuvers," the captain announced.

He shouted orders, and the sailors leapt to follow them, while Liane and the others did their best to stay out from underfoot. They found a place along the railing that was out of the way, where they could see the church's ship plowing toward them on a collision course.

The gap between the ships was shrinking, and the chain was slowly being raised from the water, thick strings of seaweed dangling from it. She held her breath as they squeezed past the church's ship and didn't let the breath go until they were zipping out between the statues, moments before the chain pulled taut.

Once they were past it and out on the open water, they unfurled the sails fully and zoomed across the water. In what felt like mere moments later, they watched as Basilia shrank on the horizon.

"On the open sea, their ships will be too slow to catch us," the captain said, leaning on the ship's wheel.

"That was certainly a close one," said the man with silver hair and a fair resemblance to Erich, coming up from the cabins.

"Liane, this is my uncle Lord Endland. He agreed to let us use his ship as our escape vessel."

"'Tis my ship," the man behind the helm said.

"That it is, but it's my geld that keeps it sailing," Lord Endland replied.

"You're welcome. Captain Endre Marcussen, at your service," he said with a flourish and a bow toward Liane.

"Thank you, Lord Endland. And you, too, Captain," Liane replied.

"Don't mention it. Anything for someone who can tame my nephew." Lord Endland tousled Erich's hair with obvious affection.

Erich endured the light teasing with a ghost of a smile on his lips. Liane liked seeing this side of him. There'd been so many secrets between them, and then a few stolen moments, but no time to share anything about themselves. There was still so much about him she had to learn. And thank the stars for this second chance. That he was alive and with her. Tears pricked at her eyes, as she was overwhelmed by relief and exhaustion.

"Even if the ship is fast, the church will chase us anyway. They're patient," Ludwig said.

"They can sure try." The captain laughed.

Ludwig rubbed his thigh where he'd been gored by a boar earlier that summer. She wondered if it had healed properly or if it had something to do with the magical speed he'd used back in the temple. That was something they'd have to discuss later.

"We're flying the Sundland royal naval flag. The church won't risk attacking us with that. We should be able to sail all the way to Sundland without incident," Lord Endland assured them.

"The Church of Sol has no domain in Sundland. I thought you'd be safest there," Erich told Liane.

"If you declare yourself at court, you could have the entire Sundland army at her defense," Lord Endland said with a pointed look at Erich.

Erich gave his uncle a pointed stare, and Liane glanced between the two of them, feeling a bit lost.

"Care to explain that long story?" Liane prompted.

Erich rubbed a hand across his face. "I told you the truth when I said I was Prince of Sundland. My father, the king, is dying or may already be dead. The deal I made with my uncle to save you was to return and reclaim my birthright to the throne."

The oracle's prophecy to go north echoed in her ears. As did the cryptic title of shield. She looked up at the dragon on the flag flying from the ship's mast and the shield behind it. These couldn't be coincidences. Her heart wanted her to go straight home, to warn Aristea and try to prevent the prophecy Liane had set in motion. But her gut told her this was where she was meant to be.

"My mother will be thrilled when she finds out." Liane laughed.

Erich rubbed the back of his neck, and Endland slapped his knee with delight.

"I like her a lot, Erich."

"It won't be easy," Erich said. "And I'm not sure how much I can do. My uncles are powerful and ambitious, and they've been scheming for years to usurp me. Until recently, I was ready to let them. If the road ahead of us is dangerous, then I know I can't keep running from my destiny. But I will not force any of you to take on this task against your will." He looked at Liane, then Ludwig, before setting his gaze on his uncle.

"You know you have my full support," his uncle said, hands turned palm up.

Liane grabbed Erich's hand and squeezed. "I am the sword, and you are the shield. I think this was all meant to be. I don't know the full scope of this, but if there's a battle ahead, we must be destined to fight together."

They both looked at Ludwig. She didn't want to make him walk into danger on her account, not after losing Luzie.

"You don't have to do this," Liane said to him.

"I will always fight by your side," Ludwig said. And she threw her arms around his neck. They'd had their ups and downs, but they'd always be friends.

Their plans settled, she felt a sudden wave of fatigue overcome her. And the swaying of the ship didn't make it any easier on her. She let go of Ludwig, and the rocking of the waves knocked her over into Erich, who grasped her by the shoulders to keep her from falling over.

"We're all exhausted. Why not rest a while, and we'll reconvene later," Lord Endland said.

Liane didn't need to be told twice, and she leaned on Erich for support as he guided her below deck to a free cabin. There weren't many rooms onboard, but as the only woman, she had a cabin to herself, while the men would share the bunks in the spare cabin. The swaying below deck was worse, and Liane thought painfully of how much Luzie had suffered on the trip from Artria. She'd never sail home again. Tears blurred her vision, and the swaying ship almost knocked her over. Erich caught her, again.

"You should lie down." And rather than let her walk the two feet to her cot, he picked her up and laid her out on the bunk, smoothing the pillows and blanket over her.

"You don't have to do all this," she said.

"I want to."

He lingered a moment at her bedside, and she felt the things left unspoken between them. She'd been so relieved to see him alive that she didn't know where to begin. The last time they'd spoken, they were arguing, and their future still seemed uncertain.

"I have to apologize to you," Erich said.

She looked at him wide-eyed, waiting for him to continue. Erich ran his hands through his hair and wouldn't look at her at first. "It's hard for me to form attachments. The thing I am, the curse I was born with, has harmed people. And the more time I spent with you, the more I wanted to be near you. To have all of you. But a part of me feared I'd hurt you as well."

She nodded for him to continue.

"Worse than that, I don't know how much time I have left before I transform into a dragon for good. So I pushed you away, rather than hurt you. But the thought of living another moment of the time I have left without you, terrifies me even more."

She grabbed his hand, and he turned toward her with a cautious expression on his face.

"I've never considered having one someone to share my life with. But when I thought you were dead, I felt as if the world had ended for me. I was willing to let the Avatheos do anything, to take away my entire self, if it meant the pain would stop."

He swallowed.

"Erich, I love you," she confessed.

"And I love you," he said in return.

He leaned forward, and his hand snaked around the back of her neck, pulling her closer as he parted her lips with his tongue and kissed her deeply. Liane wrapped her hands around his body, tugging him down to lie on top of her. They held onto one another, his hands roving over her body lazily, kissing as if they had nothing but time. She felt his erection against her belly, and she squeezed her thighs together, squirming as his hand drifted over her breast. As things got heated, and he tried to open her thighs with his knee, he slammed her knee into the wall. And she swore colorfully.

Erich pulled back to check she wasn't seriously injured. They attempted to readjust, but the bed was too narrow, and voices were filtering in from the deck above.

"Probably not the place to be doing this," Erich said against her lips.

"We've done it in worse places." Liane smirked as she kissed the corner of his mouth.

He kissed her back before leaning in to whisper in her ear. "I don't want you in a cramped cabin. This next time, I'm going to take my time and explore every inch of you." He trailed kisses down her neck. A promise of more.

His words sent a shiver down her spine. And she felt the absence of his touch as soon as he pulled away.

"We'll be in Sundland before you know it. I hope you can wait until then." He smirked, rising off the tiny cot.

She wasn't sure she could, but if that grin was anything to go off of, it would be well worth the wait.

"I suppose I'll have to," she replied.

36

Aristea felt as if she'd been living in a fog. The dreams were getting worse. The voice kept cajoling her, begging her to come down to meet her. At times, Aristea couldn't tell if she was awake or asleep. Thoughts of that dark place beneath the palace consumed her. They hadn't found Mathias, though they had Midnight Guards and City Watch alike searching for him.

Dinner with Duke Mattison had arrived. He was all smiles and compliments for her mother. Father and he discussed their hunting dogs and cattle. He was perfectly polite and charming. And far too much like Heinrich. Aristea saw her life with him playing out like a twisted play—forced to smile for his court and hers; berated for not being smart enough, pretty enough, demure enough. Worn down until she was nothing but a small pebble, something he could hold up and say—look at Princess Aristea, how easily she obeys.

"Since Prince Erich is presumed dead, I shall inherit the crown after my brother passes. My brother, the king, has assured me so. And with our marriage, we will bring the might of Sundland into the empire," he said to her mother. "And our child will rule over a stronger empire." Duke Mattison reached across the table to pat her hand like she was a simple child.

She may as well not be there. Or be a piece of furniture. Mother looked at her with a smile of encouragement. It was favorable. Ideal even. No matter that he was so much older and another man cut from Heinrich's cloth. The empire came before all else. Wasn't that what she'd taught her?

Aristea sat in place, like a porcelain doll. This is what they wanted her to do, sit, smile, and be the perfect example of a princess. Without agency. Without a choice. She wanted to scream and to run out of the room, tearing her clothes off like a madwoman. But she suspected even if she did, he'd still marry her. Because he craved power. Heinrich needed her womb. Duke Mattison didn't even need that. She'd given her blood, her tears. And now Mathias was plotting against her; he'd sided with the elves to destroy her and their family. And still she was powerless.

"Unless you come to me," the voice whispered. It seemed it was in the room with her.

Aristea looked up, and she was hovering just past Mother's shoulder, her face veiled and her withered hands reaching out to her.

"Take the power. It is your right."

"No." Aristea slammed her hands on the table.

Mother, Father, and the duke all looked at her as if she'd lost her mind. She stood and stared at the three of them. These schemers who'd plotted her life. She wouldn't marry Duke Mattison. She refused. Even if she lost everything, she would not marry this man. She'd find another way.

"I will not marry you. I will rule on my own," Aristea declared.

Her mother looked at her, mouth agape. "Aristea."

"Denounce me if you wish. But I refuse to."

Duke Mattison sputtered, and Father blinked in confusion, and then Mother set her napkin aside. She thought she would scold her or tell her to listen. Mother crossed the room, walked over to Aristea, and placed her hands on her shoulder.

"Are you sure?"

Aristea nodded slowly. "I'm certain."

"Then it is decided."

Mother turned to Duke Mattison. "I fear we'll need to end this dinner early."

"This is outrageous. You've led me to believe..."

"You were promised nothing. But presumed much," Aristea said coldly, the relief too much to express.

He glared, but with a motion from Mother, the guards moved in, ready to forcibly escort him if he didn't leave on his own. He rose indignantly and stormed out of the room. Aristea felt as if a weight had been lifted from her chest. She wouldn't have to marry Duke Mattison. Mother supported her decisions. But the problem remained. She wasn't strong enough to hold on to the throne herself. Mathias had a growing list of allies, and she had none.

"Excuse me, I have somewhere to be," Aristea told her parents.

Mother hugged her tightly. And Aristea almost gave in to the comfort of that embrace. More than anything, she wanted to rest. To let go of this iron grip she had on the throne. But she couldn't, wouldn't, give up. This was her destiny, her birthright.

"You were born for me. Your sister has the sword. But you could be so much more. I can make you an empress who will truly be feared," the veiled woman crooned to her. "Come to me, Aristea. Embrace your destiny."

She exited her parents' apartments and went straight to her own. In the safety of her room, she dismissed her guards and lady's maids, so she was left alone in her room. The tapestry hiding the secret entrance to her room twitched, as if blown by the wind. A shiver raced up her spine.

"What power can you give me?" she asked the voice. Instinctively, she knew she could hear her. That she was with her, watching, always.

"Everything. Come."

The tapestry fluttered, and the door behind it creaked. Aristea approached slowly, peered into the darkness, and then stepped into it. She walked down the stairs, into the tunnels below the palace, through the twisting labyrinth of crumbling tunnels, down, down, down into the dark, her hands holding onto the slick moss-covered stones to guide her.

Her heart was hammering in her chest as the voice led her to a room. It might have been a temple once. There were faded murals on the walls, ones she couldn't quite decipher the writing on. And at the center, there was a low-lying pool. Its water rippled strangely, and stars reflected on the surface, though they were deep underground.

"Come closer," the woman beckoned.

Aristea stood at the edge, looking over into the water, into what felt like a void of nothingness and starlight.

"Step in and be transformed."

She hesitated. The same thing had happened to Liane as a child, and she had been sickly ever since.

"Not any longer. The power has awakened. That same power lies dormant in you, Aristea. She will come to help your brother usurp you." The pool showed Liane riding on horseback, an army at her back, flying the Sundland flag. Both Mathias and Liane were riding together, against her and her Neolyrian army. Aristea balled her hands into fists at her sides.

"You're the true empress, and it's time everyone feared you."

Aristea swallowed past the lump in her throat and stepped into the water.

But what she found there wasn't a goddess' touch, or even divinity. But a darkness so deep and consuming that she could not escape. It flowed in, choking her with thick black ichor.

Sinister laughter filled her ears as she sank further and further down.

There was no way to get out of the water, and the only way out was to succumb.

She watched from a distance as her body rose out of the water. Not as herself, but a monster wearing her skin.

~ The story continues in Dragon's Devotion ~

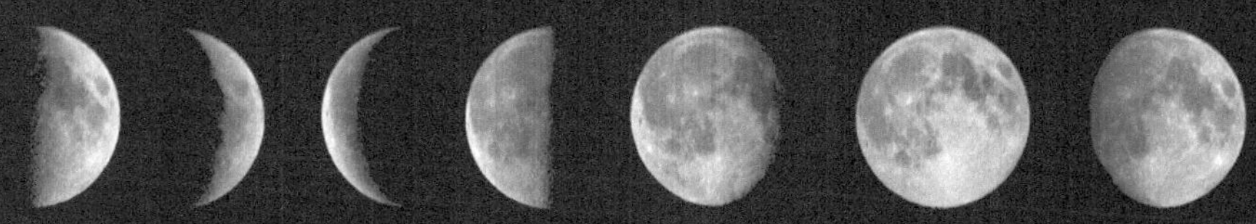

Guide to Neolyra

Nicolette Andrews

CAST OF CHARACTERS

ROYAL FAMILY

Alexander Holt Starweber—Father of Liane
Appearance(s): Empress Ascending, Dragon's Deception
Aristea Starweber—Older sister of Liane; heir to the throne of Neolyra
Appearance(s): Dragon's Deception
Eveline Starweber—Mother of Liane; Empress of Neolyra
Appearance(s): Empress Ascending, Dragon's Deception
Heinrich Meisner Starweber—wed to Aristea Starweber
Appearance(s): Empress Ascending (referenced), Dragon's Deception
Liane Starweber—second princess of Neolyra
Appearance(s): Dragon's Deception
Mathias Leopold Starweber—grandfather of Liane; former emperor; Eveline's father **(deceased)**
Appearance(s): Empress Ascending, Dragon's Deception (referenced)

Mathias Alexander Starweber—younger brother of Liane; son of Alexander and Eveline; prince of Neo
Appearance(s): Dragon's Deception
Theresa Starweber—grandmother of Liane; Eveline's Mother **(deceased)**
Appearance(s): Empress Ascending,
Viznent Meisner—former Duke Meisner, traitor who led uprising against Empress Eveline **(deceased)**
Appearance(s): Empress Ascending, Dragon's Deception (referenced)

PALACE HOUSEHOLD

Catarina—Empress Eveline's head maid; married to Falko
Appearance(s): Empress Ascending
Elias—Liane's childhood best friend (deceased)
Appearance(s): Dragon's Deception (referenced)
Falko—Head of Royal Guard
Appearance(s): Empress Ascending, Dragon's Deception
Gunnar—Master of Stables
Appearance(s): Empress Ascending
Levi—Head Attendant
Appearance(s): Empress Ascending
Ludwig Wildner—head of Liane's guard; Liane's best friend
Appearance(s): Dragon's Deception
Luzie—Liane's head maid
Appearance(s): Dragon's Deception
Aayden—Liane's guard
Appearance(s): Dragon's Deception
Simon—Liane's guard
Appearance(s): Dragon's Deception

Yvette—Aristea's lady's maid
Appearance(s): Dragon's Temptation
Jana—Aristea's lady's maid
Appearance(s): Dragon's Temptation

COURTIERS

Duke Licht—Duke of Licht; Liane's suitor; friend of Heinrich
Appearance(s): Dragon's Deception
Frey—General; Emperor Mathias's best friend
Appearance(s): Empress Ascending
Duke Holt—Ruler of Ronnenmond; Alexander Holt's relative
(father in empress ascending older brother in dragon's
deception)
Appearance(s): Empress Ascending, (referenced) Dragon's
Deception (referenced)
Duke Friesigner
Appearance(s): Empress Ascending
Duke Visscher
Appearance(s): Empress Ascending
Duke Kretschemer
Appearance(s): Empress Ascending
Dance Mistress Eleanor—Dance teacher to Aristae and Liane
Appearance(s): Dragon's Deception
Duke Schatz—Gout sufferer; Duke of Parliament member;
Empress Eveline Ally
Appearance(s): Dragon's Deception (referenced)
Count Harig—courtier; Empress Eveline Ally
Appearance(s): Dragon's Deception (referenced)
Lord Jonathan Sommerfeld—courtier; former Heinrich ally;
Aristea's former flame, father of Elisa, widower of Ida

Appearance(s): Dragon's Deception, Dragon's Temptation

Lady Ida Sommerfeld(deceased)—wife of Jonathan Sommerfeld, mother of Elisa, and daughter to Duke and Duchess Krantz

Appearance(s): Dragon's Temptation

Elisa Sommerfeld—daughter of Jonathan Sommerfeld and Ida Sommerfeld, granddaughter of Duke and Duchess Krantz

Appearance(s): Dragon's Temptation

Duke Krantz—quasi leader of Heinrich's allies after his death; husband of Duchess Krantz, grandfather of Elisa, father of Ida.

Appearance(s): Dragon's Temptation

Duchess Krantz—wife of Duke Krantz, grandmother of Elisa, mother of Ida

Appearance(s): Dragon's Temptation

Duke Wagner—Mathias co-conspirator

Appearance(s): Dragon's Deception (referenced)

CHURCH OF SOL

Aolois—Two toned stag; godling of twilight/balance created by the divine twins.

Avatheos—Leader of the Church of Sol

Appearance(s): Empress Ascending as a Vice Premier; Dragon's Deception as Avatheos

Cyra—Sun Goddess; One of the Divine Twins

Appearance(s): Empress Ascending, Dragon's Deception (referenced both times)

Church of Sol—primary religious organization on the continent

Divine Twins—First two deities born to the All Mother

Appearance(s): Dragon's Deception (referenced)

Golden Blade—Cyra's divine sword that she used to sever night from day.

Appearance(s): Empress Ascending, Dragon's Deception

Nameless Goddess, the—Moon Goddess; one of the divine twins

Appearance(s): Empress Ascending, Dragon's Deception (referenced both times)

Sun Ceremony—Summer solstice in Neolyra celebrated by invoking the sun through ritual led by the leaders of the Church of Sol

Appearance(s): Dragon's Deception

Vice Premier—Secondary rank in Church of Sol beneath the Avatheos

Appearance(s): Dragon's Deception, Empress Ascending (different Vice Premier)

Sylvie—a priestess acolyte

Appearance(s): Dragon's Temptation

MIDNIGHT GUARD

Captain Rosen—head of midnight guard; first woman head of the guard

Arne—midnight guard

Fynn—midnight guard

OTHERS

Warden Oswald—corrupt warden of the Atrira's prison

Appearance(s): Dragon's Deception

Fritz—an elf seer

Appearance(s): Dragon's Deception

Elyon—an elf

Appearance(s): Dragon's Deception

Niklas Ehrle—Leader of the Onyx Gang

Appearance(s): Dragon's Deception

Leonhard Harnisch—Head of the Hunters Guild in Basilia

Appearance(s): Dragon's Temptation

Yneas—Nameless Nameless Goddess, Moon Goddess

Appearance(s): Dragon's Temptation

SUNDLAND

Anja Endland Ostrom—former Queen of Sundland; Mother of Erich (Deceased)

Appearance(s): Dragon's Deception (referenced)

Arnfast Ostrom—Duke Mattison; Erich's oldest paternal Uncle

Appearance(s): Dragon's Deception (referenced)

Erich Ostrom—Were-dragon; Heir to Sundland Throne; Son of Harald and Anja

Appearance(s): Dragon's Deception

Freya Ostrom—Queen of Sundland; Erich's Stepmother

Appearance(s): Dragon's Deception (referenced)

Harald Ostrom—King of Sundland; Erich's Father

Appearance(s): Dragon's Deception (referenced)

Ivar Gunderson—Ambassador of Sunland in Neolyra

Appearance(s): Dragon's Deception

Greta Gunderson—daughter of Ivar

Appearance(s): Dragon's Deception (referenced)

Oskar Ostrom—Duke Ericson; Erich's youngest paternal Uncle

Appearance(s): Dragon's Deception (referenced)

Theo Endland—Lord Endland; Erich's Maternal uncle & mentor

Appearance(s): Dragon's Deception (referenced)

Duke Mattison—Brother to Harald Ostrom, uncle to Erich Ostrom,

Appearance(s): Dragon's Deception (referenced), Dragon's Tempation

Hallbjorn Geirsson—Sundland noble that Erich accidentally killed when his dragon took over.

Appearance(s): Dragon's Temptation (referenced)

COUNTRIES/ LOCATIONS

Ageless Sea—sea separating Xi'an and the continent
Artria—capital of Neolyra
Basilia—religious capital & central home of the Church of Sol
Gauldeen—province in Porroque famous for its wine
Guild Street—guild locations
Imperial Square—Artria's city center
Neolyra—Empire and largest power on the continent
Palace Street—street leading to the palace
Porroque—western coastal country known for its cheese
Rift, the—Space between the real world and the veil, used by elves for short distance quick travel
Soccicio—coastal southeastern country on the continent
Starlight Square—city square that intersects guild street
Sundland—land locked, northeastern country on the continent
Temple Street—street connecting with Church of Sol
Xi'an—large continent to the south of the continent. Known for their clever alchemists and their unusual experiments.
Velvet District—pleasure district of the city holding gambling dens, brothels, and drug dens aplenty.

TERMS & DEFINITIONS

All Mother—mother of the divine twins (Cyra and the Nameless Goddess)

Ancient(s)—godlings of lore, created by the divine twins at the dawn of time.

City Watch—city guards

Corruption, the—a cataclysmic event that destroyed light magic, and altered magical beings turning them into corrupted.

corrupted—anyone who is tainted by corruption magic.

corrupt magic—infected magic

chimera—creatures born from corrupt magic.

Eternal Light—the afterlife

Feuerster—monsters formed from embers and living flame.

Hunters—non-church sanction corruption hunters who sell their parts on the black market.

Midnight Guard—specially trained by the church of sol to hunt corrupted

Onyx Gang—an organized crime group who sells stardust.

Oracle—someone who can see into the future by reading signs in the stars and in runes and casting bones.

Ruins, the—the remnants of a lost civilization

Runes—magical markers, their uses forgotten

Valley of Darkness—the place the dead pass through on their way to Eternal Light

Veil, the—barrier separating life and death

Veins—source of magic.

Warped Mages—someone who uses corruption magic and corrupted creatures, like Chimera.

Trinity: three form goddess, (seen as maiden, mother, crone,) worshipped by Sundlanders

Wicked King—A series of salacious novels about an arrangement marriage between a woman and an evil king.

Acknowledgments

Dragon's Temptation was literal years in the making. Between roadblocks, detours, and rewrites, this has been one of the most difficult books I've ever written. if Dragon's Deception poured out of me, Dragon's Temptation was like excavating fossilized bones from deep in my soul. Dragon's Temptation is a book that is deeply personal to me, especially Aristea and Liane's points of view, both explored different aspects of my lived experience: namely, Aristea's pressures at being a perfect, oldest sister and her infertility shame. Liane's religious deconstruction also holds up a mirror to my own faith crisis and internalized shame that comes from purity culture. Writing this book was very healing for me, and I'm grateful to everyone who joined me along this journey.

Thanks to my husband, who always supports my dreams, even after he read Dragon's Deception and fell in love with Luzie after I'd already written her death (sorry, Babe). Mel, thank you for yapping with me on road-trips, selling my books better than me, and being the best sister, and #1 fan. Nicole, my soul sister, thank you for everything always. To my Arizona Wives: Marriet, Jade, Ava, & Kalista, your friendship means the world to me. Charity, I'd be lost without you. I don't know how I'd function as an author without you in my corner. Thank you, Britney Waldorf, for literally swooping in like an angel to edit this book last minute. You have my undying love and support. And last but not least, thank you again to my Kickstarter backers, especially those who backed this campaign over a year ago and waited patiently as I revised and reworked this book into something I'd be proud of. You make all of this possible!

<u>**Diviner's World**</u>

Duchess (Free)

Sorcerer (Free)

Diviner's Prophecy

Diviner's Curse

Diviner's Fate

Princess

<u>**Witch of the Lake Series**</u>

Feast of the Mother

Fate of the Demon

Fall of the Reaper

About the Author

Nicolette is a native San Diegan with a passion for the world of make believe. From a young age, Nicolette was telling stories whether it be writing plays for her friends to act out or making a series of children's books that her mother still likes drag out to embarrass her with in front of company. She still lives in her imagination but in reality she resides in San Diego with her husband, children and a couple cats. She loves reading, attempting arts and crafts, and cooking.

You can visit her at her website: www.nicolettean drews.com or at these places:

facebook.com/nicandfantasy

x.com/nicandfantasy

instagram.com/nicolette_andrews

amazon.com/author/nicoletteandrews

bookbub.com/authors/nicolette-andrews

goodreads.com/nicolette_andrews

pinterest.com/Nicandfantasy

tiktok.com/@nicandfantasy

www.ingramcontent.com/pod-product-compliance
Lightning Source LLC
Chambersburg PA
CBHW031156310726
48969CB00001B/111